PLUNGE INTO THE UNKNOWN

Daniel's kisses were different now, not gentle or re-assuring; they were demanding, decisive, and in-flammatory. Georgina's fingers dug into his back as he pushed her deeper into the pillows, but she couldn't fight him. Her mouth opened beneath his command, and his invasion left her gasping for more.

"Daniel," she whispered desperately, having no idea of what she wanted to say.

"Don't, Georgie," he whispered against her skin. "Don't say anything. This is the way it's meant to be."

He stopped what he was doing and braced himself over her, catching her gaze with his own. Georgie trembled at his strength, at her weakness, and at the abyss that seemed to open up beneath her and make her long to fall. . . .

♦TOPAZ'S CROWN JEWELS

Win $1,000 for a Romantic Weekend Getaway!

April '95
ANGEL ROGUE
Mary Jo Putney

September '95
TO HAVE & TO HOLD
Patricia Gaffney

May '95
WHITE ORCHID
Linda Ladd

October '95
PAPER TIGER
Patricia Rice

Name_____
Address_____
City_____State_____Zip_____

Mail to:
TOPAZ'S CROWN JEWELS Sweepstakes
P.O. Box 523
Village Station
New York, NY 10014-0523

Offer expires December 31, 1995

Enter with this official entry form or by hand printing your name, address, and the words "TOPAZ'S CROWN JEWELS" Sweepstakes on a 3" x 5" piece of paper.

OFFICIAL RULES

1. NO PURCHASE NECESSARY. To enter: Complete the official entry form. You may also enter by hand printing your name and complete address and the words "TOPAZ'S CROWN JEWELS" Sweepstakes on a 3" x 5" piece of paper. Mail your entry to: "TOPAZ'S CROWN JEWELS" Sweepstakes, PO Box 523, Village Station, New York, NY 10014-0523. Enter as often as you wish, but each entry must be mailed separately. Mechanically reproduced entries not accepted. Not responsible for late, postage due, lost, misdirected mail or printing errors. Entries must be received by December 31, 1995 to be eligible.

2. Winner will be selected on or about January 14, 1996 in a random drawing from among all valid entries received. All decisions are final and binding. Winner will be notified by mail and will be required to execute an affidavit of eligibility and release which must be returned within 14 days or an alternate winner will be selected.

3. PRIZE: (1) Grand Prize, $1,000.00 for winner to create their own Romantic Weekend Getaway.

4. Sweepstakes open to residents of the U.S. except employees and their families of Penguin USA, its affiliates and advertising agencies. All Federal, State, and local laws apply. Taxes, if any, are the sole responsibility of the prize winner. Void where prohibited or restricted by law. Winner consents to the use of his/her name, photograph, and/or likeness for publicity purposes without additional compensation (except where prohibited by law). Odds of winning depend on the number of eligible entries received. No transfer or substitution of prize permitted. Prize guaranteed to be awarded.

5. Winner agrees that the sponsor, its affiliates and their agencies and employees shall not be liable for injury, loss, or damage of any kind resulting from participation in this promotion or from the acceptance or use of the prize awarded.

6. For the name of the prize winner, available after January 31, 1996, send a stamped, self-addressed envelope to: "TOPAZ'S CROWN JEWELS" Sweepstakes Winner, Penguin USA Mass Market, 375 Hudson St., New York, NY 10014

Printed in the USA

PAPER TIGER

Patricia Rice

A TOPAZ BOOK

TOPAZ
Published by the Penguin Group
Penguin Books USA Inc., 375 Hudson Street,
New York, New York 10014, U.S.A.
Penguin Books Ltd, 27 Wrights Lane,
London W8 5TZ, England
Penguin Books Australia Ltd, Ringwood,
Victoria, Australia
Penguin Books Canada Ltd, 10 Alcorn Avenue,
Toronto, Ontario, Canada M4V 3B2
Penguin Books (N.Z.) Ltd, 182-190 Wairau Road,
Auckland 10, New Zealand

Penguin Books Ltd, Registered Offices:
Harmondsworth, Middlesex, England

First published by Topaz, an imprint of Dutton Signet,
a division of Penguin Books USA Inc.

First Printing, October, 1995
10 9 8 7 6 5 4 3 2 1

One

His leg ached from sitting still so long. Crossing it over his other knee, Daniel Mulloney idly massaged the rebellious muscle while staring out at the Ohio cornfields flying past. He should have ignored Evie's advice and ridden his horse up here. At least his leg would have felt better, and his pride—or whatever it was that made a man feel at home in one kind of suit and not another—would be satisfied. He was damned uncomfortable wearing this stiff collar and tie.

But the train was faster and more efficient, and he would be arriving home in some semblance of style. Evie had probably been right about that. She just didn't realize that there wouldn't be anyone there to appreciate his ceremonious return. He hadn't told anyone he was coming.

Thinking of his adopted sister's response to that information if he'd told her, Daniel grinned at his reflection in the glass. She'd have boxed his ears and insisted on coming with him. He could just imagine the reaction of the staid midwestern ladies and gentlemen of Cutlerville if Evie and her husband, Tyler, had shown up on their doorsteps. Evie would no doubt wear one of her latest Parisian gowns with feathers in her hair, and Tyler would have his boots and Stetson and fifty-dollar smile. They would have the populace eating out of their hands before sundown.

In the wake of his adopted sister and brother-in-law, no one would even know Daniel had arrived. He'd liked it that way all these years, but it was time for things to change. And the first step in that direction meant confronting the family he'd never known. He had to know who he was before he could move on to what he wanted to be.

That might be a strange thing for a twenty-eight-year-old man to be thinking, but then, Daniel Mulloney hadn't exactly led a particularly normal life. He hadn't been expected to live any life at all.

Tired of staring at his reflection and endless fields and tidy farms, Daniel returned his attention to the other passengers. There was one in particular who had caught his eye from the moment she had entered the train back in Cincinnati. She had been chattering with the conductor as he carried in her bag and helped her store it, and Daniel had been fascinated with the animation of her expression. He could tell by her expensive clothes and hat that she was a lady, but she had conversed with the colored conductor as if they were the best of friends. She'd neglected to tip the man, he had noticed, but the conductor had still gone out grinning. A woman like that could easily have that kind of effect.

He had heard her chattering with the woman in the seat beside her at the beginning, but her morose companion hadn't exactly been a conversationalist, and the young lady had grown silent after a while. Daniel turned his head slightly to see what she was doing now.

To his complete surprise, she was staring at him. A brilliant smile engulfed her face as she caught his look. She wasn't exactly what Daniel would call beautiful. She was too short and blond and round for his tastes, but she had the damnedest smile he'd ever seen, and a pair of blue eyes that laughed without even trying. He returned the smile and waited to see what would happen.

She didn't disappoint.

"I've been hoping you would look this way," she whispered loudly, nodding in the direction of the woman sleeping beside her. "You looked like you could use someone to talk to as much as I could."

He'd grown up in Missouri and Texas and Mississippi, and although the South was known for its hospitality and friendliness, Daniel didn't know a lady of his acquaintance who would have dared approach a strange male like that. He didn't think even Evie would be quite so bold unless she had something on her mind.

That thought made him restless, but Daniel gallantly tipped his hat and gestured to the empty seat beside him. "You're welcome to set a spell, ma'am."

She practically beamed at him as she gathered up her parasol and traveling bag and the long train of her skirt to transfer across the aisle. "I knew you were a Texan. You had to be with that hat. All the men I know wear black top hats, and even the shopkeepers wear bowlers. What is that thing called?"

Daniel carefully removed his broad-brimmed Stetson and set it on his lap. He was trying to keep from laughing at the same time as his senses were being inundated by a soft scent that sort of just crept up on him. He allowed his gaze to trail over her unusual costume of loose silk that showed no indication of the heavy corsets the other ladies around them were wearing. At least tight bodices gave him a good idea of what was underneath. This woman's folds of silk left him guessing, and imagining entirely too much.

"It's called a hat, ma'am. And what is that thing called that you're wearing?" Generally, he wasn't rude to strangers, but this pretty miss was setting off firecrackers with every move she made, and he had the need to defend himself.

She untied the ribbons on her old-fashioned bonnet, uncovering a tumble of loose curls gathered up in a scarf in some incomprehensibly Grecian fashion, and set it aside while she reached for his hat. Placing it carefully on her head, she strained to catch her reflection in the dirty window. "It's a bonnet, as you know full well. I do so think that clothes make the person, don't you? I mean, I could just look at your hat and know that you were a fascinating man from Texas with probably no notion of propriety and lots of entertaining stories to tell. Do you like my gown? It's the aesthetic fashion. Back in London Oscar Wilde and his set are calling for a return to simpler styles. Actually, I think they had Greek dress in mind, but most of

them are wearing knee breeches in town and calling themselves daring. I think knee breeches are perfectly silly, but
I do agree with the need for looser dress. Corsets are so
appallingly restricting."

Her mention of the unmentionable was equally appall-
ing and nearly struck Daniel dumb, but a long acquaintance with Evie had prepared him to deal with anything
and everything. Adjusting the Stetson at a jaunty angle on
the lady's head, he managed to get a word in. "So are ties
and suit coats and starched collars, but what would you
do if I removed mine?"

Ignoring the reprimand in his voice, she grinned beguilingly at him, her blue eyes dancing and catching him
in their magic. "Why don't you try it and we'll see?"

"You know you're incorrigible, don't you? That's why
you're doing this. It's a deliberate act." Daniel did his
best to sound reproving, but in the face of so much life
and laughter, he could only hide a smile.

"You see right through me, sir." She removed the hat
and handed it back to him. "My name is Georgina
Meredith Hanover. If you're going to Cutlerville, you're
certain to hear of me. I believe I'm called The Incorrigible behind my back, actually. And I daresay that's one of
the milder terms. Do you have a name?"

Several of them. It was a fact that he had debated frequently since buying the train ticket. Daniel Mulloney
was a perfectly innocuous name. He really didn't think
anyone would put two and two together. But he was a
cautious man and inclined to keep his secrets to himself.
Choosing not to lie deliberately, he replied, "They call me
Pecos Martin, ma'am. Pleased to meet you."

She seemed thoroughly delighted with the sobriquet,
but not entirely fooled by his reticence. With a twinkle in
her eye, she didn't pry for more, but merrily continued.
"Pecos Martin! I love it. I can't wait to introduce you at
parties. You will come to my parties, won't you? I'm certain there will be dozens of them."

Avoiding the question, Daniel answered, "Dozens of
parties must denote a special occasion. Are you turning
sweet sixteen?"

She smacked his arm with the fan she had removed from her traveling bag and was wielding briskly with great effect. Her tumbled curls blew in the breeze of her artful waving. "Sixteen! Honestly. Men have no sense at all. I've just come back from traveling all over the Continent and you think I'm just sixteen. Well, I'm not. I'll have you know I'm almost twenty-one and I'm about to be married. So there." The insult in her voice disappeared as she turned and peered at him impishly. "Do I really look sixteen? Did I do that right? Like a proper matron?"

Daniel couldn't help it. This time he laughed, slapping his knee and catching great gulps of air at this pixieish display of artifice, laughing even harder when a frown began to form on her forehead. She was even better than Evie at her worst. Georgina Meredith Hanover was definitely not the quiet intellectual type he preferred, but she had the bold effrontery he knew how to deal with. He felt right at home with the little imp.

"I don't see what's so funny. Do you think my getting married is funny? Or that my being a proper matron is a laughing matter?"

Daniel shook his head and recovered himself, giving her a look of amusement as he spoke. "I hope you're marrying someone with a sense of humor. He's going to need it. Does he know you flirt with strange men?"

She pursed her lips and glared at him, but the laughter behind her eyes didn't die entirely. Instead, the effect was almost winsome, as if a shadow had passed between them, revealing something she hadn't meant to be seen. She spread the fan and turned away.

"He has absolutely no sense of humor at all, and he would probably put me in chains if he knew I flirted. Why do you think I've spent the last two years in Europe? I've been trying to get all this childish behavior out of my system so I can become a proper wife."

Everything she had said up until now had been silly and flirtatious and without a grain of intelligence. Daniel wasn't quite ready for the shift to truth. Assuming this was just another game, he replied in kind. "I can see you've succeeded magnificently. You'll no doubt be staidly pouring tea from a silver pot before the week is out."

She affected a bright smile. "Well, that would be fine, if I didn't have to pour it into cups. I can think of a couple of laps that could use heating up."

That was not only not polite, it smacked of the desperate. Daniel turned her a wary look to be certain she wasn't one of these hysterical females who would soon deteriorate into tears. She was busily removing a sketchpad from her traveling bag. Damn, but she could be Evie's second cousin.

"I've decided to take up painting. Do you know anything about art, Mr. Martin?"

Personally, he knew little or nothing about it, but he had seen plenty of it in his lifetime. He took her sketchpad and flipped through the pages. The drawings were good reproductions of various architectural monuments she had visited, but they were nothing like Evie's dramatic portraits. Daniel shrugged.

"I don't know a whole lot," he admitted. "These seem to be mighty fine pictures, though. I think I've seen one like this." He pointed to the cathedral tower of Notre Dame.

"Of course, everyone's seen it." She snapped the pad closed and returned it to her bag. "That's the whole problem. I have no imagination. I don't suppose marriage stimulates the imagination."

Finally divining the source of the problem, Daniel offered what he thought was practical advice. "Well, now, if you're not interested in getting married just yet, you don't have to say yes. Just tell the man you've changed your mind."

"You try telling Peter anything. Or my father. They've made up their minds, and no amount of talking is going to change them. After all, I'm just a silly woman who doesn't know what she wants. And they're right. I haven't the foggiest notion of what I want. So I guess I'll get married."

There wasn't much Daniel could say to that. The only experience he'd had with marriage was Evie and Tyler's, and that marriage certainly hadn't started out in the most conventional manner. He'd been foolish enough to contemplate it once himself, but apparently the reasons he'd thought were good enough for marriage weren't good enough for the object of his intentions. So he scarcely qualified as an expert.

"You must have some feelings for the man or you wouldn't have agreed in the first place."

Georgina shrugged. "I don't remember ever actually agreeing. To be perfectly factual, I don't remember ever being asked. When I came back from finishing school, they started talking about setting a date. That's when I panicked and made them give me a few years of travel. I thought maybe absence would make my heart grow fonder or some such bosh. But all I can remember about Peter is that he was the best-looking man at my come-out. I really don't think that's a basis for marriage."

There was a small frown behind her eyes as she said this, but before Daniel could think of an adequate reply, she was laughing again and tapping him with her fan. "Now tell me you'll come to my parties. I'm dying to show you off to my friends. A real live Texan! Won't they be thrilled? How many Indians have you killed? Did you know Wild Bill Hickok? Can you shoot a gun?"

Her laughter was much easier to deal with. He had enough problems of his own without falling for the vulnerability behind that small frown she had shown earlier. He had a weak place for helpless females, which he meant to completely expunge one of these days. He responded to her questions in the same manner they were asked.

"Texans learn how to hold off a tribe of Indians at gunpoint before they learn to walk. Actually, we learn to ride before we can crawl. You can't invite me to parties unless you invite my horse."

She laughed and they exchanged silly pleasantries until the train pulled into the station. They were still laughing as Daniel helped her gather her things and carry them out to the platform. But Daniel stopped laughing the instant they reached the platform, and he saw the disapproval on the faces of the elegant lady and gentleman he knew at once were her parents. Georgina, however, blithely threw herself into their arms without a care in the world.

"Georgina, where in heaven's name is your companion?" Daniel heard the horrified whisper as he lowered the lady's travel bag to the ground.

"Oh, I left her in New York. She really was quite cross with me, and I told her if she couldn't be pleasant, she could stay there. I'm a world traveler now, Mama. I can handle a little journey from New York to Ohio on my own."

Daniel solemnly returned the gaze of the bewhiskered elderly gentleman frowning at him. After facing Indians, bandits, and Tyler, he could handle a pompous old goat in waistcoat and starched collar without a qualm. He didn't bother extending his hand in courtesy until Georgina offered introductions.

At the stiff silence between the two men, Georgina jumped from her mother's arms to perform the required etiquette. "Papa, this is Pecos Martin. He's from Texas and he said he'd come to my parties if he could bring his horse. Mr. Martin, this is my father, George Hanover."

As the two men shook hands, she continued to chatter. "Mr. Martin was ever so kind in helping me with my luggage. And he didn't even mind listening to my silly talk." She rummaged in her bag and produced a card case. "You must be certain to call on me so I can see that you get an invitation. Please say you will."

Daniel took the card and slipped it into his vest pocket under the disapproving frown of her father. Somehow, through all her laughter, Miss Georgina Hanover was sending distress signals loud and clear. He wasn't born a Texan, but he knew how to act like one, and there wasn't a Texan alive who wouldn't come to the rescue of a lady in distress.

He bowed, made his excuses, and limped away.

Two

C

G eorgina watched the tall cowboy disappear into the
crowd with an odd feeling of regret. She knew
perfectly well that he would never call on her.
They were from two different worlds, but it shouldn't hurt
to pretend for a little while. He had been pleasant and un-
demanding and hadn't patronized her in any way. She
needed a friend like that.

But her father was muttering words of disapproval, and
her mother was chattering to change the subject, so Georgina allowed them to lead her away. She knew there
would be an elegant black carriage waiting outside the
station to take them to the gilded cage her father had built
for them, and soon she would be back in the round of social activities that would be her life.

As she climbed into the carriage with the help of the
uniformed driver, Georgina turned to see a wide-brimmed
cowboy hat lift in farewell, and then he was gone.

"I don't see why we have to make the announcement
so soon. I just got home. Are you so eager to be rid of me
again?" Georgina asked crossly as a maid straightened the
wreath of roses woven into her coiffure. She hated pink
roses. They made her look pale and washed out.

Her mother patted the wreath lovingly. "Of course not,
Georgina. But you've made poor Peter wait for two years.
You can't expect him to keep waiting forever. The two of
you can set a date this evening, and we'll make the announcement at your coming-home ball Friday, and then

you will have all the time in the world to get used to the idea."

Georgina rather suspected "all the time in the world" would consist of the month or so it would take to make the wedding preparations, but she had no quarrel with her mother. Dolly Hanover had no thoughts of her own as far as her daughter could discern. There were times when her mother took to her room and drew the curtains closed and didn't come out for days, but those times when she was out and about, she agreed with whatever her husband told her. If George said it was time for their daughter to be married, then it was so. Georgina knew her father was the one she needed to talk with about her doubts, if only to keep her mother from fretting into collapse.

Unfortunately, her father wasn't giving her time to question. When Georgina descended the stairs to the front hall, Peter was already there, removing his hat and behaving as one of the family. He glanced up and saw her before she could retreat, and she was forced to smile and greet him.

He really was amazingly handsome, she told herself as he took her hand and squeezed it. A European gentleman would have kissed her, but Peter was all midwestern propriety. He made an appropriately innocuous comment on her appearance, greeted her mother, and returned to his business discussion with her father. Georgina grimaced and swept past him to the parlor. So much for romance.

She didn't think she was a wildly romantic person, but there ought to be something more to this marriage business than a handshake and a bit of flattery upon occasion. She felt as if she were somehow being deprived of something that was owed to her.

It was quite probably some fault of her own. When her classmates had been swooning over some male acquaintance or another, she had been out galloping through the park with the man in question. When her friends had confessed their passion for some romantic young man, Georgina had been assessing him and finding him lacking. Men were men. She just couldn't recognize any of them as the superior beings they preferred to think themselves.

If the truth were told, she found most of them downright boring.

She gave Peter a look from the corner of her eye as he took a seat between her and her father. She couldn't call him boring, she supposed. He fairly vibrated with an incandescent energy that made his every movement a thing of power. He spoke with force and command and intelligence. Even her father respected his opinions. He was only five years older than herself, yet he could command the interest of his elders. Unfortunately, he didn't command much interest from her.

Sighing, she gazed around the ornate parlor and waited for the call to dinner. The business discussion bored her to tears. She knew there was some relation between her father's factory and Peter's stores, but she wasn't much concerned about the connection. Actually, Peter didn't own the stores yet. They belonged to his father.

Thinking about Peter's father gave Georgina the cold shudders. There was a man with no conscience, one whose only concerns were his wealth and his ability to acquire more. If he were the model of Peter thirty years from now, she knew this marriage was a mistake.

But once the call came for dinner, Peter was all that was attentive. He led her to the table, held her chair, asked about her travels, and made no further mention of their impending nuptials. She would have been flattered had she not felt his interest was forced.

Remembering her conversation with the cowboy earlier, Georgina allowed the conversation to go on without her. Mr. Martin's interest hadn't been forced. She had behaved her absolute worst, and he had seen right through her. Why couldn't there be more men of her acquaintance who would actually listen to her as he had?

She had never even asked him why he had come to Cutlerville. If she had her choice of places to go, it certainly wouldn't be here. Cowboys belonged on the open range with wild horses and buffalo and other creatures of nature. Perhaps he had come for medical treatment for his injured leg.

"Georgina, you aren't listening," Peter whispered gently,

prodding her back to the moment. "Your father asked you a question. Are you ready to set the date yet?"

Rounding up her straying thoughts, Georgina pursed her lips, gazed around at the people waiting for her reply, and felt a furious surge of rebellion. Pushing back her chair and rising, she replied, "No, but since the three of you have handled it perfectly well without me until now, I'm certain you can continue to do so."

She flew from the room, leaving her parents to apologize for her behavior. As usual.

The street outside her father's factory was unpaved. The early summer dust filled the air with every passing wagon, coating already filthy buildings with still another layer of Ohio clay. Georgina frowned at the light layer of dust clearly noticeable against her dark green gown. She had rejected wearing a cloak in this heat, but she was regretting her haste now. She had meant to appear very mature and reliable when she was shown to her father's office. She feared she looked more a hoyden than ever.

Well, it was too late to do anything about it. Setting her chin, she entered the side door that she knew led to the offices.

Her father's secretary looked up from a stack of correspondence and frowned slightly before suddenly donning a fawning smile. "Miss Hanover! How good it is to see you home again. I understand congratulations are in order. When is the happy day?"

Almost all of her father's employees were female, Georgina knew, and that included his secretary. The tall, graying spinster had been with the company for years, possibly decades. She couldn't be disrespectful to the woman, but she couldn't in all truth answer the question either.

"I don't know. You'll have to ask my father," she answered simply. She hadn't spoken to him since the night before. She was about to correct that oversight. There were a few things that just had to be discussed before this comedy of errors continued. "Is he busy? I'd like to see him a minute, if I might."

The secretary looked regretful. "He's with someone right now. If you could wait a few minutes, I'm sure he would be delighted to see you."

She knew her father's idea of a few minutes. Picking up the travel bag with her sketchpad in it, Georgina gestured toward the door leading into the factory. "Would it be all right if I waited in there? I mean to learn about the business, and that seems to be the best place to start."

She spoke modestly, quietly, like any obedient daughter, but she didn't wait for a reply. For all her life her father had kept her out of the factory where his money was made, saying it was no place for little girls. Well, she wasn't a little girl any longer. It was time she started learning about life. If she were sole heir to this business, then she ought to know more about it.

Of course, she was certain Peter thought he would be acquiring the business when he married her, but she had come to a few conclusions during the wee hours of the past night. If business was what their marriage was to be built on, then she would apply herself to learning that business. She wasn't about to spend the rest of her life talking about her shopping expeditions while her husband nodded off to sleep at the table every evening.

The intense heat in the factory nearly knocked her over when she entered. There were a few windows open high up on the walls, but any breeze that passed through didn't reach the floor. The motors from the various machines clattering and banging throughout the room threw off heat to match anything the sun produced outside. Perhaps the huge room would be warm and cozy in the winter. Right now it was a furnace.

Well, if these other women could handle it, so could she. Georgina gazed around at backs bent industriously over garments in various stages of processing. No one even took the time to look up at her entrance. Perhaps they thought she was her father and were set on impressing him.

The man hurrying in her direction wasn't under any

such impression. Undoubtedly the foreman or the manager or whatever he was called, he had the look of a man who considered ladies a foolish nuisance not to be endured.

Ignoring his approach, Georgina found a seat on an empty crate and pulled out her sketchpad as if she had every right to be here. He couldn't argue with the boss's daughter, at least not until the boss came out to back him up.

By the time he stood in front of her, she was deeply engrossed in a sketch of the woman sitting at the machine directly in front of her. A shaft of golden light seeped in from the window overhead, illuminating soft tendrils of hair around the woman's face and turning her thin visage into a sheen of moisture on porcelain. Georgina wished she could capture the image, but she knew she wasn't skilled enough.

The foreman cleared his throat, and she gave him a preoccupied look. "I trust I'm not disturbing anything," she said vaguely before he could ask her to leave. "I'm waiting for my father to come out of a meeting. I shall be quiet as a mouse, I promise." She returned to her sketching without giving him a chance to reply.

He hesitated, nodded without speaking, and drifted toward the office door. If anyone were to question the boss's daughter, it would have to be the boss.

Georgina sketched a few more minutes before she became aware of a latent air of hostility shimmering in the overheated room. With the foreman out of the way, a few murmurs rose in far corners despite the constant clacking of the machines. The woman she was drawing threw her a look of annoyance, and she perceived a decided glare from the woman at the machine behind her.

She had never been an object of hostility before. Bewildered, Georgina tried to return to her work, but her hand was shaking. She gazed at it incredulously. Surely a few mutters and glares shouldn't affect her to this extent. Was she afraid?

Fear was a new experience. Wherever she had gone, wherever she was, she had relied on the people around her to see to her safety and comfort. Money provided the best hotels, the finest carriages, private railroad cars, and excellent guides as she roamed through Europe. At home she was always with parents or friends who looked after her. It had never occurred to her to be afraid of anything.

But the growing resentment she felt in this room made the hair rise up on the back of her neck.

Georgina didn't like the feeling. Laying her pencil down, she glared back at the woman she had been drawing. "If you object to my sketching, just say so," she commanded.

"And have you run to your daddy and complain? Not on your life." Tightening her lips, she returned to her sewing.

In that brief glance Georgina realized the woman wasn't much older than herself, and she drew a little confidence from that. "What would I complain about? It's your likeness, not his. I'm not a very good artist, but you looked so pretty in the sunlight I had to try. What I would really like is to take a photograph, but my father says the chemicals are too dangerous." She was chattering, she knew. She always chattered when she wished desperately to make an impression.

Her only reply was a skeptical look.

"Why don't you go dangle with your fancy feller, Miss Smarty-Pants?" a voice called out from somewhere within the chaos of machinery.

"Yeah, leave us working girls to our jobs before you get us in trouble," someone else finished for her.

A piece of bread crust came flying through the air, tangling in Georgina's elaborate coiffure. As she scrambled to pull it out, other small objects took flight in her direction. A shower of spools and screws and odd objects fell all around her, driving her to her feet, and the irate words grew louder and more daring.

"You'd better leave, miss," the pretty woman whispered quietly as Georgina stood in bewilderment at the center of the growing tempest.

Before she could retreat, the office door burst open, and

her father and the foreman walked into the room. The sudden silence fooled no one, and George Hanover's gaze focused on his daughter. He didn't have to say anything. Georgina hurried to follow him out.

"Where's Blucher? You shouldn't be down here." He practically dragged her through the office, past his staring secretary and toward the door.

"Mother needed him to run some errands. He'll be back shortly." Georgina resisted his pull. Admittedly, her introduction to the factory had been an unmitigated disaster, but she couldn't give up. This was the only hope for her future that she could see. "I want to learn about the factory, Papa. I'll start at the bottom and work up if necessary."

"That is very conscientious of you, my dear, but not in the least bit necessary." George pushed her through the door and followed her out, glancing anxiously at the street for the carriage and driver. "Peter will learn the business quickly enough when the time comes. You must have dozens of things to do to prepare for the wedding. I know your mother is beside herself trying to come up with everything that needs to be done before September. Why don't you offer her your help? I'm sure she'll be delighted."

So the wedding was to be in September. That didn't give her very much time, but more than she had hoped. "I want to know more about the business so Peter and I have something to talk about. Please, Daddy, this is important to me."

With relief, Hanover spotted Blucher coming down the street and hurried her in that direction. "You and Peter will find much better things to do than talking business." He patted the hand she held on his arm. "Now go back to your mother. I have a luncheon engagement and don't want to be late."

As the portly, gray-haired man led the beautiful blonde in green silk out to the street, the man in the window of the tall building across the way pushed his coat jacket back and shoved his hands in his pockets. Shaking his head in disbelief, he grinned and watched her climb into the grand carriage stopping for her.

Without looking at the impatient man and the massive printing press behind him, Daniel Mulloney announced, "I'll take it. You can move out by the end of the week."

Three

For the first time in her life Georgina had a goal, and she wasn't going to give it up without a fight. That factory was going to be hers, and she had every right to be there. She arrived at the office the next day to bring her father a special lunch she'd had the cook make, and she sat outside his door, chatting with his secretary while she waited for him. Her father wasn't the only person in this building who knew the business, and Georgina learned a fascinating number of things listening to Doris.

She could tell by her father's face when he came out that he wasn't pleased to see her. She jumped up and greeted him with a kiss, but the frown was still there as he held her in front of him.

"You shouldn't be here, Georgina. I thought you learned your lesson yesterday. Tell Blucher to take you downtown to buy a pretty hat. This isn't any place for young ladies, and I don't want to see you here again."

"But Papa . . ."

Gently but firmly, he escorted her to the door. "No 'but Papas' on this, Georgina. Your mother needs your help, not me. Now go on with you and I'll see you tonight."

Georgina bit the inside of her lip to hold back the tears as she found herself abruptly outside the plant and in the hot sunshine again. The factory had evidently shut down for lunch break, and many of the workers had come outside to eat the contents of their lunch buckets. She felt as if every one of them were staring at her and laughing.

As she climbed back into the carriage, defeated, she

heard a particularly musical laugh in the street ahead. Clenching her teeth with anger, Georgina sought the source of the sound, and felt all the air leave her lungs at once.

There on the side of the road, talking to the beautiful woman she had sketched the day before, stood the cowboy from the train. So entranced was he with his laughing conversation that he didn't even notice her.

Suddenly overwhelmed by the hopelessness of her goals, Georgina ordered the driver to go on. Tears of frustration stained her cheeks as she looked away from the laughing couple so evidently made for each other.

Perhaps love and romance were only meant for the poor.

Georgina was wrong about one thing. Daniel *had* noticed her. It was impossible not to see the elegant creature in flowing silk adorned in a hat that made him think of flower blooms bobbing in a garden. He could almost smell the subtle fragrance of her perfume again just by looking at her.

That was why he saw the tears. He was farsighted and could scarcely discern the print on the paper the woman in front of him was holding, but he could see distances with amazing clarity. Especially when he was staring at them with a fascination he had never intended. She was crying.

That discovery shook him. He had tried to dismiss her from his thoughts as a poor little rich girl with no need of his help, but those tears hit him hard. He was a sucker for tears, always had been. He resented that knowledge, knew it for the failing that it was, but he couldn't make the feeling go away. She was crying, and she needed a friend. He should be that friend.

He'd only been introduced to the woman in front of him the night before, but he'd already learned she was a fountain of information. "Do you know who that was in the carriage?" he asked.

Contempt replaced her earlier laughter. "Her father

owns this factory. Why? Do you think her family would let you anywhere near their precious lamb?"

Daniel gave her a placating smile. "Now, Janice, don't let your claws show. I only asked because I saw her on the train and because she was crying just now. I'm curious about people. Why would anyone with all that wealth have a need to cry?"

Janice glanced over her shoulder at the departing carriage. It looked out of place among the water wagons and farm carts and dust-covered horses that made up the only modes of transportation on this end of town. She shook her head as she looked back to Daniel.

"I can't imagine it. She has everything her heart could possibly desire, and now I hear she's going to be married to the man whose family owns the biggest department store in town, so she'll have twice as much. It just doesn't seem fair."

The handsome fiancé with no sense of humor—Daniel remembered the conversation very well. Perhaps if he just reassured himself that the man wasn't a total bastard, he would realize Georgina was no more than a spoiled child who didn't know what was good for her. That would put an end to his Don Quixote tendencies.

"What is the biggest department store in town? I haven't been here long enough to know my way around."

The end-of-lunch whistle went off, and Janice grabbed her skirt, prepared to run back to work. Over her shoulder she answered his question. "Mulloney's. The biggest store in town is owned by Artemis Mulloney. Your girlfriend is going to marry his son Peter."

She was gone before he could comment. Daniel couldn't have replied in any case. Mulloney. It wasn't possible. There couldn't be two Artemis Mulloneys in Cutlerville, Ohio.

The merry Georgina Hanover was marrying his brother.

Daniel drained his fourth beer and wiped the foam from his mouth with the back of his hand. The tavern was dark and drab, and the noise level was beginning to grow as workers just off the line filed in.

He glanced around at his surroundings and felt the familiar loneliness creeping up on him again. This certainly wasn't Texas. These men were carrying lunch buckets instead of six-guns. They wore faded blue workshirts and khakis instead of spurs and ten-gallon hats. But they were the same men just the same—men with no families or homes or lives beyond the next beer. Daniel didn't want to be one of them.

But he was. Laying his money down on the counter, he wandered toward the door. He had no head for drink and knew it, but there were times when a man just had to get outside of himself for a while. Tonight had just seemed like one of those times.

The smell of sulfur struck him as he walked outside. He had hoped for a blast of fresh air to clear his head, but the heat and humidity lingered, trapped between these narrow dark streets and towering old buildings. He would have to get out of town to breathe fresh air again.

His feet led the way. He had made inquiries earlier in the day with the thought of finding a hired cab and seeing how the other half lived, but he had never made it farther than the tavern. But now, without conscious thought, his feet were guiding him.

Riding was easier than walking with this leg of his, but he hadn't gotten around to buying a horse. Stabling it would be a problem in the city. He wasn't certain he was ready to take on the extra expense. But he was regretting his lack of transportation as he meandered through the city's main business district.

Mulloney's Department Store stretched the length of one block and the width of another. Daniel had never seen anything like it, but then, he wasn't in the habit of visiting cities. Houston had grown tremendously in the ten years since he had first seen it, but he couldn't remember anything quite the size of this store anywhere in its environs.

Daniel stared upward at story upon story of brick structure. Mulloney's wasn't satisfied with occupying just a block of land, but they needed a block of sky, too, it seemed. The amount of wealth needed just to build this monstrosity made him cringe. He didn't need to see the insides.

He could feel the rage replacing the loneliness, and he let his feet carry him on. He'd spent a lifetime learning to deal with this fury that hid behind his every action. He knew how to capture it, tame it, put it to work for him. Even Evie didn't know the depth of his deception. He wouldn't want to frighten her. But tonight the beers were working on him, and the fury was steaming through the cracks of his control.

His leg ached, and that helped to keep him in balance. Daniel went past the expensive stores—closed for the evening—and wandered into a comfortable residential district. No factory worker lived here, he wagered. Nor the clerks in those fancy department stores. The delineation of wealth was so much clearer here than back in Texas.

But he wasn't a stranger to those differences. He had grown up in St. Louis without ever considering the comforts at his command. It was only in these last ten years that he had become aware of the widening chasm between the haves and the have-nots.

There was a reason for that, but he wasn't prepared to dwell on it right now as his wandering took him farther from the business district and deeper into the bastions of wealth.

Daniel suspected these magnificent edifices gleaming with gaslights and crystal windows and hidden in the shadows behind trees and shrubberies larger than the city park would rightly be called mansions. He'd lived off and on in a mansion during these last few years, but it in no way compared to these. The mansions around Natchez, Mississippi, were falling into ruin and decay, destroyed by the war, the economy, the lack of manpower to keep them functioning any longer. Obviously, no such destruction had touched Cutlerville, Ohio.

Daniel leaned against a wrought-iron fence in front of the largest of these symbols of wealth. He could see a polished open carriage in the drive by the front door. The front door was open, and he could catch a glimpse of a chandelier glittering in the foyer. All the lamps in the house must have been lit, for light twinkled from every window. Back in the section of town from where he had just come, the cost of oil for a single lamp was prohibitive. Gaslights were unthinkable.

He had been told the house with the stone pineapples on the gateposts would be the Mulloney mansion. He could see the pineapples at the end of the street. The house and yard took up the entire block. This was it, then, the house where his family lived, the house whose portals he had been forbidden.

He had just enough beer in him to wonder what would happen if he walked up that drive and announced himself at the door. He liked to imagine the chaos that would ensue. Leaning his shoulder against the cold iron fence, Daniel remembered all those years of wondering, the years of waiting. To a child, a week was forever. He had endured years, the childhood equivalent of eternity. By the time he had learned some speck of the truth, he had developed a facade of indifference.

But curiosity had always been a strong component of his character. He couldn't help but be curious about a family that had so much it could afford to throw away one of its sons.

Just that much knowledge of the people behind this gate made him worry about the merry little imp he had met on the train. People who could throw away their own child wouldn't think twice about ignoring a bright and lovely woman whose only purpose was to bring them more wealth. Daniel hated to think of that happening. Even Evie would agree with him if she knew.

Straightening, Daniel shoved his hands into his pockets and stared at the carriage, willing its occupants to descend from the house. He wanted to know at least what they looked like before he started digging into their lives.

But no one came out, and his empty stomach was beginning to protest. It was time to get back to the real world.

He was a journalist, had learned at the hands of some of the best. He knew just how to go about digging into the lives and businesses of the Mulloney family. He hadn't been certain when he came here that he would bother, but now he had an incentive other than himself.

He would make certain that Peter Mulloney was the kind of man Georgina Hanover ought to marry. And he would find out just what kind of people the Mulloneys were before he made the decision to acknowledge them as his relations.

Hands in pockets, staring through the iron gate separating him from the family he had never known, Daniel thought he might just ride out of Cutlerville, Ohio, without ever telling them who he was.

Four

❦

The announcement was made. There would be no turning back now.

Georgina looked up at the handsome man whose arm she held and tried to will herself to feel happiness. His smile was warm as he turned it on her upon becoming aware of her stare. She gave him a vapid smile in return. If she didn't have a thought in her head, Peter wouldn't notice.

The pale blue gown her mother had chosen for her had a deep square neckline that cut scandalously low across her bust, and Georgina had felt Peter's glance in that direction more than once during the evening. She wasn't certain why men liked to look at her there, but it did make her tingle slightly when she knew he was doing it. Maybe everyone was right and she just needed to get to know him better.

It was a difficult assignment in a crowd like this. It was her duty to circulate among the guests, to dance with old and young and see that everyone was having a good time. She could do that with ease, but she couldn't figure out how to get to know her fiancé while doing it.

Not that Peter was much help. Already he had turned to one of the other male guests to discuss a problem he had down at the store, and she was forgotten. Sighing, Georgina accepted a lemonade and an offer of a dance from a young man she had known since childhood.

Much later, after she had lost sight of Peter, Georgina decided the party was doing just fine without her. Despite the open windows, the heat in the ballroom was stifling, and she could feel a fine sheen of perspiration coating her forehead.

If her fiancé wasn't around to escort her into the garden, she would just have to go herself. If she thought Peter might be in the least bit jealous, she would have another man take her outside, but she doubted if Peter would even notice. And if he wasn't going to notice, she wasn't going to waste her moment of freedom on one of these less than sober morons decorating the dance floor.

A slight breeze billowed the heavy draperies as Georgina stepped between them and through the open French doors to the terrace. The draperies prevented much of the light in the ballroom from escaping, but there were gaslights placed strategically along the paths in the garden beyond the terrace, so the night wasn't completely dark.

She saw him immediately. He wasn't making any secret of his presence. He lounged against the low wall, his wide shoulders outlined against the shrubbery, his long legs lazily sprawled in front of him. Her heart gave a strange lurch and pounded a little faster as she scanned his features to be certain she hadn't been mistaken. She recognized the slightly crooked nose, the unruly lock of hair, the almost ascetically long face that transformed into something delightfully wicked when he grinned. Which he was doing now.

He was wearing a suit, but it wasn't of the formal black worn by the men inside. The light linen stood out against the darkness of the shrubberies behind him, and the string tie was defiantly western. He was as out of place as a toad on a footstool, but relief washed over her as he came forward.

"You said I was invited to all your parties," he said softly, in a drawl she hadn't quite remembered.

"And I would have sent you a formal invitation if I'd known where to find you, Mr. Martin. You never called."

She was aware when his gaze was distracted from her face to the glittering tiara crowning her carefully stacked tresses. She wasn't certain what was in his eyes when they came back to hers, but she knew somehow that he was studiously avoiding looking at her breasts. That knowledge made her tingle more than Peter's deliberate look had. Rebelliously, she wanted this man to look at her there.

Georgina came closer, holding her shoulders back so he couldn't avoid seeing what she displayed. Never in her life had she behaved like this, but she knew exactly how it was done. She touched his arm lightly and felt the slight jerk of shock beneath her fingers.

"I thought you had forgotten me." She made her voice whisper like the breeze through the trees, and she read its effect on his mobile face.

Daniel didn't answer immediately. Instead he studied her, deliberately resting his gaze on the line of lace caressing her breasts before traveling downward, noting the hard curves of her corset beneath the silk, the full swell of her hips, the juncture of her legs beneath the clinging cloth. When his gaze returned to hers, he was smiling.

"You're doing it again, aren't you? Why don't you save your tricks for your boyfriend? There's no need for anything but honesty between us. That is, if what you want is a friend."

Georgina felt deflated. At the same time she felt relieved. She could say what she wanted to this man, and he wouldn't laugh or walk off or take her in contempt. She touched his arm again, leaving her hand there this time.

"I want a friend. Will you dance?"

Music poured through the open windows, and Daniel glanced up at the heavy draperies preventing any sight of the lavish ballroom beyond. He looked down into the plea in her eyes, and held out his arms.

"I'm not very graceful, but I'd be delighted to try. There's more room out here than in there."

The flagstones beneath their feet weren't a polished dance floor, and their motions were less than graceful as he had said, but it was a wonderful dance anyway. Georgina gave in to the sway of the music, the brush of a breeze against her skin, and the firm hold of this tall stranger's arms around her. He took a strong lead, leaving her with no concern other than the pleasure of their movements. It was like heaven. She didn't have to say a word, didn't have to be concerned about her appearance, didn't have to watch her steps. None of that mattered with this man. The dance was everything.

She was sorry when the music stopped. The cowboy's hand lingered briefly at her waist, and even when he dropped his arm, he continued holding her other hand. Their fingers entwined when he looked down on her.

"I just wanted to see if you were happy," he said in measured tones, as if the speech were practiced.

Georgina plastered on her vapid smile. "Why, of course I'm happy. I have it all, don't I?"

"That's what I thought." His gaze was curious, though, and not relieved by her reassurances. "I've decided to stay around a while. I've bought a printing press over near your father's factory. Do you still want me to call on you once in a while?"

"A printing press?" Her eyes widened in excitement. "Are you going to start a newspaper? Will you have an office with photographs in the window?" The excitement suddenly departed. "Or are you just going to print cards and posters and such?"

Even if he hadn't contemplated his own paper, he would have after that. Daniel grinned. "I'll be doing both. There's not much money to be made in a newspaper until it gets some circulation. I have to eat somehow."

This time her excitement was more muted, as if she had remembered her role as a mature adult. "I wish you would call on me sometime and tell me about it. I've always been curious about how a newspaper works."

He had hoped to invite her down to see it, but he could sense her withdrawal and bowed to the inevitability of their differences. "I would be happy to tell you what I can, but I don't know if I can get away at proper calling hours. I have a business to run."

"Give me your card, and I'll see you get the next invitation. I've got to get back to my guests."

Somehow, Georgina knew Mr. Martin wouldn't enter the ballroom with her. It was as if a curtain had been drawn between them. Even when he handed her the card and their fingers touched, that knowledge was there. There was no good reason why their worlds should ever touch again.

She tucked the piece of cardboard between her breasts and winked. She would almost swear that he colored, but he stepped back into the darkness, and she hurried toward the door as the music started up again. It felt good just knowing he was there. She wouldn't think about all the other things he made her feel.

Peter sprawled his long frame across the blanket they had spread over the grass. His dark curls fell over his forehead as he finished the chicken leg he had been gnawing on. Georgina found him an exceedingly virile specimen of manhood, but she was still searching for the magic she had hoped to find in her future husband.

At least Peter hadn't been terribly reluctant to indulge her with this intimate little picnic she had talked him into. It was just the two of them for a change. There were no other men to distract him with their talk of business, no other women to distract him with their charms. His attention was all hers.

She had worn one of her gowns from London, one of those requiring no structured undergarments. Mr. Martin had noticed that immediately when she had worn one on the train, but Peter seemed somehow oblivious to the makeup of women's attire. He rested blissfully at ease, staring up at the sky and enjoying his meal. She wanted to pour the pitcher of lemonade over him.

"What is it you do all day at the store?" She tried the soft, seductive voice she had tried on Mr. Martin, hoping Peter wouldn't think the question too unfeminine if she asked it properly. To add to the illusion, she leaned over and tickled him with a piece of grass.

"Work." He grabbed her hand and kissed it, robbing her of the grass at the same time. "What do *you* do all day?"

Georgina wanted to groan, but she obediently replied, "Play. Will you tell me about your work if I don't tell you about my play?"

Peter grinned, and the shock of it nearly made her jump out of her skin. He looked just like Mr. Martin when he did that. Of course, he didn't really look like Pecos. The cowboy's hair was light and straight and his face was much longer and leaner with that unfortunate bump in his nose, but there was just something . . .

She shook her head and willed him to make a sensible reply.

"I'm a glorified handyman," Peter admitted. "I fix whatever needs fixing."

That didn't sound very likely. Peter was always elegantly dressed in tailored coats and silk cravats. Georgina frowned. "You mean you go around with hammer and nails and pound boards all day?"

Peter laughed and reached for another chicken leg. "Not that kind of fixing. If one of the customers takes a liking to something but tries to go out without paying, I'm the one they call. The other day we had a nosy journalist asking questions of our shop clerks, and one of the managers asked me to remove him. That's the kind of thing I do."

Nosy journalist. Georgina's eyes lit up. What could Pecos be up to now? She spread jam on a roll and handed it to Peter. "What kind of questions would a journalist ask a shop clerk? I shouldn't think they'd have much to say."

"He's just drumming up a story, I imagine. There's always someone willing to complain, and newspapers will jump on their complaint just to put something on the front page. I escorted him out of the building."

"You didn't! How awful. Did you find out who was complaining or what they were complaining about?"

Talking about business was what Peter did best, and he had no objection to an eager audience. Swallowing the last bite of roll, he shrugged. "Hours mostly. And we won't let them sit down when they're on the job. I had to let one of our best workers go, though, because of the incident. She was telling the journalist how one of the new men got promoted to management over her when she had been doing the same work he does for years, without the pay he makes. She should know better. The man has a family to raise. Of course we pay him better. And you can't put a woman in management. No one would listen to her. She was a good worker. It's a shame she got to thinking so much of herself."

Peter's smug logic peeled away the last vestige of her patience. This time the temptation was too strong. The lemonade pitcher was down to the dregs, but it made a satisfyingly sticky trickle over Peter's dark curls when Georgina tilted it over his head.

Startled, he shouted and leapt to his feet, scrubbing at his hair, staring at her as if she were crazed. Georgina merely grabbed her skirts and stalked off, leaving him to think what he would.

She wanted to scream at him, "What makes you think men are so much better? Don't women have families, too? Shouldn't they be paid for the work they do?" But it was worse than useless, she knew. She couldn't change the opinion of half the populace by screaming at Peter.

But a newspaper could.

As Georgina marched out of Peter's reach, a whole new horizon spread out before her. Her dream of love and romance fell by the wayside as she imagined the front-page story she could write. At last, she had a real goal to work toward. She could change the world some day, with the right help. And she knew just where to find that.

Blucher didn't object when Georgina ordered him to take her downtown the next day. He did look slightly puzzled at the street she requested, but no one had given him orders to keep her out of photography studios. And when she sent him home with the news that she would be returning later with Peter, he obediently left her to her own devices.

Several hours later, Georgina was regretting her deviousness in dismissing Blucher, but she'd had to do it. There wasn't any way in the world she could hide the heavy satchels of photography paraphernalia, and she wasn't prepared to answer her family's questions about it. But the damned stuff weighed at least a ton.

Women turned to stare at her with curiosity as she trudged down the street in the direction of Hanover Industries. A strange man offered to help her carry the load, but his eyes were everywhere except on the equipment, and Georgina used her tripod to trip him. People stared more as the man fell on his face, but she marched on without any indication that she noticed. One of the advantages of this street was that it was almost in the respectable area of town, but close enough to the industrial side that she could walk there—providing her arms didn't fall off first.

Sweat poured in rivulets through the dust on Georgina's face by the time she reached the factory. She kept well out of sight of her father's windows, watching carefully for the name of the building listed on Mr. Martin's business card. She knew her hair was coming unpinned and was straggling down the back of her neck, and her arms were nearly numb from the weight of the cumbersome equipment, but she wasn't going to turn back now. She knew precisely what she wanted to do.

The faded paint on the wooden sign over the door was barely legible, but the building was made of substantial brick and only the bottom windows were boarded. Surely that was a promising sign. Georgina hefted one satchel to a more comfortable position and opened the door.

It squeaked. She gave it a doubtful look and glanced hesitantly into the darkened hallway. No lights flickered anywhere behind the boarded windows. She pushed the door open farther so that sunlight poured into the hall. In the center of the cavernous first floor she found a stairway, and the dull roar of machinery filtered down from the upper floors. The building wasn't entirely empty, then.

Squaring her shoulders, Georgina marched in. Her steps sounded ominously loud in the empty hall, but if there was anyone there, they didn't respond to her presence. She would have to climb the stairs and take her chances.

Groaning at the thought of carrying her equipment up no telling how many flights of stairs, she gripped her satchels a little tighter and set out. She wasn't about to appear in front of Mr. Martin dirty and bedraggled and without her equipment. She was going to show him that she was more than just a social butterfly. She was going to be a working woman, too.

Georgina didn't know why it was important that he know that, and she didn't spend any time worrying about it. She meant to take pictures to go with the stories she was writing, show the unfairness of this male-dominated world that allowed women to work long hours for less than a man and no doubt any number of other subjects of injustice when they occurred to her. She would have a purpose in life.

She didn't waste time wondering what Peter would think of that, either. If he thought anything at all, he could just take his engagement ring and find some simpering ninny to put it on. She meant to make the whole world see once and for all that she had a mind and intended to use it for something besides planning seating arrangements.

The noise from the printing press grew louder as she ascended to the second story. Her heels clattering against the wooden floor couldn't be heard above the racket. She followed the sound down still another hallway, this one much lighter and more cheerful from the light of the huge windows on either end. The heat, however, was stifling.

Finding an open door, Georgina allowed herself the luxury of dropping her satchels for just a minute, just so she could push her hair back and wipe her face off a little.

The printing press came to a crashing silence at the same time as her satchels hit the floor. The sound echoed through the nearly empty building.

Mr. Martin appeared instantly, his spectacles sliding down his sweat-coated nose, his hands rubbing a rag to remove the black ink. At the sight of Georgina, his arched eyebrows rose a fraction. At the sight of her equipment, he gaped openly, his gaze swinging back and forth between the hideously expensive camera and paraphernalia and back to the delicate blond female in silk. And then he grinned and stashed his spectacles in his shirt pocket.

"A fellow journalist is always welcome, Miss Hanover. Please come in."

Five

❦

Heaven help him, but she was the loveliest thing he had ever seen in his life. Light from the vaulted hall windows glinted off hair that was almost white-gold in its beauty. Beneath the streaks of dirt her face blossomed into a beatific smile at his words, and Daniel felt ten miles tall. He wanted to take her round little curves into his arms and squeeze them with sheer happiness. That was when he knew he was in big trouble.

She was engaged to his brother.

That knowledge wedged like a dry bread crust in his throat, and Daniel had difficulty speaking. Instead of the words of delight he wished to offer, he said, "You shouldn't be here, Miss Hanover."

The light immediately fled her eyes. "I didn't spend the morning dragging this equipment over here only to be sent away, Mr. Martin."

He didn't know why she had spent the morning dragging that equipment over here, but his gaze rested longingly on the expensive camera. He was trying to keep to a budget, and a camera wasn't in it. A newssheet like his had no earthly use for photographs. For that, he needed a downtown office and a publishing company. The idea had appeal, but not on his budget.

"You're looking to get me shot, aren't you?" Daniel kept his voice neutral as he picked up the heaviest satchel and carried it in, making room for her to step by him.

She did so without hesitation, and Daniel was suddenly aware of the shabbiness of his surroundings next to her exquisite loveliness. Her blue silk shimmered in the motes of sunlight. The yards of ruching sweeping down her boned bodice and long skirt must have cost the moon and stars. The perky hat perched atop her bedraggled coiffure had a feather that swept the air as she glanced around. He was aware that all she could see was a splintering wooden floor, soiled walls, and a mattress thrown up against a floorboard. He hadn't seen the necessity of finding an apartment as long as he had rented the entire floor. It wasn't as if he needed an office or a newsroom or any other of the accouterments that went with a professional newspaper. Not yet, anyway.

"Very nice." Her tone was too melodic for her sarcasm to have effect. She swung around and faced Daniel. "Were you the journalist Peter threw out of Mulloney's the other day?"

Daniel ran his hand through his hair, realizing it was in dire need of a trimming as he met her gaze calmly. "And if I am?"

"Then I've come to help you. Peter fired that poor woman you were interviewing. He said no one would listen to a woman. Did she have a family? Children?"

Daniel was extremely wary of gods bearing gifts. He knew his mythology quite well. And what applied to gods applied to goddesses, too. Perhaps she wasn't quite a goddess. She was dirty and bedraggled, and her tone was a little too imperious at the moment. She really wasn't even pretty, not in the same way that Evie was. Of course, Evie was beautiful. Georgina was just . . . interesting. That was the word for it. Interesting. Her lively eyes kept him captivated until he nearly forgot her question.

Her tapping toe reminded Daniel that he was expected to answer. He finished wiping his hands on the rag. "As far as I know, she was just an aging spinster with an axe to grind, but I'm sorry to hear she lost her job. That was uncalled for."

That took the wind out of her flag fast enough. She had come marching out to war for next to nothing. Daniel waited for the next installment of this emotional drama.

Georgina grimaced, but forged ahead. "If you are look-

ing for a story on how women are mistreated by management, then you have only to look to my father's factory.
I can help you with that."

That hadn't been what Daniel was looking for at all. He
had merely been trying to find out more about his family
and their operations, but he wasn't about to admit that to
Miss Georgina Hanover. He dusted off the window seat
and gallantly offered her a place to sit. He could smell the
light fragrance of her soap as she swept by him to accept
it. Lilies of the valley. Lord, but it smelled good.

"I was more interested in Mulloney's," he answered
imperturbably.

"Then you ought to be interested in Hanover Industries. They produce most of the clothing that Mulloney's
sells under their own label."

He really didn't care. The world was rife with injustice.
Daniel knew that from firsthand experience. What he really wanted to know about was the callous wealthy family
that had thrown him away, but this woman standing in
front of him was engaged to the heir apparent. He detected a slight conflict of interest here.

"Mulloney's is a big name in this town. A story about
them will generate sales. Everybody shops at Mulloney's.
Why would they bother reading a story about Hanover Industries?"

"Because those women work terrible hours under horrible conditions and make barely enough to stay alive.
Isn't that story enough?"

"That's your father's factory you're talking about, Miss
Hanover. The money he makes from his employees keeps
you in those expensive gowns and paid for that equipment." Daniel nodded at the satchels on the floor. As
much as he wanted access to that camera, he had a bad
feeling in his gut about any partnership with Georgina
Hanover. They had no ground in common whatsoever.

She really hadn't thought this through at all, he could
tell. She sighed, wiped her face with a handkerchief, and
looked miserable. Daniel suspected that what had started
out as an act of defiance to make her father or Peter take

notice was now snowballing into something quite different. But she didn't look as if she was going to give up.

Putting away her handkerchief, Georgina stiffened her shoulders. "All right, have it your way. It's your paper. But I suspect there is some connection with the factory and the store, and that's the reason my father's workers are so overworked. My father is a nice man; Mr. Mulloney isn't."

Daniel wasn't going to dive after that one. He would see for himself what kind of man Mulloney was, not dwell on gossip. "And what do you think photographs are going to accomplish on this little crusade of yours, Miss Hanover?" He jerked the topic back to more pertinent arguments.

She looked surprised. "Why, they'll show the horrible conditions people work under. Photographs are all the rage, you know. People react to pictures much better than words."

Daniel patiently let her toward the obvious. "And where will you show these photographs, Miss Hanover? Here? I think the people in this area already know the conditions they work under."

Georgina bit her lip and glanced around as if just discovering where she was. "It's not exactly like the news offices in London, is it?"

"Not exactly," Daniel agreed. Then taking pity on her, he asked, "Do you know how to use that thing?"

She brightened. "I spent all morning learning, and they said I could come back any time with questions."

"I suppose they showed you the wet process?" Daniel asked with a touch of gloom.

Georgina shook her head. "They have dry plates. They said it would be much easier if I wasn't going to use a studio. So I didn't get a tent. Do you have a room I could use for developing?"

He could feel just a hint of hope beginning to gather. Ideas swarmed through Daniel's mind as his gaze lingered on the expensive equipment. "There're rooms to spare. Do you think there's enough light inside Mulloney's to get a picture?"

"With that big chandelier overhead? Why not?"

"Do you think you could get pictures inside the store without getting thrown out? There are big clocks down there behind every counter. It would be interesting to catch one clerk in front of that clock when she came in at eight and again just before she left for home at six. People could see her standing up and know she's been on her feet for nine or ten hours."

Georgina nodded eagerly. "Peter will just think I have a silly new hobby. How about a picture of his office with the fancy carpeting and big desks? Then a picture of where the clerks live? I bet one of their houses would fit inside that office."

Daniel's eyes gleamed with approval, but his words were ones of caution. "We'll have to find a place to display them, a very public place. And you'll have to practice. I've used the dry plates before. They're very sensitive. You'll ruin your first batches until you get the exposure right."

Georgina grinned. She was going to do it. She was going to have a career. Even if she didn't know anything about photography other than the basics learned in one morning, she knew she could do it. And even if the man showing her where to set up her darkroom thought she was a tool in his employ, she would show the world that she was more than that. Then let Peter and her father pretend she was a useless piece of fluff.

Although she couldn't begin her photography assignment until the next day, Georgina took her camera with her when she left. Mr. Martin had been preoccupied with his work and not much interested in entertaining her once they had decided on a plan of action. She felt slightly insulted that he didn't feel called upon to entertain her, but she reminded herself that this was a business relationship, not a social one. She would just have to get used to the manners of the working class.

She was quite certain there was a story to be had at her father's factory if she only knew how to get at it. But her father had made it very clear that she wasn't to be caught in this neighborhood again, so she couldn't practice with her new camera there.

But the lumpy unglamorous old buildings and the wagons and the unfashionably dressed people fascinated her, and she couldn't resist viewing them through the eye of her new toy. It wouldn't hurt to take a picture or two for practice. Anything was better than returning to the house and her mother's wedding preparations.

Daniel found her there when he came down at the end of the day. He watched in amusement as Georgina beguiled a scruffy little boy and his dog into posing for her while a small crowd gathered around them. Her animated chatter kept the onlookers spellbound, and he thought she could make a fortune as a carnival barker should she ever need the money. As it was, he was quite certain these people would spend their last pennies to have their pictures taken by her.

She was smiling and laughing when he walked up, but that disappeared as soon as she caught sight of him. She glanced worriedly at the stream of people leaving the buildings around them as the church tower chimed six, took note of the long shadows indicating dusk was not far off, and hastily began packing her camera into its box.

"I think I had better escort you home, Miss Hanover. It's a little late for you to be wandering the streets." It was more than a little late, and Daniel didn't think she could possibly walk the distance to her home, but he wasn't certain he could find a hired cab in this district either.

"I don't know. My father's carriage will be here soon, but he's told me to stay away. Perhaps I could persuade Blucher to pretend I was just coming back from town." Nervously, she dusted off her gown and placed her camera over her shoulder, giving it a dubious look.

Daniel knew the meaning of that look. Her father didn't know about the camera. No amount of lies and semitruths would hide it. He took the strap from her shoulder and placed it over his. "I'll bring it to you at Mulloney's in the morning. What direction will the carriage come from? We can stop him before he gets to the plant."

Georgina directed him, but while they waited, she spied the pretty woman from her father's factory, the one she had seen Mr. Martin talking to earlier. She tugged on his sleeve and nodded in her direction. "Can you tell me who she is? She doesn't seem to like me very much, but I'd like to talk to her."

Daniel looked up and saw Janice frowning and about to cross the street to avoid him. He had met her younger brother on his first night in town. Her family was practically the only one he knew. And he knew women well enough to know the source of her frown. He took a step in Janice's direction and made it apparent he wished to talk. Her frown deepened, but she hesitated just long enough for him to speak.

"I'll walk you home as soon as I see Miss Hanover into her carriage. Janice, do you know Georgina Hanover? Miss Hanover, may I introduce Janice Harrison? Her family has been gracious enough to welcome a stranger like me."

Janice stood stiffly at his side, a glare of defiance in her eyes. Georgina smiled and offered her hand.

"I'm so glad I finally got a chance to be properly introduced. I'm not very good with pen and pencil, but I thought sometime you might let me take your photograph. Your looks are very striking, and I'm certain they would turn out well on paper."

Georgina's open flattery left no room for insult. Janice's defiance wavered slightly, but she remained stubbornly aloof. "I don't have time for such things. I've got to get home and fix supper. You needn't see me home, Daniel."

Georgina gave him an inquisitive glance at this use of a name she hadn't known, but Daniel smoothly intervened. "Janice has a younger sister who has just started working at Mulloney's. We might begin our interviews there."

The carriage came around the corner then, and Daniel flagged it down, helping a frustrated Georgina into its interior before she could ask too many questions. Janice was already hurrying down the street before he had time to get back to her.

Women. Daniel gave Janice's back a look of disgust as he loped after her. There wasn't any pleasing them. It was easy enough to make friends with a man. You had a few beers, told a few jokes, and they didn't get huffy if you talked to someone else. It would be much simpler if he could confine his acquaintance to men. Unfortunately, he rather enjoyed the company of women when they were being pleasant.

Maybe if he made them understand that marriage was the farthest thing from his mind, they would relax and learn to be friends instead of competitors. He'd have to write Evie and ask about that one.

"Georgina! What is all this nonsense? I've been told you've been here all day with this paraphernalia." Peter strode down the aisle between women's hosiery and the jewelry counter, his gaze fixed disapprovingly on the minx perched on a stepladder and balancing a camera almost larger than herself against the top rung.

Georgina glanced up and beamed. "Not all day. I came this morning and left again. I just got back a little while ago. The light is different at this hour. See how it comes through that window and lights up the rubies? Besides, I thought you would be happy to see me."

"I might if I thought I was the reason you were here. Get down before you kill yourself." Peter held the ladder with one hand to steady it and caught her waist with the other, supporting her as she descended.

Georgina tried to feel properly delighted with his concern and protection, but mostly she felt irritated. She decided against stepping on his foot, however. Peter brought out the absolute worst in her, but she wouldn't give into childish whims. She climbed down and stood toe to toe with him, giving him a brilliant smile.

"I'm honored that you are so concerned. Would you like to escort me home or shall I wait for Blucher?"

She decided that although Mr. Martin appeared taller than Peter, he probably wasn't. It was just that Peter's shoulders were so broad they negated the effect of height. She was rather frightened of the strength she sensed in Peter's grasp. She didn't like knowing that he could overcome her physically. But when he released her and ran his fingers through his thick curls, he looked more boy than man, and she relaxed.

"My father is holding a meeting over at the mill, and I'm already late. Let me see if Blucher has arrived yet, and I'll see you to the carriage."

She'd already learned today that Mr. Mulloney owned the steel mill and the gaslight company and that his other sons held positions in those places. Gossiping with store clerks could be very enlightening. She took pity on Peter and patted his arm reassuringly.

"You go on. I'll just get a few more pictures before Blucher arrives. The nice man at the door will tell me when he's here."

Peter looked relieved, and after a hasty farewell left her with the admonishment not to touch another stepladder. Georgina hummed softly to herself as she set up her next shot. The poor man had no clue, after all. It was his own fault, though. He should never underestimate the power of a woman.

Georgina found Mr. Martin leaning against a lamppost and reading a newspaper when she came out. She gave him a big grin and took his elbow, leading him toward the waiting carriage, much to the disapproval of Blucher, who looked on.

"I could go in there every day and do whatever I like and no one would think twice about it. I've already talked to half the clerks for you, but I couldn't take notes or it would raise too many suspicions. So you'll have to rely on my memory. I'll write it all down tonight."

Mr. Martin handed her into the carriage. "Give me your plates and I'll develop them tonight. If we're going to get any shots of the women at home, it's going to have to be done on Sunday. I can't take you to those neighborhoods in the evening."

"It seems to me if you can go there, I can go there," she pointed out, knowing the impracticality of the protest.

She couldn't go anywhere without a proper escort in the evening. And she had the feeling that her father wouldn't consider this man a proper escort.

Daniel gave her a grin that was impossible to argue with. "I want to issue my first edition on Wednesday. Hurry up with those notes. I can have the piece written before we go visiting on Sunday. Then all I'll have to do is lay it out and set the type. Be nice to that boyfriend of yours."

Georgina stuck her tongue out at him and signaled Blucher to pull away.

Be nice to Peter, indeed. After next Wednesday she doubted if he would ever speak to her again.

Unless Mr. Martin had some devious plan for protecting her from his wrath. And the more she thought about it, the more convinced she was that he had. He looked entirely too sure of himself.

Six

ℰ

"We've just come home from church, Georgina. I don't understand why you have to go out again. You know we are to be at the Higgins's for dinner, and we're to attend the church social afterward. You should be lying down and resting so you'll look your best instead of dashing off with that"—Dolly Hanover gave the camera in her daughter's hand a horrified look—"that dangerous piece of equipment."

Had her mother chastised her in the normal tone of an angry parent, Georgina could have brushed it off without a qualm. Instead, her mother was worrying at the beads around her high-necked dress and whispering in a tone of dread, an almost certain prelude to another "episode."

It was a form of emotional blackmail that Georgina recognized easily now that she had returned from an extended absence. When she was younger, she had always succumbed at the first sign that her mother was on the verge of a "spell." She resisted now, but not without pangs of guilt. When her mother retreated to her room and pulled the shades, her father was desolate, and Georgina always carried the knowledge that it was all her fault.

And it was going to be her fault again this time, but her shoulders were wider now. If her parents wanted to dump the blame on her, let them. She had other things to do, and saving her future was one of them.

Gently, she kissed her mother's paper-thin cheek. "I shall sleep in the carriage, Mama, and I will be back in plenty of time for you to help me find the right gown. Peter will be there this evening, and I shall want to look my best."

Her mother looked only slightly mollified, but she raised no other objection as Georgina hurried off. Dolly Hanover never raised real objections, never protested, never got angry. She simply accepted whatever came her way and retired to her room when she could no longer deal with it. Georgina supposed she ought to feel sorry for her mother. Mostly, she felt fury. That wasn't the kind of life she meant to lead.

She was humming and bouncing in the seat by the time Blucher let her out near the Presbyterian church where he thought he was taking her. Georgina couldn't see Mr. Martin yet, but she knew he was here. He was as eager as she to see this story in print. She still glowed with the praise he had heaped on her when she had given him her notes on Mulloney's Department Store. People had always praised her gowns and her hair and her smile, but no one had ever cared whether or not there was anything behind them. And since no one had ever cared, she had never tried to be anything else but what she was. That was going to change.

She was going to change, and the world around her was going to change. She wasn't going to be her mama, or anybody else's mama. She was going to be herself, and she was going to make a difference in this world. Daniel had promised her that the newspaper story would make a difference, and she believed him. As soon as people saw how mistreated these clerks were, they would insist that things change. The people of Cutlerville were proud, upstanding citizens, and they would raise a clamor at such slavery in their midst. After all, hadn't they sent a battalion to fight slavery during the Civil War?

As the carriage and Blucher disappeared around the corner, Daniel ran down the church steps and caught the camera case in Georgina's hand.

"I didn't really think you would come. I feel like I'm eighteen again and sneaking around behind my sister's back. I guess I'll have to invest in a carriage so I can pick you up at the door personally."

He shouldered the case and hurried down the street faster than Georgina could walk in her tight skirt. She wasn't certain if it was his ebullient energy that carried him or some kind of anger at himself, or maybe even her. Daniel grew more mysterious with time instead of less. But she wasn't about to let him leave her behind.

Pulling her skirt above her ankles, she hobbled after him as fast as she could. "Mr. Martin, if you can't wait for me, give me back my camera. I don't mind making a spectacle of myself on my terms, but I'll not do it on yours."

He turned in surprise, glanced down at her exposed ankle boots, then up at her irate expression, and grinned. "What kind of spectacle and what terms do you ask?"

Georgina was quite certain his thoughts weren't polite and that he was probably laughing at her, but she was too eager for this new assignment to allow him to ruin the moment. "Mr. Martin, you are rude, crude, and uncouth, and if you do not behave yourself, I'll take back my camera. How far away are we?"

Since there was no anger in her tone, he ignored the insult and extended his elbow for her use. "A few blocks. You really are going to have to find better clothes for walking in."

"I just came from church, Mr. Martin. I don't expect you to understand the need for proper attire. A gentleman adjusts his pace to a lady's."

For some reason he had a hard time thinking of Miss Georgina Meredith Hanover as a lady. Perhaps it was because she was a full head shorter than he, and he was too aware of soft round curves instead of the battleship attire of the ladies he knew. She was too young, too mischievous, too full of laughter to be one of the proud matrons he considered ladies. She was more like Evie—a lady in name only.

Except that his thoughts about Miss Hanover were anything but sisterly.

Damn, but he had trouble keeping his mind where it

belonged where women were concerned. Why in hell he had taken on a female photographer was more than he could imagine, but the deed was done and he couldn't undo it. The rustle of stiff satin against whatever getup she wore beneath that gown reminded Daniel only too well of the feminine hand on his arm, even if that haunting scent of lilies didn't surround him. He was damned glad they had almost reached their destination.

Georgina was studying the tiny wooden structures with interest. He bet she had never seen this side of town. Her carriage driver would have made it a point to avoid it when he drove her anywhere. Most of the streets were too narrow for a carriage in any event. Trash littered the dirt space between the two rows of houses, blowing up against the unpainted walls and catching on wooden steps. Here and there someone had made an attempt at cheerfulness by planting geraniums in tin cans and setting them on the steps, but the spot of brightness only served to make the surroundings more dismal in comparison.

Boys played a rough and tumble game of kick-the-can in the middle of the street, and Daniel placed himself between Georgina and the game and skirted around them skillfully. One of the boys shouted a word of greeting, and he lifted his hand in acknowledgement, but he didn't stop to talk any more than the boy stopped his game. Sociability wasn't a priority on this side of town.

"It smells," Georgina muttered as they stopped in front of the narrow one-story shotgun house that was their destination.

"There's no sanitation. No indoor toilets, no yards for privies. I won't tell you what they use." Daniel lifted his knuckles to knock at the weathered door without looking at the expression of wide-eyed horror on his companion's face. He didn't have to see it to know it was there.

The door burst open before he could lower his fist against the wood. A small figure darted from the interior, colliding with Daniel's legs before skittering around him and out into the street, shouting "Douglas!" at the top of her lungs and in a tone of terror.

Daniel staggered, momentarily unbalanced as the collision shifted his weight to his weak leg, but the cries from within forced him forward swiftly. Leaving the woman on his arm outside, he stepped into the dim interior.

Clutching her fingers over her mouth to stifle a scream, Georgina glanced after the young girl running and yelling down the street in the direction of the older boys, then back to the man who had just disappeared into the shadows of the interior. She could hear a woman's screams and a man's thundering voice and she was paralyzed. She had never been in such an unpleasant situation before, and she didn't have experience or etiquette to rely on.

So she relied on instinct. Stepping into the tiny front room, she watched a big ruffian in a derby hat and shapeless sack coat raise his hand to the pretty woman she recognized from her father's factory. The woman was cringing, and the younger girl beside her was screaming in a confusion of fury and terror. Georgina was already looking for a weapon when Mr. Martin's movement caught her attention.

The newspaperman was taller but considerably more slender than the bully. That didn't stop him from reaching for the man's collar and jerking him backward. The bully's fist missed its connection with the young woman's face. Georgina bit her hand in horror as the bigger man turned in a fury to whip his powerful arm in Mr. Martin's direction.

Daniel dodged, kicked upward in a vicious blow to the man's privates, and bent the bigger man over in a bellow of pain. Using the camera case for leverage, Daniel slammed it against the man's neck before he could straighten up, flattening him to the wooden floor.

By this time the gang of boys from the street was pouring to the door and standing outside screeching. Georgina pushed herself against the wall as the man she had considered mild-mannered and amusing pointed at the ruffian he had single-handedly brought down.

"The gentleman had a little accident, Douglas. Why don't you and the boys haul him out where he can get some fresh air?"

With whoops of triumph the boys grabbed every available limb and piece of fabric and unceremoniously hauled the huge man out into the open cesspool that they called a street.

"Who in hell was that?" Daniel demanded, turning back to the two women clinging to each other.

Now that her eyes had adjusted to the darkness, Georgina could see that there was already a growing bruise on the face of the woman she knew as Janice. The younger woman, who looked enough like her to be her sister, was sobbing brokenly. Janice lifted her chin in a defiant tilt as she first glanced to Georgina before looking at the man who had saved her form further beating.

"That's the rent collector. It's the first of the month, and we didn't have all the rent."

Her sister gulped back a sob long enough to offer the explanation Janice had proudly refused to give. "Betsy was sick and we had to use some of the rent money for medicine. We told him we would have it next week, but Egan's a brute."

Douglas came back in, brushing his hands off on his dirty corduroys. He gave a questioning glance to Georgina, but hurried to his sisters. "How did that bastard sneak up on us like that? We usually get plenty of warning when he's around."

"It's Sunday, and nobody expected him. And he came up through the back alley. He must have known we didn't have the money, so he started here first." Janice took her sister's hand and turned her in the direction of the back room. Glancing over her shoulder at Daniel, she said, "I'm sorry, but I don't think we're interested anymore. Find someone else for your story, please."

Janice was the one who had been hurt, but she was comforting her sobbing sister as if it were the other way around. Georgina wanted to go to them and help, but she didn't know what help she could offer. She felt as if she had been dropped into an entirely alien territory and spoke another language.

Georgina almost gasped when Daniel turned to her. She had grown accustomed to seeing him in wire-rimmed glasses when he was reading her notes or working on his press. She knew the laughter that lurked behind his eyes when he took the glasses off. He was always pleasant, good-humored, and patient.

Right now, he looked as if he could commit murder.

The look disappeared quickly, dipping behind the gentle gray of his eyes, lingering only slightly in the tension of his long jaw as he turned to Douglas. "Who owns these houses?"

The boy shrugged and avoided his eyes. "Anybody wants to rent, they talk to Egan. But he don't own them. He calls the owner 'boss.' "

Daniel gave the boy a hard-edged look, then curled his hand around Georgina's elbow, jerking her toward the door. "Come on, we're going to find out who 'boss' is."

One of the neighbors was already hurrying toward the little house with a basket of medicinal supplies. She gave Georgina's rich gown a look of hostility before disappearing into the interior.

There was no sign of the unconscious Egan in the gutter, but the man hauling Georgina down the street didn't seem to notice. His jaw was taut and strained, and his limp had returned. She wondered how in heaven's name he had been able to deliver that kick. She wasn't certain he was quite human.

She hurried to keep up with his furious pace. "Where are we going?"

"You are going home."

"I can't. Blucher won't be at the church for another hour or more."

"I'll hire a cab."

Georgina dug in her heels and refused to move farther. "I want to help. You said a story like this needs pictures."

Daniel glared at her. "This isn't the same story. This story needs a six-gun and a whip. You're going home."

"A six-gun?" Her eyes strayed to his narrow hips, and she breathed a sigh of relief to see he wasn't wearing a weapon. "That's barbaric. All we need to do is go to the courthouse and find out who owns the deeds. I can get my father's lawyer to do that tomorrow."

"I have a suspicion your lawyer isn't going to want to

do that. I can almost wager he already knows who owns this block. And I would wager almost as much that every damned person watching us right now knows who owns these houses. This town isn't so big that anybody can hide for long behind a bully."

Georgina's eyes narrowed. "You already have somebody in mind, don't you?"

Daniel tugged at her arm and got her moving again. "It isn't anybody living on this side of town, that's for damned sure."

"It's somebody living on my side of town, like my father. That's what you're saying." Georgina wasn't accustomed to being angry, but she was getting there now. She shook off his imprisoning hand. "Well, it isn't my father. My father is too nice to hire a thug like that."

"That's why your father hires a misogynist like Ralph Emory as foreman for a factory full of women."

"Misogynist?"

Daniel gave her a glare. "A man who hates women."

"I never heard of such a thing," she declared, halting and stamping her foot. "That's perfectly silly. Why would any man hate women, and if one did, why would my father hire him? You're making this up just to send me home."

"I don't need to make anything up to send you home. That's where you're going. You have no business in this fight. I don't know why I let you come down here in the first place. As of this moment you're fired. I'll send you your paycheck in the morning."

Before Georgina knew what was happening, they were out on the main thoroughfare and he was hailing a shabby cab meandering away from the church. She was in it and on her way, her camera in her lap, before she could think of the proper protest.

Ten minutes later, it sank in that Mr. Martin actually intended to pay her for her work. And she knew exactly what she was going to do with that paycheck.

Seven

ت

"Mr. Harmon, I am quite willing to pay you for your services. I'm not asking you to bill my father if you think he won't be pleased. This is very important to me." Georgina jerked her elbow from the man who was steering her out of the office. She was growing extremely tired of men leading her about like a pet dog.

"Now, Miss Hanover, I'll be happy to look up those deeds if your daddy wants me to, but it's not something you need be worrying your pretty head over. I hear there's to be a wedding soon. You need to be picking out a nice gown and writing invitations. You and Peter will make a lovely couple."

She had been irritated before, seriously annoyed upon occasion, but never had Georgina felt so overwhelmingly furious in all her entire life as she was now. She wanted to box the man's ears, grab his black whiskers and tug with both hands, rip them right off his smug face. and then she wished she could lift her leg as high as Mr. Martin had and kick the lawyer where it hurts.

Instead, she gave him her best vapid smile, waved her fingers in farewell, and sauntered out of the office as if she hadn't a care in the world.

And then she stalked straight over to the courthouse.

She was damned if she was going to let any more men stand in her way. She was going to find out who owned those houses, and she was going to give him a piece of her mind. And if he didn't listen to reason, she had every intention of revealing the scandal to every woman she knew until his name was black as tar all over society. She didn't know where she would go from there, but she would think of something. There must be laws of some sort. If there weren't, then somebody ought to make them. The mayor could help her with that. Her mother and the mayor's wife were good friends.

Having learned her lesson already this morning, Georgina smiled beguilingly at the clerk behind the counter labeled DEEDS. "I want to surprise my fiancé. Could you help me? I need to know how to look up the owner of a piece of property."

By the time Daniel arrived five minutes later, Georgina was up to her elbows in crumbling old books. Dust smudged her nose and stained her gloves and coated her elegant gown, but she was smiling victoriously as she ran her finger down a list of addresses.

Daniel glanced over her shoulder to see just the information he had come in search of, and it was just as useless as he had suspected it would be. But he wasn't going to spoil her triumph by letting her know that.

"What are you doing here?" he demanded. "I told you I didn't need your services."

Undaunted, Georgina stuck her tongue out at him and slammed the book closed. "Go fly a kite, Mr. Martin. I've better things to do than work with you."

Even coated in dust she smelled like lilies, and she rustled softly as she stood up right in front of him. There should be music so he could dance her around the cramped little floor. It was the only excuse Daniel could think of to grab her in his arms. Of course, what he ought to do when he grabbed her was to shake some sense into her.

"And just how do you propose to find out who owns ABC Rentals, Inc.?" Jamming his hands in his pockets, he blocked her exit.

Her lips tilted mischievously. "The same way I got the clerk to tell me how to find the addresses. I bet I find out faster than you."

He didn't like the look in her eye. And he didn't like

the look in the clerk's eye as he watched them. Daniel knew a possessive look when he saw one, and he knew what put it into a man's head to be possessive of a woman. He scowled. "And what do you propose to do with the information if you manage to get it? Start your own newspaper?"

"Wouldn't you just like to know?" Lifting her skirts, Georgina inched past him.

Daniel hurried after her. "Look, Georgina, you don't know what you're getting into. Men like that are dangerous. You could get hurt."

She shot him a glance over her shoulder. "I didn't give you permission to use my name, Mr. Martin. I'm Miss Hanover to you."

"I'll be damned if I'm going to call a spoiled brat Miss anything." Daniel hurried down the courthouse stairs in her wake. "Go ahead and try to find out who owns ABC if you want, but don't do anything until you tell me. I can put it in the paper and not involve you at all. If all you want to do is help Janice and her family, that's the best thing to do. But if you're out to show the world what a wonderful person you are, then forget it. You deserve whatever happens."

He was striding down the street away from her before the last words were out of his mouth.

Georgina wanted to throw something at him. She wanted to screech and shout and tell him what she thought of men and their arrogant assumptions. And she wanted to grab his neck and hug him. He hadn't doubted that she could find out the owners of ABC Rentals, Inc. He hadn't told her not to find out. He'd told her he would print the story when she had it.

She really thought Mr. Daniel Pecos Martin the most original man in town—when he wasn't being a pig-headed jackass.

"Georgina Meredith, I have known you since you were in diapers, and I'm perfectly aware when you are up to something that you shouldn't be, so don't play Miss Coy with me, young lady. Why in the name of heaven do you want me to inquire about something so crass as a company called ABC?"

The haughty lady affecting a lorgnette and wearing her silvered hair stacked higher than seemed possible for normal human hair looked down her nose at her young guest on the other side of the tea table. Georgina merely smiled back. The mayor's wife played the royal lady every bit as well as Georgina played the young scamp. They understood each other perfectly.

"Because they own some property I'm interested in buying," she replied demurely. "I wish to surprise Peter with my economic expertise."

The older woman's face almost cracked a smile before she forced it into retreat. "Economic expertise, my foot and eye. You're up to no good, Georgina Meredith, that I can vouch. But it should be amusing to see what you do with the information. You do realize it won't be easy to persuade Harold to tell me?"

Georgina had anticipated that. It was tit for tat with Loyolla Banks. She sipped from her cup before replying. "I fully appreciate that, Mrs. Banks. I'm not certain how I can offer my gratitude. But I have met the most interesting person—I've been thinking he would make a delightful addition to a dinner party. He's from Texas, and his nickname is Pecos, and he's the most original person I've met in a long time."

Loyolla's eyes lit up like beacons. Georgina hid her smile. She knew the matron prided herself on introducing the original and the intellectual at her exclusive dinner parties. She had no idea how Daniel would feel about such an invitation, but she had no intention of telling him he was being served as the main course.

On Wednesday morning Georgina woke up with imps of hell tap dancing in her stomach. Today was the day Daniel's newspaper would come out—and her photographs would go on display in the glass kiosk Daniel had rented as a newsstand. She would learn once and for all whether Peter was willing to have her as she was, or if all he wanted was a smiling ninny to decorate his arm. She might be throwing away a certain future for an uncertain one, but she had to know.

And she wasn't going to sit around the house, waiting for it to happen. She already knew how the photographs had turned out. Now she wanted to see that newssheet as it came off the presses. Daniel could fire her all he wanted, but he couldn't stop her from showing up if she chose to. And she did.

Besides, she had a perfectly legitimate excuse to appear on his doorstep. The invitation to Mrs. Banks's dinner party lay right there on her desk. When Daniel understood that access to the information they wanted was dependent on his acceptance of the invitation, he would have to consent. And she would have to be the one to present him with it.

The June heat was scorching as she directed Blucher to the street with the camera shop. She needed more supplies anyway, so she wasn't really lying. By the time the carriage came back after running her mother's errands, she would have had time to get to Daniel and back and still buy the chemicals. Walking quickly in this heat would have to be the price she paid for her deception.

She had dressed appropriately this time. Her white organdy skirt whispered coolly about her ankles as she hurried down the unpaved street. The matching ruffled parasol kept her protected from the worst rays. Her lace gloves let in every breath of air. The only problem with the whole effect was that it made every man on this side of town turn and stare.

Men on her side of town weren't so rude. Georgina had the urge to stick her tongue out at them, but instinct told her that probably wasn't wise. Sticking her nose up in the air and disregarding the gawkers, she hurried toward Daniel's office.

She could hear the racket of the press running even before she entered the building. All the windows on the second floor were open, and the clackety-clack bounced off the walls and up and down the narrow alley. She closed her parasol, wiped her hands nervously on her skirt, lifted it out of the dust as she stepped inside and started up the stairs.

The door was open, so she walked in. The mattress in the corner now sported a colorful quilt; an old wing chair decorated another corner. Beside the chair was a table with an oil lamp and a collection of books that covered the remaining surface and towered dangerously at several points. Georgina imagined Mr. Martin sitting there in the evenings with his spectacles on, devouring those volumes instead of food. No wonder he was so lean.

The pounding noise of the press was enough to give her a headache even from here. Crossing the room, Georgina peered into the press room with curiosity, hoping to see the newssheets as they rolled off the machine.

Instead, she saw the wide bare shoulders of a half-naked man as he bent over some obscure piece of oily equipment. The sight caught her completely unaware, and she stared. She couldn't remember ever seeing a man's naked back before. Sweat streamed in rivulets down the hollow of his spine to a narrow place just above his trousers. The trousers rode low on narrow hips, leaving a gap where she could see the difference in skin color, tanned on top, much lighter below the belt.

She gulped and flushed, but couldn't look away. His back was tanned and smooth and rippled dangerously as he wrenched at a bolt on the machine. The motion made her follow the line of broad shoulders to the bulge of muscular arms. Was that what men looked like beneath their shirts and cravats and waistcoats?

She must have made some sound or movement to warn him, although how he could hear over the racket of the press was beyond her. Daniel glanced over his shoulder, and she was caught, even as she started to back away. A big grin sprawled across his face as he straightened and turned around.

That left her even more speechless. Now she wasn't looking at his bare back, but his naked chest. How had she ever thought this man on the skinny side? True, his waist was slim and his hips narrow, but that only empha-

sized the width of the rest of him. She couldn't look at
the rest of him. She hadn't realized men had nipples, too.

She covered her eyes with her hand. "A shirt, please,
Mr. Martin."

Even over the bumps and thumps she could hear his
chuckle. She wanted to melt right through the floor and
die. Her cheeks were even hotter than the air in this stifling room, and there was a nervous twinge in her middle
that made the imps that had danced there earlier seem innocent. Stiffly, she walked into the outer room, trusting
he was finding some decent clothing behind her.

Even though she kept her eyes closed, she knew when
he came to stand beside her. She could smell him.
Strangely enough, it wasn't an unpleasant odor. It stirred
her senses in ways they had never been disturbed before.
Georgina scowled and grabbed the paper he was rattling
in front of her.

Opening her eyes, she read the banner headline: SLAV-
ERY STILL EXISTS! The subheads were sensationalism at its
best, indicting Mulloney's without benefit of trial, but
doing it in three-syllable words that made it sound legitimate.

She could imagine the display at the newsstand, these
headlines next to her photographs of the clerk looking
bright and fresh at eight that morning and wilting wearily
against the counter at six that night, the plush office with
its upholstered chairs next to the barren counter without
so much as a stool to sit on. There had also been a picture
of the Mulloney estate next to one of the rundown shack
of a worker in the final batch. She hadn't taken them.
Daniel had made free with her equipment. But if it accomplished their objective, she couldn't complain.

"Well, what do you think?" Daniel had donned not
only a shirt, but spectacles as he glanced over another
sheet. The shirt was only half buttoned and not in the
right buttonholes, and he looked like a tousled little boy.

Georgina wasn't fooled. She looked back to the story.
"It's not enough. No one is going to feel sorry for clerks
who work in a store as posh as Mulloney's and who don't
even get their hands dirty. You're going to have to go af-

ter the mill and probably the gas company. He has shares in the railroad, too, but I don't know if that will help. I still think my father's factory is your best bet. It's much easier for a reader to understand."

Daniel looked at her over the top of his spectacles and the newssheet in his hand. "Lady, you're meaner than I am. Your boyfriend is going to be screaming bloody murder over those pictures downtown and you're looking for more trouble?"

Georgina threw down the sheet and glared back. "Just because I'm rich doesn't mean I'm heartless. I saw how those people were living back there. How do you think it makes me feel to know that the clothes on my back come from the bread robbed from the mouths of those children?"

Daniel stepped closer, staring her down. "You still don't know what you're talking about. I took you to see people who grew up here, who speak English. I bet you don't realize most of these people don't even know the language. They're Germans and Jews and Italians and Poles and even Negroes from down South. They drink. They smell. They look different. Now, how do you feel about this noble cause you've taken on?"

She had never met an Italian or a Negro, but Blucher was German. Of course, he spoke English, but people could learn. After carefully contemplating his revelations, Georgina shook her head until her curls bounced. "People are people. You probably drink, too, and I know you smell." She grinned as he backed away. "Not speaking the language doesn't make them less than people. There's a lot in this world that needs changing, and what you've got in this paper is just the very tip of it. Have you noticed that women keep getting the worst end of the stick? Even in Mulloney's the men can hope to become something more than clerks, to earn a little more, to have it a little easier. What do the women have to hope for? Nothing! We are nothing in the eyes of the men who own this town. We have to marry to survive, and men like it that way. Just look at your friend Janice and see what I mean."

Daniel stuffed his spectacles in his shirt pocket and

looked at her approvingly. "My, my, we have been study-ing the situation, haven't we? And what does your fancy boyfriend think of your radical opinions?"

"Will you quit calling him my boyfriend?" Irritated, Georgina stalked to the window and stared out. "His name is Peter, and he doesn't know I have any opinions. Even if I told him what I just told you, he'd pat me on the head and smile and say, 'That's nice, dear.' But I'm going to make him sit up and take notice now. I can't go to the mill or the gas company, but I can get into my father's factory. My share of it will go to Peter when we marry, so he'll notice."

"No, he won't. I fully expect him down here the minute he sees the kiosk practically in front of his store. I'm go-ing to tell him I developed the pictures for you and stole those. And he'll believe me. He's not going to know any-thing about your radical notions."

When Georgina turned to face him, she was wearing her hostess smile. "Well, that's just fine, darling," she drawled in blatant imitation of his Texas accent. "Just don't let him smash in your pretty face too badly. You have an invitation to the mayor's house on Friday, and you're going to be there, whether you like it or not."

She dropped the invitation at his feet, picked up her skirt, and walked out.

Eight

ℰ

D aniel leaned against the front window frame, waiting for the beautiful woman in white to reappear on his doorstep. He enjoyed the sassy spoiled brat in her, but she had just shown him a side that he hadn't known existed, and he was fighting a losing battle with admiration. Spoiled, she might be, but dumb, she was not.

He grinned with another kind of admiration as Georgina sailed out the front door. She was a vision in white, trailing silken gauze and lace, and smelling of lilies, as he ought to know. The scent still lingered in the air around him. Peter Mulloney didn't have any idea how lucky he was. One of these days, Daniel was going to have to get around to telling him.

He sent the heavy vellum invitation plummeting out the window toward her feet. His aim was off. It hit the parasol first before bouncing into the dust.

She looked down at the invitation, bent to pick it up, then turned the parasol back to look up at him standing in the window. Daniel crossed his arms and called down to her, "The mayor isn't likely to want to see me after this edition hits the streets."

Instead of answering, she swung around and stalked back toward the front door.

He hadn't expected that. Or perhaps he had. Ladies didn't yell from the street. He hadn't wanted her to leave so precipitously. He wanted to share the triumph of his first creation with someone, and Miss Georgina Meredith Hanover was the ideal companion. Of course, he had in mind breaking out champagne and laughing and hugging and that kind of celebration, not a first-class, genuine, knock-down brawl, but he would take what he could get.

He rebuttoned his shirt, shoved it into his pants, and raked his hair back out of his face. He really was going to have to get a haircut. Evie would be ashamed of him. But he was grinning widely when Georgina sailed back into the room.

She slapped the invitation at the arms crossed over his chest. "You can be very certain the mayor will want to see you after the paper comes out, if only to have you hanged. But it's his wife who wants to see you. And if you don't appear, she won't give me the information on ABC Rentals. Now do you want that information the easy way, or would you prefer to work for it?"

Her blue eyes sparkled like rare diamonds, and her cheeks were flushed with heat and probably ire. Daniel couldn't help thinking that her lips were a delightfully kissable pink, but that was because she was pouting. He'd have to make her laugh and chase that thought away.

"What kind of work do you have in mind?" he asked innocently, knowing Miss Georgina Hanover had no notion of what was going through his mind right now.

She looked at him suspiciously, but since he had taken the invitation, she modified her tone. "I haven't any idea how a newspaperman works to get information out of people. I suppose if you kicked around a few people as you did that Mr. Egan, you might find one or two willing to talk. I just thought you might prefer to do it by having a nice dinner instead."

"Will you be there?" He dangled the invitation between two fingers.

"Peter and I are invited, yes." She held herself stiffly against any attack of disapproval.

"Good. I'll get to meet the infamous Peter. If I don't meet him tonight, that is."

Daniel seemed serenely unconcerned by the prospect of being beaten into a pulp by her fiancé. Georgina shook her head at his foolishness. "I'd suggest finding somewhere else to go once you send those papers out into the street. Peter is bigger than you are, and your fancy kicking isn't likely to impress him any."

Daniel bent the invitation and shoved it into his trouser pocket. "I'm not a fighter, Miss Hanover. I don't get pleasure out of hitting people. If your Mr. Mulloney can't be reasonable about this, then I'll have to show him out. How I do that will be up to him."

He didn't seem to have any doubts that he could do it. Remembering the wide shoulders and muscular arms she had seen earlier, Georgina didn't argue. She didn't know what Peter looked like beneath his frock coat and cravat, and she didn't intend to think about it. She took a gulp of air to clear her brain, but before she could give him a good reply, the downstairs seemed to erupt into commotion.

"I brought 'em, Mr. Martin! Are they ready? Can we go out now?"

Shouts and whistles and stamping feet echoed up the stairwell. Georgina turned in time to see a herd of grubby boys in all sizes and shapes pouring into the room. Corduroys and suspenders and knickers and bulky shirts and even a sporty cap or two abounded as they spread out, filling the small room with their energy.

"The first batch is coming off the press right now. You can catch the factory workers coming out for lunch. The next batch needs to get downtown. By evening, I want you all over town."

Georgina watched in amazement as Daniel sprang into action, sorting through the boys, sending two to pick up the sheets rolling off the press, setting others to folding, adjusting the carrier pouches over the shoulders of some of the smaller ones, and instructing them carefully in their duties. He had the patience of two saints as he explained the same details a dozen times. Some grasped the idea quickly, grabbing their sacks and the first papers folded and running out the door. Others hung back, uncertain, waiting for understanding to dawn.

As they understood that they were to charge two pennies for each paper and bring back one to buy more, they began to bounce in anticipation. Georgina watched as one small boy continually got pushed to the back in the jostling, shoving crowd. Swiping a carrier pouch and filling it with freshly folded newspapers, she leaned over the heads of several larger boys to hand it to the small one.

His freckled face broke into a wide grin that revealed two missing front teeth. "Thankth, mith," and he was off.

After that, Georgina joined in, leaving Daniel to return to his presses while she kept order in the folding process and saw that everyone was supplied with the same number of papers. As soon as the room cleared of one batch of carriers, the first ones started to return, their hands clutching dozens of grubby pennies.

She didn't know how Daniel was going to make any money off the pittance that she carefully divided in half, returning one half to each boy along with a corresponding number of papers. Pennies didn't buy presses. Pennies wouldn't even buy paper. She hoped he knew what he was doing.

There wasn't time to question. One of the presses stuck, and cursing, Daniel yelled for one of the boys to give him a hand. That left Georgina helping to fold papers as well as count cash and replenish pouches. Perspiration poured from her forehead, and she was in dire fear that the underarms of her gown were soaked, but no one seemed to notice. The boys just grinned and thanked her and ran out again.

As the boys spread further into the city, their returns became less frequent. By midafternoon, there was a lull, and Georgina stood up to stretch her aching muscles. Daniel appeared from the back room, ink smeared from ear to ear but grinning happily.

"They're out there, Miss Merry. We'll be the topic of discussion at every table tonight. Doesn't that make your toes tingle?"

What was making her toes tingle was the expression of warmth and admiration and approval in his eyes. Georgina wasn't used to anyone looking at her like that. And the name he had given her made her somehow feel special, as if they shared a secret between them. Avoiding these thoughts, she glanced down at her ruined gown and tried to shake out some of the paper shreds.

"I'm all a-tingle, Mr. Martin, but I suspect it's dust and fleas. Anticipating yelling and cursing does nothing but make me want to bury my head until it stops."

His grin disappeared, and an expression of concern formed lines between his eyebrows. "We'd better get you home. I don't think it's a good idea to let anyone know you're involved with this at all."

Georgina gasped as she remembered the time and Blucher waiting for her back in town. "What time is it? Blucher will think I got lost. They'll be sending out search parties. Oh, dear, I've got to go." She looked around dazedly for her parasol and whatever accouterments had accompanied her.

Daniel located the parasol in the rumpled covers of his bed, where the boys had been tussling, and Georgina found one of her gloves under his table. There was no sign of the other. There wasn't time to look. She hurried for the door, unaware that Daniel was following her until she reached the stairway.

She turned and waved him away. "Go back to your presses. I can always go to my father and tell him I got lost. He'll believe that sooner than the truth."

Daniel glanced down at her ink-stained skirt and up to her dust-smudged cheeks, and shook his head. "If you walk in like that, he's going to be after heads, specifically mine. I think we'd better smuggle you into the house and let you clean up before you go telling any stories. How good are you at lying?"

Georgina gave a radiant smile. "Not very."

"Good." Not explaining that reply, Daniel caught her elbow and hurried her down the stairs.

They met Janice hurrying up. At sight of Georgina, she froze, but she couldn't hide the desperation in her eyes as she appealed to Daniel. "The paper's all over town. Mulloney's is in an uproar. They're looking for the sheriff to get the newsstand closed down. And they fired Audrey because someone told them she had been talking to you."

Janice didn't say what they all knew: The little household couldn't survive without Audrey's meager income to supplement hers.

Georgina knew this woman disliked her, but she was determined to right the injustices of her world. "I'll talk to Mr. Mulloney," she offered at once. "I can make him see that your sister didn't do anything wrong." Her face lit up with a new idea. "I'll tell him that I'm the one who gave Mr. Martin the information!"

A flicker of hope crossed the other woman's face, but Daniel dashed it with a scowl as he pushed Georgina forward. "I don't want him to even know we've met. I'll talk to your hotheaded boyfriend myself, just as soon as I get you out of here."

Georgina grabbed the rail and glared over her shoulder at him. "You can't tell me what to do, Daniel Martin! I'm going to get Miss Harrison her job back if I have to break precious porcelain over Peter's head until he agrees. I'll have his father screaming for mercy, and it won't be over his son's broken head. He's tighter than a Scotsman. I know how to hit him where it hurts."

Daniel looked interested but not amused. "We'll discuss this some other time. Right now we're getting you home." He glanced at Janice. "Go home and tell Audrey we're taking care of it. It may take a while, but Mulloney's control over this town is ending. You have my word on it."

Looking uncertain, Janice said nothing as Daniel and Georgina hurried out into the street. A few more boys were returning with empty pouches, and Daniel directed them to help themselves to the last stack of newspapers. Then grasping Georgina's arm, he steered her toward a main thoroughfare where there was some hope of finding a carriage for hire.

"I am tired of being treated like a baby, Daniel. I can get home on my own, and I can persuade Peter to hire Audrey back."

She didn't notice that she had slipped into calling him by his given name. She was tired and worried and irritated, and her mind wasn't on the formalities. For a change, a man's insistence on seeing her home was comforting, and she wanted to surrender to the easy way out, but she knew she couldn't allow him to do it. As much as she would like to have Daniel's strong presence at her side when she arrived in total dishevelment on a day when tempers would be high, she knew she couldn't do that to him. She pulled away from him and hurried forward on her own.

Daniel kept easy pace with her. "It's late and you shouldn't be out on these streets alone. You're not getting rid of me that easily."

"Janice walked these streets alone," she pointed out. There was no use in trying to outdistance him. His legs were longer and even when he limped he could walk faster than she could. Besides, perspiration was pouring down her back and the heat was too great for any undue exercise. Words were her only hope.

"Janice isn't dressed in silk and lace and looking like a crime about to happen. She knows these people. You don't. I'm taking you home, so save your breath."

She did. Georgina held her mouth tight in furious silence as they hurried down one alley and dirty street after another until they came to the respectable part of town where Blucher had left her. Then she lifted her skirt, dodged beneath the noses of a team of horses pulling a carriage, and ducked into the nearest shop before Daniel could follow.

The shop owner looked startled as she darted inside, looking bedraggled and forlorn, but he was all solicitous kindness when he recognized her.

"I've had a small accident." Georgina smiled wryly, shaking out her skirt as she appropriated a chair. "Is there someone you could send around to Mulloney's? I need Peter to take me home."

The shopkeeper was already shouting at someone in the back when a large shadow filled the doorway. Georgina scowled at the sight of Daniel standing there in shirtsleeves and ink stains. He was going to ruin everything.

"I'll step around and speak to Mr. Mulloney. I was going that way anyway." Daniel gave the shop owner an obliging smile.

Caught, Georgina couldn't think of anything to say that wouldn't reveal she knew who he was, and she didn't think now was an opportune time for that. Mr. Daniel Martin had a propensity for wanting things his way, just like any jackass.

"That's very kind of you, sir," she murmured with syrupy politeness. "There aren't many gallant knights willing to come to a lady's rescue in this day and age."

That made him frown, and he turned around and walked out without a word to her.

Daniel was in no humor for the carpeted aisles and glittering chandelier of Mulloney's Department Store as he stalked in covered in grime and in working man's attire. The clerks stared disapprovingly, making it obvious he had no place in here. That inched his temper another notch higher. Only the prospect that he was going to come face-to-face with his brother at last kept his feet moving. Otherwise, mayhem would have been his preference.

He knew precisely where the office was. He'd had a good teacher who had taught him to always know the lay of the land. Remembering the lesson he'd learned from his good friend Benjamin, Daniel modified his step somewhat. He was in enemy territory now. It would pay to be cautious.

The office door was closed, and yelling echoed from within. The secretary who usually guarded the desk had disappeared, presumably to gossip about the free-for-all going on now in the inner sanctum. Daniel smiled a little more confidently. He had a good notion of the cause of that argument. He was going to enjoy walking in on it to tell of a maiden's need for rescue. Then he could really see what these people were made of. He already suspected he wasn't going to like what he found out.

Daniel knocked politely, but no one responded. The argument escalated into a one-sided yelling match. If that was the old man in there, he had a strong set of lungs. Hiding a smile of anticipation, Daniel swung the door

open. This was a civilized city office after all. They
weren't going to come at him with six-guns and dynamite. All they could do was yell some more, and he'd
been yelled at by the best. These people weren't going to
disturb him any.

The instant the door swung open, the room grew silent.
Two remarkably similar faces turned to stare at him. One
was older, lined with age and crowned by silver hair, but
the defiantly square jaw and glittering emerald eyes were
identical to the younger version standing next to him. The
black-haired younger man stepped forward with a scowl.

"This is a private office. Please leave."

Daniel managed to keep his hands out of his pockets
and a smile off his face by remembering Georgina's
plight. Still, he took his time taking in the man who was
almost certainly his younger brother. There wasn't any resemblance that he could see. Peter Mulloney was handsome in the fashionable sense with the broad, tall figure
and dark good looks that women admired. He was attired
immaculately in starched collar and conservative tie and
coat. The only concession he made to humanity was a
small frown between his eyes as he stared at his unwanted guest.

"Miss Hanover sent me. She's had a small accident and
seems to be in need of rescuing. She's around the corner
at the shoemaker's."

Worry and irritation crossed Peter's face in equal proportions. "Is she all right? Do we need to send for a physician?"

"She's fine, just a little shaken. I can see her home if
you're busy." Daniel had to say that. While he might have
a penchant for rescuing ladies in distress, he also had an
outrageous sense of humor. The fact that these men had
no notion of who he was tickled his fancy. To be able to
snatch Miss Hanover from under their noses would be
even more amusing. Rescuing her from their greedy
clutches just added icing to the cake.

"No, I need to talk to her." With a harried expression,
Peter shoved his hands through his hair. "Thanks for
bringing the message." He reached into his pocket and

flipped Daniel a coin as an afterthought before turning back to the irate old man behind him.

Daniel caught the coin with a grin and walked out whistling. They were going to remember this moment one of these days, and it wasn't going to be with fondness.

With that single derisive gesture, the Mulloneys had just demolished the last barrier of hesitation holding Daniel back. He felt no compunction at all about letting loose his armies and storming the bastions. The white knight would rescue the fair damsel, and in so doing, he would slay the evil dragon of injustice.

Nine

℃

"It's nothing. I was running late, and Blucher left, and I fell down and got dirty. I'm totally embarrassed, that's all. But I needed to talk to you—" The carriage hit a rut, and Georgina grasped a side handle.

"And *I* need to talk to you. How did those pictures get in that filthy newsstand? Have you seen it? There hasn't been another photographer in the store but you. Who is this fellow Martin?"

Georgina brushed a straying lock of hair from her eyes and looked steadily ahead as she answered wryly, "Thank you so much for your concern, Peter. It's good to know I have someone to call on when I'm in distress."

"For pity's sake, Georgina . . ." Peter glanced at her stubbornly set chin and modified his tone. "I'm sorry. I just had a horrible row with my father, and you know how that affects me. Are you sure you weren't hurt? You look as if you've been wallowing in the mud and got run over by a carriage."

"Thanks." Sadly enough, it wasn't even anger washing through her at this insult, although her reply hinted at sarcasm. She had known Peter since they were children. Not really known, perhaps. They never had the same interests. Boys and girls seldom did. But the town wasn't so large that they hadn't known each other since time immemorial. That made it easier to treat each other like brother and sister. And that was how he was treating her: like his nuisance of a little sister.

Remembering how Daniel's eyes lit like lanterns when

she entered a room, how he touched her arm every chance he got, how he had followed her to make certain she was all right even when she had ordered him not to, Georgina sighed. Why couldn't Peter just be a bit more like Mr. Martin? She was quite certain she could fall in love with him if he would.

Peter sent her a bewildered glance. "I didn't mean that the way it sounded. Why am I always saying the wrong things to you? I don't even know what it is I'm saying wrong. I'm glad you haven't got another pitcher of lemonade handy."

"It's not what you say. It's that you don't *listen*. I was trying to tell you something, and you didn't hear a word I said."

"I just got finished hearing more words than I wanted to hear from my father. I don't need to listen to any more lectures. You need to learn to judge a man's moods." Peter whipped the carriage horses into a trot.

"It goes both ways, Peter Mulloney. You're not God. I have moods, too. And my mood is anything but pleasant at the moment." This wasn't the attitude she had meant to take, but he had her temper riled. He seemed to do that entirely too often these days. Everything seemed to do that too often. She felt as if she were living on a powder keg about to go off. Maybe she ought to go help her mother choose a wedding gown and call this whole thing off.

"Good, that makes us even. So why don't we both go home and cool off and try this again another day?"

"Fine, but unless you rehire that unfortunate girl you fired today, I'm not likely to cool off anytime soon. I'm the one who told Mr. Martin all about Mulloney's, not that poor clerk. You owe her an apology."

"You what!" Peter screamed so loud that the horses jerked in their traces, disrupting traffic all around them.

"He's a very nice man I met on the train coming home. You can just ask him."

"And you took those photographs for him, making us look like a slave factory or something?" His voice was ominously quiet now.

"You'll need to ask Mr. Martin about that," Georgina answered smoothly. Daniel deserved a share of this abuse. If he'd just left her alone, she could have got home and cleaned up without Peter ever getting involved. Let him make up some of these answers.

"Damn him! He took advantage of you, didn't he? You chattered and he switched all the words around and made us look like fools. And then he probably admired your new hobby and somehow talked you into giving up some of your silly pictures. I'm going to break every bone in his body. Does your father know you've been seeing this scoundrel? Don't you ever go out with a chaperone?"

"They're good photographs," Georgina murmured as she crossed her arms and stuck out her bottom lip. "And nobody has chaperones anymore."

Peter ignored her. Pulling the horses up the carriage drive in front of the house, he jumped down to let her out. "Where can I find this scoundrel? I've got a thing or two I intend to tell him."

Georgina jerked her hand away as he tried to help her out. Clinging to the carriage, she let herself down. "I'm not telling you anything else unless you promise to hire that girl back. I may not ever speak to you again unless you hire that girl."

Peter glared. "Good. The silence will be a blessing."

"I hate you, Peter Mulloney." Grabbing up her skirt, Georgina fled into the house, leaving Peter to do as he wished. She wasn't about to give up yet. He would rue the day he called her photographs silly and refused to listen to a simple request.

She ran up the stairs and slammed into her bedroom. She jerked on the bellpull until the clamor could be heard throughout the house. Her father wouldn't be home yet. She would get cleaned up and plead her case with him. He might be stubborn upon occasion, but he always gave her anything reasonable she wanted. He would see that Audrey got her job back. He would understand.

Her mother had retreated into oblivion several days before, so Georgina was alone in the parlor when her father came home. She had gowned herself carefully in his favorite blue and jumped up to greet him with a smile. He frowned and threw the newssheet onto the nearest table.

"I don't know what this world's coming to. Next they'll be telling us who we have to hire and how much we have to pay. It's radicals like that who are going to be the ruin of this country. Pour me a sip of brandy, Georgie. It's been a long day."

That didn't sound in the least promising, but Georgina hurried to obey.

"I need to talk to you, Papa," she said as she handed him the snifter.

"Of course, sweetheart. Have you seen Peter today? I need to talk with the boy. Something has to be done about these radicals before they can attack other businesses."

He wasn't listening. None of them ever listened. Firmly, Georgina attempted to steer him back to the subject. "Peter fired another innocent clerk today, Papa. He blamed her for something that I did. I wish you would talk with him. I'll apologize or do whatever it takes, but he has to hire that girl back. She needs the job."

"That doesn't make any sense, Georgina," he responded absently. "What could you possibly have to do with a clerk? Is dinner almost ready? I've got to go out again shortly."

"I'll tell Nancy to start serving immediately. Will you be seeing Peter tonight?" She had to get through to him. The lives of that little family depended on her making these men understand. She was feeling a little desperate already.

Her father led her into the dining room. "Did you and Peter have a little dispute? That happens all the time, sweetheart. Don't worry your pretty head about it. I'll tell him you apologize and warn him to bring a big bouquet of flowers tomorrow."

If it would serve her purpose, she would stamp her foot and throw a tantrum right here and now, but Georgina doubted that it would get her anything more than a suggestion that she was doing too much and needed rest. That's what he always told her mother, and her mother seemed to take him literally.

Holding her smile in place, Georgina tried again. "I want you to talk to Peter about hiring that clerk back. If he doesn't, the marriage is off, Papa. I can't marry a man who won't listen."

That finally got his attention. George Hanover groomed his graying side-whiskers with his fingers as he waited for the maid to warn the cook it was time to start serving. "Don't be foolish, Georgina. Of course you'll marry Peter. He's a little young, that's all. Boys that age don't like to listen to anyone but themselves. I'll tell him to come by and you two can kiss and make up."

"He's twenty-five years old, Papa!" she protested, but she could see she was getting nowhere. Ignoring her, George started a diatribe on the subject that was irritating him the most, Daniel's newspaper.

Apparently there hadn't been time for Peter to warn her father Georgina's photographs were in the kiosk downtown. There wouldn't be any reasoning with him once he found that out. Maybe she could talk to Doris at the factory and see if a position couldn't be found for Audrey there.

She wasn't going to give up. Peter would have to listen. She would sit on his desk and refuse to move until she rehired Audrey.

She liked that idea. Wasn't there something by Thoreau about passive protest? Maybe she could chain herself to the door or something so Peter couldn't even carry her off. That would get his attention.

So she smiled and made a pretense of listening and waved her father on his way after dinner, then went to her room to make her plans.

What she didn't count on was the total irrationality of men, even one like her father who had always treated her as if she were made of precious porcelain.

Georgina had already gone to bed by the time her father came home. When he pounded on her door, she got up and quickly pulled on a robe, fearful of what she might find. Her father never came to her room in the dark of night. Something had to be wrong. Perhaps her mother was ill.

But it was her father who looked sick. In the dim light of the hall lamp, his face was a ghastly gray, and his voice wasn't that of the genial man she had known all her life. It held a hint of desperation and anger that she didn't like at all.

"Georgina Meredith, why didn't you tell me that newspaper fellow was making a nuisance of himself? I had to hear Peter tell me that he's tricked you into giving him that incendiary information and those photographs. I couldn't believe my ears! What are you doing near the likes of a man like that? Do you have any idea what you can do to your reputation with such foolishness? If word gets out, we'll be ruined in this town. Ruined! We're going to have to put a halt to this immediately."

Georgina rubbed at her eyes and tried to put this tirade into perspective, but sleep clouded her brain. "You've met Mr. Martin, Papa. He has an invitation to dinner at the mayor's Friday. He's a perfectly respectable gentleman. Just because you don't agree with his opinions doesn't mean he's not nice."

"He's trying to ruin the family you're marrying into! Don't tell me that's the work of an honest man. We've decided you've run loose too long, Georgina. I have my hands full at the factory these days, and your mother isn't well. We don't have the time to look after you as we should. We've decided to move up the wedding date. Then you will be Peter's responsibility."

Georgina stared at him in horror. "I will not! I am my own responsibility. In any case, I'm not marrying Peter unless he gives that girl her job back. I can't marry a man who won't listen to reason."

"That's exactly what I'm talking about, Georgina. You are getting entirely out of hand. What Peter does with his employees is his business and not yours. It's your business to look after the house and servants and keep things running smoothly for your husband. You'll have children to look after if you need more to keep you occupied. You'll marry Peter, child, if you know what's good for you."

This was her father talking to her. Georgina couldn't

believe he meant it. Tears pooled in her eyes, but she adamantly refused to give in on this topic. "I know what's good for me, and it isn't a man who won't listen to reason. I'll not marry him, Papa."

Her father looked older and grayer than she had ever seen him as he shook his head and started down the hall. "You will, Georgina. I can't afford for you to do otherwise. If you don't, I will have to put you somewhere where you can't hurt anyone else or until you return to your senses."

He entered his chamber and quietly closed the door, leaving Georgina to stare after him with a sense of impending doom. The words had been deceptively calm, but she knew what they meant. She had only been three or four when her mother had gone away and not come back for what had seemed forever. She'd heard the servants whisper about it for years, shaking their heads and looking frightened whenever her mother took to her room now. It had taken years for her to find out just exactly where her mother had been all those months, the place her father still occasionally threatened her mother with now when he didn't think anyone was listening.

She had no desire at all to be sent off to the Shady Rest Retiring Home for Convalescents.

"Father, you have yourself upset over nothing. He's just a mud-slinging journalist who will be out of business in a few weeks. People around here are too sensible to listen to his radical preachings."

It was nearly midnight, but the man in the black suit behind the desk had not removed one article of his formal attire and there was not a crease out of place. He puffed furiously on a cigar as he regarded his eldest son, then swept the room with his gaze to make certain the younger boys were listening.

"There are elements in any town that will use any excuse to cause trouble. You heard about the riots in New Jersey. You've seen the trouble the Grange has caused out West. We're going to nip this thing in the bud before he has a chance to cause more harm than he has. All I want you to do is take care of that spoiled brat of yours. I don't want any outcry from her when we do what we have to do."

Peter shifted uneasily in his chair. As the eldest, he had the responsibility to stand up to his father when he was wrong. John and Paul still lived in fear of the old man. Georgina had been wrong to do what she had, but she was young and naive and her mother never had brought her up properly. She would straighten out once she was married. But Peter had a sneaking suspicion that marriage wouldn't come happily if Georgina knew his father was responsible for harming her newspaper friend in any way. He had to persuade the old man to keep things quiet.

"Leave the man alone, Father. The people his article is aimed at can't read. Even if they could, they haven't got enough ambition or organization to do anything about it. Those clerks need their jobs. They can't afford to do anything no matter how much anyone complains for them. I'll take care of Georgie. But you'll tie my hands if you do anything to that newspaperman. Georgie's very adamant about protecting her friends. She's quite capable of not going through with the wedding if she thinks we had anything to do with harming any friend of hers." That thought made Peter nervous. She had been rattling on about some clerk in the store he had fired earlier. It might be wise to find out the details. He had known all his life that Georgie was going to be his wife. He'd made plans for the ticket to freedom his marriage would provide. He didn't want her throwing his ring back at him at this late date.

As if seeing the wheels go around in his son's head, the old man behind the desk chuckled ominously. "You'd better get a tight rein on that one pretty quick, son, before she has you jumping hoops like a trained dog. Just explain to her that her father's business goes down the sewer if she doesn't marry you. That will bring her around."

"Father, that's ridiculous. You can't really pull the rug from under Hanover. He's been your friend for years. He'll come out all right soon enough. He knows the business. I expect to learn a great deal from him before I take over."

The silver-haired man leaned back in his chair and blew smoke rings at the ceiling. "One of these days, boy, you'll learn that money's the only thing that gives you power. Hanover would shoot you in the back in an instant if he could. It's only that loan we hold that keeps him to his promises. Money is power, boys. Keep that in mind."

Artemis Mulloney rose and walked to the door, still tall and straight despite his years. He stopped only to turn with one more reminder, "Get that gal in line, boy, and do it soon. Elope. That's the best thing for her. Bed her and wed her, in that order. She'll come around when she knows who's boss."

Twenty-year-old John giggled as soon as the door closed. "That's one order I wouldn't have any trouble handling. Need any help with the little lady, Pete? I could entertain her when you're otherwise occupied."

"Shut up, John." Peter didn't even bother looking in his youngest brother's direction. There was something distinctly irritating about John's presence tonight. The kid looked more like their mother than their father. He had a woman's weak build and a lanky adolescent gracelessness that he hadn't outgrown. And his sense of humor was definitely misplaced.

Peter would be just as happy trouncing John as the newspaperman.

Why did the image of that stranger coming to the office this afternoon keep coming back when he thought of John? Obviously, he had too much on his mind.

It was time he paid the journalist a visit.

Ten

D aniel sat on a crate he'd brought to the roof and
leaned back against an old chimney. He was going
to have to find the fireplace that went with the
chimney if he meant to stay here this winter, but winter
was a long way off on a hot day in June. He threw off his
shirt and picked up the notebook he had been using to
keep a record of his ideas. He should be out investigating
the mill to prepare the next bombshell he had in mind, but
intuition told him it wouldn't suit his purposes to leave
the premises for too long so soon after the first attack.

Intuition served him well. He heard the sound of the
carriage carrying up from the street well before it arrived.
It cost a lot of money in horseflesh to get that expensive
clip-clop sound followed by silence instead of the unre-
lenting squeak of a farm wagon. Daniel had already seen
Hanover arrive at the factory earlier this morning. This
was a different visitor.

He couldn't help a leap in heartbeat at the possibility
that Georgina might have decided to arrive in style, but
he remained where he was, gazing upon the street below
with full knowledge that no one could see him up here.
He grimaced as he recognized the driver if not the carriage. He should have known Peter Mulloney would drive
a sporty little two-seater chaise.

Daniel made no attempt to go down and meet his guest.
He wasn't quite prepared to introduce himself to the
brother he had never known and whom he was coming to
despise as much as he had resented him earlier. Peter

Mulloney was obviously the perfect son his family had wanted. Strong, handsome, he walked with an unblemished stride that Daniel could never hope to match. He probably didn't even need glasses. Daniel adjusted his own and went back to studying his notes. The dinner invitation in his pocket was ample excuse to wait for a meeting.

The sound of a huge dog howling ferociously, then growling as his prey came close enough to strike made Daniel look up again, this time with a faint smile. Obviously, Peter had ignored the warning posted on the door. The dog had been an expensive investment, but a great burglar deterrent as well as good company.

Daniel couldn't quite hear the curses he was certain emanated from the office several floors below, but he had a good imagination. The dog was howling in frustration now. Peter must have liberated himself. Daniel counted, knowing to the last digit the number of stairs between the office and the street.

... three, two, one. Daniel glanced over the parapet to see his brother dashing out the door as if the hounds of hell were on his heels. Perhaps not quite that bad. To give him credit, Peter looked more furious than scared. His fists were clenched as he glanced up at the building as if he knew Daniel was there. Then he set the chaise off at a lethal rate of speed.

Well, that took care of the first attack on the citadel. Boiling oil might be appropriate for the next. Daniel sat back against the chimney again and pondered the logistics.

When he saw Janice run from the factory, weeping, some time later, he sighed and put his notebook aside. He hoped what he was doing was worth it in the long run, because it was certainly going to cause a lot of misery for the present.

Pale-faced and shaken, Georgina arrived in the maze of alleys leading to the Harrison household some time before noon. She hadn't slept much at all, but she had come to no other conclusions than the one she had set earlier.

She was going to help Audrey get her job back or find her a better one. For herself, she had no such clear goal. There was time yet to decide what to do about Peter and marriage. That was as far as her sleepless night had taken her.

She had held the threat of not marrying Peter over her father's head only for effect. She had never really considered breaking the engagement. She had always known she would be marrying Peter, and she had just hoped for a little time to make him see her as she was. A little romance would have been nice, too, but she had never expected miracles. So her father's threats weren't entirely effective except in their utterance. Her father had never threatened her before. The world had a whole different aspect to it this morning that she didn't like in the least.

So she disregarded her father and Peter and everything else over which she had no control and went in search of Audrey. The girl had practically been hysterical the day Egan had come for the rent. She would undoubtedly be in a similar state again, and Georgina meant to put her mind to rest. One way or another, Audrey would have a job.

She had dressed more sedately today. She wore one of her oldest walking skirts, a heavy, tan gabardine that dragged the dust but was blessedly full enough to walk full stride. She had left behind the tight, matching jacket, but the chocolate brown polonaise she wore looped over the skirt was sufficient to make her swelter. No parasol came with this outfit, and the inefficient scrap of lace and cloth that passed for a hat did nothing to keep the sun off her face. Scowling, Georgina wished she had just worn her expensive silk that required no underpinnings. It might have shocked the passersby, but it would have been cool.

But her aim had been to be discreet. She was quite certain she hadn't succeeded as she felt the stares of women garbed in full skirts and short-sleeved blouses staring at her over washing lines, but her intentions were in the right place. She couldn't help it if she didn't own a cotton skirt or an apron.

She remembered the house with the geranium on the

step quite clearly and heaved a sigh of relief. She was in the right place. It wasn't much farther.

A bit of breeze found its way through the narrow street, stirring a scrap of lace at an open window and sending pieces of paper fluttering down the dusty road. Finding the right house, Georgia removed her sweaty palms from her gloves and knocked on the door. She wanted to look humble, not haughty.

When the door opened to reveal a tiny scrap of a woman with thinning gray hair and black eyes that danced with devilment, Georgina looked more startled than humble. The woman looked her up and down with amusement, as if she had seen plenty of strange things in her life and was prepared to be entertained by this one. Nervously, Georgina began to tug on her gloves again.

"I'm sorry. Perhaps I have the wrong house. I'm looking for Audrey Harrison?"

"Inside, miss. She's moping. Company will do her good."

Georgina couldn't place the accent with which these words were uttered, but it reminded her of what Daniel had told her about the people inhabiting these houses. They were almost all immigrants. This woman didn't look foreign. Neither did her daughters or granddaughters or whatever the relationship was. But the women who had stared at her in the street had been foreign-looking, now that she knew to look.

The young girl Georgina remembered from her previous visit was sitting at a rickety kitchen table, sewing at a man's vest. Georgina recognized it as one of the styles her father sold to Mulloney's. Janice must have been able to get her piece work then. She felt somehow deflated by the knowledge that she wasn't the one to help.

"I didn't mean to interrupt. I just came to tell you how sorry I am that I've caused you so much trouble."

The girl at the table looked up without interest. Her eyes were red from weeping, or perhaps just from lack of sleep. Her gaze took in Georgina's expensive clothes and turned back to her work. "You think too high of yourself if you think you're the cause."

This really was one straw too many. She had been ignored, insulted, yelled at, and threatened for trying to help people like this ungrateful wretch, and Georgina was tired of taking the blame for everyone else's troubles. The only signal of her rising temper was a slight tightening of her lips.

"And you think too highly of yourself if you think you're the only one who suffers."

The girl looked up. Her brownish-blond hair could use a good washing, but its lack of luster had as much to do with improper nourishment as lack of water. Her face was unblemished and clean, but the color was sallow and her eyes dull. "I don't think of myself at all. What's the point?"

That struck Georgina more forcefully than anything else she could have said. It made her see the utter hopelessness of her surroundings. They would never have anything. Every day would be a struggle for survival. One blow to their precarious existence would turn them all out in the streets and leave them to starve. Where was the fun and excitement a child should be allowed to expect upon occasion? It was more than obvious the girl before her was little more than a child, but already she carried the burdens of a much older adult.

The grandmotherly woman produced a steaming cup of tea and set it on the table. "Sit. Drink. Don't listen to her. It is fine here. Much better than the old country. We will find her a good man, and she will be all smiles."

Audrey made no comment, and Georgina thought she had some understanding of how the other girl felt. Maybe she ought to offer her Peter as a choice of husbands. No doubt Audrey would be a good deal more excited than Georgina at the prospect.

"Good men are rather rare," she offered tentatively.

That brought a response from Audrey, a gleam of agreement, a flicker of something that hadn't been there earlier. She stabbed the vest more forcefully.

"In the meantime, I'm doing my best to persuade Mr. Mulloney that the newspaper article had nothing to do with you. Men tend to be unreasonable when they are angry, but he'll calm down in a day or two. I'll try again then. I'm sure he'll understand that you had nothing to do with any of it."

Georgina rather thought it was anger flushing the girl's cheeks, but she still didn't speak. Georgina supposed she would have difficulty expressing gratitude or anything at all pleasant under the circumstances, too. She sipped her tea and wondered if there was anything else she could say, but the girl's depression was contagious. She had never felt this dismal in her life.

The front door suddenly burst open, and the sound of a sob brought all of them to their feet. Before Georgina could do anything, Janice stood in the kitchen doorway, her face a tear-stained mask of grief and fury as she recognized the intruder.

"Get out!" she commanded, pointing at the door behind her. "I don't have to put up with the likes of you ever again."

"Now, Janice, the nice lady came to help." The old woman offered a placating hand to both women.

"The nice lady's father just fired me and told me I'd never find work in this town again. The nice lady can get her fancy gear out of here." Janice wiped at her face with the back of her hand, then crossed her arms determinedly across her chest.

"That isn't possible," Georgina stuttered, edging toward the door. "He hasn't been himself lately. I'll talk to him. It must be a misunderstanding."

"Do you think I'm too dumb to know when I've been fired? Get out, Miss Hanover, and don't ever come back. It's you and your kind that causes trouble. We don't need your empty promises."

Georgina didn't know what to say. She had accomplished nothing but trouble from the start, and she knew it. She had meant to help, but intentions weren't enough. Biting her lip, she turned and walked through the front room and out the door.

She was too dazed to know where she was walking. She had a vague idea of finding her father and asking what had happened, maybe pleading with him to reconsider. The knowledge that her pleas had fallen on deaf ears before did nothing to calm her. She had tried to help and only made things worse. Maybe she was good for nothing but arranging dinner tables and having babies after all. Maybe she should marry Peter and be grateful that she had a roof over her head. Maybe men were right and women had no place outside the home. She certainly hadn't seen anything to tell her differently since she began this crusade.

Tears were creeping down her cheeks and her handkerchief was in tatters before Georgina realized she didn't know where she was or where she was going. At the same time, it dawned on her that she was being followed. The scuffling noises and murmured taunts were growing louder behind her. Afraid to turn around, she walked faster, desperately trying to figure out how to get out of this maze of narrow alleys.

"What's the matter, lady? Think you're too good for us?"

As if the fact that they had been discovered made them braver, the men behind her moved in closer. At least Georgina thought they were men. She was too terrified to look, but the voice had sounded definitely low and male.

"Lost, lady? Want a map? Give you one for a kiss."

A hand reached out to grab her elbow. She shook it off and wished for her parasol. She needed a weapon. Lifting her skirts, she hurried faster.

"Not so quick, lady. You got to pay the toll if you walk this street." A grubby figure dashed in front of her, his cap parked at a jaunty angle over his forehead as he looked her up and down.

He wasn't much taller than she, but Georgina had learned to recognize a man's muscular strength, and this man could have been a blacksmith from the breadth of his chest. The bulky plaid shirt he wore did little to disguise the power of the arms crossing in front of him as he stared at her boldly. She didn't dare try to get by him.

Swinging around, she confronted a taller, lankier assailant. She couldn't tell if his skin was darkened by nature, sun, or dirt, but his teeth flashed white against his face as he blocked her path. "Toll, lady. Pay the toll." He held his arms out wide and stepped forward.

She ducked under his arm and tried to run past him, back the way she had come, but he stuck out a foot and tripped her. She stumbled, and he caught her up in a grip that was just as strong as Peter's. She gave a scream of fright and tried to shake free.

"I'd leave the lady alone if I were you," a voice rang from out of nowhere.

Georgina and her attackers swung around, searching the empty street, seeing nothing in the blank windows but the occasional flutter of a curtain. The people who inhabited these houses had learned to stay away from trouble.

"Come out and make us," the cocky, short man shouted, reaching to grab Georgina's waist.

"You don't want me to do that." A movement in a nearby alley gave an indication as to the source of the voice.

Georgina gasped as she recognized the insolent stance of the shadow leaning against a wall. *Daniel!* She had never been so glad to see anybody in her life. The ruffian grasping her waist smelled of garlic and worse, and the taller man's grip was hurting her arm. She blanked her mind against the thoughts of what would have happened had Daniel not arrived. She could barely tolerate her immediate position.

"Why not, cowboy? Whatya gonna do 'bout it?" The taller man grabbed a hank of Georgina's hair and twisted her head backward until she was looking up into his hair-stubbled face. She screamed and tried to pull away as she read his intent to kiss her, but held by two sets of arms, there wasn't far she could go.

An oddly sharp bark split the thick summer air, and the painful hold on Georgina's arm slackened. The tall man yipped and staggered backward, trying to pull his foot up.

"You want your turn?" Daniel asked the remaining man as he casually strolled from the alley, swinging something in his hand that glittered silver in the sunlight.

Feeling the hold at her waist loosening, Georgina grabbed her skirt and jerked free, running in Daniel's direction, carefully keeping to the side of the street and not getting between him and the men backing away.

"Cripes! He's got a gun. The man's crazy!" The shorter man backed toward the nearest alley. "We didn't mean nothing. We were just having some fun. Honest."

"Invite me next time you want to have some fun. I'll show you how we teach people to dance back where I come from." Daniel deliberately aimed the revolver at the shorter man's feet, sending a spurt of bullets into the dust.

The man picked up his feet and ran, his partner limping hurriedly after him.

Gasping, Georgina leaned against the nearest building, holding a hand to her pounding chest and staring from Daniel to the now empty street. She had a hard time believing she had seen that. People didn't do that in Cutlerville, Ohio. She glanced back to Daniel and watched as he slid the wicked revolver beneath his coat and out of sight. She would remember to beware of this man when he was wearing a coat.

But once the gun was out of sight, Daniel returned to being the bare-faced, mild-mannered journalist with the engaging grin as he sauntered toward her. A hank of pale brown hair fell across his forehead, making him look as boyish as the rowdies who sold his papers for him. The twinkle in his gray eyes as he took in her pose had nothing to do with the man who had just unloaded a half dozen bullets into the street.

"I don't know if I ought to be more frightened of you than of them." Pushing herself away from the wall, Georgina fiddled with her gloves. Daniel was close enough now for her to smell his spicy shaving lotion as he towered over her. She had a sudden urge to fall into his arms and feel them close around her, but Georgina Meredith Hanover didn't do things like that. She was known for her snappy comebacks and bouncy personality and her ability to keep men at a proper distance. She was just momentarily discommoded, that was all.

"Since I'm closest and I'm madder than hell, feel free to be afraid of me. Am I going to have to chase you through half the town to get you home again, or are you going to come willingly this time?"

Georgina sighed and finally met his eyes. They weren't laughing any longer. Damn men, anyway, why couldn't they let things be simple?

"I'll go, but you'll have to come back and talk to Janice. She just lost her job. We've got to do something."

Daniel caught her arm and steered her down the street. "*I've* got to do something. There is no *we* to it. Now let's get out of here before those two come back with a few friends."

He didn't have to tell her twice. Georgina moved.

Eleven

&

"I gave the photography equipment to Peter for safekeeping. He can decide whether or not to give it to you after you're married."

George Hanover was still wrestling with his tie, looking into the ornate mirror of the front parlor as he addressed his daughter.

Georgina stood woodenly on the Aubusson carpet and nodded her head. If he couldn't see her in the mirror, he would have to turn around to face her. She wondered if he dared.

He glanced over his shoulder, saw her stiff expression, and went back to his tie. "I hope you've learned your lesson. I'm glad to see you being sensible about this. Your mother and I only have your best interests at heart."

Since her mother hadn't come down yet, that was a matter of opinion. Georgina glanced wistfully toward the stairs. It would be nice if her mother would stand up for her once in a while, but that would be like asking Abraham Lincoln to come back and save the country. She fiddled with the silk ruching on the small panniers draped over her hips, and gazed absently at the toe of her slippers. Her father hadn't mentioned the shorter skirt of her new dinner gown. Perhaps the high collar would fool him, and he wouldn't notice the daring peek-a-boo netting over her bosom, either. She wondered if Peter would.

And a strange little imp inside wondered how much Daniel Martin would notice. She moved restlessly, disregarding that thought.

Peter arrived then, and her mother slowly descended from the upper floor, carrying her slight frame with an erect carriage that would grace a queen. Peter bowed low over her hand, and Dolly Hanover almost smiled, before turning to her husband. The smile disappeared again.

The party entering the carriage was an unusually silent one. Georgina normally would have filled the interior with chatter and laughter enough for all four, but she had lost that part of herself recently. She stared out the dark windows even when Peter reached over and took her hand and squeezed it. Even a week ago, that squeeze would have thrilled her, promising more. Now she saw it only as a means to keep her pacified.

It wasn't that she was without anticipation. She was looking forward to finding out the owners of that slum where Mr. Egan ruled supreme. Just making the plans to get even with Mr. Egan was enough to keep her mind busy. And the thought of Daniel showing up in front of all these sober businessmen like her father added a decided edge to the evening. She couldn't wait to see their reaction. She told herself that was the reason she was looking forward to seeing Daniel again, but she wasn't very good at lying, even to herself. She definitely had a lot of hopes for this dinner party.

The problem was that she had drifted so far from her family and friends that she had no one to share her hopes and anticipation with. Had it been her usual mischief, she would have been bouncing in the seat and describing what she hoped would happen and making everyone laugh with her foolishness. But this time, it wasn't foolishness. It was people's lives.

The real world was definitely a little scary. All she had to do to remember was to recall that encounter with those two hooligans in the alley. Maybe they wouldn't have done anything but insult her with their nasty kisses. Maybe it would have been worse. Lucky for her, she would never have to find out. She closed her eyes and saw Daniel staring back at her, his boyish grin switching to anger and concern. Mr. Martin was as scary as the rest of the world out there.

By the time the carriage arrived at the mayor's house, Georgina had found her smile. She applied it gallantly on all and sundry as she entered the foyer, teasing the mayor about a little dimple hidden beneath his newly trimmed beard, admiring the roses in a friend's hair, laughing at some jest of Loyolla's as she ushered her guests into the parlor. No one would ever guess that her stomach was tied in knots and her nerves were smoldering like a lighted fuse.

In her naivete, she had thought Daniel's newspaper would bring enlightenment. She had imagined women up in arms about the treatment of the poor clerk who had aspired to management. She had imagined men giving the Mulloneys a stern talking to and threatening a boycott if things weren't changed. She had imagined Peter standing up to his father and telling him that slavery had ended well over a decade ago. And here she was, in the center of Cutlerville society, and where were the protests?—the recriminations?—the talk of justice?

"Well, you know some of those clerks at Mulloneys are the snippiest little things. I took a pair of stockings back that had holes in them, and they had the nerve to . . ."

Georgina disregarded the woman to her right, and hearing the topic raised among the men, turned her attention there.

"He hires too many of those lazy Irish. That's the whole problem in a nutshell. All they do is drink all night and sleep all day and complain every waking moment. I heard the women are as bad . . ."

Georgina walked away, hoping for some sanity elsewhere in the room. It was almost time for dinner, and Daniel hadn't appeared yet. Maybe he had more sense than she and had stayed home. She could see Loyolla bearing down on her, and she tried to escape, but no one could escape Loyolla Banks when she had them in her sights.

"I thought you said he was coming," she whispered, pulling Georgina aside.

"After that article, are you sure you want him here?" It

was the first cynical thing Georgina had ever said in her life. Even Loyolla looked surprised.

"Of course. He's the talk of the town. Everyone is dying to meet him. He is a gentleman, isn't he? If he's one of these uncouth reporters with a cigarette hanging out of his mouth . . ."

Georgina rested a reassuring hand on her hostess's arm. "I wouldn't have you invite him otherwise. He's a gentleman when he wants to be. He's just not like any gentleman you've ever known."

Loyolla gave her a suspicious look, but turned eagerly at the sound of the front door opening. The clock was just chiming the dinner hour.

"Oh, my word. That's him." It was a declaration, not a question as the mayor's wife took in the newcomer with one swift glance.

The man entering wore an expensively elegant suit of dove gray unlike the dark suits of every other man present. With his hand in his pocket, he pulled back his fitted frock coat to reveal a white embroidered satin vest crossed by a silver watch chain bearing a fob that looked suspiciously like a silver bullet. In his lapel was a red carnation. Gray eyes gazed with amusement over the crowd from beneath an unruly swatch of brown hair that had recently been trimmed. Those eyes locked with Georgina's almost instantly.

"You'll have to introduce me," Loyolla said from Georgina's side.

There wasn't much time for introductions. More concerned with his dinner than his late guest, the mayor was issuing commands to move the party into the dining room. Georgina skirted the crowd, avoiding Peter's eyes by hiding behind Loyolla's bulk. That one pair of forceful eyes following her progress was all she could handle right now.

By the time she whispered the introductions, almost the entire party was on its way into the next room. Only Peter lingered, impatiently waiting to take his fiancée to her seat. When his eyes found the elegant stranger, they narrowed suspiciously, and he started to cross the room.

Georgina managed the introductions before Peter reached them. Under the pretense of bowing over her hand, Daniel whispered, "Better placate the hungry beast, Miss Merry. I'll talk to you later." Turning to take the arm of his hostess, Daniel walked away before he could meet Georgina's rather angry-looking fiancé.

"Who was that man?" Peter grabbed Georgina's elbow and led her toward the dining room.

Georgina smiled and announced in a triumphant whisper, "That, my dear sir, was Mr. Daniel Martin."

Heads on either side of her turned as her whisper carried while Peter seated her.

Georgina could almost watch the whisper ripple around the table as eyes turned to the man seated next to Loyolla Banks. The infamous Daniel Martin, newspaper editor. The women appeared intrigued. The men huffed out their side-whiskers and glared. Peter went white with rage.

Daniel smiled affably, whispered something to his hostess that made her laugh, and raised his glass of wine gallantly in her direction.

Georgina thought she might kill him for his insouciance.

At her side Peter bristled with outrage, but he was too much the gentleman to demand immediate satisfaction while sitting at the dinner table. Instead, he picked up his wineglass and sniffed the contents appreciatively before sipping. With an expertise he had cultivated, he announced, "Excellent vintage, Mayor. Full-bodied, with just a touch of fruit."

The mayor beamed at this approval from the acknowledged expert in the company.

Before the mayor could speak, Daniel sipped from his glass and set it aside. Looking directly at Georgina, he said, "I find it a little arrogant, and a shade *too* fruity. Too careful nurturing leads to an overripe softness that sours quickly."

She was definitely going to kill him. Daniel wasn't talking about the damned wine. He was talking about Peter. And Peter knew it. Georgina caught his hand against the table and kept him from rising.

"Why, Mr. Martin, I didn't know Texans drank wine." She turned a beseeching smile to her host. "Mr. Mayor, perhaps you ought to serve the wine you had last time. I distinctly remember Peter calling it 'humbling.'"

A few of the women tittered. A man coughed. And Mayor Banks took up the gauntlet, retrieving the party's attention from the two quarreling young men.

Daniel smiled in appreciation of Georgina's pointed reproof and turned his attention back to his hostess. Peter just glared at her. Perhaps the evening wouldn't be as much fun as she had anticipated.

Ignoring Peter, Georgina turned to the man on her right, but he had already launched into a discussion with his partner across the table. As the Irish maid served their soup, the man beside her declared aloud, "The problem is with these foreigners. They're all radicals and troublemakers. The law ought to ship them back where they came from."

The knuckles on the maid's hand whitened around the serving bowl, but she calmly continued around the table.

Georgina had never noticed the reactions of servants to dinner-table conversation before. She had scarcely noticed them at all, but her empathy was immediate. She wouldn't have been so controlled as to walk away with a soup tureen after a comment like that. Tiny shredded noodles would be dangling from her dinner partner's nose by now had she been that maid.

"It's the Jews that are the troublemakers. They keep driving up their prices as if they're better than anybody else. They scrape and cheat and make damned awful profits, then turn around and buy up everything they can get their hands on. If we're not careful, they'll be buying the town right out from under us. There ought to be laws against foreigners owning land."

Georgina pushed her noodles around in the bowl. "I thought that's why our ancestors came to this country, because they couldn't buy land in their own countries. They were immigrants escaping religious persecution, just like the Jews and the Irish."

"Georgina." There was a warning in Peter's voice as he passed the rolls.

She glanced over at her parents to see how far she could push the subject without being read a lecture later. Her mother was nervously twisting her napkin into knots and staring at her soup as if it would explode in her face at any minute. Her father was engrossed in some discussion with the mayor and heard nothing.

With curiosity she glanced at Daniel to see if he had heard. He wasn't looking in the least bit pleased about something, but she had the feeling it wasn't her. He was frowning at the ceiling in that absentminded way he had, and she could see the bespectacled journalist behind the facade of the elegant stranger.

With deliberate daring she smiled innocently at Peter. "Why, your father is Irish, darling. Should we ban him from owning land?"

"*His* father was Irish. My father lived here all his life. Now find another topic, Georgina." Peter turned his back on her and asked the woman beside him if she had attended the theological lecture the previous evening.

Georgina waited for the woman's polite response before speaking again. "I'm thinking of joining the Ladies' Society after we're married, Peter. It's all very well for them to bring in religious and scientific speakers, but I think it's time we broadened our horizons. I think we ought to hear what Susan Anthony has to say, for instance."

Her words fell into a sudden vacuum. Heads turned to stare. Georgina calmly buttered her roll. A man on the other end of the table immediately began a diatribe on women not having the intelligence to make the important decisions required in a voting booth. Georgina contemplated her roll with a little more interest.

Peter grabbed her wrist and removed the weapon. "Don't you dare," he hissed. "Remember you're in someone else's home."

Georgina stared at his large hand on her small wrist. "Yes, of course, you're quite right," she murmured apologetically. When he released her wrist, she raised it to her forehead with a small moan. "Oh, my. I don't feel well. I must have overtaxed my poor brain. Oh, please, help me."

And she fell into a limp heap against her chair back.

Georgina heard Peter cursing under his breath as he lifted her from the chair. She heard her mother give a squeak that meant she would have a spell to keep everyone on that side of the table occupied. She heard exclamations of excitement from other members of the party. And she heard Daniel's uproarious laughter.

It was all she could do to keep from laughing with him. There were cries for a physician and murmurs about brain fever and knowing tsk-tsks about too much education for a woman as Peter carried her into the parlor. She was stifling chuckles, and she knew full well that Peter wasn't fooled. He was furious. Only Daniel seemed to understand the statement she had made.

It had been a childish thing to do, but she felt good about it. Once deposited on the sofa, Georgina sat up and looked around with the same eager brightness she usually displayed. Looking at the crowd of people who had followed her in, she asked blithely, "Oh, my, is dinner over? I don't remember a thing!"

Her father had already bundled her mother into the arms of a servant and was shoving his way through the crowd. "Peter, get her into the carriage. I'll take her home."

Georgina pulled her arm out of Peter's hands and smiled. "I'm not ready to go yet, Papa."

"You've caused enough disruption for one evening, and it's time to leave, young lady." George gave Peter a meaningful look.

A tall man parted the crowd on the arm of Loyolla Banks. "I daresay the young lady is just hungry. Back home, we'd take her into the kitchen and make sure she ate a good meal. A mite of a thing like her needs lots of nourishment."

Georgina glared up into the laughing eyes of Daniel Martin. He was implying that she was too small. She wanted to tell him that most men didn't find her small, but then, most men thought she didn't have a brain in her head either. So much for the opinions of others.

"Come along, Georgina. Dinner is getting cold. George, you had better take Dolly home. I'm sure Peter will be able to look after your daughter for the rest of the evening. You know how girls are. They bounce right back." Loyolla took the situation out of the hands of the men.

The rest of the evening went comparatively mildly after that. Georgina instigated a discussion on freedom of the press after dinner that escalated into a screaming fracas, but Daniel amused himself with a stereoscope he'd found on a parlor table and didn't join in. At some point, Peter quietly confronted Daniel and demanded a retraction of the newspaper article, but Daniel merely smiled indulgently and told him that the truth never hurt anybody, especially in this town.

When Georgina attempted to intervene, Peter told her she was to have nothing further to do with "that man," and steered her away.

It was in that moment that Georgina knew what she was going to do. While Daniel vaguely retreated to some idle conversation and Peter manhandled her toward the door, Georgina discovered the courage that she had been lacking.

She had no sympathy whatsoever for the victims of her plot. If men didn't care what she thought, she could return the favor—with a vengeance.

Twelve

&

"Have you discovered who ABC is yet?" Georgina whispered hurriedly as she and her hostess went to recover her evening wrap.

"Mulloney," Loyolla whispered back, finding the taffeta pelerine and placing it on Georgina's shoulders. "You should have asked Peter. He could have told you."

Fury was an ugly emotion, Georgina decided as she smiled graciously, adjusted her wrap, and replied with calm, "That would have ruined the surprise. Thank you so much, Mrs. Banks. I had a wonderful evening."

This last was said in the presence of her host and Peter as they waited at the door. She didn't even look to see if Daniel noticed she was leaving. He had been as insufferable as every male in here all night, and she no longer cared what he thought. She had hoped he would set this company on its ears and force them to open their minds, but he had done nothing but evade argument all evening. She had hoped he would stand by her side and support her when she attempted to voice her views, but he had laughed at her instead. She didn't know the man who had appeared tonight under the guise of newspaper editor, and she didn't want to know him.

Georgina let Peter take her elbow and steer her into the humid night. There was a rumble of thunder in the distance and a flash of heat lightning on the horizon. Her father had sent the carriage back for them, and Peter assisted her into the covered interior, climbing up behind her with athletic ease. Peter was a wealthy, handsome man. He would have no trouble finding another wife.

He certainly wouldn't want her as one when she got through with him.

Artemis Mulloney owned ABC Rentals, Inc. Artemis Mulloney had hired a thug like Egan to terrify his tenants into paying. Mulloney was responsible for the squalor and misery his tenants lived in. And Mulloney told his eldest son everything.

It was more than Georgina could stomach. This whole evening had showed her that she didn't belong in this society any longer. She had thought Peter the best to be had, but now that wasn't good enough. She had thought her father a reasonable and kind man, but his actions of late had proved her wrong. She was obviously no judge of character, but she finally knew what she wanted and what she didn't want. She wanted to help those people in those tiny houses, and she didn't want to marry Peter Mulloney. And she didn't want to live under her father's thumb any longer.

Peter's smooth baritone broke the oppressive silence. "Your father is right. I think we need to move the date of our wedding to the first of the month. We can take a long honeymoon and learn to know each other better without the constraints of our families around us."

She wondered if Peter would kiss her if she agreed. Now that she had decided to be rid of him, she was curious about what she would miss. She didn't have much experience at kissing, just a few furtive attempts by slightly inebriated young men at parties. She had fantasized for years about how Peter's kiss would feel. But there had only been an occasional peck on the lips to feed her fantasy these past weeks since her return. She wanted more.

"Whatever you think best," she replied meekly, knowing the darkness would hid her lie. She was beginning to think she'd lied to Daniel when she'd told him she couldn't lie.

"Georgina . . ." Hesitantly, Peter reached for her gloved hand. "I don't want you to be unhappy. Is there something I can do or change?"

He could disown his father, pay his workers better, give them shorter hours, and stools to sit on. He could fire Egan and repair those rental houses. There were probably innumerable corrections he could make to the mill and the gas plant and who knows what other places his family owned. But that wasn't what he was asking.

"I don't suppose you could disown your father?" she asked, just as a sap to her conscience, to say she had tried to communicate her problem.

Peter chuckled and lifted her chin with his fingers. "He's not that bad. And we'll have a house of our own. You never asked about that, Georgie. Do you want to see it?"

Before she could reply, he placed his lips against hers.

It was an interesting experience. He'd been smoking a cigar and drinking brandy, she decided. She could taste the flavors on his mouth as he pried at her lips with his. His tongue came out to taste the seam of her mouth, and she gasped slightly at the sensation. It seemed an incredibly vulgar thing to do, but she knew Peter was far from being vulgar. She allowed it briefly before pulling away. So that was what it was liked to be kissed.

It hadn't been unpleasant. She had hoped for more and so felt slightly disappointed, but slight disappointments were as nothing anymore. She had all she could do to deal with the major disappointments she had run into lately.

Peter was oddly quiet as the carriage rolled up the drive. He continued to hold her hand, but there was no further demand for attention. Perhaps he was satisfied that she was in his control now. Men had that attitude, she'd noticed. She wore his ring. Soon, if he had his way, she would live in his house and have his babies. That somehow made her his possession in the minds of men. She would want for nothing.

It was a much better life than most. She would be a fool to throw it in his face.

Georgina made a gracious farewell in the foyer and left Peter to join her father in the study, no doubt to discuss the impending nuptials and whatever marriage contract they had decided on. She knew her grandmother had left her part owner of Hanover Industries. Her father had the controlling shares, so she was owner in name only, but Peter might be intent on changing that. It didn't matter any longer.

She went upstairs and quietly began packing her bags.

It was difficult to decide what she needed to take with her to her new life. She wasn't at all certain that her family would allow her back to remove anything she had left behind. They were going to be so furious that they might never speak to her again. That was her intent, but the notion was painful, nonetheless.

She consoled herself with the knowledge that it was for everyone's good. Peter deserved a supportive wife, and she would never be one. Her mother didn't need a daughter who would constantly disrupt her life and make her ill. Her father wanted a dutiful daughter and she wasn't. And Daniel . . . Well, what she was about to do wouldn't really hurt Daniel at all. Men only increased in reputation by this sort of nonsense.

She packed sensible dresses, or the closest she had to sensible dresses. She found good, solid walking shoes. In the midst of June it was difficult to think of winter, but she made sure she had a heavy winter cloak to carry with her.

She had only the one satchel, and she wasn't at all sure how she was going to carry it, so it didn't take long to fill. She would have to leave all her books and perfumes and ribbons behind. She had some pearls and a few gold-and-ivory pins that might be sold if necessary. She had her quarterly allowance in a purse she pinned to her corset. It wasn't much, but it would keep her until she figured out what she could do. She hoped Daniel would reconsider and hire her back, but without her camera, he wouldn't have much use for her. Perhaps she could learn to make those sketches she had seen in city papers.

If nothing else, she could sew. Her much-heralded education had taught her that. If the Harrisons could survive by sewing, so could she.

Georgina waited until the house was quiet before leav-

ing her note and slipping out to the small stable and carriage house her father kept. She was an expert horse-
woman, but her father kept only carriage horses. She
couldn't have saddled them if she had tried. But the
friendly pony of her childhood was still here, growing fat
and sassy for lack of exercise. She had been able to saddle him since she was a child.

He whickered willingly when she fed him sugar she'd
stolen from the kitchen. He wasn't quite as happy when
she saddled him and tied her satchel on; he was even less
so when Georgina mounted. But he was too old to learn
new tricks, and he trotted out of the barn obediently when
she applied her heels.

The thunder that had threatened earlier was directly
overhead now, and the heat lightning had become something a little more forceful. Georgina jumped nervously as
it flashed on the other side of the city and the thunder
cracked and rolled. But the rain held off, and for that, she
was grateful.

She didn't know if she would be able to keep the pony.
Feeding it might be too expensive, but she had worn her
heavy riding skirt anyway. She wouldn't have a carriage
to get around in any longer, and she would need something practical to maneuver the streets. A riding skirt af-
forded a considerable amount of freedom.

And Georgina felt remarkably free as she rode through
silent, empty streets. A cool wind blew in with the storm,
and even the air wasn't hampered by the heavy humidity
any longer. She felt light and unburdened and wildly
happy for the moment. She would have no one but herself
to account to now. It was exciting and scary and exhila-
rating beyond anything she had ever known.

Of course, the closer she came to her destination, the
more she worried. She ought to be worrying about the
dark alleys and furtive shadows and the rain that started
to drop in great splattering plods in the dust and against
her coat. But she was more concerned about the scene
that would surely unfold once her father found her gone
and read her note. It wasn't going to be pleasant, and she
was going to involve an innocent man.

But she was quite certain Daniel could handle anything. He was an odd man with many facets who revealed little of himself, but from what little she had seen, he knew how to take care of himself. If she hadn't seen him bring down a man twice his size with his bare hands—or feet, as the case might be—and watched him terrify two bullies with a fancy display of gunfire, she might have thought twice about this. He didn't seem the sort to actively defend anyone or anything. With his mild manners and spectacles and limp, he seemed more the type to hide behind books than to lash out at evildoers. He certainly wasn't the kind of white knight a girl dreamed about. But he would do.

It wasn't as if she was asking him to look after her for the rest of her life. She was perfectly content to do that herself. She just needed someone to ruin her long enough to get away from Peter and her family. Someone like Daniel ought to be perfectly adequate for that, and his reputation wouldn't suffer any for it, either.

The rain hit as she turned down the street leading to Daniel's office. In just the time it took to hitch her horse to a post, Georgina was drenched. Under the influence of her newfound freedom, she didn't care. There was no one here to complain or scold if she wished to stay out and play in the rain. She could drip across the floors with impunity. It was her skirt and her life and no one had any right to interfere.

So she climbed the stairs, satchel in hand, with a smile on her face. There was no lantern, but the rapid flashes of lightning through the upper-story windows gave her an occasional glimpse of where she stood. She probably looked like a drowned rat, but she couldn't hold back her smile. Freedom was terribly sweet.

She pounded on Daniel's door with a grin, imagining his reaction when he found her here. He couldn't even put her out on a night like this. The heavens were obviously on her side. She hummed to herself at the muffled sounds from the other side.

A dog began a frantic bark that left Georgina momentarily bemused, but the door finally fell open, and she was looking up into bespectacled gray eyes beneath an unruly cowlick. He'd removed his fancy coat and waistcoat, but from the looks of his rumpled shirt, he hadn't been to bed yet. She could see the lantern gleaming on the table beside the armchair she had noticed earlier.

"May I come in?" she asked with all innocence, pulling her dripping hat from her equally wet curls.

Daniel blinked in disbelief. "Georgina?" He glanced over her shoulder as if expecting someone to appear to save him. When no one did, he stared at her again, shaking his head. "What are you doing here?"

"Dripping wet and getting cold. If you don't want me in, may I use one of these other rooms to change?"

That was probably the wisest idea, but just the suggestion of it made him throw open the door and move out of her way.

She marched in, dragging her satchel and trailing a line of water. The German shepherd took one look, yipped in happiness, and threw himself at her. Georgina dropped the satchel and grabbed the dog as it rested its massive feet on her shoulders, staggering slightly before she got her balance. She rubbed its head happily as he slurped at her face.

"I suppose if you'd been an armed robber, he would have rolled over at your feet and panted for you to rub his belly," Daniel said disgruntled, as he came up behind her.

"He's gorgeous. Where did you get him? Papa never let me have a dog, but I love them."

"He's a . . ." Daniel halted as Georgina hugged the dog, set him down, and began to pull off her saturated frock coat. The linen shirt beneath was as wet as the rest of her—and much easier to see through. It molded to the perfect shape of breasts round as small melons.

Unaware of the cause of Daniel's sudden silence, Georgina held out the coat with despair. "Do you think it's ruined? I'll never be able to afford another. Do you think I should wring it out? Do you have a basin? I don't want to get your floors soaked."

"Georgina." Daniel coughed nervously. "I think perhaps you had better go in the other room and change. We'll worry about your wet things then."

Georgina gave him a swift look, but in the light of only one lamp, she could see little of his expression. The lamp light flickered off his spectacles, hiding his eyes entirely. "You don't mind? I had nowhere else to go."

"I don't imagine what I think has anything to do with anything at the moment," he said dryly. "It's raining out, I don't own a carriage, and you've got to get dry. We'll take it one step at a time."

She detected a note of censoriousness in his words, but that wasn't precisely anything new. He wasn't throwing her out, and she suspected she had the rain to thank for that. She smiled, lifted her satchel, and sailed into the room with the press machines.

She was more than likely going to give him heart failure before the night was over, but the idea of actually shaking up a man for a change was a pleasant one. They always had all the control. It was always their houses, their businesses, their carriages, their horses, their plans. Women had nothing to say about any of them.

But tonight, just for a little while, she was going to make the men in her life jump through her hoops. Then she would be free of them once and for all and could go on with her life.

She hadn't anticipated getting soaked in the process, but it worked into her plan very nicely. Daniel had evidently never considered her as a candidate for seduction. She would never have showed up here had she suspected he might. So if she hadn't arrived soaked, she would have had some difficulty in providing the correct atmosphere for the next scene of this play. Of course, there was every possibility that her father wouldn't show up until sometime tomorrow when she was fully dressed again and Daniel was gone to find someplace to dump her, but she meant to be fully prepared for any development.

"Do you have a towel?" she called as she pushed the heavy material of her skirt to the floor.

Georgina heard Daniel muttering in the far room before a hand came around the corner of the door, dangling a fresh towel. So he had someone to do his laundry. She was glad. She didn't like a sloppy man.

Covered by her shirt and petticoat, she stood behind the door and took the towel. She wasn't going to risk giving Daniel any ideas, even if she meant to convict him of them. The hand abruptly disappeared, and the door closed once she held the linen.

Peeling off the rest of her soaked clothing, Georgina dried herself briskly. The girls she had gone to school with had never stripped to the skin in their lives, but they hadn't been the types to get themselves soaking wet either. Georgina liked the feel of being naked.

Her hair was a saturated tangle that kept dripping down her back. Unpinning it, she tried to brush out the worst of the water, then wrapped it in the damp towel. She didn't think Daniel would look at her as any more than a drowned rat, but she was going to have to make it look a lot worse than that. With her hair secured in the towel, Georgina began rummaging through her satchel.

She drew out the filmy Parisian nightgown the girls had given her when she had left finishing school. They had told her it was for her wedding night, but she had never been able to imagine wearing it. The silk was so fine she could see right through it. There wasn't any lace or ruffles to disguise the bodice. There weren't even any sleeves to speak of, just little ropes of silk. It was the most scandalous, decadent thing she had ever seen, even worse than anything she had ever bought on her own. Even for a good cause, Georgina had doubts about wearing it.

But it was the only nightgown she had brought with her, and it would be much more effective than if she pulled on a cotton chemise with all its girlish frills and furbelows. She just couldn't decide if she ought to wear her cotton drawers under it.

At home she would have worn her drawers beneath a linen nightgown and not thought anything of it, but something about the drape of the silk told her that this nightgown wasn't made for drawers—at least not the bulky ones like hers with cotton ties and elastic at the knees and accented with eyelet ruffles.

Georgina contemplated the problem long enough for

Daniel to call out from the other room to ask if she was all right.

Taking a deep breath, she decided against drawers. She was, for all intents and purposes, naked. But she really didn't want Daniel to know that. Not just yet.

And so she called for a blanket and prayed.

Thirteen

❦

Daniel wasn't certain what he had expected when Georgina came out, but it certainly wasn't this. He could have sworn that the satchel she carried would have contained clothes, but he didn't see much evidence of them now.

Her hair was a silky wet mass falling over shoulders that were decidedly bare. Bare, as in cream and gold and softer than any human skin should be. He had difficulty even noticing that pale cream straps held up some nameless undergarment beneath the blanket.

He didn't dare look past her shoulders, but he was having a damned hard time keeping from it. With each step she took into the room, his gaze kept dropping to see if any part of that blanket moved. He was itching to know what she wore—or didn't wear—beneath it.

He finally summoned enough breath to exclaim, "Hell and damnation, woman, where are your clothes?"

Georgina's big blue eyes blinked and grew wide. "They're wet. I hung them on hooks in there. Was that wrong?"

She wasn't stupid. He knew she wasn't stupid. She was just making him crazy—and succeeding very well. "Didn't you have anything else to put on?" he asked in exasperation.

She appeared to give that some thought. "Well, I brought only the one chemise, the one I was wearing. I didn't see any reason to put on my dry gown and get it all wrinkled before morning. Which reminds me, is there somewhere I could hang it? It's going to be dreadfully crushed just from being folded into that little bag."

Daniel ran his fingers through his hair and wondered if he had somehow misplaced his mind. He couldn't keep his thoughts off bare shoulders and golden curls. He knew he ought to be getting her out of here. There were probably ten dozen questions he ought to be demanding answers to, but he could only stand here and continue this senseless argument over proper attire.

"I would feel better if you would hang the gown on yourself. The rain could stop any minute, and then we'll have to get you out of here."

Georgina pulled the blanket up more securely and looked around, finally settling on his chair as the safest place to sit. She snuggled into the cushions and shifted around a little bit until she was comfortable. Daniel almost had apoplexy just watching and imagining what was beneath that blanket, snuggling into his one and only chair, the one he had been sitting in a few million years ago.

It wasn't until she was comfortable that she condescended to reply. "But there's nowhere else for me to go. I've run away from home. My father wants me to marry Peter at the beginning of July, and you saw for yourself tonight that we're just not suited. My father will disown me if I refuse him, so I saved him the trouble. Do you think I could have my job back?"

Daniel had a broad imagination and a nagging sense of something not quite right. With suspicion he checked the street below, seeing only the pony munching on some weeds springing from the building's foundation. He contemplated checking the door again, but that seemed a little ridiculous. She was alone. With him.

"Georgina, have you lost your mind? You can't stay here; you'll be ruined. There must be somewhere else you can go until you settle this argument with your family. What if I take you to Mrs. Banks? She seems an intelligent sort."

Georgina smiled at his naivete. "Loyolla would have my father over in five minutes and the gossip around town in ten. Can you just imagine my appearing on her doorstep in the middle of the night with you at my side?" She shook her head, and a few wet curls left damp stains on the thin gown appearing beneath the slipping blanket.

Daniel caught himself holding his breath, waiting for the blanket to slip enough to reveal the shape of her breast. He was growing a trifle angry at this charade, but he wasn't certain if it was at himself or at her. He was twenty-eight years old, and while he wasn't exactly a lady's man like his adopted brother-in-law, he'd known his share of women. There was no excuse for this one to addle his mind like this. But there just seemed to be something about those baby blue eyes and winsome smile that destroyed his reasoning.

He wished for a kitchen and a coffeepot. He found his bottle of whiskey and poured himself a shot. He didn't make the mistake of offering Georgina any. "Well, you can't stay here, so you'd better start thinking. If you can't come up with any better solution, I'll be obliged to take you home as soon as it stops raining."

Georgina sighed and ran her hands through her hair in an attempt to remove the tangles. "I promise not to be a nuisance. I can sleep right here, and you can take the bed. In the morning I'll go looking for a job. You can't be making very much with that newspaper. I'll pay you rent and help with the expenses."

That left Daniel pretty well speechless for a few more minutes. Sleep? Here? It was hard enough to get past that possibility before contemplating the next one. Job? Where in hell did she think she was going to find a job? And doing what? He doubted if she could boil water or make a bed. But the idea that she meant to help him pay his expenses left him pretty well flabbergasted. No woman had ever helped offer to pay his expenses before. Even Evie knew better than that.

At this prolonged silence Georgina looked up worriedly. "I'm not going to interfere with your plans, am I? I mean, if you're courting Janice or some other lady, I can see that I'd be a problem. Maybe I could take a room downstairs."

He wished that was a possibility. Shaking his head, Daniel took another sip of the whiskey. It wouldn't clear his head, but he couldn't be any more confused if he were drunk. "The downstairs rooms have rats and spiders. Besides, I couldn't leave you alone. There's all kind of riffraff wandering these streets. I'm going to have to take you home."

"I wish you'd quit saying that." Georgina picked up a book from the table. "*Sense and Sensibility.* I loved that book, but I thought it was just a woman's novel."

"Evie sent it to me, said it would make me understand a woman's mind." Finding towering over her uncomfortable, Daniel took a seat on his pallet and leaned against the wall. He could hear the rain pouring down in buckets even though the thunder was moving farther away.

Georgina adjusted her position so she could look at him. "Evie?"

"My sister." His adopted sister to be perfectly correct, but his brain wasn't in a position to explain the details.

Georgina nodded happily. "I wish I could have had a sister. Does she live with your parents?"

"She lives with her husband and children. Maybe you better turn that lamp off and get some sleep. I've got a feeling this is going to be a long night."

When she hesitated, he turned her a quick glance. "Having second thoughts?"

"Second and third."

She looked at him with doubt, and inexplicably, that made him feel ten feet tall and stronger than Samson. That look turned him into a handsome scoundrel not to be trusted.

Daniel's laugh was abrupt and curt as he carried the thought to its natural conclusion—it hadn't been strong, handsome Peter she had run to. Peter was the handsome scoundrel. Georgina had run to good old safe Daniel.

"Well, it's too late now. I suspect we have a long day ahead of us. You'd better get some sleep."

She blew out the lamp, and the room fell into a thick darkness punctuated by the occasional flash of lightning. "Daniel?"

He was still sitting on the pallet, leaning against the wall, wondering if he should take off his shirt. He only had one clean one left. "What?" He didn't try to hide his irritation.

"Have you ever thought about what kind of woman you would like to marry?"

That was a loaded question if he'd ever heard one. Suffering under no illusion that she was interested in him, he answered honestly, "I almost married a shy one once. She liked to read a lot. She had thick black hair and eyes that looked into your soul, and she cooked circles around any one I've ever known. Why?"

"Girls always think about the kind of man they want to marry, but it doesn't seem to work the other way around. A man doesn't seem to care whom he marries as long as he's fed and warm and no one nags him. What happened to the girl you wanted?"

"She married a man with a ranch and a two-dollar smile, said we were too much alike, that I needed somebody different." Daniel pulled off his boots and made himself comfortable on the mattress.

"Do you think Peter and I are too much alike?"

"You're both spoiled brats, if that's what you mean. What kind of man did you have in mind to marry if not him? He's got everything any woman I've ever known would want." The darkness added an air of conspiracy to this conversation that Daniel found himself liking altogether too well. He would like it even better if she were lying on this mattress next to him. He could imagine her curling up to him, spoon fashion. He would slip his hand inside that blanket and test a subject that he had contemplated with curiosity for some time. Did she really fill those bodices of hers so beautifully or was that underpinnings?

"I don't know. I always imagined Peter, but I imagined him better. I wanted him to love me, to do anything for me, to be a hero. I could have loved him blindfolded if he'd just taken the time to listen to me. But considering what kind of man he really is, I suppose I'm lucky that I *don't* love him."

Suspecting he was about to hear what had precipitated her flight, Daniel asked gently, "What kind of man is he?"

"Selfish and rotten like his father, I suppose. Guess who owns ABC Rentals?"

Daniel groaned and threw his arm over his eyes. He didn't want to hear this. Just as Georgina had harbored illusions about her fantasy man, he wished to hang on to his hopes of the family he'd never known. All the evidence pointed in the opposite direction, but as long as he didn't know everything, he could continue hoping for that one piece that would prove their innocence. It sounded as if Georgina was about to hand him the final nail in their coffins instead.

"Mulloney Enterprises," he ventured.

"You knew! How did you find out? Isn't it awful? I've known Peter all my life. I can't believe he and his father are scoundrels. But I know I can't marry into a family like that. I'll starve first."

She just might starve if Mulloney had anything to do with it, Daniel reflected, but he didn't say anything aloud. Let her think him asleep.

He didn't sleep however. He wondered if he ought to offer her his bed, but she seemed perfectly content in the chair, and he knew his leg would ache like hell if he attempted it. He imagined sharing the bed with her, but his body told him instantly what would happen if she did. He'd been concentrating on his newspaper business these last weeks instead of looking for the kind of woman who would bring him relief. He was paying for that oversight. He needed a woman and he needed her right now. Daniel suppressed a moan of agony and frustration as he covered his face with a pillow on the wild theory that suffocation would exterminate desire.

Maybe it was time that he started thinking about taking a wife. A wife would have saved him from this night of agony at least. He didn't think Georgina would have turned up on his doorstep if he'd been married.

After that one disastrous adolescent encounter with Carmen, he'd decided he wasn't ready for a wife and hadn't given one much thought in years. He knew he needed to set himself up somewhere first, be a productive part of the community, have an income to support a family. Unlike Evie and Tyler, he was the settling-down kind. He didn't want to roam all over creation once he'd started a family. Circumstances just hadn't cooperated yet.

Circumstances, and the matter of his unknown family. Daniel let his body quiet as he considered this last piece of news about the family he supposed he would never claim now. He hadn't really considered taking a wife until he'd had a chance to meet his family. Perhaps madness ran in the blood. Maybe they all had two heads and tails. He'd had to know. And now that he knew, he wasn't certain it was any better than what he had feared.

But he didn't think greed was a trait that could be passed on through the blood. He could pack up, leave town, find a quiet little place to settle, and start looking for a wife to start his own family—a wife nothing like the one sleeping in his chair right now. She was too expensive, too useless, too beautiful. He would spend the rest of his life worrying he wasn't good enough for her, worrying she would find someone better. Let Peter spend the rest of his life looking over his shoulder.

He must have finally dozed. The combined racket of the dog barking its head off and furious pounding at the door jerked him back to consciousness quickly enough.

A rosy dawn sent a pattern of light across the rough wooden boards of the floor. Daniel squeezed his eyes shut and pinched his nose in an attempt to make the day go away. The gesture never succeeded, but habits were hard to break. The furious knocks were now accompanied by loud shouting and the dog's frantic scratching and howling.

He looked up to see terrified blue eyes watching his every movement. Now dry, golden hair tumbled in a sinful

cascade of curls over those bare shoulders Daniel had every cause to remember. Damn, but she was the exact opposite of everything he had ever wanted in a woman. He
liked black straight hair, thick and smooth as silk, and
dark, mysterious eyes that made his soul weep. Georgina
Meredith was as open and bright as the day was long. But
her terror roused his protective instincts.

With a groan Daniel staggered up, shoving his shirttail
into his pants. He was going to have to pay for laundry
early this week. Barefoot, he crossed the room, catching
the dog's collar before opening the door. He didn't have
any need to ask who was there. It didn't take any imagination at all to figure it out.

Georgina was the one who gave a cry of surprise when
the door flew open and Peter shoved through. She had
never counted on Peter coming. He looked furious
enough to eat nails, and her gaze flew to her father just
behind him. She was going to need all the protection she
could get.

Beneath his side-whiskers, her father's face went gray
when he saw her. Remembering what she wore, Georgina
grabbed the blanket and pulled it more securely around
her shoulders. But the damage was already done. Peter's
livid expression revealed that he had seen all she had
meant to show. She just hadn't counted on anyone coming
but her father.

She glanced briefly to Daniel. He was watching her
with an enigmatic expression that could have meant anything but almost certainly meant that he had seen what
she wore—or didn't wear—beneath the blanket. She felt
heat flushing through her at his look, and she turned back
to her father.

"You're no daughter of mine," he hissed before turning
around and walking out.

Stunned, Georgina stared after him. She didn't know
what she had imagined would happen when he found her,
but it certainly hadn't been this. How could her father
walk off and leave her in the hands of two furious and
highly volatile young men? Her gaze swung fearfully to
Peter.

She had never seen him look so dangerous. His eyes had grown stone-cold as they gazed on her, and his beard-stubbled jaw tightened menacingly as he turned to Daniel lounging against the door. It was then that she noticed Peter carried a rifle.

Fourteen

❦

"We don't treat ladies with disrespect in Ohio," Peter announced with a deceptive calm. "We have a solution for those who try."

"Peter! Stop it. You're jumping to conclusions. Before you make a fool of yourself, just listen . . ."

But Peter wasn't listening, as usual. He was glaring at Daniel. Daniel merely folded his arms over his chest, smiling back. *Smiling!* Georgina knew she should have killed them both the night before. She was beginning to prefer the bespectacled journalist to the man who smiled with fury in his eyes. Genuine fear lodged in her middle for the first time.

"The lady's talking to you," Daniel pointed out unnecessarily.

"*I'm* talking to you. I don't know who the hell you think you are, but you're going to pay for this. Did you think you could walk into town and destroy my business and steal my girl and walk away again?"

"I haven't destroyed your business—yet. And I haven't stolen Georgina. There she sits. Take her with you if you like."

"Daniel!" Irate, Georgina struggled to get up from the chair. It wasn't an easy task with the blanket wrapped all around her and in constant danger of slipping from forbidden parts, but she made it to her feet. "I'm not going anywhere with anybody."

Both men ignored her protest.

Finally stifling his fury sufficiently to face Georgina

again, Peter turned in her direction. "If you'll tell me you made a mistake and that you want to go home again, I'll forgive you this once. Just get your clothes and we'll get out of here."

That took her entirely by surprise. Shocked, Georgina stared at him, searching for some sign that Peter really wanted her to go with him. If there was any pain in his eyes, she couldn't see it. She couldn't see anything but his fury and his humiliation. She desperately wanted to believe that he would take her back because he wanted her, but she wasn't that naive anymore.

"Hanover Industries means that much to you?" she blurted out before she could stop herself.

"Your family means so little?" Peter retorted. "Get up and get your clothes and I'll get you out of here." Still clutching the rifle, he returned his attention to Daniel, expecting her full obedience.

"When my family allows other families to starve for the sake of their own pockets, they mean that little to me. I'm not going anywhere."

Daniel rolled his eyes heavenward and interceded. "You'd better take his advice, Miss Merry. You're not going to like what will happen next, otherwise."

She started to cross her arms and glare back, but remembered the blanket just in time. She grabbed it and kept it from falling, much to Daniel's disappointment, she could tell from his interested gaze. She flushed slightly at the look in his eyes. Why was it that he always made her feel so . . . so naked?

"I'm fully prepared to take care of myself," she informed him coldly, before returning to Peter. "I'm not going anywhere with you. Your family is an even greater disgrace than mine. Go back and fire another clerk and work off some steam, if that's what you want."

Peter shook his head in disbelief, then pointed the rifle at Daniel. "Get your boots on, cowboy. You're about to get hitched." Over his shoulder he added, "Find some clothes, Georgina, or you'll be going out like that."

"Don't be ridiculous. You can't tell me what to do."

Not completely understanding, Georgina remained where she was.

Daniel was the one who had to clarify matters for her. "Unless you wish to learn how a bullet works when it goes through a man's heart, you'd better get some clothes on, Miss Merry. I told you you weren't going to like this."

She had read about eyebrows disappearing into a person's hairline, and she suspected she was performing that trick right now as she stared at Peter. He wasn't watching her; he was aiming that silly rifle right at Daniel's heart. Why didn't Daniel just kick it out of his hands?

"Where are we going?"

"To the preacher. If you're not marrying me, then you'll be marrying your cowboy. Somebody has to take you in hand."

Peter seemed completely serious. Georgina was quite certain it was a joke. She sent Daniel a quizzical glance, but he merely waited with arms crossed for her to do as told. Scowling, she made an ungraceful retreat to the pressroom. She knew Daniel had something up his sleeve, but it would be a great deal easier if he would just pull it out now. This was getting downright embarrassing.

She hadn't known Peter even owned a rifle. He'd probably had to borrow it from one of his brothers. She hoped he knew how it worked or he was likely to blow someone's head off.

That thought hurried Georgina's steps. She hadn't really believed she would be putting Daniel into any danger by her impulsive decision, but he was standing out there at the wrong end of a barrel held by a man who was not exactly in his right mind at the moment. Should that gun go off for whatever reason . . .

She hadn't been able to resist bringing along the London gown that didn't require a corset. It was the easiest thing to don under the circumstances. Pulling on a chemise and drawers, she hurriedly pulled the gown over her head and adjusted the draping respectably. She couldn't get her shoes on without stockings, so she looked around for a chair to sit on. Finding none, she sighed, and sat on the floor and hurriedly jerked on the first pair she found, holding them up with tiny blue garters with rosettes. All she needed now was to borrow something and she'd be ready for a wedding.

That thought struck her rather forcefully. Surely Peter hadn't really meant that? He was just trying to make her suffer. Anyway, Daniel was certain to find some way of disarming him. And no preacher in Cutlerville was going to marry them like this. This was just a means of getting her out of the building. Well, she'd leave, but she would be back.

Fastening her shoes, she picked herself up off the floor and wished for a little more covering than the flowing sleeves of the gown. But her riding jacket was still wet, her winter cloak too heavy, and the gown didn't come with a polonaise to cover it, so she would have to go as she was.

More angry than afraid, Georgina stalked back to the front room to see the scene hadn't changed by much. The dog had settled down on the floor and gone back to sleep. Daniel was behaving most peculiarly. She had been quite certain that once she was out of the way he would have provoked some sort of struggle. But he stood calmly waiting for her, holding his jacket over his arm. He was wearing his boots, she noticed, and her heart sank to her stomach. They were really going out into the world like this.

Peter gestured with the rifle. "Come on, let's get this over. Reverend Herron will have left home if we don't get there soon."

Georgina's stomach swallowed her heart and carried it to her feet. Reverend Herron worked at Mulloney's because his congregation was so poor it couldn't support him. Herron was possibly the only preacher in town who might do what Peter told him without questioning.

She shot Daniel a look to see if he realized that fact. He merely settled his jacket around her shoulders and took her arm.

"The storm cooled things off," he murmured.

She couldn't believe this was happening. They walked

down the stairs in front of Peter, who still clenched the rifle as if he really meant to use it. Perhaps once they hit the street and were surrounded by people, they could make their escape. Peter surely wouldn't actually shoot that thing.

But it was too early for anyone to be in this part of town. In another half hour or so, workers would begin arriving at the factory, but there wasn't a sign of them now. Even the pony was gone.

That thought broke Georgina's heart as much as anything. The pony was hers. Her father had given it to her for her ninth birthday. He couldn't take it back just like that. It wasn't fair.

She felt a tear forming in her eye, but she refused to let it fall. This was foolishness. In a few minutes Daniel would find some way to get her away, and she would go on as she had planned. She had known she couldn't keep the pony.

Peter's open chaise waited for them. It was designed for only two people, but somehow, all three of them squeezed onto the seat. Georgina was practically sitting on Daniel's knees as Peter took up the reins with one hand. The other hand rested on the rifle in his lap.

"Peter, you have quite lost your mind," she informed him. "I don't want to marry anybody. I've been trying and trying to tell everyone that, but no one would listen. Don't blame Daniel just because I had to do something drastic to get your attention."

"Georgina, you always were a little fool. Up until now, I thought it sort of cute. It's not cute any longer, Georgina. You made your decision, and Mr. Martin made the mistake of going along with it. Now you'll both pay the price. People will understand an elopement. They will never understand your throwing yourself away rather than marrying me."

So that's what this was all about, male pride. Georgina squirmed uncomfortably, and Daniel caught her waist and held her still. She froze at the intimacy of that touch. She wasn't the sort who sat on men's laps, and they didn't lay familiar hands on her. She sat rigidly, trying to avoid any further contact.

"I am not throwing myself away. I mean to find a job and support myself. I'm going to make you see what your poor clerks have to do to live."

"You're going to get married and let a man look after you before you wind up in the streets. I'm surprised and disappointed that you chose this ... cowboy ... over me, but I don't mind admitting I'm a little relieved. We would never suit."

"That's what I've been telling you all along!" Excited, Georgina bounced in her seat, and almost instantly felt Daniel wince. She turned an uncertain look at him, but his expression was stoic once more. In fact, she could almost see amusement behind the enigmatic gray of his eyes. She frowned, and he tightened his grip on her waist. The blasted man was enjoying this!

She turned her attention back to Peter. "I told you we wouldn't suit. I've saved you from an unhappy marriage. You should be thanking me instead of behaving like a jackass."

"Male donkey," Daniel murmured behind her.

Georgina ignored him. "Let us out, Peter, and we'll forget this whole thing ever happened."

Instead, Peter reined in the horse in front of a modest house on a quiet side street. Picking up the rifle, he gestured with it. "Get out. We're here."

Daniel slipped out from under her and climbed out of the chaise, then held out his hand to help Georgina. If he knew what was good for him, Georgina thought, he would run now while Peter was occupied settling the horse and tying it down. She gestured for him to go, but Daniel's face closed up like a clam's, and he caught her arm and pulled her down beside him.

Damn, but he was being obstinate about playing the gentleman. Didn't he know that Peter was getting really serious about this? Whatever Peter had meant to do before—scare her, scare him, make them beg—had suddenly become something he couldn't turn back on. He was going to force them into the presence of a minister and make them go through some farce of a ceremony. She didn't know if it would be legal or not, but she certainly didn't want to have to find out.

When they were all on the ground, Daniel pulled Georgina closer to his side and away from Peter. She breathed a sigh of relief. At last, someone was coming to their senses.

"I think you'd better let me talk to Georgina privately for a minute if you really mean to carry this through. She's a mite contrary in the mornings and might not be as cooperative as you could wish."

Peter shrugged. "She can refuse and watch me shoot you. Even Georgie isn't that bloodthirsty."

"If you have any damn blood in your veins at all, you'll give us a minute. It's not as if we can go anywhere. Miss Hanover has the right to at least be asked properly for her consent, something you neglected to do, I might add."

It was the first sign of anger that Daniel had shown, and both Georgina and Peter looked at him with surprise. His angular face was taut with suppressed fury. Without waiting for an answer he pulled Georgina to the corner of the picket fence, just far enough to keep Peter from hearing.

"You and I know that we're both innocent, but the world doesn't," Daniel reminded her, keeping his voice low. "I'm perfectly willing to do the right thing by you, but I realize you've been caught by surprise and aren't any too ready for marriage. As long as you're . . . " He searched for a polite word. "Untouched, the marriage can be annulled. If you'll agree to go through with this, I promise I won't do anything to jeopardize that annulmen until you make up your mind one way or another. It': awkward, but it's one way out of the situation. People will find an elopement romantic, but a scandal won't be if word gets out that we spent the night together without marriage. We can go in there and pretend this is just wha we want and foil Peter's revenge, then correct it later."

Daniel was holding her hands between them and look ing at her as if her agreement really mattered. Georgin:

was too astonished to know how to reply. In an odd way
he was actually asking her to marry him. She wasn't at all
certain she wished to understand the meaning of "annulment" or the consequences, but she did have some sense
of what he meant by "untouched." They could be married
and not married at the same time. It was a revelation that
widened her eyes. She could be respectable but indepen-
dent.

"We could just be . . ." The appropriate word was difficult to locate, but she tried. "Friends? And be married?
Is that what you're saying?"

Daniel's smile was a trifle forced, but he nodded. "For
a while. We'd have to decide what to do sooner or later
so we don't cause any more scandal, but that will give us
more time to think than your friend over there is giving
us."

Georgina's heart was pounding a little frantically at the
decision she was being given, but Daniel had phrased it a
lot more palatably than Peter. If the world required that
she be married, she'd much prefer a man who had some
consideration for her opinions. Right now, she very definitely preferred Daniel over Peter. Curling her fingers inside his with nervousness, she nodded slowly. "All right.
If this is the only way." Realizing Daniel might not find
this arrangement as convenient as she did, not wanting to
incur his wrath any more than necessary, she sent him a
pleading look. "I didn't mean for this to happen, believe
me. I had no idea my father would fetch Peter. And I
didn't know Peter could be so unreasonable."

Daniel's smile was a little warmer as he released one
hand to caress her cheek briefly. "I'm afraid I understand
altogether too well. I'm not blaming you. I've got a feeling we're about to upset a few applecarts. Let's do it with
style."

She grinned, took his arm, and without any preparation
aforethought, stood on her toes and kissed his cheek
soundly.

That would certainly make Peter think twice.

Fifteen

&

The minister was already dressed in a dark sack coat with elbows polished by wear. His cravat wasn't quite correctly tied when he opened the door, but he didn't seem to be aware of that as his eyes opened wide at the sight of his employer on his doorstep. As he retreated to allow Peter in, his gaze fell on the two miscreants with him.

Georgina offered him a blinding smile. "We wanted to elope, but Peter has gallantly offered to stand up for us. I hope we're not disturbing you."

Daniel was quite proud of her. For a light-headed, frivolous pearl of society, Georgina was remarkably courageous. Another woman might have been hysterical by now. Of course, another woman would never have got herself into this situation.

He felt no remorse at what he was about to do. Georgina had brought it down upon her own head. Actually, Daniel found the better part of this episode mildly amusing. The hand-picked bride for the handsome heir to the Mulloney kingdom was about to be thrown away on the damaged son who had already been disowned. Daniel really hoped Artemis Mulloney enjoyed the irony of it when he discovered the situation.

And he very much feared his father would learn the whole truth of the situation much sooner than Daniel had contemplated. Marriage entailed a certain amount of honesty he hadn't anticipated revealing so soon. And he was more than certain his two companions were even less prepared for it. Well, he'd learned a long time ago to let the chips fall where they may. He just hoped those chips weren't bigger than he was.

Georgina handed him his coat, and Daniel shrugged it on. There was a grim edge to her smile that he didn't like, but he couldn't particularly blame her. Peter was at his officious worst, giving orders and instructions that had the minister and his wife running in circles. Daniel offered her a grin and tucked a straying wisp of hair behind Georgina's ear. She hadn't even taken the time to tidy it. He would have thought a socialite would have been a little more vain than that.

But he suspected this socialite was hiding one whopping load of anger behind her demure expression and vacant smile. He wasn't exactly certain that he wanted to be on the receiving end of all that pent-up fury when it was finally unleashed. The way Georgina was looking at Peter now, Daniel figured the other man would bear the brunt of it, but for one minor problem—the matter of Daniel's real name.

He could take the coward's way out and let the minister use the name Peter was currently instructing him to use. The marriage would probably be fraudulent and null and void, and they wouldn't have to go through the scandalous legal processes of annulment. But Daniel had seen the chaos that created when his adopted sister had tried it, and he wasn't prepared to deal with those kind of complications. He liked things done straightforwardly and honestly.

So he smiled and took Georgina's hand when the minister gestured for them to step forward. He couldn't think of any particularly good objections to marrying Georgina Hanover, even temporarily. She was good-humored and well-intentioned and not a half-bad photographer. She wasn't the quiet intellectual he had always imagined marrying, but a cheerful smile could go a long way toward alleviating that lack. And though she was short and blond and not the willowy brunette of his dreams, Daniel had no difficulty whatsoever in imagining her in his bed.

And if he was going to be completely truthful with himself, that was probably the major reason he was standing here listening to the minister mouth the hypocrisies of this marriage service: Georgina Hanover would make a round handful in his bed, and he was a starving man.

Of course, the degree of shock and incredulity he was about to unleash was also stimulating.

To Daniel's surprise the minister didn't use their full names when asking for their vows. As just "Daniel," he vowed to love and protect "Georgina" until death parted them. That shook him a trifle as he looked down at the woman beside him. She repeated the vows as calmly as he had, but Daniel noticed her fingers were trembling slightly. He took them in his own and marvelled at how small and soft they were against his hand. It had been a long time since he had really paid attention to any woman. He was beginning to realize that was about to change.

He didn't have a ring to give her, but she took the one off her right hand and gave it to him, and he slid it on the ring finger of her left hand. Nervously, she tried to pull away from his grasp, but Daniel held on to her as the final prayers were said over their heads. He had the oddest sensation in his middle as he held this woman's hand and heard the minister droning the words of the marriage ceremony. He had never tried to imagine what it would be like to be married. He didn't think even his imagination would have been able to quite grasp it. He was feeling nervous and scared and oddly protective and definitely very hungry.

Daniel concentrated on the hunger. There was no mention of kissing the bride at the end of the service, and he wondered what religious denomination was so hopelessly unromantic. Without waiting for permission, he tucked his arm around his new wife's waist and hauled her closer.

Georgina's eyes widened as she realized his intent, but it was far too late to resist. Daniel's lips closed over hers, and she shivered with the thrill of this unexpected intimacy. Her eyes closed instinctively, allowing her to absorb the sensation of her husband's strong embrace, the rasp of his unshaven beard, the oddly pungent flavor of his mouth. She was aware of other things, too, things she couldn't rightly name but which involved the nearness of Daniel's broad chest to her breasts and the closeness of their legs and some odd electricity that emanated from them both as a result. She was sadly shaken when he stepped back at the minister's embarrassed cough.

Georgina had difficulty tearing her gaze away from her new husband, but she forced herself to calmly turn and meet Peter's eyes. He was furious. There was a muscle jumping in his jaw that she had never noticed before. His eyes glowed with an unholy emerald green that made her wish she had never crossed his path. She had never thought of Peter as a villain, but she thought he would make a very good one right now.

"Where's the license and the register, Reverend?" Peter's voice was harsh as he turned away from the newly married couple. "We want this all tight and legal."

The minister hurriedly produced the book and a blank certificate and began to fill in the names of the parties involved. He held out the pen to Daniel. "If you'll just sign your name, then your wife can sign hers, and the witnesses will go on the lines after that."

Daniel scrawled his name boldly across the book and the paper with what looked to Georgina like a measure of satisfaction. He shouldn't be satisfied with this arrangement. He ought to be angry, or at least irritated. But he handed the pen to her with a smile that Georgina would have given money for had it been on Peter's face. As it wasn't, she sighed and took the pen and turned to the piece of paper, signing her life away.

She only glanced at Daniel's scrawl to see if he had used his full name. She blinked as her mind registered the discrepancy between what she had expected and what was there. She turned and looked at Daniel, waiting for some wink of conspiracy to tell her this was just a joke or some means of getting them out of this trap. But he had told her how he meant to get them out of this trap, and it had nothing to do with his signing Peter's name as his own.

Her hesitation made Peter suspicious. He grabbed the paper, read the signature "Daniel Ewan Mulloney," and flung it to the floor.

Raising his rifle, he thundered, "Get another one, Reverend. The gentleman doesn't seem to remember his name."

Daniel calmly picked up the paper and handed it to Georgina. Looking at her and not the man with the rifle, he said, "That is my name. You'll find it on file at the courthouse. I've got the birth certificate to prove it. If you despise the name, Miss Merry, I might consider changing it. I don't take much pride in it."

Georgina's fingers crumpled the paper at the edges as she stared at it. She had just sworn not many hours ago that she would starve rather than marry into the Mulloney family. But maybe it wasn't the same family. She had never seen Daniel in town before these last weeks. He couldn't be one of them.

She glanced up hopefully at Daniel's sincere expression. "If there's no relation, there shouldn't be room for complaint." She picked up the pen to sign her name below his.

"There's no damned relation!" Peter roared at the same time as Daniel murmured, "I'm afraid there is."

Georgina's hand halted in the midst of the first *G*. She stared at the paper as if the answer to this dilemma were written there. If she didn't sign, would the marriage still be valid? And if it wasn't valid, what would she do now? She couldn't go home. She couldn't marry a man mad enough to hold her at rifle point. She would end up walking the streets. But if she signed, Daniel was telling her she would be Georgina Mulloney. Why had he lied? Had he lied? Was he lying now? Her fingers trembled.

"Sign it, Georgie." Daniel's voice was soothing and reassuring at the same time. "I have no intention of claiming any connection with a family that lets people starve and live in deprivation so as to have expensive carriages and fancy balls. I put my real name on there only to protect you."

Against her better judgment, Georgina began to sign, but again, Peter's roar intervened. She swung around just in time to see him drop his weapon and reach for Daniel's shirt front. There wasn't time for Daniel to dodge the blow. He took it square on the jaw, staggering backward while the minister's wife wailed in dismay as he slammed into her shelf of china ornaments.

But Daniel was up and off the shelf and grabbing for the dropped rifle before Peter could reach out to repeat his earlier blow. Not using the firing end of the rifle, he slammed the stock into Peter's stomach, crumpling the other man in two. Then flinging the rifle down, he grabbed Peter's collar and jerked him up.

They stood face-to-face, and Georgina held back a gasp of recognition. It was the same sloping aristocratic nose on both men, only Daniel's was slightly bent from some earlier brawl. Their lips were pressed tight in the same straight lines of fury, and there was even a certain similarity in the jut of their jaws. Why hadn't she seen the resemblance sooner?

Because the force of their highly incompatible personalities made it impossible to see similarities where there were only differences. Daniel was easygoing, mild-mannered, and amiable, always willing to listen and eager to act. Peter was wired tighter than any rope, explosive in his manner when thwarted, stiffer than the celluloid collar at his throat and as difficult to bend. There could be no comparison, except at moments like this.

Daniel was shaking his captive and shoving him toward the desk and the still unsigned license. "Witness it, dear brother. Let us make this perfectly legal, just as you asked. Then go home to Papa and explain what you've done. I doubt that he will be amused, but he probably won't banish you to St. Louis as he did me. He'll start running out of sons after a while if he did that."

Peter turned so violently that he ripped from Daniel's grasp, but Daniel blocked the blow this time, shoving

Peter's fist away. Then he stepped back and stood by Georgina's side.

"Sign it, Peter. You don't have to tell the old man anything. Let's just try to get out of here like civilized human beings before the good reverend and his wife think we've lost our minds."

Peter grabbed the paper and scrawled his name vividly across the bottom, then handed it to Georgina to finish signing. He scowled at Daniel as he walked toward the door. "I wish you well of her, but don't think I'm forgetting this. That name on that piece of paper had better be real or I'll see that you're hanged. Georgina deserves better than scum like you."

He stalked out to the sigh of a soft "Oh, my" from Mrs. Herron. Her husband merely handed her the license to finish witnessing.

Georgina discovered she was trembling. She wasn't accustomed to scenes like this. She had always lived a staid and respectable life. Only the humbler, uneducated elements of society shouted and fought and behaved like animals. Just what was she letting herself in for?

Daniel folded the paper, put it into his pocket, and handed the terrified minister some coins for his trouble. Peter should have been the one to do that. Peter had always been her model of respectable behavior. She had only begun to realize how poor her judgment had been all these years. How wrong could she be about a man she had known only a few weeks?

Pure terror washed through Georgina as Daniel reached for her hand to lead her away. She didn't know this man at all. She hadn't even known his real name. A man who could hide his identity while attempting to destroy his real family wasn't the kind of man she wanted for a husband. She jerked her hand away and started out the door without him.

Daniel caught up with her in a few strides. She was halfway down the unpaved street before she realized Peter had taken the carriage, leaving them stranded in an unfamiliar neighborhood.

"Keep going straight. We'll be downtown in a few

minutes," Daniel advised as he walked beside her, adjusting his gait to hers.

"Go away," she whispered harshly.

"Since we're going in the same direction, that isn't reasonable."

He was acting the amiable journalist again, but now she knew better. Daniel might look quite tame, but he had a vicious streak to match Peter's any day. Anyone who could take a blow like Peter had dealt him and still return it with a fierceness that had brought Peter low was not a gentle man. She hurried faster down the street.

Daniel kept pace without complaint. He didn't even seem to be limping much. Maybe that was just a pretense, too. Scowling, she lifted her skirts and almost ran toward town.

"Merry, you can't run away. You did that last night and look where it's got you."

He was right beside her, not even breathing heavily as they entered Main Street. Street sweepers were stirring the dust on the macadam, and a few of them looked up with interest as the furious couple hurried by.

Georgina skirted around the lamp man dousing the gaslights. "I'm not running away."

"Then what are you doing? Early morning walks may be beneficial to our health, but I don't think this pace is required."

"Why don't you just shut up and go away? I have to think."

"Fine. I'll be quiet. But I'm not letting you out of my sight. In that gown you'd have every male in town on your heels within minutes."

She hadn't thought of that. She glanced down at the folds of silk blowing in the breeze created by her brisk walk. She wasn't wearing enough under it to disguise her legs beneath the thin fabric, and the neckline was shockingly low for this time and place. Even as she realized that the shadow of the valley between her breasts could be seen, she felt Daniel's gaze follow hers. He was staring at her breasts.

And he had every right to. He was her husband.

Gulping at the enormity of the foolishness she had committed, Georgina stalked on.

What if he had lied about leaving her untouched, too?

Sixteen

❦

"Merry, I'm not going to eat you alive. Why don't we stop somewhere and have a bit of breakfast and discuss this like two rational people?"

"Stop calling me that." Her response was irritable and irrelevant. Daniel's words conjured up uncomfortable sensations that she didn't know how to deal with in these circumstances, and she didn't know how else to reply. Her stomach cried out for food, but she couldn't imagine sitting down across a plate of bacon and eggs with this man just as if they were a real married couple. That was just a shade too intimate for her taste.

And the other sensation causing her agony was even worse. She needed to relieve herself, and there seemed no salvation in sight. She couldn't even remember Daniel's office having anything as civilized as plumbing. What had she done when she had thrown herself out into the cold world beyond her father's safe walls?

"You're right, you're behaving just like your father now. I ought to call you George." Grabbing her elbow, Daniel dragged her into a small side street emanating mouthwatering aromas.

The buildings along this forgotten alley were lined with grime. In wet weather the ground was like a swamp. In dry, it probably consisted of solid ruts and dust so thick a footstep could disturb it. Some of the buildings sported windows with fading letters painted on them. Signs dangling over doorways held incomprehensible names of unknown proprietors. Daniel pushed her through the doorway beneath one claiming to be "Mama Sukey's."

The scent of food in here was so strong Georgina could feel her knees weaken. Ham and biscuits came first to mind, and she had a sudden overwhelming desire for the massive breakfasts she had enjoyed when visiting a friend in Kentucky. Mounds of biscuits and bowls of gravy and platters of eggs and ham danced dizzily in her mind. She was going to faint from hunger.

Before Georgina could crumple into the nearest chair, a diminutive black woman emerged from the back and gave a holler of welcome, opening her arms and smiling warmly at sight of Daniel. "Danny Boy, where you been keepin' yo'self? I got them fresh aiggs just the way you like them, and you ain't been here to enjoy them."

The woman nearly crushed Daniel in her embrace before she discovered Georgina standing nearby. With a whoop she put Daniel aside, placed her gnarled hands on her hips, and looked Georgina up and down. "What you got here, honey? She sure enough looks like she could use some feeding up. You done brought her to the right place."

"Sukey, meet my wife, Georgina. Georgina, Sukey is the best cook this side of the Ohio, and she'd be the best cook on the other side, too, if her mama hadn't already claimed that title."

Sukey beamed. "My, my. Little Daniel done growed up and got himself a wife. Does my boy Ben know 'bout this?"

"I'm sending out the wires this morning. Is he in Texas or Natchez now?"

"He been sniffin' 'round a little girl down Natchez way, so I s'pect that's where he's at now. Those folks of yours likely to be there, too, now that it's summer. You'd best let them know what you gone and done or they'll be almighty hurt. Now you sit down here and let me whup you up a real meal."

She started toward the kitchen, but Daniel called her back. Gesturing with a modicum of embarrassment to Georgina, he asked, "Can you take Georgina back to wash up? I kind of dragged her away without giving her a chance to prepare."

Georgina sent him an incredulous look, but gladly took the excuse to hurry away. She just prayed that whatever served as a washroom in this place was clean.

When she came back sometime later, considerably relieved and in a tidier condition, she found Daniel already seated at a table mounded with just the kind of breakfast she had been dreaming of and topped off by cinnamon rolls so light they practically floated from the plate. As wedding breakfasts went, this was more than adequate.

Sighing with contentment as she sipped the steaming coffee, she missed the covert look Daniel sent her, but the half smile that appeared a moment later caught her attention. She frowned and put down her fork filled with eggs.

"Don't look so smug, Daniel Martin or Mulloney or whoever you are. I'm still furious, and I'm going to find a way to get even."

"With whom? Me or Peter or the world?" He dug into his fried ham with fervor. "And what's the point? It's over and done, and we have work to do. There isn't time for plotting revenge."

Her fork lingered uncertainly in midair as she considered his complacency after the morning's events. But the mention of work kept her tongue from flapping loosely. Georgina regarded him with a measure of caution. "You're going to let me work? Doing what?"

"Until I can figure out how to get your equipment back from your father, I guess I'll use you to do some of the interviewing. Both Mulloney and your father hire lots of women, and I think they'll talk to you easier than they will to me. I know word has got out that talking to us could cost them their jobs, but I've got a plan for that. We need to turn Audrey and Janice to our side first, then we'll be rolling."

It didn't seem possible. Georgina had already seen the trouble she had caused and the resentment that resulted. She wasn't at all certain she would be welcome in that side of town ever again, and after the incident with those two bullies, she wasn't certain she wanted to go. She was almost beginning to think she would have done better staying in the part of town that she knew, digging through the courthouse records and going to dinner parties, instead of prying where she wasn't welcome.

Her doubts must have shown on her face. Daniel looked up from his feeding frenzy to scan her expression. "You're not backing out now, are you?"

"I don't seem to be very good at it," Georgina answered miserably. "I don't seem to be very good at much of anything."

Daniel grinned and the gray of his eyes practically sparkled. "I imagine there are one or two things you might be good at with practice if that kiss was any example, but I suppose we ought to reserve them until you've decided whether or not you want to be married. I'm looking forward to our wedding night."

Horrified, Georgina stared at him. "You said this was only temporary. You said we wouldn't really be man and wife!"

Daniel shrugged and popped a strawberry into her mouth. "We won't, not until you say so. But don't take too long making up your mind. It's hard being a faithful husband when there's no wife to be faithful to."

She accepted the warning for what it was and lost her appetite. She was either going to have to move out on her own in truth, or accept Daniel as her husband. He wouldn't wait forever. It was a terrible decision to have to make. She was glad she didn't have to make it immediately.

Filled to overflowing, they traversed the streets more sedately a little while later. Georgina didn't even object when Daniel wrapped his fingers around hers and held her hand. She rather liked the casual possessiveness of his grasp. Peter had never held her hand. He had always offered his arm when required, but even a stranger on the street might do that. She liked knowing she was a little more than a stranger on the street.

She didn't like the direction they were taking, however. She recognized it instantly, and her heart beat in trepidation as the scarlet geranium came in sight. She didn't like being hated. She didn't want to deliberately walk into a place where she would be looked on with scorn. She pulled on Daniel's hand, trying to hold him back, then trying to escape when he kept on walking.

His hand crushed hers tighter as he glanced back at her. "You can't hide from the world, Georgina. You've got to confront it and shake your fist at it and go on. I've got enough battles of my own to fight. I don't want to have to fight all yours, too."

That got her dander up. Glaring at him, Georgina caught up her skirt and stalked down the street. She wasn't any vapid heroine who needed a white knight to rescue her. Janice Harrison was an arrogant pigheaded fool, and she was going to prove it to her.

She did very well when the spry old lady answered the door. Georgina smiled and greeted her and pushed her way into the house without being invited. That was when her determination faltered.

Janice knelt beside a makeshift bed in the front room, a look of worry and exhaustion painting her beautiful porcelain face in shades of gray. On the bed lay a frail golden-haired child, her closed eyelids veined in blue. Even her lips were lined with blue against the pinched thin skin of her face. Georgina halted, speechless, while Daniel came in and placed a hand on her shoulder.

Even in her weariness, Janice's anger came through as she looked up at the intruders. "Get her out of here," she whispered, not moving from the child's side.

"Georgina's my wife, Janice. We're here to help whether you like it or not. Betsy's had another of her spells?" He nodded toward the child on the bed.

"She walked clear out to the end of town, looking for wild strawberries, then some fools tried to steal her pail, and she had to run all the way home. The doctor said she shouldn't overexert herself. Her heart's too weak to stand it." Janice gave Georgina a curious look, but didn't comment on her new status.

That didn't keep the old woman from cackling over it. "Found yourself a good man, did you?" She gestured toward a lumpy stuffed chair near the door. "Have a seat. It's good to see a smiling face once in a while."

Janice scowled, but taking one look at Daniel's expression kept her from driving their visitors away. Instead, she gave Georgina a malicious glance. "What happened to your rich beau? Frighten him away?"

"I couldn't marry a man who would hire a scoundrel like Egan." Georgina took the seat offered although she was certain her light gown would be soiled forever. There wasn't any way these people could beat out the grime that coated this neighborhood.

Janice snorted. "I could marry a man with two heads and horns if he could give me everything Peter Mulloney could give me. You're a fool."

Georgina smiled sweetly. "I'll introduce you two sometime."

"If you'd married him, you could have persuaded him to fire Egan and fix up these places," Janice pointed out, dipping a sponge into a basin and carefully mopping her sister's forehead.

"If I'd married him, I could have grown old talking to the walls. It would have done as much good. The only way to persuade Peter to do anything is from the wrong end of a gun." Georgina looked up to Daniel hopefully. "Could we do that? Could we hold him at gunpoint and force his father to sign over the houses or something? I'd dearly love to see Peter at the wrong end of that rifle."

Daniel's lips quirked up in agreement as he gazed on her, but then he jerked his gaze away and back to the woman at the bed. "Do you have more of that medicine the doctor prescribed last time? That seemed to work."

Georgina felt a breeze of emptiness pass between them as she, too, turned back to look at the small tableau. The rapport she had found with Daniel before had just been wishful thinking, after all. They were two completely different people with different backgrounds and different goals. How could she have imagined that he needed her, even for a single minute? Like Peter, he was all business. It was just that Daniel's business was more to her liking than Peter's.

She turned her attention back to Janice who was evading Daniel's question by murmuring something about medicine not being necessary. Georgina didn't think it took a woman to understand that Janice was too proud to admit that they couldn't afford the doctor or medicine, but it might take a woman to tactfully suggest a solution.

Before Daniel could reply, she interrupted. "Which doctor do you use?"

Janice frowned, but said, "Dr. Phelps."

Georgina nodded her head knowingly. "Dr. Phelps owes me a favor or two. I think it's time to call them in. Why don't I send him over here just to make certain Betsy doesn't need something else? He won't charge you if he knows what's good for him."

Daniel's hand closed over Georgina's shoulder as he talked over Janice's protest. "We'll go do that right now. But if you don't mind, I'd like you to think if there aren't some other women from Hanover Industries who might be interested in talking to us—maybe some who don't work there anymore. Make a list, and we'll come by to get it later. Is Douglas still going to help with the deliveries? I'm expecting this next edition to really raise dust."

He understood. Georgina gave a sigh of relief and stood up, taking Daniel's arm as he led her toward the door with Janice's assurances that her brother would be ready. He had not only understood what she had tried to do, but he had helped her. She would dearly like to meet the family that had raised this marvelous man. And then tell them to break his habit of telling lies.

Outside, as they hurried down the street, Daniel glanced down at her and asked, "You don't really know Dr. Phelps, do you?"

Georgina smiled blithely. "Never heard of him. But I've got my quarterly allowance and I'm certain he will go anywhere we ask with the proper enticement. That child looked horribly ill to me."

"She had a fever that injured her heart. She probably won't live to be an adult. Are you sure you want to throw away your coins? There won't be any more where those came from."

Georgina jerked her hand away and glared at him. "Stuff it up your shirt, Mulloney." She stalked away without a backward glance.

Daniel's laughter followed her up the street.

It was a heck of a way to start a marriage, but much better than contemplating what would happen in the night to come.

Seventeen

"**Y**ou did what?"

The man behind the massive desk leapt up and glared at his eldest son as if he had taken off his head and bounced it on the floor.

Peter shoved his hands in his pockets and glared back. "I wasn't going to let her be ruined by that scoundrel. It serves them both right. What I want to know is where he got the name. I haven't been down to the courthouse yet, but he swears his name is Mulloney and that he's my brother. Even an ass wouldn't make that claim unless he has something to back it up."

Artemis Mulloney went white, whether with rage or some other emotion wasn't easily discernible. His fingers locked around the desk, and the light from the window behind shadowed his face, making it impossible to read his expression. "The lying, conniving son of a . . ." He halted in mid-curse, straightened up, and took his seat. "His intent is evident, of course. It's a simple enough matter to forge documents. I'm not certain how he found out, but he has evidently done his research. We've not mentioned it to any of you because it never seemed important, but there was a child born before you, a son. He died within three days of his birth. He's buried in the family cemetery. You can see the stone for yourself. It reads 'Daniel Ewan Mulloney.'"

Peter took the first deep breath of the morning. His stiff stance relaxed a shade. "I knew there had to be an explanation. The bastard is trying to pass himself off as one of us so he can walk in and claim his share of our wealth and Georgina's, too. Do you think he means to take it to court? Surely forged documents can be detected?"

Artemis reached for a pen and began to scribble across a piece of letterhead. "I suspect he will opt for blackmail. He won't want to get the courts involved. I'll notify our attorney. We'll stop this before it can even begin." He looked up and glared at his son. "Marrying him to Georgina Hanover is the stupidest thing you've ever done. But I'll take care of that. You get back to work."

Peter stiffened again. Biting his tongue, he swung around and stalked out. Sometimes, he had a great deal of difficulty liking his father, but he didn't have to like him to obey him. The old man knew what he was doing, there was no doubt about that. But just this once, Peter would like to be a step ahead of him.

He would start with a visit to the courthouse.

Georgina stared out the window of her new home to the dirty street below where a farm cart rattled past loaded down with fresh produce from the country. It was a little late to be arriving for the Saturday morning market. Perhaps the farmer had been so successful he had gone back for a second load.

Turning around, she gazed at the nearly empty room that she and Daniel would now share. This wasn't even a house. It was a warehouse. These rooms were made for offices and stock and hordes of dirty, sweating men. The walls hadn't been painted since the building had been built. The floors were worn and scraped with years of machinery and feet crossing them. They had never been sanded and polished for the feet and delicate shoes of women.

At least there was some semblance of plumbing, she had discovered much to her relief, but that was as gracious as it got. The windows had no curtains. The floors had no rugs. The rooms had no furniture, unless one counted a printing press, a pallet, and an old armchair.

Her eyes strayed to the pallet Daniel had slept on the night before. Surely he wouldn't expect her to share that?

Raising her chin, Georgina started for the door. Daniel had left her here while he went to run errands. She didn't know what he expected her to do with the time, but she knew what she wanted to do. She set out to explore the other possibilities of this filthy building.

When she was done, she was even more depressed than before, but at least she had some ideas. There was another room across the hall she could use for herself. She just needed a broom and a pail and a mop to clean out the dirt and the spiders and the cobwebs that had accumulated with years of neglect. She hoped Daniel didn't have to pay much rent for this pile of garbage.

She counted the coins left in her purse after she had given Daniel some for Dr. Phelps. Her allowance was generous, and she could calculate the number of new dresses and shoes she could purchase with it, but she didn't know the cost of anything else. It seemed wisest to hang on to every penny until she knew where the next would come from. Why should she waste her precious money on brooms and mops when she knew where she could get some for nothing?

Her father would have a conniption fit, but Hanover Industries belonged to her as much as it did to him. Or almost as much. She could see no reason in the world why she couldn't use their brooms and mops if she liked.

Deciding action was better than inaction, Georgina unpacked her satchel, shook out the simplest cotton gown she had, and hastily changed. She kept one ear open for the sound of footsteps, terrified Daniel would be back before she could dress, but all she heard was the whine of the dog wanting his ears scratched.

After she smoothed the gray skirt over her oldest petticoat and tied her shoelaces, she let the dog in and gave him the requisite pat. His tail wagged eagerly, and she debated taking him with her, but Daniel needed him to guard his machines. Leaving him with a scratch and a promise, she hurried into the hall.

Doris stared when Georgina sashayed into the office in a gown that looked like it had never been pressed and should have been worn by a servant. Georgina gave her a big smile, commented on the weather, and swept into the next room. The women at the machines had their backs to her and didn't dare to turn to see who entered, but the foreman was quick to note any invasion of his turf. Fortunately, he was on the other side of the room and had to dodge boxes and machinery before reaching her. Georgina waved tauntingly and opened the maintenance closet door.

She had the required equipment in her hands before Emory could reach her. Praying that her father had not mentioned her disgrace, knowing he wouldn't breathe a word of it for the sake of his own pride, she pretended she was still the spoiled daughter and merely smiled at the foreman's shout.

Gathering up her tools, she called, "I'll bring them back shortly. Don't worry about me! I can handle them." Then with an insouciant calm she didn't feel, she swung her hips deliberately and walked out.

Georgina waved at Doris as she went by. She didn't realize she was holding her breath until she got outside and let it out again. She had done it. She hadn't exactly bearded the lion, but she had staked a claim. And she would keep on staking that claim until they realized they couldn't keep her out.

It was just a matter of time until she ran into her father, but she would worry about that when she got there.

When Daniel returned from his errands sometime later, it was to find his bedraggled wife covered with the grime that had once coated the floors and walls of his home. The pale gold of her hair was hidden behind a scarf sporting cobwebs instead of spring flowers, and a smear of dirt instead of powder adorned her nose. But her lips carried a smile brighter than dawn, and beneath the smudges, her cheeks were as pink as roses. He hoped the tug at his heartstrings at the sight was just admiration for her pluck.

He gestured for the men behind him to enter, and she gave a squeal as they began carrying in the bedposts.

"Not in here!" she cried, shooing them away with her feather duster as if they were dust balls and not two-hundred-pound men with arm muscles bigger than her waist.

They halted and turned to Daniel for direction. He shrugged and turned to Georgina. "Where else would you put it?"

"In the bedroom." Skirting around the movers, she crossed the hall and threw open the door to the spacious room she had just finished cleaning.

The windows sparkled in the sun, flooding the room with light, and on one wall, Daniel noted the outline of the missing fireplace. She was right. This would make an ideal bedroom. Daniel's gaze swerved to take in his remarkable wife. He wondered how she would react when he moved in here with her.

But he let her bustle and peck like a mother hen without disturbing her excitement. It was kind of nice having a woman to look out for his creature comforts. He hadn't thought Georgina would be the type to give in to housewifely instincts, but he certainly wasn't going to complain. He had fully expected to come home and find her curled up in the chair with a book, waiting for him to take her out to lunch. That she had made an effort to make this place into a home warmed him inside.

When the bed was where she wanted it and the mattress tested for plumpness and the movers gone, Daniel crossed his arms and waited for Georgina to remember he was still here. The flush on her cheeks and the way she took the duster to an imaginary cobweb told him she was having some difficulty accepting the fact that he wasn't going to disappear and leave her to this fantasy world she was creating.

"The place looks great, Miss Merry. I appreciate it. I suppose now I ought to get a desk for the other room so we can work like professionals."

She swung around and eyed him uncertainly. "I thought you were saving your money for the paper."

Daniel leaned against the doorjamb and shoved his hands in his pockets. He was suddenly aware that he wore only shirtsleeves and not proper gentlemanly attire. He didn't know why he should think of that when she looked at him that way, but he moved his shoulders restlessly beneath the light cotton. It was suddenly very, very warm in here.

"The paper won't make money for a long time, but I've got a number of printing jobs already. That's another reason you'll be good to have around. You can go out and get the information while I get those jobs out. Since Max likes you so well, you can take him along as bodyguard."

She nodded doubtfully, and Daniel took pity on her. The poor little rich girl had faced enough harsh reality for one day. He shouldn't be so damned soft on her, but he couldn't help it. The hero instinct died hard.

"Why don't I bring you some water so you can freshen up and then we can go out to eat? There's a place owned by some Italians not so far from here, and they have the greatest food you've ever tasted."

Georgina brightened, and her hand instantly went to her hair. When it came away with the filthy scarf, her smile dimmed, and Daniel couldn't stop himself from crossing the room and burying his fingers in the soft curls revealed. It felt good to have the right to touch her. He swelled with the intensity of some emotion he preferred not to name. He just enjoyed the sensation of soft curls against his fingers and left it at that.

"You have hair like spun sunlight. Nothing can detract from it. I'll get you a mirror so you can see for yourself."

The words were what she needed to hear, but Daniel's touch was unnerving. Georgina jerked slightly, but didn't move away when he wound his fingers more tightly in a strand. She found herself staring up into gray eyes that smoldered, and her heart skipped a beat and began to pound erratically. Surely that look couldn't mean what she thought it meant.

She glanced away, and he released her. Trying not to sigh with relief, she murmured, "I'll be ready quickly," and said nothing when he turned and left the room.

Thank goodness she had thought to clean a room for herself. Last night she had thought their relationship was purely platonic. Today, she was beginning to think men didn't understand the meaning of the word. She was much better off staying as far from them as possible.

Daniel knew something was wrong as soon as he woke from his pleasant daydream.

He had just finished delivering a load of posters to the grocery and was on his way home, picturing Georgina greeting him at the door. He was mentally contemplating a soothing evening relaxing with a book and gentle conversation, anticipating the moment when they could retire to bed when he became aware of the footsteps following him. He tried to imagine the seductive persuasiveness that would entice Georgina into that first kiss, but his feet were already carrying him around a corner and into the nearest alley. It was a little difficult imagining how that kiss would turn out while waiting in a dark doorway to see if the footsteps would go on by.

They didn't. They hesitated.

With a sigh of regret Daniel found a better position. He should have known better than to drift into daydreams in this area of town. Those two bullies he had scared off would have friends they would dearly like to set loose on him. There were even real thieves and low-life scum waiting in the alleys like this one for anyone unfortunate enough to display any sign of wealth. He knew better than to be caught unprepared. The wariness he had learned in Texas hadn't been left behind when he hopped the train. He had just momentarily misplaced it while dreaming foolish dreams. He definitely knew better.

He could hear their whispered consultation at the end of the alley and wished he had brought his Colt. He didn't often carry it. It was a shade melodramatic for the sleepy town of Cutlerville, Ohio. But if he were going to continue producing radical papers attacking the Mulloney establishment, he had better learn to be better prepared. He had the sneaking suspicion Artemis Mulloney was a man to be reckoned with.

And no doubt he was already on the rampage if Peter had gifted him with the information of Georgina's hasty marriage. Daniel almost felt sorry for his brother, only he had difficulty thinking of Peter as a real brother. He was twenty-eight years old and the only brothers Daniel had ever known were Evie's cousins. He'd take those two heathen rattlesnakes over the civilized copperheads bearing the Mulloney name any day of the week.

Bracing himself, Daniel waited for his followers to attack.

They entered the alley unarmed. That was a good sign. Leaning his shoulder against the brick wall beside him, Daniel called, "Looking for someone, gentlemen?"

They gaped, jerked around, searched the narrow alley, and finding nothing, glanced upward.

Daniel smiled beatifically down upon them from his perch on the windowledge. "Better talk fast. I've got an appointment with a beautiful lady."

They weren't dumb; he had to give them credit for that. Finding themselves in an unexpected position, they cut right to the parleying rather than the usual fisticuffs to warm him up.

The tallest wore a checked coat and a striped waistcoat and looked very much like Egan except for the bulbous nose. Maybe Mulloney kept a stable of matched bullies, Daniel thought whimsically as the man yelled up at him.

"Come down here where we can talk to you!"

He smiled and crossed his arms and leaned back against the painted window.

"We got something to say that'll be worth your time," Checked-coat called in an almost wheedling tone.

Daniel shrugged. "I said to hurry it up. If you have something to say, spit it out."

The shorter man developed a fierce scowl that turned his face into a shriveled potato with eyes. "We'll spit you out, you highfalutin turd." He reached for Daniel's boots.

Daniel caught the wall on either side of him, adjusted his weight, and swung his foot outward. The kick caught Potato-head right beneath the chin. He went wheeling backward with a scream as much of fury as agony.

Checked-coat immediately retreated to a safer position. "We've got an offer to make, like I said. There's someone as wishes you to leave town. The faster you do it, the more he'll pay. We've got tickets here for tonight's train. If you're on it, there'll be someone at the station with a bag of greenbacks for you. If you wait until the next night, he takes out a hundred, and a hundred every night thereafter. And if you take it and try to come back, that same someone will be there to greet you with a knife."

Daniel leaned against the window again. "How exceptionally generous of you. Tell your employer if the man meets me with a packet of deeds for the houses owned by ABC, I'd be much more likely to cooperate. I'll be even more generous than he and offer to wait until tomorrow. But for each day I have to wait after that, I'll demand the deed to another property. The one the department store is sitting on would be pleasant."

"Why you little—" The curse was lost in the scuffle as Checked-coat leapt to grab one of Daniel's legs while Potato-head went for the other.

Prepared for his action, Daniel shoved off the window ledge and jumped before they could grab him. His boots landed squarely in their faces as he did so.

He had a hard time keeping his balance as they went down, but he caught himself up a good deal quicker than they did. Giving his good sturdy Mexican boots a mental word of thanks, Daniel swung at the first man up.

This was certainly going to make a long day even longer.

Eighteen

℃

"**D**aniel!" Georgina screamed as he staggered through the door, one side of his face already puffy, blood streaking his shirt, and water spots showing his hasty attempts to wash the worst away.

His grin was slightly lopsided. "You should have seen the other guys."

She wanted to smack him for that careless male attitude toward violence, but that wouldn't have been appropriate under the circumstances. She shoved him into the chair instead.

He went without protest, leaning his head against the back as she hurried off to get water. If she weren't so frightened, she would almost feel sorry for him. Those bruises had to hurt.

"What we need is an ice pack," Georgina murmured as she applied a cold cloth to his face a few minutes later. "You're not going to be able to see out of this eye if it swells any more."

"I'll squint," he replied manfully, wincing only a little as she cleaned the cut on his lip.

"Are you going to tell me what happened?"

He shrugged and winced again, drawing Georgina's attention to the tattered shirt covering his chest. She had been unconsciously avoiding tending lower than Daniel's battered face. But from the looks of it, his face wasn't the only part of his body needing care. Taking a deep breath, she began unfastening what remained of his buttons.

Daniel tensed slightly at the brush of her fingers, but he

managed a jovial answer. "Minor disagreement with some thugs who wanted to rearrange my face. It won't happen again."

He helped her pull the shirt off, and Georgina bit her lip as she contemplated the mass of bruises forming over his ribs. When Daniel was fully dressed and wearing his glasses and joking with her, she felt safe in his friendship. But seeing him this way with his broad shoulders uncovered, his chest and stomach tight with muscles, and his upper arms bulging in ways that a woman's never would, she was reminded all too well that he was a man, and not just any man. He was her husband. It was a terrifying notion.

But also a comforting one. There was nothing shocking in tending her husband's body. She could satisfy her curiosity with impunity. Hesitantly, she applied the wet cloth to the muscular bulge over one male nipple, wiping away the dust and blood.

"Your face wasn't all they wanted to rearrange. Don't you think we ought to call a doctor?"

Daniel smiled as her fingers brushed over him. It was almost worth the price he had to pay to have Georgina touching him like this. And she wasn't fussing or nagging or yelling at him. Just looking at that angelic expression of concern on her face made it all worthwhile. He expected she would get around to berating him sooner or later, but it was nice just letting her take over for a few minutes.

"Dr. Phelps is with Betsy right now. It probably wouldn't be a good idea. As long as none of the ribs are cracked, I'll be fine. I've survived worse."

"Worse!" Georgina stared at him incredulously, trying to imagine worse. It didn't seem possible.

Daniel had let his eyes drift closed. He opened them again when her soothing touches halted. Her blue eyes were wide with horror, and he offered a sympathetic smile. "Broken bones are much more painful, I assure you. Why don't you go fetch me a clean shirt and I'll finish up here?"

Gritting her teeth, she returned to her ministrations.

"Men are animals. I can't imagine how the world has got this far in their care."

"Because of women," he murmured contentedly. "They patch us up and send us back good as new. You don't know how good your touch makes me feel."

Georgina wanted to throw the wet cloth at him and run, but she seemed to be caught in some magnetic spell that held her bound to him. She pressed a particularly impressive bruise over one rib, and he cringed.

"Might be a crack there," he admitted. "I'll see about it in the morning. We'd better go find something to eat before I'm too stiff to move."

Georgina had never been more frightened in her life. Even when those two thugs had attacked her, Daniel had been there to help and she'd had her home and family to run to. But now she was on her own, and the man she had relied on to help was injured so badly she feared for his health. And she could do nothing. She didn't know how to treat his injuries. She couldn't cook his meal so he didn't have to go out. And she didn't even know where to go to buy food so he wouldn't have to move. And if the villains who had done this to him came back, she could do nothing to stop them. Was the world outside her father's home always like this?

"You shouldn't go out," she murmured in protest as he sat up and started to rise.

"There's a little restaurant not far from here. If I don't scare them with my pretty face, we'll be all right. Will soup and sandwiches be enough for you?"

Georgina didn't know how he had made it home. He was swaying just standing there, and she knew he couldn't see out of that one eye. She might be terrified, but she wasn't inhuman. She shoved him back into the chair again.

"Tell me how to find it. I'll take Max and bring something home. Do stoves cost very much? Maybe we should look into finding one."

She was bustling around the room, tidying her hair, looking for a wrap, checking her pockets for coins, and calling for Max. Daniel closed his eyes and let the pound-

ing in his head have its way. He knew better than to let
a lady loose in these streets, but he simply didn't have the
strength to argue. His hero instincts had had enough for
the day. The idea of buying a stove together tickled him.
He would have to give that some thought.

"Just say, 'now, Max,' and he'll go into attack position
if someone threatens you. Don't say 'attack' unless you
have no other choice. He'll go for their throats. I don't
think you'll have any trouble. There's no one around this
time of night."

Daniel looked so pale and worn lying there that Georgina felt an unexpected surge of what must be sympathy
just looking at him. Tucking the money into her pocket,
she brushed the unruly cowlick back from his face and
dared a quick peck on his cheek. "You're the bravest,
silliest man I've ever met," she whispered.

Daniel grinned and let her go with Max and his instructions to guide her. Georgina Meredith was made of stronger stuff than he had first imagined.

Georgina nervously rinsed off the plates they would
need to take back to the restaurant in the morning. Had
she married Peter, a maid would have been carrying off
the crystal and china they would have received as wedding gifts. But her thoughts weren't on their lack of
proper wedding gifts. They centered on the man resting in
the easy chair by the room's only table.

Daniel had only sipped at his soup and coffee after attempting to chew a bite of sandwich and declaring it not
worth the effort. She wished she had gone for the doctor.

He needed to be in bed. Georgina threw a glance at the
pallet still lying against the wall. That was where she had
intended for him to sleep, in here with his machinery and
his dog.

But he looked so pale, she knew he was in pain. And
the bed in the other room would be a hundred times more
comfortable. She had moved all her clothes into that
room, but she supposed she could carry some back here.
It wouldn't hurt to sleep on a pallet for a few nights. She

would feel much better when Daniel was back to normal, and that time would come sooner if he slept comfortably.

Having made that decision, Georgina started for the door, meaning to fetch her night things and some clean clothing for the morning.

Daniel opened his eyes and pushed himself from the chair. "Good idea. I don't think I can stay awake any longer."

Georgina stared in horror as he came up behind her, carrying the lamp, and reached for the door. Trying to calm herself, she said sensibly, "I'll just get a change of clothes before you go to bed."

Daniel whistled at the dog and pointed to the presses, "Guard," he ordered. The dog whined and dropped obediently in front of the pressroom door, tongue hanging out and paws crossed. Daniel pressed his hand to Georgina's back. "He'll be fine. Come on. Let's test that new mattress."

Obviously it was the flames of hell washing through her at the touch of Daniel's hand at the small of her back and the sound of his words in her ear. Georgina's face burned with heat that coursed through the rest of her body. This wasn't the way it was supposed to be. Even on a proper wedding night, the groom was supposed to leave the bride some privacy. She balked halfway across the hall.

Daniel looked down at her quizzically. "Did you forget something?"

"No, you have." Gathering the shattered remnants of her courage, Georgina tried to explain. "I'm not really your wife, remember? I can't share that bed with you. I'll get my things and sleep in the room with Max."

"Don't be foolish. There's plenty of room in that bed for both of us. And I'm not in any shape to take advantage of you, if that's what you're worried about. You'd probably fracture the rest of my ribs if I tried." He pushed her toward the opposite door.

And she went. It was madness, but she went. She was tired and scared and lonely, and she didn't really want to sleep alone on a pallet with a dog as company. She didn't think she really wanted to sleep with Daniel, either, but he wasn't giving her much choice. She opened the door and went into the room she had thought of as her own.

Daniel surveyed it with a grim shake of his head. "It's not as if I was exactly prepared to bring a bride home, I suppose. We'll get a dressing screen on Monday. Shall I blow out the lamp?"

Georgina nodded and hoped he would see. She wasn't certain she could make her tongue form a word.

The lamp went out and the room plunged into darkness. The uncurtained windows formed pale rectangles against the walls, but provided little light. Georgina took a deep breath and wondered if it was necessary to undress at all. These clothes couldn't be any more ruined if she slept in them.

There was a rustle behind her, and then Daniel's voice spoke over her shoulder. "Do you need some help?"

Her one stroke of genius this day had been to wear a gown that buttoned down the front. Her hand went protectively to cover the buttons. "No. Go on to bed. I'll be there in a minute."

He touched her shoulder anyway, skimming his hand along the bone, then up her throat to her chin. He held his finger there and turned her face slightly so he could place a kiss on her cheek. "It will work out, Merry. Smile, and everything will be fine."

He turned away after that, and she could hear the bed springs creak as he sat and tried to use the bootjack on his boots. His words and touch had burned right through to the bone, and she was paralyzed. How was she ever going to go through with this?

By smiling, as he said. This was an adventure. She had wanted a hero to rescue her from Peter, and now she had one. Perhaps Daniel wasn't the most romantic of heroes, but he was better than any other she had found. Unfastening the first buttons, she forced herself to smile. It was much better than bewailing the fates.

When she slid in beside Daniel, Georgina was wearing only her chemise and drawers. She felt scandalously undressed, but not nearly as naked as she had been last night in that indecent nightgown. Daniel hadn't touched her then. She doubted that he would touch her now.

"How did those other men look when you got finished with them?" she whispered.

Daniel chuckled. "Their noses will never be the same again. And they may walk with permanent stoops. Don't worry. They won't be back. Go on to sleep." It was easy to reassure her, not so easy to reassure himself. They might not be back with the same kind of attack, but he could swear on a stack of Bibles that Artemis Mulloney wouldn't give up with one defeat. And there wasn't a doubt in his mind that it had been his father trying to bribe him to leave town.

There was no point in worrying over it now. He had put on a clean shirt before supper, and out of politeness, he had left it on to come to bed. He was stifling in the folds of cloth, but having Georgina in bed beside him made all the day's troubles worth it. He reached to fold his fingers into hers.

In a day or two he would think about doing more—after he'd had time to consider how much trouble he was going to cause his father by taking this particular woman to wife.

Fighting the sun in her eyes, Georgina tried to roll over and go back to sleep, but a heavy weight held her hair pinned against the pillow. She tried to wake enough to free herself, only to discover that a hand was resting boldly across her breasts. Blushing clear to her roots, she squeezed her eyes shut and tried to squirm away.

The hand woke then. It formed a cup to cradle her breast. Even through her chemise she could feel the heat of the fingers wrapping around her. Her blush went deeper, burning somewhere inside her. When strong fingers began a stroking motion, she jerked away, trying to push herself into a sitting position. The weight on her hair held her down.

"You feel good, Miss Merry," a masculine voice murmured in her ear.

She nearly leapt from her skin. Her eyes flew open to

confront the bruised and swollen face of her husband. It was not a reassuring sight. Even through the swelling, Daniel was grinning at her, and the light in his one open eye twinkled with mischief. The hand found its place on her breast again and stroked upward until it found the peak.

Georgina squealed and tried to break free. "You promised, Daniel Mulloney! You promised. Now stop that, this instant. I want to get up."

He sighed a deep sigh of regret. "You don't know what you're missing, Merry. But I suppose it's asking too much to have the princess kiss a beast like I must look this morning. Maybe I should go beat up Peter and you can compare us at our worst."

He moved away, freeing her hair, and Georgina escaped. Hands on hips, she glared down at him and prepared to deliver a tirade, until she really saw him. He was wearing nothing but his shirt.

Color blazed in her cheeks as her glance ran down Daniel's bare legs. They were covered in a soft dark down until they reached his long, bare feet. She gulped, and her gaze drifted back up again. His shirt moved oddly over his hips, and she swung around, keeping her back to him.

"I'd thank you to leave until I can get dressed."

With his arms crossed beneath his head, Daniel contemplated the slender back she presented him. The light from the window silhouetted her body beneath the thin chemise. She had a tiny wasp waist without the benefit of a corset. Her hips flared roundly to firm thighs and straight legs that peeked out from beneath her knee-length drawers. His gaze lingered on bare calves, and he contemplated them with longing, wondering how they would feel when they were wrapped around him. That thought made his loins surge dangerously. Daniel let his gaze drift upward again, wishing he could see the curve of her breasts from this angle.

"I'm not sure that I can," he said lazily. "I ache all over. I may need you to massage me until I can move."

Her back stiffened. "I'm not coming near you until you're dressed, Daniel Mulloney. This isn't funny."

Glancing down at the rebellious part of his body pushing up his shirttails, Daniel agreed wryly, "No, it's not."

Georgina rigidly kept her back to him as she heard the springs squeak and his feet hit the floor. For the millionth time in the last twenty-four hours, she wondered how she had got herself into this.

"It's all right, you can look now," Daniel called from the other side of the room.

She swirled around, her hair tumbling over her shoulders and down her back, and Daniel took a deep breath of admiration. That revealing light behind her told him everything he had wanted to know, reinforcing everything his fingers had discovered this morning. She was magnificent.

Her hair shimmered in spun silver and gold over breasts that jutted wickedly against the thin cotton of her chemise. The prim buttons were fastened all the way to her throat, but a blue ribbon pulled the fabric into gathers beneath her breasts, revealing their grace and form to his eager gaze. He didn't think he'd ever had a woman like this one. He had always favored the tall, willowy types. Maybe it was time for a change.

But her frozen expression warned now wasn't the time to test his theories. Brushing his hair out of his eyes, Daniel attempted a smile through cracked lips. "I've got some work to do on the press. Let me know when you're ready and we'll go get a bite to eat."

He walked out, closing the door softly behind him.

It wasn't until then that Georgina allowed herself to breathe again. Daniel's admiring stare had twisted something loose in her insides, and it was fluttering wildly there now. He'd looked at her, really looked at her, and he'd liked what he'd seen. It came as a startling revelation.

She was really a woman, and one a man could desire.

It was a turning point in her life. Until now, she had been treated as a precocious child, patted on the head and admired and sent from the room, and she had thought of herself the same way.

But Daniel saw her as a woman. The knowledge bore a terrible burden of responsibility Georgina wasn't certain she wanted to carry. For one dreadful moment she wanted to go back to being a little girl with a cowboy for a friend.

But that little girl didn't exist anymore.

Ignoring the odd feeling in her middle that thought disturbed, Georgina reached for her dress. She was not only a woman, but a married woman. She didn't know the full meaning of that yet, but she knew a small portion of it. Marriage was a partnership, and she meant to uphold her side—for as long as it lasted.

Nineteen

"I think the best thing to do is start talking to the women over at your father's factory." Daniel paced the open space they now thought of as their front room. The pallet lay rolled up against the wall, unused since Saturday night. Two nights in bed together and his mind was already deteriorating into a shambles, he decided, shoving his hair back from his face.

Georgina sat at the table, going over a page of printing, checking for errors before the final product was turned out. She didn't look up from her work as she replied. "Leave the factory out of this. I want the heads of every Mulloney on a pike."

Daniel swung around and glared at her. "You're the one who has been telling me that your father's factory is the best place to start. I'm just agreeing with you. It's right there, across the street, easily accessible, and you said yourself that there's some connection to Mulloney's."

Irritation edged his voice, but Georgina kept on with what she was doing. He had been pacing the office like a caged tiger all morning. He ought to be aching in every fool bone in his body and lying around groaning, but he had set this type and written several pieces for the paper and still found time to pace. She wished he would go out and find some other bully to beat up.

"That was before when I thought Peter was going to end up owning it. Now it's part mine, and I'll take care of it. I think we ought to stay with an exposé of ABC Rentals and the living conditions of their tenants."

Daniel stopped in mid-stride. "What's part yours?"

Georgina finally glanced up. "Hanover Industries. My grandmother left me forty percent of it."

Daniel continued staring, waiting for an explanation.

Georgina shrugged. "My father had to borrow the money from his family to buy the business. He gave them a forty-percent share in return. When my grandfather died, he left it to my grandmother. My grandmother left it to me. She probably meant it for some sort of dowry. I'm certain my father intended for Peter to take it over when we married. But as far as I know, it's legally mine when I turn twenty-one."

"And when do you turn twenty-one?" he asked ominously, glowering through one swollen eye.

Georgina dimpled sweetly. "July fourth."

Daniel opened his mouth to speak, shut it again firmly, swung around, and strode to the window. "Then you'd better hire yourself a damned lawyer real soon. I'm going after Mulloney Enterprises, and if my hunch is correct, they've got a piece of Hanover Industries somehow or another. If so, it's going to come tumbling down with all the rest when I get through with them."

"I'll be there to pick up the pieces." Finishing her proofing, Georgina stood up and dusted herself off, then reached for her hat and gloves. "I'm going to see the Harrisons. I'll be back with lunch."

Daniel swung around and glared at her as she calmly pulled on her short white gloves. "You'll do no such thing. You're not going out there alone."

Georgina gestured for Max. "And who's going to stop me?" she asked, still smiling sweetly.

And before he could offer argument or logic, she was gone.

"Betsy is looking much better today," Georgina commented as she took the seat the old lady showed her to.

Janice sent her visitor's gray dress a disparaging look.

"You're not. Where's your fancy silks and lace? Isn't Daniel going to take you on an expensive wedding trip like your other beau would? What are you even doing out of bed?"

The pretty little girl sitting on the floor playing with a broken doll looked up at the harshness in her sister's voice. Seeing Janice's expression, she turned worried eyes to their visitor.

Georgina blushed, but kept her back straight. "Daniel has work to do, and I'm trying to help him. He was attacked Saturday, you know. I think that's a sign that he's causing people like Mulloney some sleepless nights. We're going to do more than cause them sleepless nights before this is over."

"What is over? What do you think you can possibly do to a man who owns half the town? He probably had Egan and his cronies beat up Daniel as a warning. What do you think he will do next?" Janice asked scornfully.

Georgina hadn't thought about that. Peter had always been nice, if distant. She hadn't thought him capable of violence. But then he'd pulled that rifle trick, and she'd had to rethink her judgment. Perhaps it was time she began rethinking a lot of things. Would a prominent, wealthy businessman stoop to hiring thugs to beat up journalists? Especially if that journalist claimed to be his son?

Georgina cringed at the notion. This was definitely not the nice world she had thought. But it could be. The good people just had to band together against the bad guys.

Relieved by that thought, she smoothed her gloves and stood up. "I've been reading about unions. I think that's what we need here. If all the women working for Mulloney's Department Store got together and demanded raises and better hours, they could force Mr. Mulloney to do what they wanted. He couldn't sell a thing without them."

Janice sent her a cynical look and picked up her piece-work, "He would just fire them all and hire new ones. I read, too."

Georgina shook her head and glanced at Audrey, who had been listening listlessly until the union had been mentioned. "Explain it to her, Audrey. Tell her how difficult it is to hire just the right sort of person for a place like Mulloney's."

"She's never been inside Mulloney's. She won't believe me," Audrey whispered.

"I never saw such a defeatist attitude," Georgina declared, glaring at both women. "Mulloney's is a public store. Anyone can go in at any time, but they've scared you into thinking otherwise. Audrey can look after Betsy, and Max can stay here. Come with me, and I'll show you what I mean."

Janice looked down at her mended cotton gown and shook her head. "I'm not going in there to make a fool of myself just for your pleasure. They would throw me out if I tried."

Georgina smiled brilliantly. "Oh no, they won't. I'm very good at creating scenes. If they so much as try, they'll have a scene the likes of which the town won't forget in a hundred years." She pulled off her gloves. "Here, if it will make you feel better, we'll dress you like a lady. Put these on."

She unpinned her hat, studied Janice's loose chignon, found the best angle, and pinned it to her thick hair. "There, instant style. What do you think, Audrey?"

The other girl studied her older sister carefully. "It would be better if she had a parasol or a mantle or a rope of pearls." Her eyes brightened. "Mama's cameo! That will be perfect."

The cameo was produced and declared satisfactory. Janice stood still for the demonstration for her sister's sake, but when they were done, she held out the plain drape of her blue skirt and shook her head. "It won't do. They'll know I'm an impostor."

Georgina adjusted the bonnet brim so it covered more of Janice's face. "They can think whatever they like, but you'll be going in with me, and they know I'm not an impostor. And you speak beautifully. Better than I do, actually. Not to be nosy, but how did you accomplish that? I thought that's why I went to school."

Janice shrugged. "Our mother was Irish, but Father was English, the younger son of a vicar. His family disowned him when he married our mother. Contrary to popular thought, most immigrants come from good families. Just because most speak foreign languages and have to work for a living doesn't mean they're beasts of burden."

Georgina frowned at the hidden sarcasm. "And just because some people come from good families doesn't mean that they're not as inclined to behave as much like jackasses as the rest of the world. I was just curious. You didn't have to give me a lecture."

Janice began to peel off the gloves. "You've made your point. If you don't mind, I've got work to do."

Georgina grabbed her arm and pulled her toward the doorway. "So do I, but I'm setting it aside until I show you what we can do. You want your sister to get her job back, don't you?"

That was the impetus that sent Janice out the door, however unwillingly. She glared at Georgina, then down at the evidence of her plain clothing in the glaring sunlight. "I feel ridiculous."

Georgina caught up the simple gray serge of her skirt and started down the street. "We all ought to be ridiculous every once in a while. Even the Mulloneys. Let's see if we can't help them out."

The reaction of the Mulloney employees as soon as they entered the store was much as Janice had predicted. The doorman in his formal black suit and stiff white collar hurried to intercept them, but stepped back in confusion when one of the two dowdy customers turned a familiar dimpled smile to him.

"Good morning, Jerome. Excellent day, isn't it?" With a regal nod, Georgina swept past the stunned doorman and into the interior. The blazing chandelier couldn't compare to the sunlight outside, and the glittering glass counters of expensive perfumes and jewelry held as much shadow as light, concealing the expressions of many of the clerks as the two shabby customers walked the carpeted aisle.

"How may we help you?" A stiffly erect woman in rustling cascades of brown taffeta hurried to their sides as Georgina lingered over a counter of expensive bracelets. The woman's hair was properly arranged in thick knots high on her head. Her gown buttoned all the way to the throat. And she reeked of the gentle scents of lavender sachet.

"See what I mean?" Georgina whispered as Janice tried to tug away. "She talks like her mouth is full of marbles." Looking up to the clerk, she smiled. "Good morning, Miss Whalen. My cousin and I were wondering if the Mulloney employees ever get together after work just for fun? I should think a company picnic would be pleasant. I really must talk to Peter about it. Do you think anyone would be interested?"

The woman's mouth gaped open as her gaze swept over Georgina's improper attire, but she managed a stiff smile. "I'm certain we would be delighted with the opportunity if it were offered."

"Personally, I think better wages and better hours would be more meaningful," Georgina said thoughtfully, tapping her lips with an ungloved finger. She looked up innocently. "And job security. I hadn't thought of that before. Loyal, hardworking employees should know they always have a job, even if their views don't agree with management's."

The clerk was too stunned to reply, and Georgina swept on to the next counter, trailing Janice behind her.

"You're insane," Janice whispered.

"No, I'm angry. I hadn't realized Peter had hired such snobs. I'm not certain they're worth saving." Georgina smiled pleasantly at a few more clerks who turned and stared as they walked by. "I think I'll gather up all the workers at the factory and bring them over here for a shopping spree."

Janice stifled a small giggle at the thought of some of the loud and rambunctious women at the factory suddenly being thrust into the pristine quietude of Mulloney's Department Store. It almost bore thinking about. Instead, she caught Georgina's arm and led her toward the hat counter.

A terrified young girl of petite stature clasped her hands in front of her as the two women stopped at her counter. Upon recognizing Janice, she offered a shaky smile. "Is there anything I can do to help you?" she inquired hesitantly.

"How's Clarence?" Janice asked, giving Georgina no time to stage another performance.

The girl gave a fleeting look around her, then seeing no one close enough to hear, she whispered, "He's just fine, Miss Harrison. You tell Audrey that I'm awful sorry. She didn't deserve what happened."

"Well, we're going to try to stop it from happening to anyone else. Pass the word around. See how many are interested in getting together to talk about better wages"— Janice threw a look at Georgina—"and job security. Miss Hanover and Mr. Martin are offering their help in any way they can. Mulloney can't fire everybody."

The girl's eyes widened, but she gave a hasty nod before they strolled away.

Janice knew several more of the clerks and made her little speech a few more times before the distraction they were providing finally caught the notice of management. Georgina was quite proud of her as Peter came storming out of his office and down the stairs. Janice only whitened two shades and turned toward the door.

"It's too late," Georgina whispered before Janice could make good her escape. "I'm not running."

"Georgina, what in hell do you think you're doing!" Peter's usually well-modulated voice soared through the building as he approached. Realizing his error as heads swung to stare, he waited until he was upon them before continuing. "Do you think to shame me by coming in here looking like that?"

Georgina smiled and took his arm, deliberately steering him toward the doorway. Janice fell in behind them, out of the line of fire.

"Why, no, of course not, dear Peter. I was just showing

a friend from out of town the quality of the shopping that can be had here in Cutlerville. I just didn't think about changing. Daniel and I have been working so hard that I'd quite forgotten what I wore. Quite silly of me, I'm certain. What one wears is so important, isn't it? But I'm certain you don't need to be told that. Why don't you come over and visit us sometime? We'd be delighted to have you. You could bring my father and my camera and we could make a party of it."

Georgina's smile was almost malicious as she made a quick curtsy at the door and walked out. Janice hastily skirted around the frozen gentleman left standing in the aisle and followed Georgina into the street.

She didn't say a word as Georgina strode furiously down the walk, steam practically pouring from her ears. The very proper lady was in the midst of a very improper temper tantrum, and Janice hung back to enjoy the sight. It was good to know that the other half didn't have everything easy. She'd very much like to know what was behind that little scene, but she wasn't prepared to find out.

"All right, I see what you mean." Judging the temper about out of steam, Janice finally caught up with her companion. "Those clerks talk and dress like proper ladies. There can't be too many people in this town with those accomplishments who are looking for jobs at menial wages. If they all walked at once, Mulloney would have a devil of a time replacing them."

Not particularly mollified, Georgina managed a curt nod. "They would have to close the doors. The task will be persuading all those snotty department managers to join in. Peter pays them a little more and pats them on the back occasionally so they think they owe him their lives. If they don't stand with the rest of them, Peter will try to keep the store open with just their help."

"He can't," Janice announced decisively. At Georgina's questioning look, she explained, "We'll get the people in the back, the people you never see and don't know anything about: the seamstresses and hatmakers and storeroom clerks and delivery boys. Mulloney's doesn't buy everything ready-made. They sell service as well. If customers lose their favorite seamstress, they'll go where they can find her."

Georgina stared at her newfound partner in crime. "You have a devious mind, Miss Harrison. We're happy to have you on the team."

Twenty

ð

"Georgina Meredith, I'm going to have to put you in chains. Now will you quit your meddling and go to bed? I'll be there just as soon as I get this last piece set."

"I'm not meddling. Something like this could blow up in both our faces if it's not done right. I have just as much right to go over it as you do."

The frightening part about it was that she was quite right. Daniel shoved his glasses back on his nose and glared at the back of her head. In the lamplight, Georgina's hair gleamed almost silver. She had stacked it untidily on top of her head after washing it earlier in the evening. Daniel had known Georgina had a penchant for anarchy from the first moment he had met her. He just hadn't known what it was going to mean to his own life. She was destroying every defense he had ever erected.

Reaching for the pencil behind his ear, he growled, "I've been doing this a lot longer than you have. Have a little confidence in me, if you please. You can go over it again in the morning."

The truth was that Daniel would prefer it if she would go on to bed now and be sound asleep before he got there. That reduced the temptation to a certain degree. She had worked as hard as he these last few days to put together this next edition, and he would be a heel to disturb her sleep. But she sure as hell disturbed his.

It was his own damned arrogant fault, and he couldn't blame Georgina for his predicament. He just hadn't thought his unwanted wife would cause him so much trouble. He wasn't like some men, thinking and dreaming sex day and night. He lived in his head as much as his body, and the two had got along well all these years. It had never occurred to him that his body would suddenly rebel and demand a satisfaction that his head told him he had no right to take.

Georgina yawned and stretched. Daniel knew damned well she wore only her chemise and drawers under that wrapper, and he had difficulty keeping his eyes from watching the folds of material gape at her movement. Now that he had some idea of what she kept so coyly concealed beneath all that material, he could think of little else. In the midst of a fiery editorial he found himself wondering how it would feel to slip his hand beneath that cover of cloth over her breasts, and he frequently cursed himself for not having taken the chance when it had first been offered—as he cursed himself now for even thinking about it. It was perfectly obvious that Georgina didn't think of him in the same way that he found himself thinking of her.

It was almost a relief knowing that she would come into part of Hanover Industries in less than a month. He would hire a lawyer and see that she got her share of the profits. Then they could work out an annulment, and they both could get on with their lives. It was the only solution that might save his sanity.

Daniel held his breath as Georgina finally gave in to exhaustion, crossed the room, and pressed a simple kiss against his temple before retiring. It was those light, innocent touches that drove him into his worst frenzies. He wanted to grab her waist, pull her down on his lap, and make mad, passionate love to her. For hours. On the floor. On the bed. Anywhere. Everywhere. He didn't think he could stop once he got started.

So he couldn't get started. Georgina knew nothing of passion. She thought of him as little more than a brother. And that was the way it should be. He was a loner, always had been. Outcast by his real family, he had made his way through his early years with the limited aid of his adopted family, and he had been on his own since. The women in his life always looked on him as a friend, never anything more. There was no reason anything should be different now.

It was very late that night before Daniel put down his proof pages and dragged himself across the hall to where his sleeping wife awaited him. Even though he was practically asleep before he hit the bed, he was a long time in finding slumber once he had Georgina's welcoming body beside him. Hell couldn't have found a more artful temptation.

Georgina laughed as Douglas raised his fists in a gesture of triumph as he returned for the last stacks of papers. All the sheets were on the streets now, and the boys had been delirious with excitement at how quickly they sold. It meant pennies in their pockets for the boys, but it meant a great deal more to Daniel. People were waiting to hear what he had to say, and willing to pay for it. He could start taking subscribers soon.

"How are they reacting to it down at Mulloney's?" she asked, stuffing his bag with the last papers on the floor.

"I listened as they left for the day," Douglas bragged. "They said there wasn't anything from the office. No shouting, no nothing. But they were all talking, Miss Georgie. They were all whispering. And Janice has heard from a lot of them already. I think they're coming around. Nobody likes being ex . . ." he stumbled for the word.

"Exploited. No, they don't," she answered with conviction. "We'll get your sister her job back if we have to shut down the whole store to do it. Everybody ought to have rights."

He grinned and ran out the door with his load. Pennies were more important than politics to a twelve-year-old.

Daniel returned not long after that, grinning from ear to ear as he threw himself down in their one armchair. "It's a pity we won't be having dinner at the mayor's tonight. We might hear a little more than complaints about those uppity Irish this time."

Georgina settled in his lap and kissed his cheek. Nights

of sharing a bed with this man had made her bold indeed, and she had no compunction about allowing her natural exuberance loose in his presence. "It was a stroke of genius comparing the cost of milk for one child to the weekly wages of its mother. It shouldn't take any imagination at all to know the mother would have to starve herself to feed her children. There isn't a mother alive who won't weep over that. I just don't think men are going to pay attention to those statistics, and even if the women see them, what can they do? Women have no power."

Daniel wrapped his arms around Georgina's waist and settled her more comfortably against his thighs. If his hands wandered in the process, she made no complaint, and he grinned and planted a kiss beneath her ear. "You underestimate your sex, my dear. Mulloney's caters to women. Women do all the shopping. They even buy their husbands' shirts and socks. If the ladies of town should decide to stop shopping at Mulloney's, the doors would close overnight."

Georgina gave a cry of excitement and bounced in his lap. Daniel caught her and settled her down a little with a judicious use of his hands on the rounded curve of her hips and buttocks. He wasn't even certain he completely heard what she said next as he settled back in the chair and enjoyed his predicament.

"That's what I can do! I know those women. Their husbands probably won't even let them see that editorial, but I will. I'll call at Loyolla's during one of her afternoon teas and make certain everyone hears of it. I'll be certain to make Loyolla understand what it means to mothers and babes, and she'll be on the bandwagon before I say another thing. If all the ladies in town refuse to shop Mulloney's until they pay their workers better, they'll have to close the doors!"

Daniel dared another kiss to her throat as he murmured something agreeable. At this moment he didn't give a damn about department stores or babies or teas. He had one thing only on his mind, and it was so close, he could feel it.

"Don't you think it's time to retire for the night?" he murmured as he nibbled his way up to her ear.

Too excited to sit still, Georgina jumped from his lap and rushed to the door. "Let's go out and see what they're talking about over at the café."

Daniel closed his eyes and stifled his groan of agony. He'd rather be punched in the face any day than suffer another moment of torment with Georgina. Apparently, he had a masochistic streak he had known nothing about.

He got up and followed her out.

"Yes, Georgina, dear, I did read Mr. Martin's extraordinary newssheet. It's made me quite anxious. What if my favorite seamstress over at Mulloney's has a starving child at home and is so worried she sticks me with pins or ruins my rose organdy? After reading those articles, I'm quite surprised some of those clerks don't come after my purse with a knife. It's quite scary."

Loyolla Banks took a deep breath and gently chided the preacher's wife. "Now, Lolly, you've missed the *point*. Just think how much you paid Mulloney's for gowns last year. Don't you think your favorite seamstress should have got a little more out of them than the cost of a few quarts of milk?"

"Now, Loyolla, don't you get started on women's rights again. This has nothing to do with our rights. This has to do with clerks who take their money home to be spent on whiskey every Friday night." The wife of the man who owned the local lumber mill spoke up. "That's where the money goes. Not on baby's milk. Why, my Harry can scarcely keep the mill open on Saturdays after he pays the help. They all stay home sick or come in so hungover he has to send them back home again. If he paid them more, they wouldn't come in at all. They're little more than animals."

Georgina wanted to reach over and pull the woman's hair from her head, but she demurely spoke over the top of her teacup instead. "I'm quite familiar with a number of Mulloney's clerks, Mrs. Garrison. One family comes from an English vicarage, others are descendants of well-respected craftsmen driven from their homes by religious or political persecution. Their families try hard to learn the language and the customs and make a new life for themselves here, just as our families did when they first came to America. Most of the clerks at Mulloney's are second-generation Americans, but due to deaths or illness in the family, they have very little money and must work hard for a living. I should think Mr. Mulloney could give up a carriage or two to let them live a little better."

"Well now, you remember to tell Peter that, Georgina, when he offers to buy you your first carriage. You just tell him to put that money into a clerk's salary. Just see how well that goes over."

How odd. Peter hadn't mentioned their broken betrothal to anyone. And if her family hadn't mentioned her marriage, these ladies would have no idea she was living on the other side of town. They didn't talk to their servants.

Georgina sipped her tea and let the silly conversation go on without her. It was patently obvious that selfishness and a lifetime of never thinking for themselves made these women worse than useless for her purposes. It wouldn't improve her position to tell them she was married to the newspaper's editor, but she'd dearly love to stand up and announce it to them all just to see the shock and horror on their faces. But if neither her father nor Peter had made the announcement, she wasn't going to take it upon herself.

With a sad shake of her head Georgina set her cup down and made her excuses to Loyolla. This was the wrong group of women to talk to about forming a ban on Mulloney's. She would have to think of another route.

Loyolla accompanied her to the door, holding her hand and patting it gently. "You've just tried to do too much at once, dear Georgina. I know your heart's in the right place, but standing up to Mulloney's isn't going to make the world better. Why don't you wait until you're married, and then you'll understand things just a little more. Women do have power, dear, but we must use it wisely."

To get bigger carriages and newer gowns, Georgina

supposed as she thanked her hostess and took her leave. She couldn't see what else they were using their power for.

With a grimace of disdain she set out for the church where Daniel was distributing some of his literature. She hoped he had been a great deal more useful today than she had been.

She looked up in surprise at the sight of her father's carriage rolling down the street in her direction. It was the middle of the day, and he was usually up to his ears in work at the factory. Perhaps it was just Blucher out running errands for her mother. She rather missed the stiff old man. She waved, and the carriage slowed.

To her surprise her father sat behind the driver. To her greater surprise he jumped out and held out his hand to her.

"Georgina, thank goodness I found you. It's your mother. She's gravely ill. I need to take you to her at once."

There wasn't any mistaking the gray lines of worry and fear on her father's face. Georgina took his hand and instantly climbed into the carriage. Despite all her mother's failings, she loved her dearly. It had gone against the grain to stay away this long, but without an invitation from her family, she had felt as if she would be disgracing their doorway by returning. This wasn't the kind of invitation she had been expecting.

"What is it? Has the doctor said? How bad is she?" Anxious, she turned to her father as he sat beside her.

"I'm afraid it's the worst, Georgina. I'm afraid we're going to have to send her back to the hospital. The doctor has her sedated now. I hoped she would come around before I had to send for you."

Clenching her hands in her lap, Georgina prayed for the wisdom to handle this ordeal. She wished she had Daniel beside her. She needed his experience right now. He knew a great deal more of the world than she did. Perhaps there was something else they could do, someone else they could send for. It didn't seem right to send her mother away just because she had difficulty coping with the world. Surely they must be doing something wrong, and if they could just somehow make it right . . .

Several hours later, Georgina was the one who was sedated.

As George Hanover carefully removed the cup from her inert hand, the physician shook his head behind him.

"It's a classic case, I'm afraid. It must run in the family. I'm sorry to see it, George. But the doctors can work wonders these days. We'll have her right in a few months. I hope this won't hurt her chances with young Mulloney. This kind of brain exertion doesn't occur in males, so he won't have to worry about sons. And Georgina will be just fine once he learns to keep her quiet and away from excitement. I'll explain the technical details to him if you like."

"That's kind of you, Ralph. If you'll just signal Blucher, we'll carry her out of here. I'm certain a good long rest at the sanitarium is just what she needs. I should never have sent her away to school, but with her mother . . ." George gestured helplessly.

Ralph patted him on the back. "I know. It was a hard decision to make. I trust Dolly is strong enough to make the trip with you?"

"She's rested. She'll be fine. You might want to leave me some more of that medicine just in case she gets agitated while we're traveling."

Ralph removed a bottle from his medical bag. "You might need to keep Georgina under control while you travel. This should be sufficient to get you there. Just remember the dosage I told you. And God be with you."

As Blucher entered to carry his employer's daughter to the waiting carriage, George tucked the bottle of opium into his pocket and went in search of his wife.

Daniel paced the street in front of the church one more time. Georgina had told him Loyolla's teas never lasted past five o'clock. He pulled out his watch and glanced at it again. Seven.

He should have paid more attention to the time. She should have been here hours ago. He had expected her here to help him long before this. What kind of crazy side trip had she made this time?

His leg was beginning to ache from the day's exertion, but he set out down the street to the mayor's house. Maybe Loyolla Banks would have some idea where Georgina might have gone after she left there.

The servant ushered Daniel into the mayor's office. He stood, frowning, looking pointedly at his pocket watch as Daniel entered.

"I won't keep you for a minute, sir, but my wife was here earlier, and she hasn't come home yet. Is Mrs. Banks available? I thought Georgina might have told her where she was going."

The mayor frowned. "Your wife, Mr. Martin? I wasn't aware that you were married. Mrs. Banks is visiting a sickbed at the moment. I fail to understand why Georgina Hanover would know where your wife went, but she won't be able to help you now. She's had some crisis of the nerves like her mother some years ago. They're taking her to the sanitarium as we speak."

Daniel's weak leg nearly gave out from under him, and he grabbed the desk's edge just in time to keep from falling.

"The sanitarium, sir? What sanitarium?"

"Don't rightly know. You'll have to ask Dr. Ralph. It's some place out in Illinois, I believe. I know the train to Chicago just left, and they were on it."

As a man in a daze, Daniel thanked the mayor politely and wandered out. They were sending Georgina to a sanitarium. Beautiful, bright, flighty Miss Merry—his wife.

Damn, but he was going to have to rescue her.

Twenty-one

Heart hammering so fast he feared the excess of blood raging through his brain would make him incoherent, Daniel hurried to the railroad station, again cursing his parsimony in not buying a horse. He had to have been mad to come north to the civilized environs that used carriages on city streets. He had no use for carriages, but his leg had little use for walking. He needed a horse.

Pain shot through his cramped leg muscles as he reached the ticket office and leaned against the counter. "When did the train to Chicago leave?" he demanded of the startled clerk.

The man checked the big clock on the wall. "Twenty minutes ago. There's not another out until tomorrow morning."

This couldn't be happening. Daniel shut his eyes and tried to think clearly. They flew open again an instant later when another thought occurred to him. "Were the Hanovers on it? I was supposed to meet them here."

The clerk pulled a long face. "They certainly were. Mr. Mulloney gave them his private car. Sad story, isn't is? Poor Miss Georgina, she was always a smiling mite. Darned pity she had to inherit that condition from her mother. Goes to show that money can't buy everything, don't it?"

Money could buy a damned lot. Grinding his teeth together, Daniel swung around and tried to think what to do next. The livery. He had to find a horse. He swung back to the ticket clerk. "What route does that train take? It's not direct, is it?"

The clerk checked his schedule. "That one goes back to Cincinnati tonight. Then it changes and heads north again toward Indianapolis. If you were to take a buggy straight across from here, you could probably catch up to it around Brookville or somewheres, if that's what you've a mind to do."

That's what he had a mind to do. Before he could put his plan into action, however, he heard his name called from the other end of the platform. Annoyed at the interruption, prepared to ignore it and go on, he started away from the office in the opposite direction.

"Damn you, Daniel, if you leave us stranded here at this hour, I'll come after you with a whip!"

With a sudden impossible flare of hope, Daniel swung around to watch the two figures hurrying toward him. One sailed along in a skirt that swept the dusty platform in ruffles and a hat that skimmed the air with a bushel of roses and feathers. The one carrying an enormous satchel wore a fawn suit tailored to fit broad shoulders and narrow hips to perfection and guaranteed to attract the notice of all eyes in the sea of dark suits surrounding him. *Tyler and Evie.*

"Oh lord, you're a sight for sore eyes." Forgetting the state of his bruised face, Daniel hurried to pump Tyler's free hand and grab Evie in a hug that left her breathless and wide-eyed. "But I haven't got time to greet you proper. My wife's being kidnapped and I've got to go after her. You'll have to put up at the hotel until I can get back."

He was already hurrying in the direction of the livery, trailing his adopted family behind him as he spoke, ignoring the curious looks they exchanged.

"I thought you'd outgrown those damned fairy stories, Mulloney," Tyler growled as he caught his wife's waist and hurried her after him, swinging the enormous satchel jauntily. "People don't get kidnapped in broad daylight in a respectable town like this one. And even if they did, you're supposed to wait around for the ransom note."

"It's Georgina's father. I haven't got time to explain. I've got to cut off the train before Brookville."

"It's a little difficult to stop a train by yourself, Danny," Evie informed him as she escaped her husband's hold and hurried to walk beside her adopted brother.

"I'll blow the damned thing up, if that's what it takes." Daniel kept walking. The livery was now in sight.

Tyler and Evie exchanged glances with a soft "uh-oh." Daniel had been known to blow things up before.

"I doubt that Evie's carrying dynamite in this thing"— Tyler glanced at the satchel he carried—"but we'll come along for the ride. We came all the way up here to meet your bride. Seems a shame to miss the chance. It's been getting boring sitting around the house anyway."

Daniel threw Tyler a look over his shoulder. Nothing was ever boring around Tyler Monteigne. The man drew trouble like a magnet, just like Evie. The two of them had probably been drawn here right now because of that unerring instinct for making a nuisance of themselves. But it was the kind of nuisance he appreciated having around.

He threw Evie's fancy gown a knowing look. "This isn't going to be any fashion parade. I'm riding like hell."

Arriving at the livery, Evie looked the solid stable up and down and gestured for the satchel in her husband's hand. "I'm sure there's something I can change into." She nodded at the stable hand coming forward to check their business. "While these gentlemen choose our horses, might I borrow an empty stall for a few minutes?"

The stable hand stared at the beautiful lady in fashionable silks as if he didn't understand the question. When he didn't respond, Evie swept past him and disappeared into the dark interior. Tyler and Daniel took no notice of her going and immediately set out to choose the horses they needed. The stable hand checked over his shoulder every once in a while to see if he had been imagining things.

By the time they had decided on three solid horses, Evie reappeared in an elegant riding outfit with a split skirt of her own design. When the stable hand started to put a sidesaddle on her horse, she stopped him and pointed at the appropriate male saddle. "I mean to keep up with the gentlemen, sir."

Daniel shook his head, but kept his mouth shut. Evie had never ridden a horse in her entire life until Tyler came along. He wasn't exactly certain that Tyler's lessons had been appropriate for a lady, but if they hastened his progress, he wasn't going to protest. Evie was certainly old enough to know what she was doing.

Tyler roped Evie's ever-present luggage to his saddle, then assisted his wife in mounting. When all three were seated, he turned to Daniel. "Lead on, Pecos. Where to?"

"Due west, straight as the crow flies. We've got a train to catch."

As they maneuvered city streets with caution, Daniel explained events as hastily as he was able. Evie was furious by the time they reached the edges of town. Tyler was thoughtful.

At thirty-five, Tyler Monteigne had developed into a man of powerful build and some authority. He turned steady eyes to the young man he had known as a dreamy boy and watched grow into a determined, well-respected journalist. Daniel Mulloney had never been distracted by the feminine gender since that first disastrous encounter of his youth. And now he was married to a woman obviously not of his usual sort and whose family thoroughly disapproved to the point of kidnapping her. Tyler suspected there was a small portion of this story missing, but he didn't question Daniel's privacy.

"If they're using the same engine that brought us in, we'll catch them in time. It's an old eight-driver, probably built just after the war. If it's going south while we're going west, we'll catch it coming north all right."

Since Tyler had spent half his life touring the country on steamboat and train, Daniel took his assurances with some degree of relief. He spurred his horse into a gallop at the first stretch of straight road.

Evie had no difficulty keeping up. The trio rode into the night, letting Daniel set the pace.

He knew the horses had to be rested occasionally, but he had difficulty forcing himself to halt even for water.

Racing a train was a mad thing to do, but he couldn't live with the image of Georgie trapped on that train, terrified and not knowing what to do. He didn't know by what means her father had got her on that train or how they held her there or if she would try to escape. He only knew he had to get to her before anything disastrous happened—before they locked her up behind the closed doors of some cold institution where they would permanently douse the shining light that was his Miss Merry.

Daniel wouldn't say he needed her. He had quit needing anybody once he had turned eighteen and learned the ways of the world. He couldn't say he loved her. He didn't know a whole lot about love except to know there wasn't much of it in this world.

But he could say she was his wife and belonged by his side and in his bed, despite whatever crazy promises he may have given. Georgina Meredith Mulloney very definitely belonged in his life. And if her family didn't want her, he most certainly did.

So he drove his horse and himself and the plucky pair behind him until the point of exhaustion. They rode through sleepy little towns that had retired for the night. They rode through vast fields of corn and wheat where only the hoot of an owl gave evidence of any other life besides themselves. They rode past solitary farmhouses, dark with sleep. And at no time was there any evidence of trains or rails or a steam engine chugging down tracks toward Chicago.

Daniel began to fear he had taken the wrong route, chosen the wrong star to follow, and they were riding hellbent for nowhere. He tried to count the miles in his head, figure the speed of his horse, calculate the distance he was cutting off, but he didn't know this territory. He hadn't scouted ahead as Ben had taught him. He hadn't known his enemy was out here, among the corn and wheat fields. He could only keep riding and pray that Someone was watching over him.

The first low moan of the train whistle nearly startled Daniel into stopping. He glanced madly about, searching for the crossing, the station, the reason for the signal echoing across the distance. He saw nothing but waving acres of grain.

It was then that Daniel realized how sound traveled through the night air, covering untold distances. The train was out there. He just had to find it, to stop it, to board it, and to find Georgie.

One thing at a time. Without glancing at Tyler and Evie, Daniel spurred his horse down the road.

Off to the side he could see the headlight appearing out of the darkness as the whistle grew louder. The train had to be approaching the station. There had to be a town somewhere ahead. And he had to get there before the train did.

He felt sorry for his horse. Daniel promised it all the hay it could eat and a lifetime in pasture, but he had to have just a little more speed. He wished he had the thoroughbred he'd left getting fat and sassy at Tyler's plantation. That horse had wings. This one was meant for reliability, not speed. He cursed as the train whistle whined again. It was coming into the station.

At last, Daniel saw the silhouettes of buildings in the open field ahead. He didn't know where the hell they were, but there had to be a station there. The train was slowing down. He could hear the distinctive clacketyclack of the wheels now. They weren't going to make it.

"Leave the horses. Get Evie on the train. I'll be right behind you." Tyler came up to Daniel's side, throwing his words over his shoulder as he pressed his horse faster.

Daniel didn't ask what he intended to do. Tyler was capable of anything, but he favored fast-talking his way through most situations. Daniel let him go. Talk wasn't going to get him to Georgie.

He brought his horse to a panting halt just outside the low-slung building that had to be the station. The massive shape of the train already hissed and rattled at the platform. Light shone occasionally through curtains not completely closed, but for the most part, the train cars looked as dead as the town. There was no sign of Tyler, and Daniel reached to help Evie down.

She was looking for Tyler, too, but she ran obediently

with Daniel, holding up her riding skirt and clicking her heeled boots down the wooden platform. Daniel caught the railed bar of the nearest passenger car and grabbed her hand, hauling her on to the steps without speaking. The train wouldn't idle long in a place like this. They would be filling up with water and fuel and moving on. Even the ticket office would be closed at this hour. They would pay the conductor when they found him.

Daniel gave a sigh of relief as they entered the silent car. A few men in the corner playing cards looked up with interest at Evie's appearance, but they went back to their game when Daniel came in behind her. Almost everyone else was asleep. Evie sent him a questioning look.

"She's in a private car. I didn't see it at this end. They probably hooked it on last. We'll wait for Tyler, then the two of you can have a seat while I find it."

She nodded. The engine gave a mighty belch and heaved forward. Evie grabbed the nearest seat and glanced worriedly toward the door.

Tyler came sauntering from the next car just as the train rolled from the station. He took Evie's arm and led her down the aisle, not even bothering to glower at the poor benighted souls who could only look at Evie and drool. Even after their mad ride she was a picture of radiant loveliness.

"They're carrying a private car at the rear. It was designed by Pullman, so there's an emergency hatch in the roof. There aren't any more stops between here and Indianapolis. How far do you want to go?"

Tyler's whispered asides to Daniel took them through one car and into the next, steadily progressing toward the rear of the train.

"Not any farther than I have to. We'll need to find out how many people are in the car. Most of them should be sleeping at this hour, though."

Tyler nodded in understanding, found a seat for Evie, and set her in it. Then he took off his dusty coat, folded it over a seat, and started for the nearest card game. "Come on, we'll get what we need and break."

Evie made a vile face at them as they left her, but since

Tyler had dumped her satchel on the floor, she began rummaging in it and didn't make any other protest.

There was room for only one more player, and Daniel stayed out of it, standing to the rear and listening as Tyler began his spiel. The older man had made his fortune at card tables and kept his hand in for practice upon occasion still. But it wasn't his talent with cards that he was employing now. Daniel listened with admiration as Tyler wished aloud that he had thought to bring his own private car as someone else evidently had, complaining the journey was taking much too long for his tastes. Tyler Monteigne dressed with the elegance of the wealthiest robber barons, and spoke with the authority of power. The men around him listened without a trace of doubt to his lies.

It didn't take long or much persuasion to pump them for every bit of information they had. Daniel was edging for the far door before Tyler could unravel himself from the game.

"You're not going to walk in there and carry her out, you know," Tyler murmured as he caught up with Daniel. He made no comment on the name of the man who owned the private car they were heading toward. The problem between Daniel and the Mulloneys was an old one. Daniel would inform him of any new encounters with the family he had never known when he was ready. Obviously, they hadn't been pleasant ones.

"I trust you two didn't think you were going to do this alone." Evie swished up behind them, carrying her satchel and Tyler's coat. "I might just make this easy for you if you'll tell me what's going on."

Daniel had to smile at that. Evie was his elder by two years and had always been the one to march forward into the fray first in their younger days. Having children of her own now apparently hadn't changed her any. He wondered if Georgie would be like that after they'd been married ten years. Daniel couldn't believe he was thinking like that.

He hugged Evie briefly as they came to the darkened dining car. He had always been taller than she, but now she actually felt small beside him. Not as small as Georgie, but small enough to protect. "I don't know how you're going to lie us out of this one, Evie. I just wish I'd brought my guns."

Evie slanted a warning gaze at her husband. Tyler always carried his somewhere, but she didn't want him using them. It took something from him every time he had to use violence. Besides, it wouldn't do to shoot Daniel's new family.

"Tell me the story, and then I'll decide what we can do," she announced.

Twenty-two

ℰ

"Well, if there's only her parents and two guards in there, we shouldn't have any problem," Evie decided after Daniel and Tyler told her what they knew. "Everyone but the one man will be asleep at this hour, I wager."

"He's not likely to come to the door and hand Georgie over," Daniel pointed out unnecessarily. "I want Georgie in my hands before you two do anything."

Tyler grinned and leaned against the door frame. "Why don't you two just go ahead and make the plans and wake me when you need my muscle?"

Although it was a long-standing joke in the family that Tyler was too pretty to need brains, Daniel knew his brother-in-law better than that. Tyler thought fast and acted faster. He was just the man he needed with him now.

"I'm going up on the roof. If they're all asleep, they won't hear me. I imagine the guards are posted at the doors, but they won't be at the hatch. I'll go in and find Georgie. You'll have to provide some distraction so I can get her out."

Evie looked worried at this idea, and Daniel knew she was concerned about his ability to climb the train and maneuver across the roof with his bad leg. She hadn't worked herself up to the worst part of it yet, but he could see Tyler had. Daniel waited stoically for his decision. He couldn't do much to help Georgie on his own, but he couldn't see any other way out of this.

Tyler glanced down at Evie in her elegant riding clothes, carrying her precious satchel of belongings, then back to Daniel. "You do know what you're doing, don't you?"

"They can't do anything to you and Evie. I'm willing to take my chances with Georgie."

Without saying what both men knew would happen even if they could get Georgie out, they came to an unspoken agreement. Tyler nodded and looked out at the darkened car just a few steps away. "No time like the present, I suppose. We'll give you time to get in there and look around."

Without a look back, Daniel stepped out of the dining car, across the coupling, and over to the series of hooks leading to the roof of the attached private car. Placing one hand on the highest he could reach and the other hand on the next, he began pulling himself up until he was over the edge and out of sight.

Evie turned to Tyler and murmured softly, "I don't suppose we can settle this amicably and stop at some decent station down the line for our return journey, can we?"

Since that was precisely the point they had been trying to keep from her, Tyler grinned wryly and pushed his hat back on his head as he gazed down on his beautiful and too perceptive wife. "I don't think even you can talk that fast, my dear."

Although Daniel was certain Tyler was right about the train's lack of speed, the wind rushing past him as he pulled himself across the roof did nothing to confirm his estimate. Maybe a trainman could walk across this blamed thing, but he wasn't about to make the attempt. He wanted to be all in one piece when he finally got Georgina in bed beside him again.

That was the thought that kept him placing one hand in front of the other as he eased himself across the rocking, rolling train with little or nothing to grasp should they come to a sudden halt. Those nights with Georgina beside him had been a kind of hell, but it didn't take his vivid imagination to know what kind of heaven they could be.

A bed could be a damned lonely place when there was no one to share it. It was even lonelier when he got up in the morning and knew there would be no other face at the table but his own. And he was finding it harder and harder to imagine any face but Georgina's across that table.

Daniel found the hatch door toward the center of the car without any great difficulty. The only sound he could hear was the roar of the train as it raced across the fields. The night was clear, sparkling with stars and no moon as he lifted the latch and door. He didn't know what he was going to face when he got down there, but he reckoned it was worth whatever it took to get Georgie back.

He couldn't make himself believe that rescuing her would overcome his lack of looks and great wealth, but he couldn't consider doing anything less. He'd read too many of those damned Pecos Martin books when he was young, he supposed. He was beginning to believe in them. If he ever wrote this adventure up, his publisher wouldn't believe it, though. Even Pecos Martin drew the line at climbing over rail cars. His fearless hero would have used guns.

Grasping the sides of the hatch, Daniel lowered himself into the compartment below. A faint light at the far end of the car showed that he was in some kind of hall between the parlor and presumably, the bedchambers. Calculating that the front of the car would be the public rooms, he made his way toward the rear.

He had two doors to choose from. The tiger or the lady, he muttered to himself as he contemplated this decision. Judging the tiger didn't have very sharp teeth, he threw open the right-hand door.

She was asleep. Hints of light caught in the silver-blond length of hair spilling across the pillow. She had always worn it in a braid when she had gone to bed with him. Daniel hovered a minute, just enjoying the sight. But when she moved with a restless moan, he sprang into action.

Kneeling beside the bed, Daniel shook her slightly. "Miss Merry, you've got to wake up. We need to get you dressed and out of here." Even as he said it, he was scanning the room for clothes. As much as he enjoyed seeing her in a chemise that appeared to be untied, he didn't mean for any other man's eyes to see her that way. He would wrap her in a sheet and carry her first.

Georgina lay suddenly still. Daniel glanced down at her and saw that her eyes were open, but they didn't seem to be focusing on him. He handed her a wrapper he found on a nearby chair. "Sit up, Georgie, and get this on. It isn't much, but we don't have time for more."

She continued staring at him in some confusion.

She didn't resist when he pulled her up and put her arms in the sleeves of the wrapper. She allowed him to pull it into place and tie it firmly. Her quiescence made Daniel uneasy. Georgina was many things, but quiescent wasn't one of them.

She stood obediently at his urging, then hesitated. He had his arm around her, guiding her, but she pulled slightly away, staring at him with a flicker of something in her eyes. Daniel wished he had more light to see by, but the one faint lamp on the far wall was all there was.

"We're getting out of here, Georgina," he reminded her. "I'm not going to let them take you away."

She touched his face with her left hand as if uncertain of his reality. Then catching sight of her ring on the wrong finger, she smiled grimly, clenched the hand into a fist, and glanced quickly around.

Daniel breathed a sigh of relief when she silently caught up a pair of shoes and took his hand. He almost had her back.

He wasn't going to take her out on the roof in her present state, however. He was going to take her right down the middle of the car and out, and to hell with everybody in it.

The guard posted at the door had his chair tilted and his feet propped against the wall and across the opening as he dozed. Daniel kicked the chair's legs out from under him.

The man gave a yelp and reached for his gun as he tried to untangle his feet from the chair, but the car door behind him swung open with more force than was necessary. It connected neatly with his elbow, sending the gun skittering down the hall toward Daniel.

Daniel grabbed the weapon and gave Tyler a curt nod of thanks just as a bedroom door behind him burst open with a yell. Calmly palming the gun, Daniel jerked Georgie behind him, against the wall, and turned to meet the furious gaze of the bewhiskered, stout old man standing in his nightshirt.

"You! What in hell are you doing here? Get away from my daughter, you animal, before I have the guards shoot you."

A second guard staggered sleepily from the rear of the car and halted. Hanover stood between the gunman and Daniel. The narrow corridor wasn't made for athletic displays. The gunman glanced to where Tyler was neatly occupying his partner, and shrugged.

Still holding the gun, Daniel nodded acknowledgment of the wisdom of the guard's decision not to interfere, then turned his attention back to Hanover. "Apparently someone failed to inform you that your daughter is now my wife. Shooting me may temporarily solve Georgina's financial problems, but not yours. I'd recommend that you take a nice long vacation while we go back and straighten out whatever you've told Mulloney. I have a number of very unpleasant surprises for him, and you really don't want to be around when I spring them."

Dolly Hanover crept quietly from the bedroom and clutched her husband's sleeve as she caught sight of Daniel's gun. Her gaze strayed worriedly to the strange man holding the guard in the doorway, then back to her daughter hovering in Daniel's protection.

"Georgina?" she inquired anxiously.

"Get back to bed, Dolly. I'm handling this." Hanover tried to push her away, but she clung more fiercely.

"It's all right, Mama." Georgina touched Daniel's shoulder. "This is my husband. You remember Mr. Martin, don't you?"

Dolly smiled and nodded. "Pleased to meet you again, Mr. Martin."

Daniel could almost hear Tyler grinning behind him. It

seemed perfectly natural that he was marrying into a family that was as mad as the one he had adopted. Daniel gave a pleasant nod. "Happy to see you again, ma'am. If you don't mind, I'm taking your daughter home now. I'll take real good care of her, so you just go on back to bed and rest."

Hanover was ominously silent during this exchange. His gaze darted back and forth from the one disarmed guard to the one waiting patiently for orders. A shot fired in these close quarters could kill anyone. He grunted and glared at Daniel.

"She doesn't come with a dime, I promise you. If that's what you're thinking, you're better off leaving her to Mulloney. He can support her the way she's used to."

Daniel reached behind him to encompass Georgina's waist with his arm. "Sorry to disappoint you, but it's not money we're after. Merry's doing just fine without it. I hate to break up this fine party, but we've got to be going. Good night."

He gave a wry nod of his head and pushed Georgina ahead of him, out of reach of the only other man in here with a gun. Behind him, Daniel heard Hanover shout at the guard to go after him. Giving Georgie a shove toward Tyler, Daniel swung around to hold them off, continuing to back toward Tyler and freedom.

Tyler caught Georgina and deftly handed her through the doorway into Evie's hands. When Daniel was close enough, Tyler shoved the first guard toward the second, sending them both into a sprawling heap on the floor.

With a quiet yell of triumph, Tyler and Daniel slammed out of the private car and raced into the dining car after the women. Just as someone rattled the door behind them, they threw the bar across and ran.

"They'll shoot it loose!" Evie yelled, just as a splatter of gunfire proved her words.

"Hang on to your satchel, my dear, we're going for a ride." Tyler grabbed his wife by the waist and fled from the dining car.

Daniel snatched Georgina in the same way, leaving her no time to question as they reached the platform between the cars. Without any further thought, he flung his arms protectively around her and leapt from the slowly moving train.

Georgina screamed as they slid down the embankment and rolled to the ground, bits of dirt and pebbles flying around their heads. Although she felt Daniel trying to take the brunt of the fall, when they reached the grass at the foot of the embankment she was lying beneath him. Gasping for the breath knocked out of her, Georgina felt Daniel's heavy weight pressing her into the ground and heard him panting as loudly as she. The arms braced on either side of her head reassured her, however, and she grasped them in a grateful daze. The laudanum was dissipating rapidly, but her head still seemed to be spinning.

Against the backdrop of the night sky, Daniel's eyes gleamed like the stars in the heavens above. When her gaze met his, the connection was almost physical. Stunned, Georgina just lay there, looking up at him.

"You came for me," she finally managed to whisper.

"Of course." Without another word, he leaned down and kissed her.

Georgina had never known a kiss like this in her life. Perhaps it was the aftereffect of drugs. She could feel the roughness of Daniel's lips as they pressed against her mouth. They sent a kind of magic spiraling through her middle that had been missing before. Her fingers gripped his arms tighter as she became aware of his masculine body pressing into her. But then her lips seemed to part of their own accord, and she felt his breath fill her mouth, and everything that was happening between them seemed perfectly natural. She didn't even notice the press of gravel and grass against her back or feel the heat of the night wind against her skin. Her entire universe consisted of this man above her.

Georgina's hands flew to circle Daniel's neck and pull him closer. He came willingly, cradling her in his arms as he pressed his kisses deeper. She felt the rasp of his tongue, the heat of his passion, and she arched upward with a groan to experience more. It couldn't be like this. The fall from the train must have knocked something loose inside her. But she couldn't stop kissing him back. She couldn't stop anything he wanted to do to her. She moaned against his mouth as Daniel's hand came between them to circle her breast.

The impact of two other bodies falling somewhere down the line didn't intrude upon their reverie. The scrambling sound as the other pair righted themselves didn't come to their attention. Even when two pairs of feet stopped almost on top of them, they were too engrossed in these explorations to notice.

The sound of a masculine voice right overhead brought Georgina abruptly to her senses.

"I trust that isn't a pile of cow dung you found to wallow in. We're going to have a hard enough time finding shelter for the night."

Above her, Daniel choked and pulled partially away, but his arms kept her protectively surrounded. Georgina gradually became aware that she was wearing little or nothing and Daniel's legs seemed to be sprawled between hers, but she made no effort to move. Her gaze traveled with interest to the pair of boots standing beside them, then moved carefully upward until she measured the source of this unwelcome invasion. She had never seen the man before, and in the darkness, she couldn't tell a lot about him, but he had the whitest grin she'd ever seen on a man.

"You and Evie find shelter. We're fine just where we are," Daniel answered gruffly, keeping Georgina carefully covered with his body.

The stranger chuckled as a woman peered around him, and Georgina began to feel the first flush of embarrassment. She shifted slightly and released her grip on Daniel's neck.

"Aren't you going to introduce us, Danny? After we came all this way, it's the least you can do."

There was laughter in the woman's voice, and Georgina closed her eyes in shame. It was obvious from the disorder of their clothes that these two had just jumped off the train with them, but despite their dishevelment, they were garbed elegantly, and they knew Daniel. She was about to meet his family while half dressed and making love in a cow pasture.

Daniel didn't seem to find their presence particularly amusing either, but reluctantly, he assumed a seated position and pulled Georgina up with him. She hastily wrapped her robe around her and looked for her shoes.

"Evie, this is my wife, Georgina. Georgie, my sister and brother-in-law, Tyler Monteigne. Like bad pennies, they turned up at the train station after you left."

Georgina couldn't think of any etiquette that covered greeting new relatives while sitting in a cow pasture after jumping off a train. She wasn't certain if she was more shaken by the jump or by Daniel's kiss. But this unexpected introduction left her speechless. She just buried her head against her knees and hoped it would all go away.

She heard Evie laugh and say, "That's the most honest reaction I've seen in a long time. I'm certain it will be a pleasure getting to know you, Georgina, but let's try it in the morning. I see a farmhouse down the line. We'll meet you there."

"Are they gone yet?" Georgina whispered as the feet moved away.

Daniel chuckled and pushed a strand of hair away from her forehead. "They're out to fast-talk some chickens out of their roost, I suspect. We ought to get your shoes on and catch up with them. There's a few hours left in the night, and I can use some sleep before we start looking for a way out of here."

Sleep. Georgina lifted her head and stared up at Daniel. His arm was still around her waist, and she could feel the heat of him against her. She wasn't at all certain that sleep was what he had in mind.

It very definitely wasn't what she had on hers.

Twenty-three

&

"Mama Sukey tells me Ben's been courting. Is it serious?"

Daniel hobbled up behind the other two and spoke as if they were gossiping at a house party. Georgina tried to pull her wrapper tighter, but the pair in front of them didn't notice her dishabille.

"It's serious. He's cleaning up the old overseer's house for her. She's a quadroon from down New Orleans way, pretty as Ben is ugly."

"Why doesn't he move into the big house? Seems to me that would impress her a whole lot more."

Daniel's hand strayed to brush proprietarily along Georgina's hip as she walked. She gave him a quick glance, but his attention seemed to be solely on the conversation as they ambled toward the farmhouse ahead.

Both Tyler and Evie laughed, but Tyler was the one who replied. "You're a newlywed, you figure that one out. The big house is bursting at the seams with my relatives, Evie's relations, and Ben's. Even the terrible duo came in for the summer, and Kyle and Carmen came up with them to see Natchez. You never saw so many people in one place in your life."

Georgina watched as Evie sent a concerned glance over her shoulder at Daniel as if expecting some reaction from him at the mention of these names. Daniel only smiled and pulled her a little closer. Evie turned around, satisfied, but Georgina smelled a rat.

"Who are the terrible duo and Kyle and Carmen?" she asked innocently.

"Evie's cousins," Daniel replied.

"Daniel's partners in crime," Evie answered at the same time.

"The banes of my life," Tyler intoned when the other two laughed. "Evie took in her cousins when they were orphaned. I thought I would get rid of them as they got older; instead, the numbers seem to be growing. When Carmen married Kyle, I thought we'd got rid of at least one, but instead we've got the two of them popping up all the time. And now they've got a kid of their own to drag around. Evie's father is ostensibly supposed to be the kid's guardian, but I spend more time prying him out of taverns than he spends looking after them."

"He can't see well enough to paint anymore. He has to do something," Evie responded defensively. "And he doesn't drink. He just talks. You're exaggerating, Tyler Monteigne."

"Exaggerating is Daniel's job." Tyler glanced over his shoulder at them. "I read that book you sent Evie, Danny Boy. I don't ever want to hear you say another word about my fast-talking again. Just because you put it down on paper instead of saying it out loud don't make us any different. And I'm going to get even, just see if I don't."

Daniel grinned. "I call it the way I see it. You're just mad because I let Pecos get the best of you."

"A damned riverboat gambler he made me." Tyler turned his complaint to Georgina. "Now tell me, do I look a riverboat gambler to you?"

Now that he mentioned it, Georgina thought the answer ought to be yes, but she wasn't feeling any too certain of herself at the moment. She turned a helpless look to Daniel. "What are we talking about?"

Evie started laughing and caught Tyler's arm, turning him back around. "He hasn't told her, you fool. Now we're in for it."

"Haven't told me what?" Georgina was quite certain the effects of the drug hadn't worn off. She would wake up in the morning and discover that this had all been a dream. She couldn't really be walking down a railroad track in the middle of the night in her chemise and a wrapper, discussing riverboat gamblers and quadroons and multiple cousins with two people too beautiful to be real. She wouldn't even think about those minutes with Daniel on top of her and his mouth on hers. There were words for dreams like that.

Daniel bounced a pebble off the coat Tyler had thrown over his shoulder. "You never have learned when to keep your damned mouth shut, Monteigne. Next time I'll have Pecos put a bullet through it."

"Daniel!" Exasperated, Georgina smacked his hand off her hip and stood out of his grasp. "You said you were Pecos. Have you taken leave of your mind?"

Tyler and Evie were hurrying away, laughing. Daniel shoved his hands in his pockets and glared at her. "I'd like to get some rest this night, if that's all right with you. Do I have to explain everything right now?"

"I figure you've got a lifetime of explaining to do, but I just want to hear about this Pecos right now. Are you or are you not Pecos Martin?"

"Pecos Martin is a figment of imagination. I got called that because I was always reading books about him, and when I was a kid, I thought Tyler was the real Pecos. The name stuck to me instead."

Georgina waited. He hadn't explained everything, she could tell by the way he stood and shifted from foot to foot.

He grabbed her arm and marched down the track after the other two. The farmhouse was almost directly ahead.

"When I got laid up with a broken leg, I decided to write my own Pecos Martin book. I sent it to the address in the front of the books, and they bought it. I've been turning out one or two a year ever since. It won't make me rich, but they're selling well and I earn a few extra dollars, more than the newspaper is going to bring in for a long time."

Georgina looked up at him, eyes wide. "You write books?"

"Pecos Martin books," he corrected, as if that made a difference.

"Any kind of books. Real books. You take what other people dream and talk about and put it into real words where people all over the world can see them and dream about them and maybe do something about them. You're a writer!"

Her words were little short of hero worship, and Daniel glanced down at her in surprise. "Of course I'm a writer. That's what I do on the newspaper."

"But those are facts. You don't make those up. But you make up the Pecos Martin books, don't you? You take pictures and people out of your mind and paint them on paper like an artist paints on canvas. I've never met anyone who can do that. I mean, I met Oscar Wilde once, but that doesn't count. That was just shaking his hand. This is different. Why didn't you tell me?"

Daniel shook his head in incredulity, but a note of pride crept into his voice. "Because it's not important. The newspaper is what's important. Newspapers can make a difference in people's lives."

"Pecos Martin made a difference in your life, didn't he?" Georgina pointed out. "He showed you what a hero should be, and you came after me just as he would have, I bet. Somebody else would have just stayed home and moaned and complained and not done anything."

Daniel didn't need to be reminded of that. He'd done some damned foolish things in his life in the name of heroism. It wasn't anything he liked to brag about. Seeing Tyler and Evie disappear inside the barn without any eruption of noise from within, he pulled Georgina after them.

"Words are meaningless without action," he said obliquely.

They felt their way through the darkness of the barn. A horse nickered somewhere in the rear. A cat prowled around their ankles and finding them useless, disappeared through a hole in a stall door. There didn't seem to be much other life in here. Seeing Tyler and Evie find an empty stall and disappear, Daniel decided that was the wisest thing to do for the moment. There wasn't any use in raising the household at this ungodly hour, not in their present states. Much better to wait until morning.

Finding a horse blanket, he opened the nearest stall and gestured for Georgina to enter. She looked at him dubiously, but he didn't leave her much choice. Throwing the blanket on a pile of hay, he pulled the door closed behind them.

"I'm not sleepy," she whispered in muffled tones behind him.

"I don't doubt that, but I'm dead on my feet. Give me a few hours, and we'll find our way out of here when it's light."

When she continued to hesitate, Daniel sat down and began pulling off his boots. He doubted that Georgina Meredith Hanover had ever been inside a barn in her life and had certainly never slept in one. He was bringing her down to new lows, but fate was giving them little choice in the matter. When she continued to hover, he impatiently pulled her down beside him.

"Just lie here and close your eyes. We'll be fine."

She lay stiffly on her back, arms crossed over her chest. That was probably the best possible course to take, but the crazy emotions wheeling through him at this moment wouldn't settle for reasonable. Daniel reached over and pulled her into his arms.

"That's better," he murmured. He was asleep in an instant.

Georgina lay awake a long time after. She had a lot to think about, and the man beside her was a major part of those thoughts. That, in itself, was terrifying. That she wanted his hand to stray again to places she had just discovered ached was even more terrifying.

"Mama!" The screech shattered the rafters, sending cascades of chaff from the loft. "Mama! There's thieves in the barn!" The last words drifted from a little less than the close range of the first, indicating the warning siren was running toward the house.

Having finally drifted into a light sleep, Georgina

nearly jumped from her skin at the first screech. The second screech sent Daniel rolling on top of her, burying his face in the cascade of hair she hadn't taken time to braid. She caught her breath at this unexpected closeness.

"Tell me that was a nightmare and it's not dawn yet," he muttered into her shoulder.

"That was a nightmare and it's not dawn yet," she replied obligingly, only to be rewarded by a finger tickling her ribs. "Ouch, Daniel, stop that!"

"Obviously, the two lovebirds are awake already." The sleepy male voice came from the other side of the stall. "Let's send them in to make explanations. We're too old for this."

"You're too old, you mean," his feminine counterpart replied. "I'm only a little older than Daniel."

"And if you keep it up, you'll be younger than he is any day now," Tyler replied grudgingly.

Daniel's chest heaved with laughter against her, and Georgina wound her arms around him and surrendered to the silliness. She had never known the luxury of this kind of closeness before. She had never had brothers or sisters or friends close enough to giggle and play with. She thought she might just get used to the experience.

But reality was an unpleasantness that kept intruding. From outside came running footsteps and a shout of more authority than the earlier childish screech, "I've got a rifle. Get yourselves out here with your hands up!"

"Oh, no, please don't!" Daniel moaned with helpless laughter as he rolled off Georgina and held his sides. "I can't put Pecos in a barn with a woman! He'd purely die of embarrassment and probably melt into shame. Tyler, get out there and hold off the posse!"

Evie's giggles were as helpless as Daniel's from the other side of the wall. A boot gave the thin stall partition a solid kick, but a moment later, a golden head appeared above the door. Georgina watched in utter astonishment as a golden-brown eye glanced down at them with amusement, winked casually, then disappeared behind a broad-brimmed hat that sat on his head like some kind of halo.

Georgina collapsed in laughter at Daniel's side. "He's

not real, is he? I thought I just dreamed him. Nobody really does look like that, do they?"

Daniel held her against his side and patted her shoulder. "Of course not. I dreamed him up for you. Shall I make him disappear?"

"You do, and I'll rip your head off, Daniel Mulloney!" Evie sang from the other side.

That sent them both into paroxysms of laughter until Evie stormed around the corner and flung her satchel in their direction.

"You'd better find your wife some clothes real quick, little brother. We're going to have a hard enough time explaining this without explaining why she's running around in her undergarments."

Georgina covered her mouth and choked on her laughter as the magnificent rose-and-feather hat marched past and out the door. From outside, the sound of Tyler's smooth Southern drawl placating the terrified farm woman carried through the open barn door, soon joined by Evie's cheerful feminine tones. The poor woman didn't have a chance.

Daniel was rummaging through Evie's things without concern, pulling out anything that looked mildly useful. Georgina looked down on her partially open wrapper and gasped at the amount of skin revealed. Hastily turning her back, she berated him, "Why didn't you tell me I was half undressed! Whatever must they think of me?"

"That you were kidnapped and carried off without any clothing," Daniel replied prosaically, throwing his findings over her shoulder. "We all know what women look like, so it's not as if we're seeing anything we haven't seen before."

"You haven't seen me before!"

"There's that I suppose, but it's not from lack of trying."

The devil of it was, she could almost hear the grin in his reply. They were getting to know each other much too well. Irritated, Georgina informed him, "You're going to have to leave. I can't put these on while you're sitting there."

"You're not going to be able to put them on unless I sit here. Evie has Tyler and probably ten dozen other people to help her put those getups on. You'll tie yourself in knots trying to do it yourself."

He spoke the truth, Georgina realized as she examined the exquisite walking dress he'd thrown to her. It buttoned down the back in a million tiny jet buttons, tied in a dozen places between skirt and bodice and petticoat and required another half dozen tapes in the bustle and lining. It would take her all day to do it herself.

Carefully tying her chemise closed at the top, she reached for the petticoat to pull over her drawers. She was quite certain she and Evie weren't the same size, but under the circumstances, she had little choice in the matter.

Daniel quite efficiently tied off the petticoat tapes for her, and Georgina threw him a quick look over her shoulder. "You've done this before."

He reddened slightly. "Upon occasion."

Sniffing delicately, she struggled into the shaped corset. "I suppose you consort with low women."

"Well, high women don't take it kindly if I consort without marriage." Daniel caught the corset strings and pulled them tight.

Georgina gasped as her breasts were pushed upward to preposterous proportions. Evie wasn't exactly built the same as she was. She felt Daniel gazing over her shoulder with interest, and she hastily covered her bosom with her hand. "The gown, please, Daniel."

He chuckled and dropped the violet silk over her head. "You're made for a man's hands, Miss Merry. When are you going to let me show you?"

"When birds fly backward," she informed him stiffly. But she knew her resolve was faltering as she felt those hands efficiently fastening the buttons at her back. Daniel's closeness was doing extraordinary things to her insides. Just the thought of his fingers on her bosom made her mind whirl. Such ideas had never entered her head before.

And the awful part was that she really didn't have any

choice any longer. Daniel was her husband, and if she gave herself to him, he would have to support her. And she was going to have to give herself to him if she wanted to live.

Even if the drugging incident hadn't effectively severed her relationship with her parents, it had become perfectly clear from her father's conversations with her mother that she would no longer be able to rely on him or Hanover Industries for support. They were bankrupt.

Twenty-four

𝒞

"**W**ell, I think it was perfectly kind of the widow to feed us so handsomely before bringing us to town." Evie gazed up at the substantial brick building with the slightly ostentatious label of HAMPTON INN hanging over the door.

"She just wanted to know all the gossip and talk about fashion," Tyler replied, slightly disgruntled at the sight of a town without a single saloon. Temperance had apparently taken strong roots out here in farm country. "If she'd taken us to town right off, we could have made the train."

"Well, we can catch the one in the morning. Besides"—Evie's voice dropped to a whisper as they watched Daniel shove his hands in his pockets and walk stiffly beside Georgina to the mercantile store window—"I think the newlyweds need some time to themselves. You really are going to have to talk to Daniel. There's something wrong here, or I miss my guess."

"There's nothing wrong here that I can see. Georgina's just bigger than you are in the bosom department, and Daniel can't keep his eyes off the way she's about to spill out of that gown. Give the poor girl a shawl and the world will right itself again." Tyler grinned as he watched the pair.

"Men!" Evie huffed, lifting her skirt to enter the hotel. "You can only think of one thing at a time and that one thing unfortunately seldom changes. Daniel was never like that. That's what's wrong."

Smiling, Tyler followed the sway of her bustle inside. "Daniel just never met a woman like that before. You know what I think?"

Evie turned with a questioning look. He linked his arm with hers and led her toward the desk, leaning over to whisper in her ear, "I think he hasn't gotten under her skirts yet."

Evie looked shocked, then threw a thoughtful glance over her shoulder to where the young couple could just barely be seen through the plate glass window. "Do you think I ought to talk to her?"

Tyler looked properly horrified. "Hell, no. Even Daniel doesn't deserve that fate. He'll straighten her out when the time is right."

He turned to the clerk who was listening with great interest. "My wife and I would like a room, and the pair out there"—he nodded toward the street—"want the honeymoon suite."

Georgina gazed in trepidation around the room the clerk had led them to. A huge vase of flowers filled the dresser. She was rather certain most hotel rooms didn't come provided with flowers. She had some experience with hotel rooms, and the only time flowers appeared were when some suitor sent them. But she'd been with Daniel all this time. He couldn't have sent them.

Her gaze lingered on the bucket of ice with a bottle that suspiciously looked like wine of some sort sticking out. She knew perfectly well that ice in summer and wine in Ohio didn't appear without a great degree of monetary persuasion.

That led her to the bed. It was a massive bed. It looked like something out of one of the castles she had toured in England. Damask draperies were tied back from the mahogany canopy, and the bed linen was already turned back invitingly. Something very odd was happening here.

She turned her gaze to Daniel, who was leaning against the window frame with his arms crossed, surveying this splendor with the same interest as she. Feeling her gaze, he looked up with a slight grin.

"I didn't mention that my adopted family comes from a race of genies, did I?"

She shook her head slowly. "There's a whole lot of things you didn't mention, if you want to talk about it."

Daniel's gaze swept from the crown of Georgina's silver-blond hair to the tip of her tapping toe, lingering knowingly at the full curve of her bosom and the small circumference of her waist. "Talk isn't exactly what I had in mind," he mentioned nonchalantly—a little too nonchalantly.

Georgina shivered at the tone of his voice. He'd been acting oddly ever since he had rescued her last night. She caught her elbows in her hands and tried to steady herself. "We need to talk, Daniel."

He nodded and pulled out a chair, then held out a hand to help her into it. "I'm not much good at it, but I'll give it a try."

His hand was dry and warm and reassuringly strong as he took hers. Georgina's felt small and damp and disappointingly weak to herself, but Daniel didn't withdraw in disgust. He merely stepped back, pulled out a chair for himself, and straddled it, settling his arms over the back as he waited for her to open the conversation.

Georgina gulped at all this masculine proximity and attention suddenly focused on her. She lifted her chin defiantly. "My father owes Mr. Mulloney—your father—a great deal of money."

Daniel nodded. "I knew that. My father makes it a point to get a firm grip on every business that he deals with."

She dipped her head and looked at her fingers. "Did you know that the debt can be called at any time, and that there isn't any money to cover it?"

"That's rather stupid of your father. He should have known what kind of man my father is." Daniel frowned. "I suppose that's the bait Artemis used to force your father to agree to the marriage with Peter."

Georgina nodded, but didn't look up. "With my shares and what my father gave as dowry, Peter would have controlling interest in the factory."

"No, he wouldn't, Artemis would. I've studied his methods rather thoroughly these last weeks. He doesn't let anything out of his hands, not even Peter. I don't know what your beau thought he was going to get, but I bet there were more strings tied to that agreement than a team of lawyers could tear apart."

Georgina shrugged. "It doesn't matter now. Whether Peter knew or not, my marrying you destroyed the agreement. My father will have to sell the factory and our house and everything we own to repay Mr. Mulloney."

Daniel whistled. "That was some debt."

"I don't exactly understand the details. It was something about my father expanding when prices were high and now prices are low and things aren't worth as much and it would turn around in a few years, but not right now."

Daniel nodded. "He gambled. It would have made a lot of money for you and Peter one day, but the cash isn't there right now." He reached across the chair and rubbed his knuckle against her cheek. "You're telling me your forty percent is worthless."

Georgina stared at her hands again. "If I can get my camera back, I'm sure I can sell my photographs. There are photographers in New York who make huge fortunes. I won't starve."

"Not after the first few years while you learn your trade, I suppose." Daniel pushed her chin up so she had to look him in the eyes. "I won't let you starve, Miss Merry."

"You didn't want a wife," she reminded him.

His lips twisted into a wry grin. "I wanted a wife, all right, or I would never have married you in the first place. You're the one who isn't ready for marriage."

"But you don't love me," she protested.

It was Daniel's turn to shrug. "Maybe not, but I sure like you a whole lot. That ought to count for something. And I really do want a wife. I like waking up in the morning with you in my bed."

Georgina blushed beneath Daniel's uncompromising gaze. She had dreamed of love and romance, but she had known she wasn't going to get it. She had been willing to settle for less with Peter. Why shouldn't she settle for less with this man who at least listened to her?

There wasn't any reply she could make. Before she could try, Daniel leaned over and grabbed the bottle of wine from the bucket. "We'll settle this in Western fashion." He picked up the glasses on the table and filled them, handing her one. "We'll play for it. I win, you agree to be my wife. You win, and you can choose what you want to do."

Georgina sipped the wine, then choked. She stared at it a little incredulously. "I think your genies mean to get us drunk."

Daniel tasted the wine and laughed. "I think you are quite probably right. Since we're stranded here with nothing better to do until tomorrow morning, it's probably a fine idea. We'll drink and gamble until dawn. How about it?"

Something wilder than the strong wine swirled inside her as Georgina looked up and met Daniel's gaze. She felt as if a trapped bird in her middle frantically flapped its wings to get free. The sensation made her giddy. Or perhaps it was the intensity of Daniel's stare and the wine. She took another sip and smiled determinedly.

"What kind of game did you have in mind?"

Daniel grinned. "Poker."

Georgina frowned. "I don't know how to play."

"I'll teach you. Wait right here. I'll ask our resident genies for some cards. That will set their smug expectations back a little."

Georgina laughed at the thought of Tyler's and Evie's faces as Daniel asked for cards to while away the hours. The laughter held her until he was gone, but then she had to face herself and what she was about to do. She was about to deliberately lose a game of cards and become a wife.

She didn't have any doubt that was what she meant to do. Winning might mean she could choose what she wanted to do, but what she wanted to do and what Daniel could offer her were two different things. He couldn't give her back her father's factory. He couldn't support her until she could support herself without calling her wife. He couldn't give her a man who would love her and want her for herself.

So she was going to give Daniel a wife. She was going to make a lousy wife, but surely he knew that. She couldn't cook. She would never be obedient or docile. She wasn't an intellectual. She wasn't as pretty as Evie. She really didn't have any idea how to go about being a wife, but she was going to learn. It had to be better than learning to work in a factory or to be a maid. Those were about the only other alternatives open to an unmarried woman, and they wouldn't be open to her, not in Cutlerville anyway. Too many people knew her. She really didn't have any choice, but she wouldn't tell Daniel that. If he wanted a wife, he had one. She just wouldn't let him know that quite yet.

He came back a few minutes later, whistling. He really was the nicest man Georgina had ever known, even if he was occasionally a little peculiar. Perhaps Daniel wasn't as handsome as Tyler, but he wasn't hard to look upon. The laugh lines around his mouth and eyes made her happy. The admiration beaming from his face when he looked on her as he was doing now made her feel strange inside. She wouldn't think about those times when his face got hard and his hands turned into fists. She knew he would never turn that side of him against herself.

"All right, Miss Merry." Daniel pulled the table and chairs into order and threw the deck of cards on it, then refilled their wine glasses. He lifted one in salute. "To winning."

Georgina sipped hers, then searched his face anxiously. "You're insane, you know that, don't you?"

Daniel pulled out a chair and gestured for her to sit. "Most writers are. Have you thought about what it's going to be like married to me? Does playing this game make you a sane woman?"

Georgina relaxed slightly. "No, it makes me as crazy as you. If you win, what are you going to do with a crazy wife who can't cook?"

Daniel beamed happily. "Make love to her, of course." He broke the cards, shuffled, and dealt her five. "The object of this game is to get a higher hand than the other person. Would you like to make any side bets to make it interesting?"

Georgina decided it was going to take a lot more wine to make this easy. Daniel's calm pronouncement of his intention of making love to her made her insides tremble, and she took a good gulp of her drink. Before the night was over, they were going to ... Her glance shot nervously to the majestic bed and back. It wouldn't do to think about it.

"I don't have any money to wager." She looked at her cards with interest. What constituted a high hand?

Daniel flicked his cards into a fan like a professional, then gazed over them at Georgina. His scrutiny fell on the curve of her bodice. "We could start by wagering buttons," he offered.

Startled, she stared up at him. "Buttons?"

Daniel pulled a pad of paper and a pencil from his coat pocket, then neatly buttoned his coat and vest. "You have a heck of a lot more than I do, but then, I have more experience at the game. That should make it fair. We wager buttons. At the end of the hand, the loser unbuttons however many the other won."

As his intent became clear, a deep blush colored Georgina's cheeks. The wager wasn't fair, and he knew it. She could tell by the wicked gleam in his eye. She would be sitting here in her undergarments in a few hands, and he would still be wearing his shirt. She had meant for him to win, but she hadn't meant for it to be easy.

She held her chin up. "Tapes and hooks get to count as buttons," she proposed.

Daniel groaned, but nodded agreement. "All right, but the clothes have to come off so I know you're not cheating. The last one with clothes on, wins."

She didn't think she could blush any deeper, but she felt warm clear down through her middle. Not daring to meet his eyes, Georgina stared at her cards. "Tell me what a high hand is."

Twenty-five

ℰ

The remains of their meal of cold chicken and potato salad lay stacked on a corner of the table. It had taken them several hours to actually eat it, and they had ignored the rap on their door of the servant come to carry it away.

Their second bottle of wine was only half empty, but they were making inroads on it. Sunlight still seeped through the window, but from an entirely different angle than at the start of the game. Shadows began to form around the room as they studied their cards.

Daniel's coat lay across the back of his chair and his vest was unbuttoned down to the last button. Georgina's gown gaped all the way down the back, the millions of tiny buttons completely unfastened, but the train of the gown was still clinging by a tape, so she refused to remove it.

She couldn't, however, keep the front of her gown from falling forward without holding it, and it was increasingly difficult to hold her cards, her glass, and her gown. But she noticed this worked in her favor as often as not. Lifting her glass to sip, she let the gown fall forward, and Daniel's gaze instantly focused on the rise of her breasts above the corset.

Georgina smiled and helped herself to another card. "I raise you two buttons."

Daniel marked down the bet and spread out his cards, his eyes still focused on the display before him. "Two jacks, my dear. Off with the gown."

Georgina glared at the two tens in her hand. He might be distracted, but that didn't help her luck any. With a shrug that came as much from the wine as composure, she let the gown fall off her shoulders as she untied the bustle tape.

"You're down six buttons, my dear. The tape is only one." Daniel watched in fascination as Georgina stood, letting the gown fall to her feet.

She was still fully covered in corset and petticoat, drawers and chemise, and if the truth were told, she'd be delighted to lose the corset. She just didn't want to lose it too quickly. The numbers of buttons and tapes remaining were becoming rapidly few, and the bed loomed ever larger in her mind.

Georgina unhooked the first five fastenings of the corset, and wished instantly that she had started at the bottom. Her main concern had been breathing, but now it became the spill of her breasts from the loosened garment.

Daniel was grinning blissfully as he looked his fill, and Georgina sent him a hostile glare. "Look while you can, mister. When you're down to your last buttons, I'm going to be buttoning up."

"I can't wait." Still beaming, he shuffled and dealt.

Daniel's stare was making her feel funny inside again. Georgina squirmed in her chair and picked up her cards, but she had difficulty concentrating. She took a sip of wine and tried to make herself think, but all she could think about was the way the warm air felt on her uncovered skin.

It was hot in here. She could feel a trickle of perspiration roll between her breasts. She reached for the napkin that had come with their dinner and patted herself dry as she stared at her cards. She heard Daniel make a noise suspiciously like a groan, and she looked up, but he was staring grimly at his cards. He must have a bad hand.

Georgina gazed at the hand dealt thoughtfully. A nine, ten, and jack of hearts stared back at her. It had possibilities. She made another mark on the pad, discarded, and took two more cards.

The buttons were piling up, but now she had the eight of hearts. Georgina eyed Daniel's fastened shirt thoughtfully. She had seen him once without it. She wasn't at all certain she could concentrate for long if she had to sit across the table from him while he was half naked. But she thought she'd like to try. It was better than the alternative.

Daniel had recovered his equilibrium to some degree and now doubled his bet, daring her to match it. She needed a seven or queen of hearts. They hadn't been discarded. They could be in there. She met his bet and took another card. The queen.

Keeping her smile to herself, Georgina let him raise her again. She was really going to enjoy this hand. He was hanging on to his cards as if they were the crown jewels, but he couldn't beat what she held. She took another drink of wine. She was going to need fortification when Daniel began shedding his clothes.

When he finally called and she spread her hand out for his edification, he looked at it in amazement. Then a slow grin began to spread across his face as he unfastened his last vest button.

"It was getting a mite warm in here, anyway," he mentioned casually as he threw the vest over his coat.

Georgina watched with avid interest as Daniel discarded his collar. He wasn't wearing a cravat or tie, but he had links in his cuffs. He held them up for her perusal.

"Do these count?"

She nodded. Mentally, she tried to tally her points and the number of buttons he had remaining. She was beginning to wish men still wore those old-fashioned trousers that buttoned up both sides. Her gaze inadvertently went to the band of that article of clothing. The cloth flap prevented her from seeing how many buttons were behind there.

Daniel was counting the buttons of his shirt out loud as he unfastened them. Georgina's gaze reluctantly lifted to watch as the shirt gaped open. She had hoped he might be wearing some form of combinations underneath, but she should have known he wouldn't. There was nothing beneath that gaping cloth but pure male flesh.

He kept pulling the shirt from his trousers, sliding out one button at a time, until she wondered if the material reached to the floor. He finally reached the designated number, two buttons shy of the end, but that was scarcely a saving grace. The shirt gaped wide to reveal tantalizing glimpses of tanned smooth skin that moved with muscular grace as he returned to his seat. Georgina gulped and reached for the cards.

"More wine?" Daniel picked up the bottle and refilled their glasses without waiting for her response.

Georgina gulped it hastily. Things were getting a little fuzzy around the edges, and she was learning to appreciate the sight of Daniel sitting there so casually with his shirt open. She was even beginning to like the feel of his admiring gaze as she reached across the table, exposing more of herself than she had ever exposed to anyone before. She was beginning to think that getting drunk was a very good idea.

"Are you hungry? Shall I order something else brought up?" Daniel asked carefully, eyeing the level of her wineglass.

"No, I don't think so," Georgina answered hazily, letting the cards fall from her hands as she dealt them. It wasn't professional, but her head was too light to do more.

Ascertaining that she was still upright and functioning, Daniel sifted through the hand dealt while Georgina stared at hers in confusion. She was losing track of her purpose here. Was she supposed to be winning or losing? Every time she looked up and saw Daniel across the table, she got more confused. If he took off all his clothes first, did she win?

She had this rather odd feeling that she wouldn't. It didn't matter much. The hand she held was a loser, and no amount of discarding was going to improve it. She spent this round calculating the number of hooks on her corset that she could afford to lose.

Oddly enough, she didn't feel in the least embarrassed

as she folded her hand and began unfastening the hooks. Daniel had helped her put the thing on this morning. It didn't seem strange to have him see her take it off. She ought to be horrified at sitting in a hotel room with a man while wearing nothing but her underwear, but it somehow felt perfectly natural. She even gave a seductive little wiggle as she undid the last hook and shook the corset off. Daniel sat there with his arms crossed over his chest, calmly watching her, but Georgina noticed his eyes became slightly glazed and he seemed to stop breathing when she sucked in her stomach and pushed out her breasts before sitting down. This was getting interesting.

Daniel dropped one of his cards and had to pick it up off the floor. Georgina crossed her stockinged legs beneath the table and wiggled her ankle at him while he was down there. He was a long time in coming up.

They both had lousy hands for the next round, but Daniel lost his last two shirt buttons and had to add the shirt to the growing mound of discarded clothing over his chair back. Georgina's fingers ached to touch the bulge of his shoulders, and she had difficulty keeping her eyes away from the ridge of muscles across his chest. Her mild-mannered journalist was built like a stevedore.

Daniel looked up questioningly when she hesitated too long over a discard. "You can fold now, if you like. It will only cost you those two pretty ribbons." His gaze indicated the ones he meant, the ones tying her chemise closed across her breasts.

That was getting dangerously close to shameless, but Georgina did as he suggested. It was easier to unfasten two ribbons than gamble more and lose the whole piece. She didn't think she was brave enough to sit there as bare-chested as he.

Daniel sighed in ecstasy as the chemise gaped enticingly, revealing almost the entirety of the valley between her breasts. "Why don't we retire this game until later and explore the possibilities of that bed now? It's perfectly legal, you know."

"I could win," Georgina reminded him, but she pushed her arms against her sides slightly until her breasts rose against the thin fabric of her chemise, threatening to spill over. Victory was already flooding through her veins as Daniel rose from his chair.

"This way, we both win," he murmured, pulling her up out of her chair.

He tasted of wine and masculine heat and his tongue took such rapid possession of her mouth that Georgina couldn't control her spinning senses. Her hands circled his neck, and the broad chest she had just been admiring from afar was now rubbing disconcertingly across her own, sending screaming warnings careening through her body.

Daniel's hands caught her waist, circling it, lifting Georgina closer until she could feel his hips pressed near hers in a proximity that even in her innocence she knew was dangerous. And seductive. She pressed closer, wanting more, but Daniel's hands were exploring elsewhere now, rising higher until they rested just beneath her breasts. They teased at the covered curves, creating desires over which she had no control. In a minute she would be jelly in his hands, and there would be no turning back.

Gasping, Georgina pulled away. Placing her hands on Daniel's chest to hold him off, she stared at him in astonishment. This wasn't Daniel, the mild-mannered newspaperman with spectacles and an endearing grin that she knew so well. This was a man with only one thing on his mind. She read the truth in the flare of his nostrils, the darkening of previously clear gray eyes, the twitch of a muscle over a broad jaw. She didn't need to know more. She backed away slightly.

"We're not finished with the game," she said lamely.

His eyes darkened further, but he nodded curtly and took his place again. This time, his face was ruthless as he dealt the cards.

She was going to lose. She could see that in his eyes. What had been a game had become something else. He was playing to win, and she was the prize.

Georgina bent her concentration on the cards, discarding wine and desire and all other encumbrances to clear thought. She felt as if she were suddenly fighting for her life. She didn't know how or why the game had changed that way, but she knew it had become a winner-take-all dispute.

She had two deuces in the hand he dealt her. She played them for all she was worth, but in the end, his pair of fours won. Rather than remove any more ribbons on her chemise, Georgina lifted it under the table and untied her garters and her drawers, throwing them both on the stack of clothing she had accumulated.

Daniel grimly shuffled and dealt the next hand. She was sitting on the chair with nothing but one thin piece of cotton between the wood and her skin. She had never felt so naked in her life. Daniel's knowing glance didn't help. The place between her legs tingled, and Georgina began to have some idea of what she was about to lose. She glanced helplessly at the massive bed. Her mother had never told her what happened in a marriage bed, but her body was telling her things she would rather not know.

Daniel dealt again. This time he folded quietly after drawing two cards. He stood and began unfastening his trouser buttons.

It was then that Georgina noticed the bulge pushing at the tight fabric of his pants, and she went red clear to her hair roots. The wine finally took control of her brain, and she felt as if she were spinning giddily.

Daniel was beside her before she could fall. He caught her up and carried her to the bed, and suddenly the spinning was something else, something much more serious, and Georgina grabbed for his shoulders.

That was undoubtedly her undoing. His skin was hot and smooth and slightly moist with the heat of the nearly airless room. Georgina couldn't resist touching even as Daniel laid her back against the cool sheets. She wanted to touch all of him, and her hands spread around his sides and went forward, touching his chest as she had longed to do all afternoon.

Daniel was on top of her before she could say a word. His kisses were neither gentle nor reassuring; they were demanding, decisive, and inflammatory. Georgina's fingers dug into his back as he pushed her deeper into the pillows, but she couldn't fight him. Her mouth opened beneath his command, and his invasion left her gasping for more. The wine and the heat and her own desire had her spinning out of control.

When Daniel's hands came to cup her breasts, Georgina moaned into his mouth and felt her bones melt beneath his touch. She was liquid wax and he was the mold shaping her.

When his kiss strayed elsewhere, her eyes flew open. She hadn't even realized she'd closed them. She trembled as the rough stubble of his chin grazed against her cheek, but then his fingers found the peaks of her breasts, and she was lost again.

"Daniel," she whispered desperately, having no idea of what she wanted to say.

"Don't, Georgie," he whispered against her skin. "Don't say anything. This is the way it's meant to be."

Daniel's lips found her earlobe as his hands played skillfully at her breasts, and Georgina couldn't speak had she wanted to. It was all beginning to make sense now. She was coming alive, and he was showing her how. Passion and desire and hunger flooded through her, and nothing he did was enough. There had to be more.

Her hands raced to touch him, to consume him as he was doing to her. The unbuttoned trousers were an inconvenience easily disposed of. Daniel helped her push them off and they fell to one side. Her chemise quickly followed, and they were naked between the sheets.

Daniel didn't let her hesitate. He bent to suckle at her breast, and Georgina rose straight off the bed with a small scream of delight. His arm circled her waist and held her there, pressed against him, and she felt a hardness she had never guessed at probing between her legs. Her hips angled tentatively in that direction, and he helped her, cupping her bottom with his hand, letting her feel the heated length of him.

"Daniel, please," she whispered, not knowing what she asked.

He stopped what he was doing and braced himself over

her, catching her gaze with his own. She looked up into
the steely gray of his eyes, as he pushed her legs apart
with his knees and came between them. She saw the hard
possessiveness in that stare, the look a male animal must
give his mate when he takes her, and she trembled.

"Man and wife, Georgina, till death do us part." It
wasn't a question, but a promise.

She was utterly terrified by the immensity of the moment. This was their wedding then. This was what it
meant to be married. She nodded, and he kissed her, then
his hand came down between them to caress the place
where they would join.

Twenty-six

𝒞

She was wet and ready and heaving anxiously against him, and Daniel couldn't wait any longer. This wasn't a noble or heroic thing he did. It was selfish all the way to the bone. She was innocent and drunk and he was starved for a woman, any woman. It was just convenient that the one in his bed was his wife.

And the moment he moved, she would be his wife forever. Daniel positioned himself carefully and thrust deep within her.

Georgina cried out, but he caught the cry with his mouth, kissing it away as he tried to hold himself still. He was shaking with the need to move, to thrust deeper, to push himself all the way into her until they were both screaming for release, but he could taste the tears on her cheeks. He kissed them away and soothed her with words that made no sense to his ears.

Then he began touching her again, arousing her to that peak where they had been before. He didn't think he could wait much longer. She was so tight around him that it was just a matter of time before he lost it all. He ached too much to do this right.

Then Georgina moved under him, arching herself into him, and Daniel gave a cry of relief and sank deep within her welcoming body. He was beyond caring that she hesitated again. He was finally inside her, making her his own, and nothing could stop him now.

She was still struggling to keep up with him when he made one final thrust and cried out his release with a pleasure that nearly swept him away. Too much wine had made him giddy; he'd never had a head for drink. But nothing could take away the pure ecstasy of having Georgina naked in his arms and crying with need beneath him.

Daniel opened his eyes and looked down into hers. The sparkling blue contained suspicious hints of moisture, but her cheeks were a becoming pink. He pressed a quick kiss to her trembling lips.

"I think . . . I might come to like that," she whispered a trifle breathlessly.

He had shown no self-control and made an utter baboon of himself, but she still tried to make him feel good. Daniel shook his head in disbelief but didn't move from his position. He wasn't ready to leave her yet. It might be a month before he could work off this need he had denied too long. He could feel himself growing hard within her already.

"Good," he murmured, kissing her ear and fondling her breast. "Because we have only just begun."

She looked mildly alarmed, but Daniel was in better control this time. The wine still buzzed through his brain, what remained of it, but he did know one or two things about pleasuring a woman. Knowing he was the first to show her these delights made it doubly sweet for him. He sought her mouth with his while his hands found her breasts, and she was soon moaning with hunger beneath him again.

This time, he plied the place between her legs with care, until she was begging for more, writhing her hips and clutching his arms and pulling at him until neither of them could stand it any longer. This time, when he lifted her buttocks, she was wholly with him.

Daniel tried to be careful, to be conscious of her newly opened tenderness, but Georgina was thrusting as wildly as he had earlier, and he went down in a self-destructive swirl of desire, caught up in the whirlpool of her passion. It was like nothing he had ever done before or would ever do again. It was pure crazed lust that drove him into her again and again until she was exploding with the same ecstasy that she had given him earlier.

His release wasn't any less frantic this time than last, but Daniel had the satisfaction of knowing he had carried Georgina with him. And as he rolled over to his side, momentarily sated, he had the satisfaction of knowing they would never be parted again.

He just hoped the tears she was weeping now were tears of joy.

"Get up you two lay-abeds! The train will be coming any minute now. Daniel, move it!"

The all-too familiar male voice resounded outside the door in accompaniment with a violent knocking. Daniel closed his eyes tighter and groaned. There had been too many mornings in his youth when Tyler had roused him from a warm bed like that. He'd like to throw something at the door right now, but he had the uneasy feeling that he was forgetting something.

The wine caused a mild ache behind his eyes, but it didn't take long to rouse him to the feel of warm flesh beside him when he moved his hand. She moved cautiously away, but memory was returning rapidly. Daniel turned and caught Georgina's waist and stared down into wide blue eyes as the noise continued outside.

"Shut up, Monteigne. We're up and awake," he shouted at the door, but his gaze was busy taking in the dawn-flushed sight beneath him. "Lord, but you're beautiful," Daniel whispered with a certain amount of amazement as his hands curled in thick strands of silver-shot hair and his gaze traveled over the fullness of upthrust breasts to the curve of a tiny waist.

"Shouldn't we be getting up?" she whispered back, lying still and slightly frightened beneath him.

Frightened. Of him. Daniel sucked in his breath and smoothed her hair back. What in hell had he done last night to make her fear him?

He had a vague recollection of a truly violent lovemaking session, of an uncontrollable passion that he had never released before, and he winced, closing his eyes and touching his forehead to hers. He had taken her with less care than he had given experienced whores.

It had to have been the wine. He would never touch a drop again. Taking a deep breath, he touched her cheek and murmured, "I'm sorry," before rolling off her and out of the bed.

Georgina watched him go with trepidation. She didn't know why he apologized. She was terrified of the needs he had aroused in her. She was lying here now trying to deny them but wishing he would come back to bed and show her more. She was starved for more, and she was terrified he would discover how she felt. She was quite certain ladies didn't feel like this. She'd heard enough conversations between her mother and women like Loyolla Banks to know she ought to be grateful that he was getting dressed now. She should be hoping he wouldn't want to do that again until next week. But she lay here like a wanton whore hoping he would change his mind.

This wouldn't do at all. She had promised to learn to be a wife, and wives didn't behave like whores. Carefully pulling the sheets up around her, Georgina looked for a washbowl and wished for a convenience.

As if sensing her desires, Daniel pulled his wrinkled shirt on over his trousers and started for the door. "I'll send someone up with warm water."

He was gone before she could say anything.

The room seemed hollow without him. With the sheet wrapped around her, Georgina wandered to the window, but it overlooked the street. She assumed Daniel would be heading out back to the privy.

Daniel, her husband, until death did them part.

She closed her eyes and offered a fervent prayer. They would be sharing toilets and washbowls for the rest of their lives. She was going to have to learn to live with these terrifying desires coiled up and rattling inside of her. She was going to have to pretend she was a perfectly normal person going about her everyday chores when all she wanted was to be back in that bed with her husband.

She was out of her mind.

She forced herself into the prosaic chores of preparing herself for the day. She was sore between her legs, she discovered as she washed with the water the maid brought up. She had bled, and a hasty glance to the bedsheets showed the stain. She blushed and cursed herself for blushing. She was a married woman now. She was expected to know about these things.

The room smelled of what they had done, and Georgina threw open the window to air it out before anyone could notice. Once washed, she dressed hastily. Daniel would be back at any moment, and she would feel better insulated against these desires if she was buried in clothing.

When he came back, he had his shirt properly tucked in, and he was carrying a paper bag full of rolls and muffins.

"There isn't time to find breakfast. Maybe these will hold us until we get to Cincinnati."

Daniel was unrelentingly attentive as he fastened her buttons, gathered their things, and led her out to join the others to walk to the train station. He was everything an overzealous husband should be to the point of driving Evie and Tyler to exchanging laughing glances and keeping out of their way. But Georgina knew it was all for show. The Daniel she knew had retreated somewhere behind that pleasant facade. His mind wasn't on the false attentions with which he showered her.

That was nothing more than she had expected. His mind was back on his business already. She ought to be glad she hadn't horrified him with her wanton ways. But a trace of her still longed for that romantic encounter of the prior day when his attention had been solely on her.

Well, now that he had what he wanted, that would never happen again, so she might as well get used to it. Despite his protests, Daniel was still a Mulloney, and she had reason to know their single-mindedness. She should be grateful he had agreed to take her as wife so she had a roof over her head. She wouldn't ask for more than he could give.

So she smiled pleasantly and blushed at the Monteignes' gentle teasing and clasped the bag of baked goods tightly in her hands as they found seats on the train. Evie ordered Daniel to sit with Tyler on the other side of the aisle, informing him that he had the rest of his life with Georgina so he couldn't protest a few hours apart. Then she spread her elegant skirts and took the seat beside Georgina for herself.

Georgina offered her the bag, and after they each selected a roll, they passed it over to the men. She felt shy with this elegant woman who seemed so very certain of herself. She had never felt shy in her life. Perhaps it was just because everything in her life had suddenly become so strange. Georgina picked delicately at her roll, conscious that the gown she wore was Evie's and not even her own.

"I must tell you, we were terribly worried when Daniel telegraphed us that he was married."

Georgina looked up, startled. The woman certainly didn't believe in social amenities.

Evie smiled back at her. "Well, we only have a few hours, and I didn't want to waste them. Tyler said we would be imposing if we went home with you, so we're going to stop in Cincinnati."

Georgina crumbled her roll some more. "I'm certain Daniel would love to have both of you. We would have to put you up at the hotel, though. We haven't had time to . . ."

Evie shook her head and touched her hand. "Of course you haven't. I don't care what anyone says, getting married is a shock to the system. You've always been one person and suddenly you're two and it's not easy making all the adjustments." She sent Georgina a penetrating look. "And if you don't do anything to prevent babies, you'll be three real soon. I don't suppose Daniel bothered to take care of that, did he?"

Georgina's eyes widened with shock. She hadn't even given that any consideration. Babies. Good lord above, what would she do with babies?

Evie took her silence for agreement. "Bother the man. I hope Tyler is giving him a good talking to right now. You can't have known each other very long. It's obvious Daniel has gone on one of his heroic exploits again and you've got caught up in it. I can't say I'm sorry. He's needed a wife, but there hasn't been time enough for you to know each other. Drat it, I wish Tyler would let me go back with you. You're going to need help."

Georgina had to offer a smile at this amazingly accurate assessment of their predicament. Evie obviously knew Daniel very well. "I mean to make him a good wife, Mrs. Monteigne. You don't need to worry."

Evie rolled her eyes heavenward. "You would have to be a true heroine to make a wife to Daniel. Call me Evie. We're family, and we're going to be friends. You're going to need one if you mean to live with Daniel."

Thinking of the man with the six-gun, the one who had apparently climbed over a train roof to get to her, Georgina began to have some inkling of what Evie was saying. She bit her lip and asked anxiously, "He isn't always that way, is he? I mean, he seems so nice, and he laughs all the time, and he's so easy to talk to."

Evie nodded, and the flowers on her hat bounced. "Yes, he is. Don't get me wrong. Daniel is special. You'll not find another man like him in all the world. My children love him. He always plays with them. He has the patience of a saint sometimes."

She turned and gave Georgina a sharp look. "He hasn't told you about his childhood, has he?"

"He hasn't told me anything," Georgina whispered sadly. "I didn't even know he was a Mulloney until the day we married."

Evie sent the two men laughing across the aisle a furious glance. "That figures. And I thought Tyler would make a good example for him to follow. I should have known better." She turned back to Georgina. "Daniel has his reasons, and you'll have to blame his less honest moments on me and Tyler. We weren't a very good influence."

She tucked the pin more safely into her hat and sought words to explain. "Daniel is a Mulloney in name only, you know," she began thoughtfully. "His family sent him away right after he was born. He never knew them until recently."

"Right after he was born?" Shocked, Georgina stared at her. "How could they send a baby away?"

Evie shrugged. "I've never met them. I've always thought they must have horns and tails, myself. But the excuse probably had something to do with the fact that Daniel wasn't expected to live. Something went wrong when he was born. Now that I know a little something about childbirth, I imagine it must have been a breech. He may have been born blue and they thought even if he lived, he would never be right. And then there was his leg." She lowered her voice to a whisper as she glanced in Daniel's direction. "Whoever delivered him broke his leg when he was born, and they didn't set it. He came screaming into this world and didn't stop even when he arrived in St. Louis and was delivered to the nurse who raised us."

Georgina stared at her in shock. "St. Louis? They sent a sick infant all the way to St. Louis? They had to be mad."

"Nanny was very good. I'm certain they thought they were doing what was best. And St. Louis was on the river, more easily accessible than most places. It made sense. Even if Daniel lived, he was going to be a cripple, or worse. If they sent him far enough away, they probably figured he would never work his way back again."

"A cripple?" Georgina threw a hasty glance to her husband, who was now playing a game of cards with Tyler, the crumpled bag empty of baked goods between them. "He limps sometimes, but I certainly wouldn't call him a cripple."

"But he was." Evie rummaged in her satchel and found a pot of lip cream which she applied carefully. "Daniel grew up unable to walk without the help of a cane, and his balance then was precarious. He could never play with other children, so Nanny kept him home with her. He grew up learning about life from books. I thought you ought to know that. Daniel still has this funny idea that life ought to be like books, that right should always prevail, and heroes always win."

"And fair maidens should always be rescued," Georgina finished what Evie had left unspoken.

"Exactly." Satisfied with the result in her mirror, Evie set it down and turned to the woman beside her. "That gentle, sweet-natured man still thinks he ought to be more like the Pecos Martin of his childhood dreams, and that devil of a husband of mine and his friends taught him just how to go about it. You didn't marry one man, Georgina, you married two. And one of them hasn't the foggiest notion of what to do with heroines after he's rescued them."

Georgina leaned her head back against the seat and stared out the window at the fields rattling by. She rather thought Evie might be just a little bit wrong about that last part. Pecos Martin knew what to do with women, all right. Unconsciously, she pressed a hand to her abdomen and felt the aching in the place where they had been joined. She just thought maybe it was whores and not heroines with whom Pecos might be most familiar.

Twenty-seven

%

They waved Evie and Tyler off at the train station in Cincinnati. Then Daniel took her hand and led her down the platform.

"Well, Mrs. Mulloney, shall we go home, or would you prefer to wait for the next train and go wherever it takes us?"

Georgina started slightly at the sound of her new name, but his words rapidly captured her attention. There was nothing she would like better right now than to run and hide in some faraway city where no one knew her, where she could learn to deal with her embarrassing predicament without the watchful eyes of people who had known her all her life. She wanted to be the child she once was, the one who knew the world was a happy place and everything would be all right because Daddy made it so. But she wasn't.

Georgina turned her eyes up to her husband's concerned face. They had been stiff and nervous with each other ever since Evie and Tyler had gone. She didn't see any immediate resolution, but she knew enough now to know the answer he expected. "Your father still thinks he's running a slave plantation. Who's going to correct that if we don't go home?"

Although there were shadows of strain behind his eyes, Daniel smiled and brushed her hair with his hand. "Then come on, Miss Merry, the train's fixing to leave. It's time to head back."

They had made this trip together once before. That

time they had laughed and teased and behaved outrageously with each other. That had been before, when she was still a child. Perhaps she had given herself away even then. Had Daniel seen it? Was that why he had allowed her into his life? Because he had seen the wanton that she was and wanted her the way a man desires a whore?

Georgina's cheeks flooded with embarrassment. She clutched her hands in her lap and stared out the window. She didn't want to know what Daniel thought of her. They were married. They would have to make the best of it.

Daniel watched sadly as Georgina closed her eyes and pretended to sleep. He had taken something magical away from her and destroyed it. He didn't know how to undo whatever he had done. She was afraid of him, and rightly so. He didn't know himself anymore.

His stomach clenched in a spasm of pain as he remembered how he had taken her last night, not once, but twice. She had every reason to fear he would lose control and do that to her again. He couldn't even tell himself that he wouldn't do it again. Even knowing he must have hurt her very badly, he was aching to have her again. He couldn't keep his thoughts from straying to their bed, of dragging her up the stairs and tearing her clothes off, and of making mad, passionate love to her for the rest of the day and night.

He was becoming obsessed with the notion. Sex had never been an extremely important part of his life. It was something one did when the time was right. The rest of the time he had been quite content with his books and printing presses and horses and whatever interests he was involved with at the time. He had always been surrounded by women. They were there to laugh with, to talk to, to flirt with upon occasion. But they hadn't been the kind of women he would take to his bed and practically rape. Neither was Georgina. But that's what was on his mind now. He was sitting here peaceably beside her on a public train, but he was so hard his trousers pinched.

Loins aching, Daniel struggled with this new problem life had dealt him. Surely, his obsession with his wife was a temporary aberration that he would overcome with time and work. Georgina was a lady, and he had a proper respect for ladies. It was just a matter of getting back into their regular routines. He would give her time to get over the discomfort, then he would take her properly, with the gentleness that she deserved. He didn't want her to regret marrying him. He adjusted himself uncomfortably while his wife slept.

Georgina woke when the train pulled into the Cutlerville station. Determined to do things properly and not to frighten her anymore, Daniel talked of what needed to be done when they got back to the office. She brightened somewhat as she made suggestions for his next edition. This was something they could share without the shadows and restraints that marred their hasty marriage, and he felt a measure of relief that one island of sanity still remained in their lives.

Seeing the half-grown boy being towed down the street by the powerful German shepherd as they arrived at the office, Daniel wasn't certain that perspective could be relied upon for long. Leaving Georgina at the door, he rushed to grab Max's leash before the dog could strangle himself with unrestrained joy at his arrival.

"I took care of Max while you were gone," Douglas proudly announced the obvious.

"And Max and I thank you. Come upstairs and let's see if we can't give you something for your trouble. How're your sisters?"

The boy rushed up the stairs ahead of them, chattering as he ran. "They've been holding meetings and talking to the other ladies and acting like everything is going to be all right, but I think something's wrong and they're not saying. Egan was over the other night."

Daniel and Georgina exchanged glances, but Daniel was the one who spoke. "What did he want? It's not the first of the month."

Douglas slid to a halt in front of the office door. His eyes were as old as an adult's as he turned to face them. "I know. That's why I know something is wrong. I think he's going to evict us."

Daniel cuffed the boy's head gently and opened the door, pretending an ease he didn't feel. "Well, then, I guess you'll just have to move into this place with us, won't you?"

The boy shouted his approval and slid across the wooden floor. "We could turn out papers every day then. We'd be rich."

Daniel gave Georgina a rueful look. "I think we need to teach the lad a little about labor and economics."

"Not to mention marketing and sales. Why don't we send him out to solicit advertisements?"

"Miss Merry, you are a genius." Daniel bent to kiss her cheek and felt her stiffen. He brushed his lips across her hair instead. This was going to be harder than he thought.

He handed Douglas a few pennies for taking care of Max, then pushed him gently toward the door. "Tell your sisters they may hold their meetings here if that would help and have them let us know when the next one will be so we may attend. And if Egan comes around again, let me know at once."

"Yes, sir!" Douglas danced happily out the door, jingling the coins in his hand.

Daniel turned to his wife, who had frozen into a motionless statue at his touch. "Well, Georgina, this is it. Behold your new home to do with as you wish. I had better go and see what Egan is up to now."

Daniel departed with an odd sense of relief at having something constructive to do to keep him away from his wife. He refused to start counting the hours until he dared approach her physically again.

Georgina stared out the window at the workers filing slowly into the factory across the street on Monday morning. She hugged herself against the struggling sense of emptiness inside her.

Daniel hadn't come to bed these last nights. She'd found him asleep in his easy chair in the office, books lying open and scattered all around him. She wasn't certain what to make of it.

She didn't know what to make of these aching feelings

inside her, either. It had been over two days since Daniel
had first taken her to his bed, and she could still feel him
inside of her. She could easily recall how he had felt beneath her fingers, the heat and texture and strength of
him. And she could scarcely stop thinking of how he had
lifted her in his palms and come into her until she was
filled to overflowing with him, until she was convulsed
with the need of him. It had seemed so perfect and right
at the time.

She closed her eyes as the throbbing began again. She
had felt very married at that moment. She had felt valu-
able and wanted. Daniel had been shaking with desire
when he had taken her. She knew she couldn't be mistaken in that. The need in his eyes had been as strong as
the desire she felt. She had been certain that feeling
would grow stronger and become something special.

Instead, they were farther apart now than they had been
before he had taken her. It had to be her fault, but she was
at a loss as to how to repair it. She had gone over Evie's
words forward and back, but she couldn't find a single
clue to Daniel's behavior. She could only conclude that
either her wanton behavior had appalled him, or his need
was only a temporary and fleeting thing.

In either case, she was going to have to find a life of
her own to fill this emptiness. She wasn't made for sitting
around and moping all day. She had time and energy to
spare, and she had an inkling of an idea of how to use it.

But first she would have to retrieve her clothes.

When Daniel came home some time later, she was
gone. Terror swept through him as he searched all the
rooms and the roof, finding the only trace of Georgina in
a trunk of clothing that hadn't been there before. Had she
left him? That was difficult to believe if she had gone to
the trouble of recovering her clothes. And if not, had she
been kidnapped again? The terror of that first time still
lodged deep in his heart.

He didn't know where to begin to search. Should he
start with the Mulloneys under the assumption they were
responsible for her disappearance? Should he go to the
Harrisons in hopes she had just gone visiting? As his gaze

drifted to the window, his lips set in a tight line. He at least had a starting place.

Daniel knew he had found her the minute he opened the office door to Hanover Industries and heard the laughter. It took a moment before anyone turned to see him standing there, and he used the time to study the scene.

Georgina was modeling a lady's chemise on the outside of her gown, pointing to the lace and trimmings as she explained what she wanted done, occasionally striking a mocking pose as she pictured the garment with the neck opening tied too tight or the ribbons falling loose. Daniel was reminded vividly of how she had appeared with a similar chemise partially undone and nothing on under it. He was beginning to believe Evie was right. Men had only one thing on their minds.

Two of the seamstresses from the factory were laughing at her actions while correcting some of Georgina's suggestions with their working knowledge of what it was possible to do with the machines that they had. The gray-haired secretary Daniel remembered from a previous visit was presiding over this with a notepad and pencil, but he wasn't certain how she managed to take notes from a conference like this one. Sheer exuberance seemed to be the name of the game here, but she wasn't complaining, and neither were the participants.

When Georgina climbed up on a crate to model a wrapper over the chemise, she finally saw him, and a smile instantly lit her face. Daniel felt the warmth of that smile seep straight into his bones, but then she remembered herself, and she hastily disrobed and came forward to greet him properly.

"Daniel, what are you doing here? I thought you were out digging up dirty details on Mr. Egan."

"I was hungry, and I came looking for my wife." Daniel watched carefully as the double entendre went right by Georgina's innocent little mind.

Her brow puckered with worry. "I hadn't realized it was that late." She threw a glance over her shoulder at the workers discreetly waiting out of hearing. "Could you wait just a little while longer? I want to get them started on these new style changes right away."

"I can wait, but Georgina"—he took her hand—"are you certain you ought to be doing this? Your father could come back at any minute. Or my father could come in and order the place shut down. Or he could send Egan over here to clean house. This isn't the safest place in the world for you to be."

Daniel had never noticed the obstinate set of Georgina's chin before. He marveled at it now as she spoke.

"These women won't have jobs if this place closes down. Even if there isn't any money, I still own part of this business, and until someone comes to tell me otherwise, I'm going to do what I can to keep it going. Give me one of your guns and I'll shoot the first person who tries to stop me."

The thought of Georgina with a gun in her hand was not a pretty one, and Daniel shuddered. "No, ma'am. If there's any shooting needing to be done, I'll be the one doing it. You just send over to the office for me. I'll be right there if you need me."

She smiled vaguely, patted his arm, and returned to her fashion show. Daniel had no choice but to wander back to his office alone.

She didn't appear even after the lunch whistle blew. When it whistled again to indicate it was time for the workers to return to work, Daniel fixed himself a sandwich from bread and cheese and went back to working on his lead article. He had spent the better part of his life amusing himself. There was no reason he needed a wife now to fill the empty hours.

The furious knock at the door with the resulting crazed bark of the dog some time later startled him out of his concentration. Yelling at Max to settle down, Daniel called for the visitor to enter. The door was never locked. He thought everyone knew that.

The man entering now knew it, too, but Daniel supposed Peter was showing an excess of politeness by not walking in on a newlywed couple. Daniel hid his amusement as his brother looked carefully around before entering entirely. He wasn't certain which Peter feared most: walking in on a revolutionary committee or Georgina in dishabille.

Daniel set his pencil down and leaned back in his chair, crossing his arms over his chest as he looked his younger brother over. Peter didn't look like he'd slept in a week. He was still dressed in his normal immaculate suit and starched linen, but an aura of untidiness clung to him. The handkerchief in his coat pocket was crushed, the suit was slightly rumpled, and his thick, dark hair needed cutting. The boy's mind was obviously tackling a problem he hadn't solved.

"Georgina isn't here," Daniel said conversationally when Peter didn't immediately speak.

"It's you I want to talk to." Peter's voice was harsh, but a hint of uncertainty edged it. He glared at Daniel. "I want to know who you really are and what you want. And don't give me any more cock and bull about being my brother. Your grave is in the family cemetery."

Daniel chuckled. "How touching. Did I get a monument? Did I rate an angel and an inscription about being known for so short a time but loved just the same?"

Peter scowled. "Daniel Ewan Mulloney is dead. Did you really think you could walk in here and claim to be heir to Mulloney Enterprises?"

"Hell, I hadn't even intended telling anybody who I was until you pulled your little stunt. But the more I look at what Mulloney Enterprises is doing to this town, the more I think somebody with a backbone ought to step in. Can those pretty suits mean that much to you that you'll allow a family to be thrown into the streets to keep them?"

Peter leaned over the table and grabbed Daniel's shirt front. "Mulloney Enterprises is none of your business. If you know what's good for you, you'll get the hell out of town now."

Daniel grabbed his brother's wrists and applied pressure where it would hurt most. The grip on his shirt immediately slackened, and he shoved Peter away. "This is Georgina's home even if her family resorts to kidnapping to save the family business from our father's clutches." Peter's look of startlement gave Daniel some sense of satisfaction.

He plunged on. "I'm not going anywhere until Georgina's ready to go. After you leave here, why don't you go look for my death certificate? Then find the midwife who delivered me and ask about the baby with a crooked leg born to the mighty Mulloneys. If you an get that far, then you're ready to talk to your father's attorneys. They have the records showing the checks mailed to St. Louis for every month of my life until I came of age." Daniel rose behind the table and leaned over it. "Then do us both a favor. Go ask my mother if she knew I was alive. I'd like to know what kind of monsters created me."

Daniel caught Peter's furious swing and shoved him toward the door. The huge dog coming to stand at his feet and growling prevented any further attack.

Eyes glaring with fury, Peter stopped at the door before leaving. "I'll make you regret this, whoever you are. I'll not let you hurt my mother. She's suffered enough as it is."

He turned around and walked out. Daniel ran his hand through his hair as he watched him go. His mother was the one missing piece in this entire puzzle. Could the woman who had borne him really have let her first-born son be given away? Or did she even know he was alive?

So far, he hadn't had the heart to find out.

Twenty-eight

G eorgina came through the office door that evening dragging an unwilling Janice after her.

"Janice says Egan means to evict them at the first of the month. What are we going to do about it?"

"*We*, my dear, are going to do nothing about it. *You* are going to stay out of it entirely." Daniel stood up and stretched the knotted muscles of his bad leg. He was relieved to see Georgina home and in fine fettle, but he had to put a stop to her dangerous notions.

She dropped Janice's hand and placed her fists on her hips. "All right, Mr. Know-it-all, what are *you* going to do about it?"

Daniel sent Janice an apologetic look. "Technically, there is nothing anyone can do about it. ABC has a right to remove any tenants they consider undesirable. The houses belong to them."

Janice looked resigned. "That's all right. We really can't keep up the rent much longer anyway. My great-aunt knows of a boarding house that is much cheaper."

Daniel crossed his arms over his chest. "I didn't say that was the only alternative. ABC could be bought out by someone else. The management of their houses could be turned over to someone a little more conscientious than Egan. Or lacking that, the tenants could strike the owners where it hurts."

Both Janice and Georgina looked at him with interest. He could almost see their minds spinning, ready to keep up with him. They both seemed to catch on at the same time, but Georgina was the first to speak.

"If all the tenants refused to pay their rent until their conditions were met, they couldn't throw everyone out, could they?"

"They could, but if those houses are heavily mortgaged and they need the rent money to cover the payments, they won't."

More certain of Daniel than Janice was, Georgina said, "And the houses are mortgaged, aren't they?"

Daniel beamed at her in approval. "Mulloney believes in leveraging. Everything he owns is mortgaged to the hilt."

Georgina threw her arms around his neck and kissed his cheek. Before she could realize what she was doing, Daniel caught her waist and held her beside him. He figured he was grinning like a fool, but he liked having the little firecracker in his arms. She didn't put up a struggle, he noticed.

"I don't expect you to handle this one, Janice," he said to the wide-eyed woman watching them. "You do whatever you think is best for your family. I'm going to start talking to the men tonight. I figure word will get to their wives soon enough, and it should be all around the neighborhood by the end of the week. I don't think we'll have any difficulty persuading people not to pay rent."

"What about Egan?" Janice whispered. "He likes hurting women."

Georgina jerked away and glared at Daniel even before he gave the answer she expected. He shrugged at the accusation he saw in her eyes. "I'll take care of Egan and his cronies when the time comes."

Janice left with an obvious look of relief on her face, but Georgina wasn't so easily seduced by easy promises. As soon as the door closed behind Janice, she demanded, "Who do you think you are? Pecos Martin? You're not a figment of imagination, Daniel Mulloney! You can get hurt just like real-life people."

Daniel knew that. His tendency to ignore it was regrettable, but it wasn't any of her business either. It was his problem, and he would deal with it. He merely smiled and replied, "The people Egan hurts are real-life people, too. Now let's go find something to eat. I'm starved. And then I want to take you dancing."

"Dancing?" Georgina backed away from him and stared at him incredulously. "It's Monday night. Where would we go dancing?"

Daniel smiled into her upturned face and pulled gently on one loosened curl. She was so incredibly lovely, he had difficulty keeping his mind from straying to where he meant this evening to end. "They're giving lessons over at the church. I've always wanted to take dancing lessons."

"Don't be ridiculous." Georgina's tone wasn't anywhere near as harsh as her words. She seemed to be wavering slightly beneath his touch, so Daniel touched her again, stroking her cheek. Her blue eyes blinked helplessly. "I learned how to dance a million years ago. Why would you want to take me dancing?"

"Because a local orchestra will be playing, and because I've never had a chance to woo you. Wouldn't you like to be courted just a little bit?"

A trifle breathlessly, Georgina asked as his fingers strayed down her throat, "Why would you want to court me? You have what you want already, don't you?"

Daniel wished she was wearing one of those gowns that buttoned down the front. His hand had to be satisfied tracing a line of braiding down her bodice to seek what he could find beneath the layers of clothing separating his flesh from hers. He played with the tip of her breast as he shifted his gaze to hers.

"I have your body, if that's what you mean. Is it too selfish of me to court your affections, too?"

Georgina stared at him, her breath coming shallowly as her heart beat a rapid tattoo beneath his hand. "I didn't think affections mattered to men. They're not inclined to the gentler emotions."

Daniel smiled and brushed his lips across her cheek. "There are a few preconceived notions in that head of yours that need correction." He straightened and released her, and she stepped hastily away, watching him with wariness. A wry look crossed his face as he noted her expression. "I never had a family, Georgina. I've always wanted a real family. I've always thought if I married, it would be for love. I'm willing to work to earn yours."

She was speechless. She stared at him in incomprehension. Men didn't say these things. Men talked about business and politics and sports. Men either didn't care if their wives loved them or took their love for granted. Didn't they?

But Daniel was standing there expectantly, waiting for some response from her. His expression still held some of the elements of boyishness that she found so endearing, but there was something else there behind his eyes, something else she had denied or ignored or never seen through her own selfish blindness. She knew he was a man. She'd never had any doubts about that. He was a strong man, one who had confidence in his own abilities and didn't need to show them off as a weaker man might. He had humor and grace and intelligence enough for ten men. She was quite certain her judgment wasn't faulty in that. Daniel might not be the kind of man who made heads turn at first sight, but he was the kind of man who could command loyalty and respect for a lifetime once a person got to know him.

But he was showing her something more, something he probably had never shown any other woman in his life. He was showing her his weakest point: his loneliness.

That shouldn't be so difficult to believe, but it was. Daniel had everything to make a woman love him. He could easily find someone much better than she, someone who could cook and clean and be the kind of wife he deserved. But he was stuck with her, and he was willing to make the best of it. He wanted her to love him.

Georgina didn't think she could refuse. She wasn't at all certain that she hadn't loved him since the moment he came through the train roof to rescue her, except that events hadn't been terribly clear at the time. They were even less clear now. With her father temporarily out of the picture, she had a factory to run, and Daniel had a family to destroy. She wanted to unite the workers of Mulloney's Department Store, and Daniel wanted to tear his father's throat out and shoot everyone who got in his way. He wanted to bed her as one does a bought woman, and she wanted to be a proper wife, except he treated her like a wife and she behaved like a bought woman. It was all terribly confusing, and she didn't trust her judgment one iota, but she wanted to believe that was sadness and disappointment in his eyes as he turned away at her prolonged silence.

She held out her hand and caught his arm. "Daniel?"

When he turned back, the shadows were gone from his face, and he was smiling vaguely and reaching for his glasses.

She wanted to shake him. Instead, she took the glasses away and put them back in his pocket. "Take me dancing, please?"

"It will be my pleasure, Miss Merry." He smiled and bowed and offered his arm.

Her hesitation had ruined the moment, but it wouldn't happen again, she vowed.

Georgina's vow was already wavering before they had been at the church for less than half an hour. She had bathed and donned her simplest evening dress and put her hair up with a yellow rose Daniel had filched for her from some garden, but she had yet to dance with her husband.

The orchestra was warming up for a waltz right now, and Daniel was across the room, talking with a few men she didn't recognize. She hadn't realized the church he was taking her to wasn't the Presbyterian one her family attended but the Catholic one to which many of the factory families belonged. There were young children here learning their first ballroom dances. And there were young people here who already knew how to dance, but seized the opportunity to meet, talk, dance, and flirt just like at any society party. And then there were the adults who watched over this mélange with amused interest and an occasional cruise across the floor themselves. It was to these adults that Daniel turned his attentions.

So much for romance and affection, Georgina thought glumly as she looked around for something to do. She knew Daniel had promised Janice that he would talk to some of the men about the rent strike, and the opportunity had opened the minute they walked through the door. She had just thought they might have a minute or two to themselves, to start building those affections he claimed to want.

Georgina sensed more than heard the first angry murmurs as they began around the room. Her gaze went to Daniel first, but he was engrossed in a discussion that involved many gesticulations from his companions. He didn't seem to be aware of the undercurrent. She looked over the large hall for some sign of the source, and her gaze fell on a newcomer standing at the door. *Peter*.

It didn't make sense. He had no right being here. These people hated him, but had to work for him, so they could do nothing to show their fear and hatred of the power he wielded. Yet he stood there as if he had no notion of the commotion he was creating, just as she had that first day she walked into the factory. She winced at the memory.

The couples waltzing on the dance floor didn't notice his entrance. Perhaps she could get him out of here before someone created a scene. She had already seen Audrey turn to some of her young friends. They were just the right age to cause trouble. Georgina hurried forward to greet him.

Peter saw her at once and came forward quickly. Perhaps he understood what kind of danger he was placing himself in. Georgina hoped he hadn't come with bad news about her parents. As far as she knew, they had not yet returned. Perhaps something had happened? She caught up with him halfway across the floor.

"Georgina." Peter halted and looked her over closely. "You look lovely. I've been worried about you."

Georgina brushed this nonsense aside. "What are you doing here? Is something wrong? Have you heard from my father?"

Peter took her hand. "I came looking for you. There was a boy at your office playing with the dog, and he said you'd come here." The music hit a high note, and he pulled her toward the dance floor. "Dance with me, Georgie?"

She jerked her hand from his. "I wouldn't dance with a villain like you if you were the last man on earth. Now why are you really here?"

His jaw tightened as he stared down at her. "Do you hate Daniel so much that you must hate me now for forcing this marriage on you?"

Astonishment kept her from answering immediately. Recovering her tongue, she struck out. "Why should I hate Daniel? I abhor violence, and that's what you used against us. Go back where you came from, Peter. You don't belong here."

She started to turn away, but he caught her arm and pulled her back around. "Daniel isn't exactly nonviolent, you know that, Georgie," he reminded her. "I've been gathering a lot of information lately. I'm not the only one he's used his fists on."

Georgina glared at the hand holding her arm. "Get your hand off me, Peter," she replied through clenched teeth. "I'm trying very hard not to create a scene."

"It's too late." The voice came from behind her, a familiar voice with a not-so-familiar edge to it. Georgina didn't even have to look up to know whose arm came out to pull her away. "Daniel," she murmured, stepping back beside him.

Steely gray eyes glared at the handsome young man in rich clothes. "Stay away from my wife, little brother. You gave her up. She's mine now."

A jaw set as stubbornly as Daniel's clenched tighter. "You don't own her. If she's unhappy, I can get her away from you."

Daniel carefully set Georgina behind him and stepped closer to Peter. "Try it, and see what happens."

Georgina pounded her fist against Daniel's back. "Stop this at once, you apes! You're making spectacles of yourselves for no reason. Stop it, or I'll slap you both."

A solid *thunk* smacked against Peter's back before either of the two men could step away. Georgina gasped as the seeds of a green tomato shattered across his coat and slid down his back. As Peter turned furiously to confront his attacker, a barrage of ripe strawberries spattered across his immaculate shirtfront, bouncing off him and striking Georgina and Daniel as well.

Furious that her gown was ruined before the evening had even begun, Georgina leaned over and picked up a handful of the juicy fruit, heaving it at the young man she saw darting into the crowd.

As her wild throw splattered against an elderly lady in widow's weeds, Daniel groaned, "I wish you hadn't done that," and pushed her toward the door.

The room suddenly seemed to erupt in splattering fruit and cookies, flying lemonade, and thrown fists. Daniel caught a chair heaved in Peter's direction and flung it to the floor, but he couldn't drown out the curses and threats that came from all around them. Peter grabbed the chair and used it as a shield against two young men who rushed in with fists upraised, but he couldn't shield himself on all sides. More fruit struck his turned back, and bright patches of red bled together with the green.

With a sigh of regret Daniel swung his fist and floored the man coming up on Peter from behind. Shoving his younger brother through the shouting, cursing melee and capturing Georgina by the waist, he pushed his way through the rioting crowd.

They were no longer the main attraction. Fights had erupted all across the floor as old grievances gave way to new, and flying objects sent tempers soaring. Leaving Peter to fend off his latest attackers with the chair, Daniel grabbed Georgina, swung her up in his arms, and pushed and shoved his way to the door. Peter followed close on his heels.

The brawl was already spilling out of the lighted hall and into the darkened alleys around it. Still carrying Georgina, Daniel hurried to the safety of a lighted thoroughfare. The sounds of the melee soon fell far behind them. ►

"Daniel, put me down." Georgina struggled to gain her

feet, succeeding only as Peter came up behind them, wiping strawberry juice from his forehead.

"There for a moment I almost imagined you were defending me." Peter gave the tall, lean man shielding the woman behind him a look of curiosity.

"You brought it on your own damned fool self. I was protecting my wife. You'd better get the hell out of here before some of them come looking for you."

Georgina heard the odd note of defensiveness in her husband's voice. Daniel had every reason to despise Peter, yet he did nothing now to show his contempt. She had seen him divert the blows meant for Peter. Another man would have used the opportunity to beat his enemy to a pulp, but Daniel had protected Peter with his fists and strength. Uncertainty kept her from intervening.

"I wanted to talk with Georgina."

Whether that was an excuse for his appearance at the dance or a demand for her attention now couldn't easily be discerned. It didn't matter. Daniel kept Georgina protectively behind his back.

"Get lost, little brother. She's my wife now and none of your concern. And don't come back this way again if you know what's good for you. You're persona non grata in these environs."

"The cowboy speaks Latin. How fitting." Shoving his handkerchief back in his pocket, Peter turned his tailored back on them and strode away.

It was only then that Georgina realized Daniel had just flung a red flag in his brother's face for her sake. He had given up all hopes of coming to terms with the only family he had in favor of the one he hoped they would make together.

She wasn't certain if she was honored, terrified, or just plain dismayed at the thought.

Twenty-nine

ℰ

They were both silent as they climbed the stairs and by mutual agreement entered the bedroom rather than the office. Georgina was glad that Daniel stayed with her rather than going to his easy chair, but now that he was here, she was nervous of his presence. Somehow, tonight, he seemed to fill the room with his energy, and she was acutely aware of their physical differences. She didn't mistake him for an older brother or a platonic friend anymore.

She almost jumped when Daniel caught the back of her gown and began unfastening the hooks there. Her stomach knotted as she realized what this action must mean. She had to remember she was a lady and behave circumspectly so she wouldn't disgust him again, but what she wanted more than anything was to turn around and throw herself into his arms and beg for his kisses.

That was a rather dismaying notion, and Georgina stood silently for his ministrations. She wanted Daniel to care for her, but she hadn't the slightest idea of how to go about it. She was terrified she would drive him away as she had every other man in her life. She just wasn't the type of woman who attracted men. She knew that. It had never mattered until now, and she had given it little thought in the past. She was regretting her carelessness now.

"Well, Pecos Martin was never much of a ladies' man." Humor tugged at his drawl as Daniel unfastened the last hook and stepped away. "I guess I'd better find another hero to emulate if I'm going to try this courting business."

Georgina held her bodice in place as she turned around to look at him. His cowlick had fallen in his face again despite all his attempts to keep it slicked back. She wanted to brush it back from his forehead, but something in the glitter of his eyes kept her from reaching out. They stood in the light of only one lamp, and the shadows between them were too great.

"I've been courted before," she murmured uncertainly. "This is not a particularly unusual end to my relationships. When I was twelve, I went to a garden party with a boy and fell out of a tree and broke my arm while racing him to the top. Last year, in London, I attended a perfectly extravagant ball with a viscount. We ended up arguing over my mode of dress, and when I threw champagne at him, he poured wine on me. When I looked around, we had an audience laying wagers on the outcome. I won't bore you with all the other disasters in between those two episodes."

Daniel chuckled and pulled a pin from her hair, sending a carefully arranged curl tumbling to her shoulder. "The Incorrigible Miss Merry. Maybe we're made for each other. Did Evie tell you I once blew up the main street of town?"

"Really?" Laughter came easily with Daniel, and Georgina felt a surge of warmth as he continued taking down her hair. She wasn't certain if it was for his understanding or his closeness, and she didn't care.

"When this is all over, I want to take you down south to meet some of my friends. They'll like you." Daniel dropped the handful of hairpins on the stacked crates she used as a dressing table.

Georgina didn't want to know what "this" referred to. She prayed he meant the fight with Mulloney's and not what was between them. She didn't want what was between them to ever end. Daringly, she placed a hand on his chest and fiddled with his shirt stud. "How can I make you like me?" she asked softly, staring at his chest, not daring to look upward to meet his eyes. She felt his soft intake of breath, but didn't dare look up.

"I've liked you since the first day we met, Georgina. To tell the truth, I more than like you." Daniel caught his fingers in her hair and pulled her head back until she met his eyes.

Georgina tried not to gulp at what she saw glittering there behind the gentle gray. His brows were a sharp brown line that pulled together with the intensity of his emotion, and his lean jaw set with a determination she was beginning to recognize too well. Perhaps she was beginning to see deeper than a person's surface after all. It certainly wasn't the genial journalist she was seeing now.

"I want you, Georgina," he murmured, lowering his head until his lips brushed against her ear. "I don't want to frighten you again, but I don't want to sleep in the chair, either."

She didn't know what she was supposed to do. Should she turn her back and begin obediently undressing so he could assert his husbandly rights? Should she slide her arms around his neck as she longed to do and show him that she wasn't in the least frightened? Should she just wait and let him do as he would?

Taking a breath, she dared to do as she wanted. Let him think her a loose woman. She had never spent much time trying to be something she wasn't; why start now? Georgina lifted her arms and slid them around Daniel's neck and stood on her toes to reach his lips with hers.

He grabbed her waist with both arms, lifted her from the floor, and eagerly accepted everything she gave him. Georgina's joy shot through them both as she returned his kiss with a ferocity that nearly had them tumbling into bed before they could undress.

Georgina's bodice had fallen down with her impulsive gesture, but she scarcely noticed until she felt the skirt tapes give way beneath Daniel's quick fingers. Her gown lay in a puddle on the floor as he lifted her out of it and carried her down to the bed.

She lay in corset and petticoat beneath him as he leaned over her, and she didn't feel in the least ashamed.

Georgina drew her fingers over Daniel's lean jaw and smiled as he bent to ply her mouth with kisses again. She was beginning to like his kisses much too well.

Daniel pushed himself off her and stared down into her face as one hand went to unfasten the hooks of her corset. "How do you feel about children, Georgina?"

The sensation of his strong, long-fingered hand inserting itself between her corset and her breasts clashed with the cool control of his words, but the combination made some insane sense in her mind. Georgina reached to tangle with a man's shirt studs for the first time in her life.

"I always wanted brothers and sisters," she murmured irrelevantly as she dropped the first stud to the floor and found her fingers brushing warm flesh.

"They start out as babies, you know. Tyler told me we should have had this discussion before we married."

The corset came unfastened, and Daniel lifted Georgina's back and pulled it free to fling it to the floor. The exquisite freedom made her tingle even before his hand came to circle her chemise-clad breast. Delicious waves of warmth swept through her as Daniel's fingers found the aching tip through the thin material.

She wasn't even certain she was capable of speech, but valiantly, she tried to reply to the question he wasn't asking. "I'll give you babies, Daniel. I think I would like to have your baby very much."

"I've always wanted several, Georgina," he warned, even as his hands went to the fastenings of his trousers.

"Then we had better get started, hadn't we?" Just the idea of it surged through Georgina with a primeval need that sharpened every touch to an unbearable intensity. She wanted to make a baby, and she wanted this man to give it to her. She put her hands around Daniel's neck and pulled him closer so she could feel all of him against her.

That movement probably saved him from grievous injury. Glass spattered across the room at the same time the street echoed with the sound of a shotgun blast.

Diving down to the bed, Daniel grabbed Georgina's waist and rolled them both to the floor. More blasts followed. Glass shattered and spun crazily across the bare floor. He rolled them under the high bed and out of the hurricane of flying shards. Across the hall Max began to howl with rage.

"Stay here." Pulling the cover down from the bed, Daniel rolled himself in it and started out into the room.

"Daniel!" Georgina tried to hold him back, but it was akin to holding back the wind. He was gone before she could do more than touch a hand to his arm.

The many panes of the towering windows gaped with splintered holes as Daniel bent over and ran to the door, crunching the glass on the floor beneath his shoes. Georgina cried out as another blast sent more glass and pellets flying through the room, but Daniel made it to the door without any noticeable injury.

She knew where he was going, and her heart lodged in her throat as she waited. He kept his guns locked in a chest in the pressroom where the boys couldn't get at them. She knew he was cursing his caution right now, but she was thanking the good Lord. She wanted those villains gone before a shoot-out ensued.

It looked as though her prayers were going to be answered. The street grew quiet, and the few remaining panels of glass were left unshattered as Daniel came back carrying his rifle. Georgina stayed where she was as he stood against the wall and searched the street. She hadn't known how hard her heart was pounding until she saw Daniel standing there, looking murderous with a rifle cocked and ready in his hands. She held her fist to her mouth to keep from crying out while he scanned the street. He was fully capable of shooting anyone who emerged from the darkness.

He cursed and blew out the lamp and waited a while longer, but apparently none dared show their faces, not even the police. Georgina gingerly reached for her fallen corset and used it to sweep a path through the glass beside the bed so she could get out.

Still cursing, Daniel set the rifle aside and came over to help her. When they'd cleared a safe place, she rolled out and found herself clasped tightly in strong arms. She gave in to the urge to cling to his greater strength. Wrapping her arms around his waist, Georgina buried her head against his chest and let him soothe the shivers quaking through her.

"Why would anyone do that?" she whispered against his shirt.

"I haven't exactly made myself welcome in these parts," Daniel reminded her. "I just hadn't thought they'd endanger you, too." He stroked her hair, smoothing it down her back as he held her.

"But everybody around here likes you," she protested. "It's just Mr. Mulloney and my father that you've made mad."

"And the other businessmen like them, and the thugs that they hire. The circle grows wider with every editorial I publish. If this was Texas, they'd have tried to tear up the press by now. I'm sorry, Georgina, I just thought it would be a little more civilized here."

"What are we going to do?" Georgina didn't want to let go, but she felt the tension in him building. She was beginning to learn that when Daniel got tense, unpleasant things happened. She stood back and looked up at him.

He was glaring at the shattered windows with a thoughtful frown. When she pushed away, he turned his gaze to her, and his expression softened slightly. He pushed a fallen curl from her face and smiled. "We're going to take that old pallet back to the pressroom and sleep where there aren't any windows tonight."

That seemed reasonable. Georgina shook out a sheet and gathered up their pillows. The broken glass could wait until morning when she could see what she was doing. It crunched beneath her shoes as she followed Daniel across the hall to the office.

The office hadn't been lit, and the vandals had left the window in here alone. Max came trotting up to lick Georgina's hand, calm now that the danger had ended. Without a lamp, the room was filled with shadows. She stood back and waited as Daniel dragged the pallet to the windowless pressroom. This wasn't exactly the romantic encounter that she had anticipated.

It didn't get any better, either. Once they had the bed

made up, Daniel picked up his rifle and kissed her cheek. "Get some sleep. I'll find a safer place for you to stay in the morning." And he walked out.

Georgina stared down at the empty pallet incredulously. She'd made her bed, and now she supposed she would have to sleep in it—without her husband. Why did that not surprise her?

She jerked open the door between the two rooms and found Daniel settling into the chair, the rifle across his lap and Max at his feet. "If they're coming back, I don't want to be asleep." She stepped through the doorway, suddenly aware that she wore nothing but her chemise and drawers.

"There isn't anything you can do. One of us ought to get some sleep out of this night. Go on to bed, Georgina. I'll be fine."

He wasn't even looking at her. That annoyed her more than his words. She wanted him to look at her. "I didn't marry Pecos Martin, I married Daniel Mulloney. I wish you would make up your mind who you are."

He looked up then, but she couldn't see his face in the darkness. "I'm still Daniel Mulloney. Pecos would be out chasing the varmints down. Now go to bed, Georgina. I'll catch up on my sleep tomorrow when you're up and about to keep an eye on things."

She went then, knowing there was no other argument she could offer if he didn't want what she tried to show him. She shut the door softly behind her.

Daniel stared at that closed door for a long time afterward, feeling the ache deep down inside him, longing to take those few steps to where she waited.

But she deserved a whole lot more than he had to offer right now, and he wasn't starting any babies until he could keep them and their mother safe, no matter how much the rest of him longed to do so.

Ignoring the pain in his loins, he waited patiently for their attackers to come back and investigate the damage they had done.

He must have dozed sometime after dawn. Daniel woke to the sound of Max's low growl, and his eyes instantly lifted to the door separating him from Georgina. The door was open, and she was standing there, the morning sunlight caressing the tumble of curls down her back. One strap of her chemise was falling off her shoulder, but she held the cloth carefully in place with her arms crossed beneath her breasts. She couldn't disguise the full swell of those lovely curves however, and Daniel swallowed hard at the sight revealed. She was doing this to him deliberately.

"What happened to that slinky piece you wore the night you came here?" he couldn't keep himself from asking.

"You didn't give me time to put it on last night," she informed him coldly.

He caught what she didn't say easily. "You mean you've been wearing it the other nights?" The nights he hadn't come to her bed.

She nodded, and a golden curl fell over her shoulder. Daniel drew a deep breath and started from the chair. He was only a man, after all. The admission wasn't difficult for him to make while she was standing there, a goddess of the morning emitting a siren call that even he could hear. Vows made under duress weren't valid when exposed to the morning light.

As Daniel rose and started toward Georgina, Max began a furious howl and dashed to the door, scratching and barking for it to be opened. Torn between the temptation in sheer linen on one hand and warning signs of danger on the other, Daniel halted in mid-stride. His lame leg locked and sent a shooting pain through his muscles.

The door slammed open and Peter stood there. His gaze instantly swept from Daniel still in his formal shirt and trousers to Georgina leaning against a doorjamb in her underwear. His eyebrows shot up as he respectfully returned his look to Daniel, giving Georgina time to duck back into the other room.

It was more than Daniel could stand. With a bellow of rage he reached for Peter's shirtfront and hauled back his fist, slamming it solidly into his brother's jaw, sending him flying backward into the hall.

From behind the pressroom door came the distinct sound of a ladylike voice sighing, "Oh, damn it to hell." A moment later, Georgina stood in the center of the office, wrapped in a blanket, golden hair flying over bare shoulders like a Valkyrie, glaring at Daniel and the man sprawled outside the door.

Without another word she stepped over Peter and disappeared into the bedroom with a loud slam of the door to shut them out.

From his position on the floor Peter rubbed his jaw and commented thoughtfully, "If that's the way you both get up in the morning, you damned well deserve each other."

Thirty

They could hear her crunching across the floor in the other room. A moment later, a trunk lid creaked and they could hear more muttered cursing.

"I'm going to have to go in there and help her," Daniel advised the man still sprawled across the hall, his expression daring Peter to stop him. "Her gowns were all designed for a maid, and we don't seem to have acquired one yet."

Peter propped himself on one elbow and rubbed his aching jaw, testing for broken bones and teeth. "What do you carpet your rooms with, glass? I never heard a floor that crunched before."

"Is that supposed to be a declaration of innocence? Because if it is, I'm not buying it. Save yourself some grief and disappear while I'm gone." Daniel stepped over him and entered the bedroom, carefully closing the door behind him.

A moment later, a hard object crashed against the other side of the door. Sitting up, Peter listened as a few murmured words were exchanged, followed by another distinct crash. He moved out of the line of fire and leaned against the wall just in time for the bedroom door to fly open again. This time when Daniel emerged, he reeked of expensive perfume and the front of his half-open shirt clung to his skin with the smelly liquid. The door slammed behind him.

Shoving his hair back out of his eyes with his hand, Daniel glared at the man sitting on the floor watching with interest. "Are you still here? You like to live danger-ously, don't you?"

"What are you going to do, set Georgina loose? At least she only used lemonade on me. You stink like a polecat. Want me to rub you down in tomato juice?"

Grunting, Daniel stepped back into the office and rum-maged around for a towel in his scattered belongings.

Feeling momentarily safe from another attack, Peter stood up and followed him in. "I never could figure out what sets her off. One minute she's all smiles and flirty eyelashes, and the next she's flinging things and scream-ing. Must be a woman thing." He eyed the rifle by the chair with curiosity.

"Are you still here? A glutton for punishment, aren't you?" Daniel toweled off his chest and glared at his youn-ger brother. Peter was dressed casually this morning in tweed jacket and khaki pants instead of his usual formal suit. Daniel's eyes narrowed with suspicion. "Just what the hell are you doing here anyway?"

Peter shrugged his broad shoulders and shoved his hands into his pockets. "There's no death certificate on file. And I found the midwife. She's a drunk of no use to anyone now, but someone sends her money regularly ev-ery month. She wouldn't tell me anything. I doubt that she remembers anything to tell. I'll have to tell our father that he's wasting his money there."

Daniel's hands clenched into fists at the subtle admis-sion of Peter's words. He responded coolly. "Not filing a death certificate was a rather stupid mistake. I'm certain it could have been done easily enough. There's enough dead babies in those slums to provide as many death cer-tificates as anyone could wish."

Peter shrugged again, but the tension in his stance was evident. "He might have been afraid that he wouldn't have any more sons and kept his options open. That's typ-ical of him."

"How good to know. He might have dragged me back, lame leg and all, if none of you had been born. Now I've got another reason to resent the hell out of you all. Will you get out of here now? I smell something worse in here than Georgie's perfume."

The bedroom door crashed open again. A highly irate figure stalked past and down the hall. Peter turned in time to catch a glimpse of trailing silks and little more. Daniel drifted toward the window overlooking the street.

"I don't suppose you're going to tell me what's going on here?" Peter asked casually.

Counting mentally, Daniel didn't answer until Georgina emerged on the count of one. He watched as she stormed across the street and entered the factory office. "She just walked out on me. I'm going to have to go get her." He turned and glanced without curiosity at Peter. "Why are you still here?"

Peter's face stiffened expressionlessly. "I talked to Mother this morning. She wants to see you."

"Good for her." Daniel started unfastening his shirt studs as he walked toward the hall.

Peter grabbed his arm. "Don't you understand? I had to tell her the whole sordid story. She's thought you dead for twenty-eight years."

Daniel shrugged him off and continued across the hall. "As far as the whole damned family goes, I *am* dead. I don't want any part of it. I've got a wife to look after."

He stepped into the bedroom and closed the door.

Struggling with emotions of his own, Peter clenched and unclenched his fists, waited a few minutes, then started down the stairs. In the past few weeks his life had become a nightmare from which he still hoped he would wake. Losing Georgina had only been the first stroke. Now it appeared as if everything he had once taken for granted would be lost. He wanted to fight the horrifying sensations of loss and betrayal, but in a way, they were opening up a whole new world. Peter didn't want to quite contemplate that yet. He had been taught duty at an early age, and he still had a few duties yet to accomplish.

Daniel listened to him leave without any sign of regret. Last night had finished off any hopes he might have harbored of becoming reconciled with his family. There wasn't any doubt in his mind over who was responsible for almost costing them serious injury, if not their lives. Apparently, his father drew the line at actually killing his unwanted son outright. He just hired thugs to threaten him. But when it came to threatening Georgina, Daniel drew his own line. What had first been an exploratory venture was now full-scale war.

Georgina wasn't surprised when Daniel appeared in the factory office a short while later. She was only surprised that he hadn't come sooner. Ignoring him, she turned back to the foreman she had just been castigating.

"I know you've worked for my father for years. You can work for him again when he returns. But right now, while I'm here, you'd better just get out of my sight. I'll not have that kind of behavior in my factory." For all she knew, her father could return from Chicago or wherever tomorrow, but she derived a great sense of satisfaction from her command.

"You can't fire me. You don't own this place. You're going to cost your daddy a lot of money if you try to get rid of me." Only slightly taller than Georgina and of a wiry build, the foreman pulled himself into a threatening posture as he glared at her.

"Then don't consider yourself fired," Georgina answered sweetly. "Just consider yourself on unpaid vacation. But if you show yourself in this building again, I'll call the police."

Daniel leaned against the wall, not saying a word. The furious foreman sent him a look, but if he'd expected any help from that quarter, he got none. With rage he demanded, "I want the wages owed me right now."

Georgina nodded at the secretary. "Doris, give him a check for what he's owed."

"Your father advanced him a week's salary some time ago. He's never paid it back." Checking her calendar, Doris looked up without expression. "He owes us for three days' pay."

"How fortunate." Georgina continued to smile sweetly. "I'll dismiss you with three days' pay bonus, Mr. Emory. Good day."

She turned around and walked into the office, closing

the door after her without acknowledging Daniel at all. Crossing his arms over his chest, he met the foreman's gaze with equanimity. Emory glared at him, then departed without another word.

Daniel shifted his gaze to Doris. "Tell my wife I'm going to be out for a few hours. If she needs anything, she should send for Douglas Harrison. He'll know where to find me."

Like the good secretary she was, Doris expressed no comment and asked no question, she merely nodded her head and jotted down the name on her notepad.

When Daniel didn't storm her office or send Doris in to fetch her or any of the other things any normal man would have done, Georgina was left to pace restlessly. She didn't dare leave the office for fear he would still be standing there, waiting disapprovingly for her to acknowledge him. And she didn't send for him because she didn't want to face him.

She didn't know what she wanted. It wasn't an unusual state of mind for her, she admitted to herself. She thought she'd wanted to make this factory work as she had wanted to make her marriage work. And she had wanted to help those poor clerks at Mulloney's and the ones forced to live in those deteriorating houses under Egan's jurisdiction. But she didn't know how to do any of that, and the events of last night had left her doubting the wisdom of trying.

She had enough sense to know that whoever had shot out their windows hadn't meant to kill them. They were incredibly careless of their safety and serious injury could have been done, but she was quite certain that would have only been a pleasant side effect for the terrorist. The man had accomplished exactly what he had set out to do: he'd terrified her.

Georgina pulled in her stomach and straightened her shoulders as she realized this. He had meant to terrorize *her*, not Daniel. No one knowing Daniel would think he would be afraid of a few shotgun pellets. Was her father still trying to separate her from Daniel? Or was Artemis Mulloney trying to reach Daniel by scaring her?

She didn't know, but she couldn't let them win. She hadn't walked out this morning because of the shotgun blasts, though no one would know that but she and Daniel. She was going to have to go back and face up to the shambles of their marriage just to defy whoever was after them.

At least Daniel and Peter hadn't been killing each other when she left. That had been the final straw, hearing Daniel fell his own brother with his fists without any provocation whatsoever. Or perhaps there had been some provocation. Daniel probably thought Peter was involved in the shooting. She could have told him that Peter wasn't like that, but Daniel wouldn't have believed her. Her judgment so far hadn't been all that spectacular, so she could scarcely blame him. She just knew it wouldn't solve anything for the brothers to be at each other's throats.

If they were truly brothers. Throwing up her hands in defeat, Georgina slammed out of her office. Thinking wasn't what she did best. She needed action. Relieved to find the office empty of all but Doris, she headed for the factory. The women in there might resent the hell out of her, but they obeyed orders. A few changes in design, and she'd have orders from every department store in Ohio. Mulloney's was falling behind the times.

By the end of the day she had streamlined the undergarment line by producing a more modern pattern which required less fabric. Extremely pleased with herself, she declared five o'clock to be the new closing hour, and listened with no small amount of self-congratulation as the women hurried home in trails of laughter and excitement. Today she had managed to make a difference.

At least she knew about sewing and fashion. What she didn't know about was accounting and finance. Sitting in the deserted office, Georgina stared at the company books as if they were tomes of Greek. She didn't like the numbers written in red. There were too many of them, and the color wasn't reassuring. She thought it might be simpler to just heave these books out and start new ones.

She rifled through the files in her father's desk, finding stacks of bills from assorted manufacturers that hadn't been marked paid. Nothing showed how much was owed Mulloney. That was all right; there weren't any invoices showing the cost of how much was shipped to Mulloney's, either. She hoped the men knew what they owed each other, because she was going to pretend the debt didn't exist until someone showed her a piece of paper with numbers on it.

She wouldn't know what to do with it if they did, but she would worry about that when the time came. Glancing out the office window and seeing the lengthening shadows, Georgina realized the time had come to decide what to do about her personal life. That wasn't quite so easily done as manipulating a few pieces of paper and cloth. Objects could easily be handled. Daniel couldn't.

She was going to have to face Daniel. Straightening out the desk, she reluctantly blew out the lamp and locked up.

The sun was still shining down the length of the street between the buildings as Georgina stepped out. These bricks and boards weren't quite the same as the spacious tree-studded yard of her parents' home, but she didn't particularly miss the difference. Her world had always been made up of people, not trees. And the one important person in her world right now was in that building across the street.

She was going to have to get used to the idea that Daniel was important to her. Georgina rebelled against the notion, not wanting to admit that a stranger who had been thrown into her life a few weeks ago could suddenly become the most important thing in her existence, but deep down, she knew the truth. Daniel was inside of her in more ways than she was willing to admit, in more ways than he knew. Cutting him out would be impossible now.

Sunlight still streamed through the hall windows as Georgina climbed the stairs, but when she opened the office door, she was greeted by the shadows of lamplight.

She looked at the boards covering the room's one window, then looked for some sign of Daniel.

The *thump-thump* of the press told her where he was. Closing the door behind her, Georgina allowed her eyes to adjust to this artificial dusk. She finally realized in addition to the boards on the window, a new object had been added to the decor. A heavy black stove now stood in front of the boarded window, its pipe connected to the board and presumably by some arrangement to the outside. Heat emanated from that end of the room, and a pot sitting on top bubbled and steamed, sending out delicious aromas.

She knew absolutely nothing about kitchens, but the contraption drew her to investigate. She was cautiously stirring a spoon around in the bubbling brew when the press shut down and Daniel appeared carrying the first run of the next day's paper.

Georgina hastily covered the pot and laid down the spoon, discreetly hiding her hands behind her back as she turned around to greet him. He was examining the headline, his spectacles perched on the end of his nose as he frowned at some error needing correction. When he finally looked up, his smile was vague.

"You're home, good." Giving the front page one more glance, Daniel reluctantly laid it aside. "I bought some things down at the market and threw them in a pot. They ought to be done by now."

Nervous now, Georgina glanced about uncertainly. "I suppose we can set that table if I clear off the books. Do we have any plates?"

"Plates?" Daniel took off his spectacles and finally returned to the world in front of him. His blank look turned to a sheepish grin. "I usually just eat out of the pot. I've got some forks around here somewhere."

How could anyone stay angry at a man like that? It simply wasn't possible. Georgina cleared off the table by the chair, turned up the lamp, and neatly laid the forks that Daniel produced beside their places. He took the wooden chair that he had bought some days before, and she settled into the easy chair. Her seat was too low; his was too wide. They looked up at each other and grinned.

"All right, so maybe we're missing a few amenities. I'll find you a proper house just as soon as a few things settle down." Daniel tasted the stew in the pot, burned his mouth, and held the fork away from him to let it cool.

Georgina nodded cautiously, blew on her forkful of food, then gingerly tasted it. Once she got past the heat, she ate the bite hungrily. All it took was an empty belly to appreciate the humbler things in life. "It's good. I didn't know you could cook."

"I can't. I just watched a lot. I was always starving and hovered around the kitchen whenever anyone would let me near. It didn't look like too complicated a task."

They spread the front page out on the table and studied it as they ate. Daniel pulled out his pencil and marked errors as Georgina made suggestions. There hadn't been much time for sensationalism for this edition. Daniel had settled for listing the grievous conditions of the housing owned by ABC Rentals, reported tales of beatings and terroristic tactics by the company's rent collectors, and then listed the owners of ABC as Artemis Mulloney and Mulloney's Department Store.

Georgina didn't know where he had gotten that last piece of information, but Artemis and the store were one and the same to her. She just wished she had her camera so she could have taken pictures of those humble dwellings with their falling roofs and rotten privies. Photographs would have been a good deal more eloquent than words.

Full, she sat back in the chair and opened the paper to peruse the inside.

From across the table Daniel said softly, "You'd better pack your satchel, Georgina. We need to take you over to the hotel."

She lowered the paper without a word and stared at him. She knew that determined expression setting his jaw, and right now, she hated it.

Just as she was beginning to settle in, he was going to throw her out.

Thirty-one

ᘓ

"I'm not going to a hotel." Georgina carefully laid the paper aside and got up, heading for the door. Daniel followed her. "It's not safe here, Georgie. I've got some savings. When the next check comes from my publisher, we'll find a house."

Georgina crossed the hall and entered the bedroom. He'd boarded up these windows, too, and swept up the glass. She should have been the one to do that. She was pretty much a failure at being a wife. She hadn't even been here to cook his dinner—not that she knew how anyway.

"Will you stay in it with me? Or will you be sleeping with your damned press?" Georgina grabbed her satchel and examined the contents. Without a dresser, she had been pretty much living out of suitcases anyway.

"I've got to stay with it right now. Last night was just a warning. They'll be back with worse. I've been through this before, Georgie. You've got to understand . . ."

Georgina threw the satchel on the bed and headed for her trunk. "I understand. I understand you never meant to be married, that I'm in your way, that I'm just another burden for you to bear. I'm tired of people wanting to be rid of me. I'll admit, I'm pretty useless. So I'll just get out of the way. I can learn how to take care of myself."

"Where do you think you're going?"

"To the office. There's a couch there that will suit me just fine. I don't need you. I don't need anybody." Georgina suspected she was beginning to sound hysterical, so she shut up and shoved fresh clothing into the open satchel. She felt tears watering behind her eyes, but she had no intention of weeping in front of Daniel. She'd save that until she was alone.

Daniel grabbed her arms from behind, keeping her from stuffing any more garments into complete ruin. "Stop being childish, Georgina. This is just temporary, for your own safety. You don't have to act as if I'm throwing you out."

She broke loose of the grip on one arm and swung around, standing up to him, even if her chin measured to his shirt button. "You *are* throwing me out! You have as much as said that I'm a nuisance, that I'm in your way. Of what earthly use am I to you, anyway? Just let me go, Daniel. I know when I'm not wanted." She jerked the other arm free and reached to snap her satchel closed.

Daniel grabbed the satchel and threw it across the room. He caught her waist and jerked her around to face him again. Before Georgina could scream a protest, his mouth was covering hers, filling her with heat and desire and a passion that flared out of control much too easily. She had used the wrong phrase when she had said she wasn't wanted.

Whatever point he had meant to prove went up in flames as their suppressed desires erupted in this kiss. Georgina cried out her surrender, digging her fingers into Daniel's shoulders as he clasped her so close she could feel the length of him hardening against her abdomen. Excitement flared instantly, and she responded with what little knowledge she possessed, returning his plundering kisses, running her hands up and down his back, pulling him into herself.

Daniel groaned against her mouth, but his hands moved to her breasts, pushing at them helplessly through the layers of clothing. Heat burned in places Georgina didn't know how to name, but she knew what to do about them. She reached behind her and began unfastening her bodice.

He knew what she was doing. He hesitated, pulling away to look down at her as if questioning her reasoning, but then he lifted her to the bed and fell down beside her.

Daniel's hand pulled up her skirts, finding the opening in her drawers with calculated ease. Georgina cried out in surprise when he touched her there, his rough fingers rubbing sensitive flesh, then exploring deeper. Had they really done this that night they were both drunk? It couldn't be possible. She couldn't possibly . . .

His fingers elicited a long drawn-out groan as they plunged into her. She ought to protest. She ought to show some semblance of shame. But her body had a mind of its own. Her hips raised off the bed to meet his thrusts.

Daniel came over her then, kissing her until Georgina was too breathless to say anything. She wanted his fingers back again. He had opened a void inside her that desperately needed filling. Panic began to build that he wouldn't come back into her. She writhed beneath him, trying to tell him what she needed with her body.

"Time, Georgina," Daniel murmured in her ear, "everything in its own time." Even as he said it, his fingers were somehow finding their way beneath her bodice, lifting her from her corset, sending shivering waves of desperate heat right through her middle as he caressed her breast.

It wasn't enough. It simply wasn't enough. Georgina tore at his shirt, trying to find some ounce of flesh to ease the need for contact. She jerked open enough buttons to run her hands up his chest, and victory surged through her as he groaned when she found his nipples. This worked both ways then.

"Georgina, we can't . . ."

But they could. Her skirt and petticoat were up around her waist, her bodice was falling off, and she was poised eagerly for his taking. She wasn't going to let him get away this time. If it worked both ways, then she could . . .

Her fingers found the buttons of his trousers, and Daniel gave a groan of surrender. Within seconds, he had them unfastened for her. She was too shy to touch him and retreated instantly to the safer territory of his chest, but he had no such inhibitions. He pulled the strings of her drawers and eased her out of them.

"Daniel." She was scared now. He was heavy over her, and she wasn't at all certain of his mood. And she felt completely vulnerable like this, with the place that was burning open to inspection. She closed her eyes tightly as Daniel shifted to look at her there, and his hand came to cover her.

His finger intruded once more, and she cried out, forgetting her fear, forgetting everything but the need welling up inside of her. She didn't like being in his power. She wanted to protest, to assert herself in some way, but she could only succumb to his stroking fingers. In another minute, she would surely burst. She couldn't hold back any longer.

And then he was shoving inside her. He was large, much larger than she remembered, and her eyes flew open to find his eyes staring gravely back at her. She lifted her knees, and he thrust home, their gazes still entangled as they waged a silent war. And then she quivered with the ecstasy of his possession and closed her eyes, letting the power of Daniel's body take over.

He was strong and swift and knew exactly what she needed. Georgina cried out as the explosion hit her, erupting in wave after uncontrollable wave. He kept going, taking her with him, until she felt the intensity building again, felt her entire insides opening to his thrusts, felt him in the very center of her—where he gave a triumphant cry and took his release, filling her with the liquid of his loins.

Perhaps, in some male way, he had won that war. Daniel knew what he was doing, and she didn't. He had the power to control her body, to take her to heights she hadn't known existed, to fill her with the life-giving seed that would one day make them one. And he had the power to deprive her of the same. But in some quiet, female sense, Georgina knew she had won another kind of war. They were no longer separate people leading separate lives. His need was for her as much as hers was for him.

They lay tangled in the wreckage of their clothing, catching their breaths, clinging to the warmth between them where they still remained attached. It was a very odd sensation, having this male body inside hers. Perhaps she ought to be ashamed, but she wasn't. She liked it too much, and she didn't think Daniel was objecting too strongly.

Georgina wanted to ask him if she could stay now, but she was afraid to say anything that might disturb this temporary peace. Daniel shifted his weight to one side and pulled her with him, and she snuggled contentedly into the curve of his arm. She would sleep like this if she had to.

He pulled the pins from her hair until he had loosened a curl. Then he wrapped it around his finger and used it to caress her throat. The touch was soft and arousing. She opened her eyes and met his.

"You can't stay," he whispered, the agony clear in his eyes.

"I won't leave," she answered calmly, too calmly. Her heart was beating furiously, and the effort to maintain control was taking its toll.

It was a draw of sorts, Daniel realized. He couldn't carry her to the hotel over his shoulder, particularly not in her current half-dressed condition. And he couldn't allow her to run away to the office to sleep unattended. He could insist. He could get up from here right now and refuse to be a part of her foolishness. But even if he won the argument, he would lose what he wanted most.

"Georgina." Daniel slid the rest of her bodice off her shoulder, focusing on the creamy skin that had been his undoing that first time she had revealed it.

"I want to be a real wife," she whispered against him.

It was almost a plea. He didn't want his carefree Miss Merry to be reduced to begging. He wanted her just as he had found her, full of life and love and all the good things she deserved. Daniel's lips curved silently as his hand drifted down between them to cover her bare stomach. Those good things could include his babe by now. So much for protecting her.

"You're more wife than I deserve, Miss Merry." Gently, Daniel untied the tapes of her gown and pulled the sleeves down until she could wriggle out of them.

Then he pulled the whole thing off and threw it over the side of the bed.

He took the time to admire her rounded legs still encased in garters and stockings. It wasn't often he got to admire a lady in her undergarments. He thought he might get used to the idea very quickly. He returned his gaze with interest to the casing of her corset and the spill of her breasts through the open chemise at the top. Twin pink peaks stared back at him, and he couldn't resist.

Georgina squealed when he touched his tongue to temptation, but she didn't make any other maidenly protests. Daniel had a vague notion that they were supposed to be doing this in the dark with nightgowns and nightshirts encumbering them, but he had never been one to bow to convention. If he had his way, he'd do this in the middle of the day with bright sunlight pouring through the windows. Had they any windows.

That thought stopped him. Glaring up at the boards that gave evidence of the precariousness of their privacy, Daniel pulled himself to a sitting position. Georgina hastily pulled her chemise together and stared up at him.

"They're likely to come after the press tonight, Georgie. I can't stay in here." He looked down at her regretfully, pulling her hands away until he could caress her breasts again. Her nipples puckered eagerly beneath his fingers. He had never met a woman as ready for him as she was. He liked knowing he affected her that way. "If you won't go to a hotel, you'll have to stay with me in the pressroom. I can't leave you alone in here."

"Fine." She drew her hand down his chest to the point where his trousers ought to be fastened, only they weren't. He gave a gasp as her fingers explored a little lower, and she smiled up at him angelically. "If you're going to be Pecos Martin, then I'm going to be the kind of woman he likes."

That was quite enough of that notion, and Daniel started to remonstrate when her hand began to do things he wasn't prepared to resist. Staring in astonishment at his lady wife, he grinned, caught her wrists, and pinned her to the bed.

"I think we'll deal with each other real fine, ma'am, just as soon as you learn to take orders."

Daniel buried his bristly chin against her throat as he bit her ear, and when she squealed and bucked against him, he lifted her from the bed, slid his feet to the floor, and carried her out of the bedroom to the pallet he had prepared in the pressroom.

Georgina didn't think she would ever remember that night again without blushing. Daniel did things to her that she was quite certain no man had ever done to a woman before, or at least no gentleman to a lady. And she not only allowed it, but encouraged him, loving every minute of it.

They were so engrossed in their play that even when Max began to bark a warning, Daniel merely bent a kiss to her forehead and whispered, "I'll be right back, sweetheart, keep a place warm for me," and Georgina watched in languid ease and let him go.

It took a minute before she realized he was pulling on a gun belt with his trousers. Even then, she didn't feel any great alarm. He was moving unhurriedly, as if he had everything under control. She merely wrapped a sheet around her and sat up to watch him leave. Idly, she realized she was still wearing her stockings and garters and nothing else. Was that the way hired women did it?

As she heard Daniel order Max to silence then cross the office, Georgina rose to stand in the doorway and watch. She couldn't find anything dangerous in the warm summer night. There was nothing here that could rouse a man to anger. Even the soft glow of the dying embers in the stove gave a gentleness to the scene.

She watched as Daniel eased open the door and looked out. It wasn't until she heard the light tread of shoes in the hall below that she woke from her love-struck lethargy. Daniel's bare chest and shoulders looked strong and wide and rippled with muscle, but they were also very, very naked and vulnerable. She didn't want to imagine what would happen to them if the intruders below carried guns.

But it was too late now. There was nothing she could

do but stand here helplessly, listening to the sounds below and waiting for whatever would follow. Daniel had both his guns and his rifle. She had only Max and a crowbar she picked up from the toolbox. It scarcely seemed enough.

It was more than they needed. As the footfalls drew closer, Daniel reached for a rope tied next to the door. Georgina watched in fascination as he unknotted it and let it go. Her gaze saw the rope disappear into the hall somewhere, then she heard the clatter and bang of tin pails. In the next moment there were screams of rage and anguish and thuds as the intruders fell back down the way they had come.

Daniel glanced up to where she waited, and his smile was almost apologetic as he shrugged his shoulders. "I had considered boiling oil, but I didn't want to stay up keeping it hot." He glanced back out the doorway, his hand on his guns as he waited for someone to try again.

None did. They could hear the curses and wails, someone giving orders, others refusing. Within minutes all was quiet again.

Daniel closed the door and pulled the bar across it. When he turned back, Georgina was still waiting for him, a sheet wrapped around her, but slipping to reveal most of the curve of one breast.

"So what did you use?" she asked patiently.

Daniel unbuckled his belt and began heading toward her. "You don't really want to know."

Georgina backed away, knowing the gleam in his eye too well. "I really do."

He reached for her and came away with a handful of sheet. His gaze dropped with satisfaction to her bare form, taking in rounded curves and a gold triangle of curls and gartered stockings with a swift glance. "What'll you give me if I tell you?"

Georgina beamed and placed her hands on her hips with a seductive wiggle. "Whatever you want."

"Good." Dropping the sheet, Daniel stepped across it and placed both hands on the firm curves of her buttocks.

"I want this." His mouth swooped down to claim full lips moist with desire as his hands pulled her into him.

It was only much later that she learned the contents of those buckets, and she giggled into her pillow at people's astonishment when they discovered a privy had been bailed out in the dead of night.

Thirty-two

ℰ

Georgina could hear the call of the newsboys hawking Daniel's newspaper outside the factory at noon. As the work shift broke for lunch, she could hear the women calling for their papers, and her lips curved slightly upward as she listened to the excited discussions erupting outside her office window. At least someone was reading the fruit of Daniel's labors.

Janice came through the open office door without knocking. The open-door policy had been one of Georgina's better ideas, but the truce between the two of them was still a fractious one. The other woman resented her inexperience, didn't trust her wealth or background, and wasn't prepared to accept Georgina as a working woman. Georgina figured Janice was waiting for her to get bored or tired and walk out complaining. There were times when she wanted to. What Janice didn't count on was that Daniel would be waiting for Georgina back at the newspaper if she did give up, and she couldn't face Daniel feeling a failure. So she gritted her teeth and kept working.

"Audrey says the Mulloney workers are ready to strike." Janice contained her excitement in a whisper as she glanced over her shoulder to make certain no one was listening.

Georgina sat back in her chair and allowed a sense of satisfaction to roll over her. "All of them?"

"All the ones that count." Janice threw the latest edition of the paper on the desk. "If the strike goes on for long, they're going to get mighty hungry."

Georgina picked up the paper and spread it out so the blaring headlines about ABC Rentals could be seen. "They can use their rent money to eat. This article will see to that."

"Sooner or later, though, they'll have to pay the money. We'll all be in debt so far we won't see our way out."

Georgina frowned and glared at the newsprint. "I wish I knew an easy solution. If we had a real union and paid into it for weeks and months until we had a balance built up . . ."

"Nothing would ever get done," Janice said firmly. "It's got to be done while everyone is fired up. And they're furious because Mulloney has told them they're going to have to work July Fourth. That's when the big parade and celebration are held downtown, and he wants to take advantage of the crowds."

"That will do it!" Georgina looked up and grinned. "Independence Day. How symbolic can you get? We can stage a parade of our own right through Mulloney's front lawn."

Janice managed a small smile of appreciation. "I'd like to see that. Of course"—her smile disappeared—"I'd like to see them march right through your father's front lawn, too."

Georgina waved a hand. "Go ahead. There isn't anyone there to appreciate it at the moment, but if it makes everybody happy, I won't deprive them. Anyway, from what my father said, it will be Mulloney's front lawn before long, unless something changes. I just keep waiting for the other shoe to drop."

Janice sank into the nearest chair and crossed her hands in her lap. "Then the rumors are true. This place is going under and we're all going to be out of work."

Georgina's lips straightened into a thin line. "Don't say that. Words have a tendency to make themselves true. I don't know a lot about bookkeeping and selling and such, but Doris knows everything there is to know about that end of it. She's helping me. We've already picked up several new accounts. It's just a matter of getting their purchases made up out of existing stock and getting the money for them so we can buy new material. I don't think anyone is going to sell us material on credit anymore."

Janice nodded thoughtfully. "All right. We'll cut the patterns so as to limit waste as much as possible. We'll be able to squeeze a few extras out of every bolt. If I spread the word, there's half a dozen ways we can cut waste. That should give you a little extra cash to make a bigger purchase for the next sale."

Georgina gave a sigh of relief. "If I had any authority, I would make you foreman—or forewoman—or whatever it would be called. But if you can manage to cut waste, I'll try to see that there's a little extra in everyone's paycheck when that sale comes through."

Janice stood up and prepared to leave. "The money has to be there somewhere. Your family lived off it for years."

Georgina stood up with her. "I'm thinking my family lived off Mulloney for years. He owns us. I don't want him owning me."

Janice grimaced. "He owns the whole town. If you can figure out how to get us out from under him, you're a genius."

Georgina didn't even see her go. Janice's words had started the wheels spinning, and she was afraid to contemplate the results. Daniel was a Mulloney. Daniel was the eldest Mulloney son. Somehow, Daniel had the means to force his father to release his heavy-handed grip on the town.

Those facts still churned uneasily through her mind as she set out for home that evening. *Home.* Georgina looked up at the boarded windows of the nearly empty warehouse across the street and marveled that she could call such a place home. She had to be out of her mind. But the thought that Daniel was waiting for her there, that he would be sitting there with his newspaper, eating from a pot of some concoction heated on that old stove, sent her feet hurrying in anticipation.

Georgina stopped short as she noticed the man pounding nails into boards across their front door. She had thought him a hired workman come to repair some of the damage. The stink on the front stairs had been enough to nearly bring her breakfast up this morning, and Daniel had assured her he would have it cleaned before she returned. But this man wasn't cleaning anything. He was nailing boards across the door.

"What on earth are you doing?" Georgina demanded as she came up beside him.

The workman pulled on the bill of his flattened cap in a mocking salute, spit a wad of tobacco in the street, and resumed hammering. "This building's condemned. It's unsafe for human habitation. Owner's going to have to tear it down."

Georgina froze, unable to juggle the variety of panics coming instantly to mind. Her gaze flew to the boarded windows where Daniel ought to be waiting. This just couldn't be. Everything they owned was in there. This was their home.

She heard Max's howl, and it jarred her back to action. She grabbed the man's hammer and began ripping out the boards. "My dog is in there. You can't board up a dog."

The man had little choice but to stand aside and watch her rip off the board he had just installed. He had never seen a lady in silk gown and bustle and fancy hairdo tear into a boarded door before, but he sure wasn't going to touch her. And nobody had mentioned any dog to him. He could wait. He stuffed a new rope of tobacco into his cheek as the lady swung open the door and raced into the darkened interior.

There weren't any lamps lit in the office as Georgina threw open the door. Max leapt out of the semidarkness and licked her exuberantly, but there wasn't any sign of Daniel. Pushing her fear deep down inside her, she snapped Max on his leash, ordered him to stay, and went to search through the rooms for what seemed most portable.

She grabbed her satchel, added some of Daniel's shirts, and went to the pressroom where he kept the locked chest. Realizing she still held the hammer, Georgina slammed it into the lock, splintering it. She didn't think Daniel would keep gold in a chest so easily opened, but his guns were there. She wasn't going to leave them behind.

The chest was filled with yellowed manuscripts. She hoped they were ones already published because she couldn't possibly carry them. The gunbelt was there. The rifle wasn't. She didn't know what that signified, but with Daniel and his rifle missing, it didn't sound good.

Adding the belt and guns to her satchel, Georgina took one last glance around and found nothing else that she could carry. She glanced over her shoulder at Daniel's printing press. Surely there was some way he could come back and save that. There had to be.

She marched down the stairs with Max in one hand and the satchel in the other. Somebody was going to hear about this, and they weren't going to enjoy one minute of it.

"Who's responsible for condemning buildings?" Georgina demanded as soon as she hit the bright light of the street.

The workman shrugged and took the hammer from her. "Mayor, I imagine. I just take orders from my boss." He backed away from Max's threatening growl.

Georgina gave him her best vapid smile. "Then I'd suggest you don't trouble yourself too much with those boards. They'll be down again tomorrow. The mayor is a friend of mine."

"That's what they all say." The man went back to hammering.

Fuming, Georgina stalked down the street. She couldn't go to the mayor's house dragging a satchel and Max, and looking like this. She needed to know where Daniel was. She needed something in her stomach. She was about to starve. And she needed to know where she was going to sleep tonight.

She certainly hadn't got much sleep the night before. Remembering what Daniel had done to her last night, Georgina felt the heat rush through her cheeks. She was still sore, but it was a soreness she was more than willing to suffer again. If this was what it meant to be a wife, she was sorry she hadn't started years ago. Even now, her need to know where she was going to sleep tonight had little to do with sleep and much to do with Daniel. She wanted his arms around her right now.

She didn't even know where to begin to look to find him. He had always been right there, where she needed him. It felt very odd to be wandering around without him, without even knowing where to find him. It was like losing a part of herself, the better part.

But she couldn't stand in the street, looking lost. She had to do something. And the nearest place she knew to go was the Harrisons.

When she reached the street where the Harrisons lived, she knew she had made a wrong decision. The narrow dirty alley was swirling with angry young men, screaming women, and crying children. As Georgina approached, some turned their attention from the center of this chaos to glare at her and yell curses.

Max growled and kept the worst of the crowd at bay. A stone sailed over her head, but it had been a halfhearted throw at best. The worst of the fury was focused on something just out of her sight—something terrifyingly close to the Harrisons' little hovel.

Having just experienced what it was like to be arbitrarily thrown out of her home, Georgina felt the leap of fear in her throat. Daniel had managed to get his paper out despite threats and shotguns and intruders in the night. The person behind those threats would have to vent his fury and frustration in some way, especially since the contents of that paper would now be the talk of the town. The Harrisons had already been targeted for vengeance, and they weren't as strong as Daniel.

With Max's help Georgina shoved her way through the crowd. Just as she had feared, she could see Janice holding a weeping Betsy in her arms, while Douglas danced up and down on a table, screaming and cursing at the top of his lungs. The objects of his curses calmly continued dumping loads of furnishings into the growing pile in the street.

With relief, Georgina found Daniel's tall figure filling a wheelbarrow with some of the Harrisons' smaller possessions. Behind him a man filled a pony cart with furniture. Other men arrived with wheelbarrows and carts as she pushed through to this inner circle, and an insane idea began to dance in Georgina's mind.

As if there were some magnetic current between them, Daniel's gaze lifted to find her as soon as she broke through the crowd. Sweat was pouring down his forehead, and his partially opened shirt clung to his back. Georgina could see the helpless fury in his light-colored eyes as their gazes locked, but she reacted with a laughing smile that set him back.

Throwing her satchel into the nearest cart, Georgina sent Max into Douglas's waiting arms, then approached Janice and Betsy with an insouciance she could portray easily in her rich traveling silks, but one she couldn't feel inside. The men carting furniture from the house snickered at her approach, but she ignored them. Janice looked immediately suspicious, and Audrey turned away, but their aunt met Georgina's laughing approach with a bright look. The old lady was ready for anything.

"Remember that parade we talked about earlier?" Georgina addressed the question to Janice who responded with weary bewilderment at first. "The one across my father's front lawn?"

Recognition lit Janice's eyes briefly, but wariness replaced it. She nodded, and her gaze went to encompass the procession of carts and barrows and donkeys forming in the alley.

"Since Daniel and I have just been kicked out of our rooms, we have to go somewhere. You might as well go with us." Georgina grinned as Janice looked startled and Douglas jumped down to join them.

Daniel came up behind her then, putting a hand on her shoulder and squeezing it. Georgina glanced up and gave him a slightly wavery smile. "They condemned the newspaper building," she whispered. "They're boarding up the doors right now."

Daniel's hand was hot and sweaty, and Georgina could

see the weariness in his eyes as he nodded in understanding. She was so physically aware of him that she knew his leg hurt even without seeing his limp. She could smell the male musk of him beneath the odor of perspiration, and she would have given anything to be able to dive into his arms right now. But she couldn't stop to think about things like fear or she would collapse in sobs right here in the middle of the road.

"I thought it would be a nice night for a parade. We have to march past Mulloney's before we get to my father's house. I don't think the servants can stop us from getting in, can they?"

Even through his weariness, Daniel grinned. "You have a malevolent mind, Miss Merry. I really do appreciate it."

No one had ever appreciated her mind before, and Georgina felt an extra jolt of electricity shoot through her as Daniel pressed a kiss to her hair. And coming from a man as smart as Daniel, it was an extra special compliment. She just hoped she could live up to it.

As word spread through the crowd of what they meant to do, the anger of the mob shifted to a holiday jubilation. In a gesture of defiant insolence, hats appeared to adorn the heads of the donkeys and ponies pulling carts. Bright streamers of cloth were tied to wheelbarrows and wagons. Women dashed into their houses to pull on their gayest blouses and fasten ribbons in their hair before running out to cart an armload of linens or a box of clothes. Children carrying nothing at all responded to the gaiety with laughter and excited headstands and yells of happiness as they traveled beside the ungainly procession working its way down the alley.

The men who had been sent to empty the house scratched their heads in puzzlement, but diligently continued their duties. Janice insisted that her elderly aunt sit with Betsy in one of the carts and sent it on its way while she helped fill others with the last of their precious possessions.

With his arm still around Georgina's shoulders, Daniel supervised the loading, yelling at Douglas and his friends when their overexuberance threatened to topple a wagon, assuring Audrey that she could take her cat, and casually keeping an eye on the crowd. It was that casual eye that warned Georgina, and she glanced around, finding Daniel's rifle leaning against the house, close at hand. He was expecting trouble.

"Can't we leave now?" Georgina whispered, nervously watching as the procession started off without them. "I'll need to be in front when they reach the house."

"We need to keep Janice and Audrey with us, and they won't leave until they've seen everything safely in the carts." Daniel's tone was preoccupied.

He was waiting for Egan. That knowledge sent Georgina into action. She wasn't going to stand here and watch Daniel fight with the bigger man when it was evident he was already dropping from exhaustion. Whatever damned possessions the Harrisons had left could take care of themselves.

Giving Daniel a look of irritation, Georgina removed herself from his hold and hurried to Janice. With a few whispered words she apprised the other woman of the situation. Janice sent a quick look to the quiet man staunchly guarding the crowd, nodded her head, and went after her sister.

By the time Georgina returned to Daniel's side, the sisters were smiling and waving their good-byes to their neighbors and running to catch up with the boys yelling and laughing at the front of the procession.

Daniel gave her a frown, but Georgina returned it with a dazzling smile. "We're going to do it, Daniel," she informed him happily. "We're going to turn this whole town on its ear, and we're going to do it smiling."

As Daniel watched the parade of gaily decorated carts and people chattering in half a dozen languages snaking their way out of the dingy alley into the broader thoroughfares of the town, he nodded agreement. There were better ways than violence, and his own Miss Merry would find them. He was damned proud of her.

As he hurried her down the alley to catch up with the others, he raised his head to catch sight of Egan standing in the shadows of a cross street. Daniel grinned, grabbed a ribbon from Georgina's hair, and stuck it like a banner into his rifle barrel.

The other man scowled and turned away.

Thirty-three

T he parade attracted considerable attention as it wended its way through city streets on the way to the better residential section of town. Janice and Audrey waved cheerfully to acquaintances among the clerks pouring from Mulloney's at day's end. Others among the crowd waved at friends and neighbors and relatives emerging from other stores along the streets. And carriages and horses lined up to take their owners home were caught in the traffic as the parade spilled through the crowded thoroughfares.

Georgina caught sight of one of Peter's younger brothers astride a horse trapped by the masses, and she waved gaily. He looked startled, then grinned so much like Daniel that she warmed to him instantly.

She poked Daniel and pointed. "That's your youngest brother, John. Wave."

Daniel turned reluctantly to where she indicated and was startled to see a younger version of himself staring back. All the boy needed was a pair of spectacles and a bad haircut and he could almost be the eighteen-year-old Daniel had once been. The youngest in the family hadn't followed the Mulloney tradition for Irish good looks, then. With a rather foolish grin at that thought, Daniel waved as directed.

The boy looked mildly puzzled, but he nodded back, then eased himself through a break in the crowd and disappeared down a side street. Daniel watched him go with a feeling of disappointment that he would never have the chance to know the lad. It had never really bothered him before that he hadn't had an opportunity to know his brothers. He wasn't going to dwell on it now, when it was too late. He turned his attention back to the disorderly parade.

The straggling procession of carts and poorly dressed people seemed to be growing in size. Neighbors joined neighbors as word spread, and there was a definite air of defiant celebration as they passed Mulloney's with ribbons flying. Daniel glanced up and caught the brief shadow of a man in an upper-story window, and he lifted a victorious fist with thumb upraised at his father. This wasn't the significant moment he had hoped to share with the man, but it certainly was what he deserved.

As they moved into the quieter residential area, the party became a little more subdued. Many of them had never been here before, and they stared around at the immaculate grounds behind iron fences with awe. They passed respectfully around an elegant carriage containing an elderly lady, making a path for it to continue on its way undisturbed. The woman didn't even turn her head to acknowledge them.

Janice worked her way around the crowd to walk beside Georgina. "This idea is beginning to lose its appeal," she murmured. "We don't belong here."

"Just as I don't belong on your side of town?" Georgina challenged her. "Just as Betsy won't belong in Mulloney's when she grows up?"

"Betsy can be anything she wants to be when she grows up. I'll see to that," Janice replied defiantly.

"Then you'd better start teaching her about this side of town. It has the same kind of people in it as your side; they're just dressed fancier and more of them speak English." Georgina waved at a startled Loyolla Banks as the mayor's wife came out to stand on her porch to see what was happening. Loyolla only stared back.

"Your father will have us all arrested for trespassing."

Daniel stepped between the two women and took their arms as he pushed them toward the head of the procession. "Her father is in Chicago trying to borrow money, a little bird tells me."

Georgina threw him a suspicious look. "How do you know that?"

"The little bird works in the telegraph office." With a wink Daniel linked their arms and steered the parade up the driveway to the Hanover home.

Carts and wheelbarrows spilled over the lovingly groomed lawn as the newcomers stared up at the sprawling mansion with its hundreds of mullioned windowpanes glittering in the late afternoon sunshine. Screaming with laughter, children scrambled up the stately maples and pelted one another with pine cones gathered beneath the towering evergreens. Women stopped to stare at the wanton beauty of dozens of multicolored roses filling beds along the walls. The men assessed the number of lifetimes they would have to work at current wages to earn a structure only half as magnificent as this one.

Georgina scrubbed away a tear and marched up the front steps. She tried the door and finding it locked, she removed a key from her pocket and unlocked it. With a welcoming gesture she bade them enter.

The crowd held back. Noting the tremble of Georgina's lower lip, Daniel caught Audrey and Janice by the arms and led them up the stairs to join her. Their aunt followed with Douglas and Betsy.

"We need food and drink," Daniel whispered to Georgina. "What do you think they have in the kitchen?"

Georgina instantly beamed again. "Punch by the gallons. I'll see about food."

The Harrisons were staring in stunned awe at the gleaming foyer, their gazes going from the crystal gaslights on the walls to the delicate Aubusson carpets covering polished oak floors. Even though he was familiar with the comfortable homes in the neighborhood in St. Louis where he had grown up, Daniel still found himself impressed with the extent of the riches displayed in Georgina's home. And he had brought her to live with him in an empty warehouse. He was just beginning to realize the enormity of his folly.

Terrified servants began scampering through the hall with buckets of punch and trays of crystal glasses and cups under Georgina's direction. Daniel imagined all that expensive glassware in the hands of children who had scarcely known anything better than a tin cup and shuddered. But it was doubtful that the Hanover household had anything so demeaning as tin cups, so he let them pass. He'd figure out how to pay for the damage later.

"Audrey, you and Douglas go out there and see everyone gets a cup. Janice and I better go back and see what we can do to help Georgie. Our guests deserve a little refreshment for their hard work, don't you think?"

Jarred from their stunned awe by this request that spoke to their inbred courtesy, the Harrisons immediately threw themselves into the spirit of the occasion. Within the half hour, the front lawn was filled with women sitting in spread skirts, men crouched and sitting cross-legged, and children capering over the grass, all snacking on tiny sandwiches and sipping at fruit punch while admiring the summer beauty of this parklike yard.

"Just imagine how many people we could crowd onto my father's front lawn," Daniel mused out loud as he sat on the front step, munching a sandwich much too delicate for his tastes. He peeled open the bread and tried to identify the pastel-colored paste, wrinkled his nose, and gallantly bit into it.

"The whole Independence Day parade." Georgina didn't dare look at Janice as she made this pronouncement. Ideas were spinning in her head so fast she didn't dare look at herself.

"We won't change anything," Janice replied gloomily. "We can't stay here. Someone will call the police sooner or later. Everyone will go home shortly, and we'll still be out of a house."

"As far as that goes, Mulloney will probably come to take possession of this place as soon as he finds out we're here, but at least we're here for the night. It's a pity we can't keep everyone here. I'd like to see him throw everybody out."

Even as Georgina said it, they could see people drifting

out through the gates, seeking their homes before it grew too dark. It had been a spectacular gesture and a kind of holiday for otherwise humdrum lives, but it wasn't reality. Reality was waking up in the morning and wondering where the money was going to come from for the next meal.

The Harrisons' careful store of possessions was unloaded and left in tidy piles on the porch where they wouldn't get wet if it stormed. What had made such a magnificent parade now seemed pitifully small and shabby in comparison to the grand structure around them, but no comments were made. Each person depositing another small piece of the past shook one of the small family's hands, made comforting gestures, and disappeared into the growing dusk.

"I've put Betsy and your aunt to bed in the nursery," Georgina said as she returned to join the dwindling party on the front stairs. "A maid is making up a guest room for you and Audrey. Douglas says he wants to sleep in the stable with the grooms. Do you think that's all right, or should I have a room made up for him?"

Janice blinked back a tear and stared at the smaller woman nervously clasping her hands beside her. Georgina's elegant gowns always made her seem grander, larger than life. Her laughing smiles and engaging manners always made her seem to be in charge of the world. But standing here now, bedraggled and tired, her golden curls falling in dishevelment about shoulders bent with uncertainty, she was just a woman, like all the rest.

"The stable is fine. He'll think he died and went to heaven. *I* think we've died and gone to heaven. How are we ever going to live anywhere else after seeing this?" Janice gestured at the foyer they were entering.

"The same way I did." Georgina reached for Daniel's hand. "You go where your family is. That's the only place in the world that is real."

Janice gave a scornful shake of her head. "Love doesn't put a roof over your head or food in your belly. You have a lot to learn, Mrs. Mulloney. But I thank you for your generosity, anyway. In the morning, we'll look for a boarding house."

At the words "boarding house," Georgina murmured "hmmm" and began to look around her with a look of calculation in her eyes. As Janice disappeared up the stairs in search of her family, Daniel jerked his wife's arm and brought her down to earth.

"Even if you rented every room for fifty dollars a month, it wouldn't pay for this monstrosity, so get that idea out of your pretty head right now, Mrs. Mulloney."

Georgina made a face. "Couldn't you change your name? I'm really going to have a hard time getting used to being called by that one."

"To Martin, maybe?" Daniel grinned and hugged her tighter. "Go on up to bed. I figure someone ought to go quiet the staff before they decide to make a break for it by morning."

Daniel wandered off to the rear of the house, leaving Georgina to stumble upstairs to bed. She hoped he knew how to find her. Maybe she ought to stick labels on the doors so everyone could find each other.

Her room seemed much small and fussier than she remembered it. The pink ruffled curtains and bedcovers had been her mother's idea, but Georgina had never protested them. The dresser was still filled to overflowing with perfume bottles and lotions, and she wondered what she had ever needed all of them for. All she cared about now was a hot bath, and that was one blessing that was easily bestowed in this place.

Running the bathwater in the next room, Georgina poured a bottle of her favorite bubbles into the steaming waters and struggled out of her clothing. It was going to be sheer bliss luxuriating in a full tub for a change.

When Daniel finally located her sometime later, Georgina was lying with her head on the back of the tub, nearly asleep in an ocean of bubbles. He hesitated in the doorway, taking in her luxurious surroundings with a pang of something he wanted to ignore. This was his wife's natural setting. She was meant to be surrounded by the finer things in life. She functioned best here, where she knew the people and the etiquette and the forces of society.

He had been a blind fool to think she was as adaptable as he was to the harsher side of life.

Thirty-four

ॐ

Georgina woke with a jump when Daniel climbed into the tub with her. She stared at the amazing image of a naked man sitting in her own bathtub and wasn't certain if she was still sleeping. Daniel's strong legs sliding wetly along her own confirmed his reality.

He really had the most amazing face. Long lean bones and a mobile mouth and those electric eyes lent themselves to an astonishing number of characters. One minute he could be vague and scholarly, the next he could be the very picture of a furious cowboy out to protect his claim. At the moment he possessed a look of seductive tenderness that turned her insides to quivering jelly.

"Did you stave off mutiny?" she whispered lightly, trying not to reveal the effect he was having on her.

"They were quite reassured to know the master of the house is in Chicago, that we are temporarily looking after the household, and that we don't intend to hold any more unexpected parades. It's just a matter of telling them what they want to hear."

"And you're an expert at that. Daniel, what are we going to do about the printing press? Will they tear it up?" Georgina strived for a tone of reasonableness as she watched him soap the light hairs across his broad chest. She hadn't noticed before, but the wet mat made a pattern that seemed to trail into an arrow that pointed directly downward. And she was trying her best not to look directly downward.

Amusement laced Daniel's voice as he watched her watching him. "They'll wish they hadn't if they try. There are laws, Georgina. Artemis may have the local lawyers tied in knots, but I know how to reach some of the best in the business. That press is private property. If the city takes it upon themselves to close that building, then they are legally responsible for what happens to it and anything in it. I'll retrieve our things tomorrow."

Georgina suspected Daniel was talking off the top of his head just to reassure her, but she let herself be reassured. If he wasn't worried about the press, neither was she.

"Have you ever made love in a bathtub, Miss Merry?"

The switch of topic was disconcerting. She stared at him and found that even her toes were quivering at the idea he had so casually suggested. She shook her head slowly, not daring to speak.

"Neither have I, but I've always wanted to try."

Before she could offer any kind of reasonable protest, Daniel caught her wet waist, lifted her over him, and slid beneath her so she was sitting on his lap.

As he gently soaped her breasts, Daniel kissed Georgina's lips and murmured against them, "I'm going to take good care of you, Miss Merry. Don't you worry about a thing."

And because she wanted to believe him, she did. What else could she do while her head spun dizzily with the things he was doing to her? She let him take her, she welcomed him, and she gave herself with all the heart and soul of which she was capable.

Because she loved him.

Daniel was dismantling his printing press in the heat of a late June afternoon when Egan walked into the room. Wiping his hands on a dirty rag, Daniel cursed himself for leaving behind the boards he had pried from the first-floor windows. They would have made great weapons.

The piece of heavy iron in his hand would serve, but only at close range. Daniel hefted it casually as he nodded at the thug. Egan looked like a small-time hoodlum in his derby and checkered vest. No man in his right mind would sit down to a poker game with a man like that.

"Thought I'd find you here." Egan looked around, and finding no one else in the enclosed space, relaxed and stretched his large arms. "You and me got a few things we need to work out."

"Wouldn't, if I were you, dog-face. Haven't you heard? My daddy doesn't want me dead, just out of town."

Egan stared at him, and Daniel threw the iron part from hand to hand, admiring the effect of honesty. Why did men like that always think they knew everything and no one else knew anything? Positively fascinating the way the human mind worked.

"He don't mind if you get messed up a little before I take you to see him." Egan advanced a pace or two closer, forcing Daniel backward against the heavy machinery.

"Well then, he won't mind if I eliminate the middleman, will he?"

Before Egan could figure out what he was saying, Daniel kicked high and hard, striking the larger man right where it hurt the most. Egan really was a trifle slow. One would have thought he'd have remembered that maneuver.

The man screamed with pain but threw himself forward like a bull, aiming his head at Daniel's stomach. Tuttutting, Daniel nimbly stepped aside and let the idiot ram his head into the printing press. He really wasn't much of an opponent at all.

As Egan slid to the floor, Daniel picked up his tools and the various parts of the press he had dismantled and started down the stairs. It rather sounded like his father was summoning him. That suited him just fine, because he had a thing or two to say to the old man himself.

Daniel worked up a full head of steam on his way downtown. The rejection he had felt as a child was as nothing to the fury he felt now as an adult at his father's callous refusal to acknowledge his eldest son. Perhaps there were very good reasons for not acknowledging him, but there were no good reasons for the strong-arm tactics

Artemis was employing. If the man wasn't so damned old and his father to boot, Daniel would have enjoyed cutting him down a peg or two physically. But it was with words he would have to win this battle.

Just before he reached the store, Daniel was brought to a halt by the sight of the crowd gathered around the kiosk he had rented for Georgie's pictures—a kiosk which should be empty now that she had no camera. Curiosity prevailing momentarily over anger, he pushed his way through the crowd. Whatever was there must have just appeared for so many people to suddenly be taking an interest.

With the calm eye of a professional, Daniel examined the display of black-and-white photographs. Some were overdeveloped by inexperienced hands. The composition of others left much to be desired. There was no doubt that the photographs had been taken by an amateur, and one without an eye as good as Georgie's.

Be that as it may, the photographs packed a significant wallop. The crowd of ladies in trailing silks and bustles and feathered hats gazed in dismay at pictures of nearly naked, grubby children sitting near gaping holes in sagging porches. Rooms where the ceilings threatened to cave in on neatly set dining tables vied with rats sitting on piles of garbage while children played nearby. A family dressed in their Sunday best beamed solemnly at the camera from in front of a house that seemed in imminent danger of collapse.

Someone with a cynical eye had caught these scenes, and Daniel wondered who could be any more cynical in this town than himself. He wandered around all sides of the kiosk, looking for some clue to the photographer and finding none. He knew it wasn't Georgina. While she might see the contrast between the people and the living conditions, she was prone to dressing things up in ribbons and bows. Whoever had done these pictures had gone for the jugular.

Remembering Peter was still in possession of Georgina's camera, Daniel shook his head and backed out of the crowd. Artemis would have his brother's scalp if he learned Peter had taken these pictures. He couldn't imagine the stiff and proper Peter doing anything so defiant, especially when it wasn't in his own best interests. ABC Rentals would be Peter's one day, and the houses in those pictures belonged to ABC.

Not believing what logic was telling him, Daniel hurried across the street to Mulloney's. He had an appointment to keep with his father, an appointment that had waited twenty-eight years. It was time to keep it. He would worry about those photographs some other time.

He wasn't exactly dressed for the occasion. His white shirt was stained with oil from the press, and he hadn't bothered with collar and cravat or coat and vest in this heat. His hair was undoubtedly disheveled as usual, and his hands were grimy with the same oil that marked his shirt. At least he hadn't marred his knuckles on Egan's chin, Daniel reflected wryly as he ignored the stares in his direction and headed up the stairs to the office. He didn't think his father would appreciate his restraint.

The secretary opened her mouth to protest as Daniel stalked past her, but she wasn't in a position to tackle him as he threw open the door and marched into the inner sanctum. She sank back to her desk as he slammed the door behind him.

Peter wasn't available for this particular confrontation, Daniel noted. Only the old man behind the large desk near the window occupied the room. He couldn't see any resemblance at all between his own image in the mirror and the broad, handsome man behind the desk, but that man's name was on his birth certificate, and it was time for some explanations.

Daniel threw himself into a comfortable chair and propped his boots on the desktop. Arms crossed over his chest, he depicted insolent defiance even before he opened his mouth.

"Well, Dad, Egan says you want to see me."

The distinguished silver-haired man gaped blankly for a moment, then stared at the tall, lean stranger he had seen once before. The memory of the stranger's laughing insolence at the time burned brightly still. No son of his would behave that way.

But even as Mulloney denied it to himself, Daniel's mouth lifted in a familiar grin and gray eyes sparkled with a light identical to those of his youngest son. Artemis gritted his teeth and gripped his desk.

"Had I ever wanted to see you, I would have paid for your fare to come back here. I don't know what you thought you would accomplish by coming to Cutlerville, but I have given you all I ever intend to give you. You ought to be damned glad that I bothered to support you while you were growing up. I have no intention of doing so anymore."

Daniel continued smiling. "You don't need to. I'm doing a very good job on my own. Chip off the old block, I suspect. Making money is one of the easier of life's chores, don't you think?"

Artemis scowled. "You are getting nothing from me. Had you appealed to me with some respect, I might have considered finding you a position in my holdings, but you have done your damnedest to bring me down ever since you got here. I want you out of this town and out of my sight, and I will do whatever is necessary to bring that about."

Daniel shrugged. "I came here only to see what kind of family gives away its children. Now that I know, I don't feel under any obligation to claim you. As a matter of fact, I'm seriously contemplating changing my name. My wife objects to being related to a nest of vipers."

Mulloney's face turned a mottled purple as he obviously restrained himself by clenching his fingers around his desktop. "I paid good money to see you brought up to show some respect to authority. I have a good mind to demand my money back."

"If you can get blood out of a turnip, I suppose you can get money out of a dead woman. But I suspect Nanny taught me a great deal more about respect than you ever learned in a lifetime. I have a great deal of respect for people who scratch and save and try to make a living while a bloodsucker like you steals them blind. Forgive me if I don't recognize you as the kind of figure of authority I'm supposed to respect."

The man behind the desk grew dangerously quiet as he pushed his chair away and stared at his visitor. The city street below him went unnoticed as he crossed his arms in a gesture unconsciously similar to his son's.

"You'll learn to respect me before I get finished with you. Even as we speak, I have lawyers preparing the papers to take over Hanover Industries and that hideous monstrosity of a house that your wife calls home. You'll both be on the streets before evening. You thought you were clever in stealing Georgina Hanover away from me, but you'll soon learn what it's like to keep a woman like that in the streets. She'll make your life hell until I take pity on her suffering and offer to pay for a divorce so she can mend her childish errors. You'll never get your hands on Hanover Industries while I'm alive."

Daniel sighed and shook his head. "You just don't get it, do you? I suppose I should have known, but it's difficult to believe one's own father isn't human. I don't suppose you want to tell me why you found me so repulsive that you banished me from your kingdom?"

Dark eyes gleamed from behind the grim mask of the older man's features. "Because as far as I'm concerned, you're no son of mine. You might bear my name, but not an ounce of my blood. Are you beginning to get the picture?"

Daniel shrugged nonchalantly, but the stiffness of his posture indicated some of his inner turmoil. "Since I don't know my mother, I can't very well defend her. I'll take your word for it." He swung his boots to the floor and stood up, prepared to depart.

"You don't leave here until I tell you to leave!" Artemis shouted, rising from behind the desk.

Daniel kept walking.

"I'll make a deal with you!" When Daniel still didn't halt, he added, "It concerns your wife, so you damned well better listen."

Daniel sent a questioning look over his shoulder.

"I want you out of this town. I don't want you bothering my wife. She's ill and I won't have it." Artemis clenched his fists against the desk. When Daniel still made no reply, he continued, "I'm prepared to put the mortgage to Hanover's house in your wife's name so she effectively will own the property. All you have to do is get out of town and not come back."

"And Hanover Industries?" Daniel asked carefully.

"That's mine. I'll do with it what I wish. If your wife's bleeding heart can't bear to see the place shut down, then she can damned well divorce you and marry my son the way it was intended. Then the decision will be up to Peter."

"I'm certain that makes perfect sense somewhere in your cold heart. I fail to admire the logic of it, but I'll give it some consideration. But if intuition serves me, you might not find Peter as cooperative as you seem to think. I'll get back to you."

With an assurance bordering on the insolent, Daniel walked out.

When he was gone, a tall man wearing oddly western clothes for a city of this sort stepped out from behind a concealed door in the wall. His hand went to scratch thoughtfully at his two-day old beard.

"You heard that?" Mulloney demanded.

The stranger nodded. He hadn't bothered removing his badly stained Stetson earlier. He took it off now and examined a bullet hole through it.

"Then you understand why I want him out of town. You said you were looking for him yourself. Here's your opportunity."

The man adjusted the hat over his eyes and hooked his thumbs in his belt. "He ain't 'zactly what I expected. These writer fellers are usually shrimps that squeak when you look at 'em. This one ain't like that a'tall."

Mulloney gave him a look of disgust. "I thought you were a gunfighter. You can't be afraid of a callow youth."

The man shrugged and rocked back on his heels. "Ain't afraid of no man, not even you. What I'm sayin' is that I like the man's guts. He stood up for himself. I was plannin' on scarin' a mouse. Now I ain't so sure if I shouldn't get to know him better."

Mulloney scowled. "Get out of here, Martin. You're a broken-down has-been. I don't know why I bothered with you in the first place."

" 'Cause I was lookin' to kill the boy and you thought I'd save you the trouble." Pleased with himself, the cowboy spun around on his tall heels and let himself out.

Thirty-five

D aniel sat on the front step of Georgina's home and watched his wife playing with the two youngest Harrison children. Janice had found a boarding house to take them in and they would be leaving tomorrow, despite Georgina's vehement protests. This huge old house would seem empty without them.

As it would be empty and lifeless without Georgina. Daniel watched as she flung a ball to Betsy and laughed as the little girl caught it. Georgina was meant to be wealthy. She had a generous heart that would break if she couldn't help others. She was meant for having children, too, even though she wasn't entirely aware of it yet. Daniel watched indulgently as she dodged Douglas's throw and laughingly drew him into a race across the lawn. The boy hadn't looked so young since he'd known him.

He wasn't a poor man. He could buy Georgina a modest house and support children, but the cost would eat into his capital quickly. He would have to make money to keep her comfortably for the rest of their lives, but he couldn't do that here. Artemis would see to that. Daniel was realistic enough to know that he could cause his father untold grief, but he could never stop him entirely. On his own, he would have stayed to fight. A wife and children were another matter entirely. They would have to leave Cutlerville if they wanted to live any kind of life at all.

But this was Georgie's home. She had friends and family here. Daniel knew the power of family, and he didn't want to deny her that, even if her father was cut of the same cloth as his father. He didn't want to destroy the sheltered world that had created a gem like his Miss Merry. He was accustomed to living without family, to traveling without a home, but Georgina wasn't. He couldn't do that to her.

If this had been a love match, had Georgina married him because she loved him in defiance of all else, Daniel might have considered other options. For the love of a woman like Georgina, he would have climbed mountains and swum seas, anything she might ask of him. And he would have expected her to do the same for him. As it was, he couldn't even ask her to leave home for him.

It was a dilemma he didn't like. He could stay and try to destroy his family for her sake. He could take her with him and force her to leave her family behind. Or he could give her her freedom and walk away.

Selfishly, he preferred the first two alternatives to the last. Georgina was the best thing that had ever happened to him, and he didn't want to give her up. Remembering how she had looked in the bathtub last night, her wide blue eyes stunned and delighted as he had taken her in the most erotic experience of his life, Daniel groaned slightly and forced his thoughts to the practical. He couldn't be practical while dreaming of the full globes of her breasts glistening wetly in the lamplight. He would never think further than their bed at that rate.

They were good together in bed, there was no doubt of that. But how long would that last if he took Georgina away from her home and family and friends to a place totally alien to her? From his experience, women made love with their brains as much as their bodies. If they were unhappy, they weren't satisfied physically or emotionally. He would destroy what little they had together when he destroyed her happiness.

So he would have to do the unselfish thing and make Georgina happy. He was damned tired of playing the hero, but he couldn't make himself do anything else. As much as he despised giving in to the man, he would have to take his father up on his offer, for Georgina's sake. All he had to do was scribble his name on the document in his coat pocket and disappear. It shouldn't take any effort at all.

But it did. As he left the porch to find a pen, Daniel heard his wife's laughter drifting from the front lawn. He had imagined living the rest of his life hearing that laughter. He had daydreamed of how she would look when she grew round with his child. He had wanted to take her south with him to meet his friends and the rest of his adopted family. He had invested a lifetime of wishing for love in his desire for Georgina Meredith Hanover. He would rather keep those dreams intact as dreams rather than see them destroyed by the reality of a loveless marriage.

Trailing slowly up the stairs, Daniel imagined he could still smell the fragrance of lilies of the valley wafting from the room they had shared last night. The bare room they had shared in the warehouse had been his. This frilly concoction in her father's house was hers. He wondered what kind of room they would have created together had they been allowed.

He wasn't destined to find out. Sitting at Georgina's desk, he penned his name to the agreement, went over the newly written mortgage to make certain of its legality, then placed the latter in Georgina's desk and the former in an envelope to be delivered to his father. With that done, he stared at the empty blotter and Georgina's stationery for a minute longer. Writing was his business. Surely he could come up with something that would make her understand.

As he wrote, Daniel tried to tell himself that he didn't have to do this tonight. He could stay and spend another night in Georgina's arms, memorizing all those things he would miss when he was gone. If he took enough memories with him, they might last a lifetime. He hadn't even begun creating the memories he would have liked to have had.

But he would feel like a traitor if he stayed, now that he had signed the papers. It was better to make the break swift and clean. Georgina was much stronger than anyone imagined. She would see to the workers at the factory and the department store. She would lead them to victory over his father's machinations. He could count on her to finish what he had started. There was no reason to linger over sentimental maundering.

Leaving the letter under her pillow, Daniel packed his few belongings and slipped down the back stairs and out through the kitchen.

At twilight Georgina sent the children off to bed and went in search of Daniel. She had been aware of him the whole time he had watched her from the porch. She had known when he had gone inside. She had hoped he would join them, but Daniel had never learned to play as a child and probably didn't know how. She would have to teach him someday.

She figured she would find him occupying the study, either writing or reading, but the light was cold as if he had never been there. In hopes that he had decided to bathe after his miserable day dismantling the press, she slipped into her bedroom and partially disrobed. Two could play at this game.

But he wasn't there. Sighing, she filled the tub and finished undressing. Maybe he would find her.

He didn't appear by the time she had finished. Wrapping herself in a cotton robe, Georgina found a book and settled in her bedroom chair to wait. Daniel was quite capable of anything. She couldn't possibly pin him down and didn't want to try. She loved him too much the way he was.

Something had been bothering him all evening, she knew. Perhaps it was those photographs mysteriously appearing in the kiosk. She hadn't been down to see them herself, but she'd heard about them from the Harrisons. Daniel hadn't mentioned them, but he hadn't asked questions either, so he knew about them. Maybe he had gone to find out who had put them there.

Secretly, she hoped it had been Peter. Peter had her camera, after all, and he had access to all those houses. Daniel needed to get to know his family, and Peter ought to be the easiest one to get to know. She really thought they had been making overtures of a sort the other night, but nothing had come of them that she had seen. Maybe she could devise some way of bringing the brothers together.

The day at the factory had left her bone weary, and her head began to nod over the book. Glancing up as the mantel clock struck eleven, Georgina frowned and set the book aside. Where could he have gone at this hour?

Putting on her slippers, she went downstairs to see if any of the servants knew anything, but they had long since retired, as had the Harrisons, she discovered, as she noted their darkened room. There was no one up and stirring but herself.

Making certain the front door was unlocked so Daniel could get in, Georgina dragged herself back upstairs to her empty bed. It was amazing how quickly she had become used to sharing a bed. She wanted to snuggle against Daniel's warm, bare chest and feel his arms close around her. She liked feeling his breath blowing across her ear and his fingers entangling in her hair. She didn't know how she had ever lived without him before.

Somehow, she was going to have to tell him that. Would that scare him away? It might some men, but she didn't think it would scare Daniel. She rather thought he might flash that wide smile of his and kiss her until she was dizzy. He might even try to love her back if she made it easy for him. Perhaps they hadn't started out with the traditional romantic courtship, but they already had the most romantic marriage Georgina could think of. Daniel's constant thoughtfulness had seen to that.

Throwing her robe over the chair, she climbed into bed, resting her head wearily on the pillow. She probably didn't have the strength to make love tonight anyway. She didn't think she could really sleep until Daniel came home, but she could rest her eyes.

Turning on her stomach and running her hands beneath the pillow to hug it closer, Georgina felt the brush of stiff paper beneath her fingers at the same time as it crackled in her ear. Something unpleasant clenched at her stomach as she curled her hand around the envelope, crushing it slightly as she drew it from its hiding place.

She was tempted to leave it until morning. She could just lie here and wait for Daniel to return, and they could read it together in the daylight. Daniel would make any unpleasantness go away. Notes under pillows could only be unpleasant.

On the other hand, it might be a love note. Daniel could be waiting for her somewhere, wondering why she didn't come in answer to his romantic overtures. It would be just like Daniel to dream up something like that.

With a mixture of anticipation and fear, Georgina sat up in bed and lit the lamp. The bold scrawl of her name on the outside was definitely Daniel's handwriting.

Holding her breath, Georgina carefully slit the envelope. By the time she removed the sheets of paper, her hand was shaking. It didn't take this many sheets to make plans for a romantic tryst.

She didn't want to read it. She squeezed her eyes closed and tried to put it aside, but the first line—"My dearest Miss Merry"—swam in front of her eyelids. It was like hearing Daniel's voice in her ear to see that line. Tears formed beneath her lashes, and irritated, Georgina wiped them away and opened her eyes again.

She read it through the first time hastily, waiting for the punch line, waiting for that line that said everything would be all right if she would just be patient. It never came. Puzzled, trembling, she tried to read it more carefully, but tears kept blinding her to the words.

He was leaving her. He had already left. He was on the seven o'clock train to Cincinnati. He would write whenever he got wherever he was going. He would keep in touch. If there was a child, he wanted to know about it, because he wouldn't let any child of his go without a father. But he wanted her to have her house and her freedom and her life back just the way it had been before he had come into it. He wanted her to be happy, and he would only cause her grief and trouble.

It was just like Daniel. She could hear him speak every word. He was very eloquent, astonishingly sincere, and heartbreakingly honest. He was also the biggest damned cad she'd ever had the misfortune to run into, and she was going to make him pay for this.

Georgina didn't even bother looking for the mortgage he had assured her was in her desk drawer. Damn the mortgage. Damn the house. Damn all damned Mulloneys. He wasn't going to do this to her. He had played the hero for the very last time. This time, she was going to shoot him down.

Raging inwardly, Georgina leapt from the bed and began jerking on whatever clothing came to hand. It was the middle of the night. The last train had left with Daniel on it. But she knew how to find him. She had one ace up her sleeve that he obviously didn't believe she would play. He was about to learn differently.

She was going to telegraph Tyler and Evie.

Daniel watched the brief show of lights as some unnamed town flashed by. He had passed the last stop between Cutlerville and Cincinnati. There would be no turning back.

He tried to look ahead, to plan a future that seemed suddenly empty. He didn't think he would go back to Natchez right away. Tyler and Evie would be full of questions, and they wouldn't be pleasant ones. Perhaps he would go back to the *Despatch* in St. Louis. Pulitzer had been a good teacher. He would hire him back.

Or he could go to Texas and find a town that didn't have a paper. He wouldn't get rich, but he could make a comfortable living. He'd find some pleasant little girl who would make a good wife and wouldn't require rescuing and they could settle down and have twins or something. He'd like to have roses in the front yard and a picket fence. His needs really were very few. Surely he could acquire these basic desires.

Or he could risk it all and have Georgina.

The wheels of the train slowed to make a long curve, and Daniel found himself putting on his hat and picking up his bag. Without a thought to what he was doing, he meandered down the aisle past the sleeping passengers, walking faster the closer the train came into the curve. He was practically running before the train could pick up speed on the other side.

Dashing out the car door, Daniel grabbed the pole on the outside, threw his bag into a corn field, and leapt into the dark of night.

A man in a stained and crumpled Stetson watched him go, then pulled his hat farther over his eyes and smiled as he settled more comfortably into his seat. The boy had gumption, he'd say that much for him.

Thirty-six

T he pounding on the front door echoed the pounding behind her eyes as Georgina jerked her hair tightly into a knot and stabbed another pin into it. She had just spent the most wretched night of her life, and she didn't need this infernal pounding. Maybe she ought to find one of her mother's bottles of laudanum.

She couldn't expect Evie and Tyler to respond to a telegram sent in the middle of the night. She should have waited until morning. But she couldn't just sit here and do nothing. If she had any idea at all which train Daniel had taken after he reached Cincinnati, she would be on the next train out. But she didn't, so she couldn't. Not until she'd heard from the Monteignes.

A servant discreetly tapped on her door, and Georgina scowled as she looked up.

"Mr. Peter Mulloney to see you, ma'am."

Peter? At this hour? Georgina glanced at the mantel clock. She didn't think Peter even knew what the sun looked like at this hour.

She nodded her head in dismissal. "I'll be down in a minute."

It would only take a minute to gather her wrath and fling it at him. Had she been a violent person, she would blast the entire male population this morning. Georgina was almost grateful that Peter had presented himself as a target for her ire before she exploded with the need to release it.

She had put on a fresh dress this morning, but she

wasn't at all certain which one or how it looked and didn't really care. She had stayed up all night in hopes of hearing something, anything, and she was operating on temper alone right now. Any Mulloney would serve to divert her fury.

Peter was standing in the front hall, his hands filled with familiar cases and equipment. The fact that he was in possession of her cameras only increased her fury.

"You have your nerve coming here, Peter Mulloney! Any man with an ounce of conscience would hide himself from the face of the world after what you and your family have done. Just put those things down and get out of my sight. You disgust me."

Stunned by this virago who wore the same face as the laughing girl he had once known, Peter slowly lowered the camera equipment and stared at her. Bouncing golden curls were tied back in a severe knot that did nothing to detract from her delicate beauty, but the dark shadows under her eyes were not natural to the woman he had known. The cloud over laughing blue eyes stabbed at his heart.

"What's wrong, Georgina? You still can't be mad at me for making you marry Daniel. I thought you were happy about that."

"Happy?" Her voice nearly reached a screech. "Happy to be forced to marry a man who did absolutely nothing other than to be kind to me? If I had a rifle, I ought to force you to marry some poor woman who did nothing more than suffer from your selfishness. Did you know your father had Daniel's newspaper building condemned and the Harrisons evicted from their house? Did you? Now stand there and act innocent, Peter Mulloney. I dare you. Get out of my sight. If I never see another Mulloney again, it will be too soon."

She turned around and started back up the stairs, only to see Audrey and Janice peering down at her from the upper hall, their eyes wide and frightened. Swearing to herself, Georgina turned around and glared at Peter. "Get out."

"I didn't do it, Georgina!" Growing angry, Peter focused his attention on the woman in the hallway. He couldn't see the ones above. "I have nothing to do with those rental properties. I'd think they would be happy to be thrown out of the rat-infested traps anyway."

"Oh, tell me another one, Peter," Georgina responded sarcastically. "Tell me Mulloney's Department Store doesn't own part of that rental company. Tell me you're not in charge of the department store." She placed her hands on her hips and minced forward. "Tell me you're not a Mulloney, and maybe I'll even believe you."

"Georgina, what in hell is wrong with you this morning? I brought back your camera in hopes of a truce. I just wanted to ask a favor of you." Peter held his ground until Georgina was practically on his toes, then he backed toward the door. "Will you listen to reason just for a minute? My mother wants to see Daniel. You know she's an invalid. She's scarcely been able to eat since I told her about him. You've got to persuade him to come visit. Believe me, Georgina, I'm not the villain you want. I've argued with my father about those properties, but he doesn't listen to me. There isn't anything I can do about it."

Ignoring his plea, Georgina concentrated on her fury. "And there's nothing you can do about those employees you fired, either, is there, Peter?" Her first question was deceptively calm. "And there's nothing you can do about the hours they work or the salaries they make or the promotions you give only to men. And buying stools for them to rest on would undoubtedly bankrupt you." Georgina's voice rose with each new accusation until she was shouting. "Get out of my house, Peter Mulloney, and don't you dare show your face here again!"

"All right, thank you, I will!" Jamming his hat back on his head, Peter stalked out and slammed the door after him.

Wanting to collapse on the floor, Georgina held herself straight and stiff a few seconds longer, letting the fury race through her fingertips and out of her body before she turned to face her audience. She had never done anything remotely like this in her entire life, and she wasn't at all certain that she ever wanted to do it again. Life had been much easier when she could face it with a smile.

She tried to paste one to her face now, but it faltered slightly as she turned and found Janice already at the bottom of the stairs.

"He won't do anything, will he?" she asked calmly.

Georgina shook her head. "Won't or can't. I don't know which."

Janice nodded in understanding. "It's all right. We'll get by. The boarding house is much cheaper, actually, since it comes with two meals a day. And if you can keep the factory open, Audrey will make much better wages working for you." Tentatively, she touched Georgina's arm. "You'll feel better after you have a bite to eat. Did you know that Egan tried to collect the rents the other day?"

Georgina listened listlessly.

Janice guided her toward the dining room. "He didn't collect one penny. The men followed him everywhere so he couldn't even take out his wrath on any of us. The boys have set up shifts at all the corners now so he can't get past without everyone knowing. We sent a list of demands to Mulloney himself."

Georgina nodded and smiled and let the words fall around her. The only thought in her mind, however, was how soon she would hear from Daniel's family.

Georgina dug her fingers into her hair and contemplated pulling it out as she stared at the figures on the paper in front of her. On the best of days the figures made no sense to her, and this wasn't the best of days. Her gaze strayed to the crumpled telegram on the corner of the desk.

The Monteignes hadn't heard from Daniel, but they were making inquiries. In the meantime, they were on their way north. She should expect them shortly.

What in the world was she going to do with Evie and Tyler Monteigne while her whole world crumbled around her? Maybe she ought to send them over to visit Peter's mother. That plea had nagged at her all day long with all her other problems. Why hadn't she considered Mrs. Mulloney earlier? She had never heard anything against the woman. She even vaguely remembered her as a sweet and rather fragile piece of her past. Artemis Mulloney had probably walked all over her until she was no more than a shadow inhabiting the upper stories of the house.

The men in the Mulloney family were like that. Georgina scowled and stared at the figures some more. But she wasn't going to be like the women of the Mulloney family. She wasn't going to be like her mother, either. She was going to fight back, if it killed her. The way this day was going, it just might. At least she'd be out of her misery then.

Rubbing at a wayward tear, Georgina glanced up as one of Janice's assistants entered. Janice had taken the day off to move into the boarding house. Even the Harrisons would be gone when she got home this evening. Maybe she could eat dinner in the kitchen with the servants.

"Miss Han . . . Mrs. Mulloney?"

Georgina nodded impatiently.

"We've got two crates full. Do you want to ship them tonight?"

"That's not enough to fill the Norton order, is it?"

"No, ma'am, but it's enough for the Rottingham one."

"I want to fill the large orders first. They pay faster and they might order more quickly if we're prompt. We'll wait until you have the rest of their order together."

"Yes, ma'am." The woman bobbed a brief curtsy and disappeared through the doorway.

Georgina stared after her, rubbing her head. Lack of sleep was catching up with her now. She would wish the day at an end if she only had someone to go home to, but the thought of that empty house made even the factory a welcome haven. Maybe it wouldn't be such a bad thing to have the Monteignes come to stay for a while.

But her new five o'clock closing time came all too soon, and the happy laughter of departing workers quickly grew into the deadly silence of an empty building.

Refusing to give in to it, Georgina bent her head over

her work. Now that there wouldn't be any interruptions, she could get something done.

From his vantage point at the window of the warehouse, Daniel watched the workers leaving the factory for the day. Georgina's carriage waited outside, but one of the women stopped to talk to the driver, and a moment later, it lurched away without Georgina in it.

Blast the woman, she shouldn't be working in this part of town at this hour. He'd like to go wring her neck. Surely she didn't think Artemis was going to let her keep the place?

But he had thrown away his right to interfere, so Daniel could only fiddle with what remained of his press and wait for Georgina to appear. He just wanted to see her, to be certain she was holding up all right. He knew she was in there. He had seen her at lunchtime talking with the workers on the front lawn. He bet her father had never bothered to do that.

He didn't know how good a plant manager Georgina would make, but she would make a darn good personnel manager. Peter should have married her. He could have managed the factory, and she could have dealt with the employees. Together, they would have made a fortune.

The idea of Georgina turning to his brother for comfort made Daniel grit his teeth and go back to cleaning the ink from the piece he held in his hand. He ought to let her go, but he couldn't—not until he was certain she would be happier without him.

It was pure male conceit that made him think she might be better off with him than without him. He knew that, but still he sat, staring out the window, waiting for Georgina to show her face. He didn't expect her to be smiling. He didn't know what to expect. He just wanted to keep an eye on her for a few days and make sure Artemis kept his promises.

It was still light out when he looked up and saw the first curl of smoke coming through the factory window. Daniel wasn't certain he was seeing right, and he put the piece down that he was working on and tried to get a better look. Normally, he could see distances much better than up close, but he couldn't believe what he was seeing.

Why would there be smoke coming out of a window?

Trying not to panic, Daniel set himself an easy pace out the door and down the stairs. That jump from the train last night and the resulting long hike to civilization had worked at his weak leg muscles. He didn't want to go tumbling headfirst down the stairs right now.

By the time he reached the street, his heart was pounding like a frantic drum. The smoke could have been just an illusion in the warped glass. Georgina might not even be in there. There was no reason to believe there was a fire in a factory that had been there for decades. No reason at all.

Except for the flame now leaping through the window where the smoke had been earlier.

Screaming fire at the top of his lungs in hopes that someone would hear, Daniel ran for the office across the street. Couldn't Georgina smell the smoke?

He heard other shouts behind him, heard the harsh gallop of a horse as someone raced for the fire department. Fire in these old buildings could be deadly. He would have help in minutes, but he couldn't wait that long.

Smoke poured through the office doorway as Daniel flung open the front door. Heat washed over him in waves, but there was no sign of fire in this part of the building as yet. Covering his mouth and nose with his handkerchief, Daniel shoved past the chairs and secretary's desk and made his way to the tiny room in the back of the building, Georgina's office.

By the time he flung open the door, he was coughing heavily and sweat poured off him from the heat. Smoke made the dim interior even murkier, and it took a moment to focus. He prayed she wasn't here. Surely she would have smelled the smoke and left earlier. Surely she wouldn't have gone into the factory to investigate the source of the fire. If there was a Lord in the heaven above, He wouldn't let someone like Miss Merry die in an inferno like this.

He found Georgina with her head resting on her arms

on the desk as if she had gone to sleep and hadn't awoken. Daniel gripped her shoulders and called her name, but she didn't stir. Panic raced through his veins as swiftly as the trail of fire coming through the wall.

There wasn't time to think or grieve or pray. Pulling Georgina into his arms, Daniel started back for the door, only to see another trail of flames creep up the wall to the ceiling out there. Whatever was burning on the other side of that wall had finally reached a state of combustion that would ignite the entire building in minutes. He didn't have time to cross both offices and get out, not carrying Georgina.

Without a quiver, Daniel turned and crashed his shoulder against the windowpane behind him. The glass shattered instantly. Flinging Georgina over his shoulder, he used his coat sleeve to knock splinters of glass from the frame. Only when he was satisfied the exit was safe did he lower Georgina through it.

She crumpled lifelessly on the ground outside. Daniel had already stopped feeling any emotion at all. His brain had stopped functioning the instant he'd touched her and felt no response. Like the machines on the other side of the wall, he moved stiffly and without reason, going through the motions for which he was made.

He climbed through the window and bent to lift Georgina from the ground. He could hear the excited shouts of people carrying a water line to the pumps. In the distance he heard the clang of a firebell. None of that mattered. His life was in his hands now, and Daniel carried her gently through the darkened alley to the street. If she lived, he would survive. If she didn't, he had died in the fire with her. He knew that as certainly as he knew where his feet were carrying him.

No one saw them as he lifted her through the un-boarded window of the warehouse across the street. He needed no light to carry her up the familiar stairs to the room they had shared together.

He laid her on the bed that had been left behind when they abandoned the building. She unfolded like a lifeless doll, spilling arms and legs across the cover. This was more than sleep, then.

Daniel reached a trembling hand to Georgina's soft cheek, whispering her name. He sat beside her, willing her to respond as he stroked her face. Desperate, he leaned over and applied his lips to hers. They were warm, but seemingly lifeless.

He pulled her into his arms, forcing her upright, holding her over his shoulder as he hugged her and murmured senseless words in her ear. He ran his hands up and down her back, gently at first, then more vigorously. His murmurs became anguished cries of pain when she didn't respond.

"Georgina, answer me! My God, don't leave me like this! You can't leave me. You're all I have, Georgina. Wake up and wish me to the devil, Georgie, but don't go away. Please, Georgie . . ."

Daniel was crying now, huge tears rolling unashamedly down his beard-stubbled cheeks as he rubbed her back and buried kisses against her throat. "I love you, Georgina," he whispered desperately, suddenly knowing it was true, recognizing it with a stab of bitter anguish. "I love you. I just want you to be happy. Please, God, let her live. I'll do anything. I'll never curse. I'll never take Your name in vain. I'll honor my father. Lord, anything! Please . . ."

Daniel's voice trailed off in waves of sobs as he rocked Georgina back and forth, waiting for some miracle in a life that had been filled with anything but miracles.

In the silence left by his tears, a low moan sounded, followed by a wracking cough.

Daniel ran his fingers deep into Georgina's hair and gave a heartfelt prayer of thanks even as she bent double with a spasm of coughing that shook them both.

Thirty-seven

❦

He was afraid to let her go, afraid she would slip away from him again, but he needed to get her water. Daniel held Georgina tightly as spasms of coughing struck her again and again until he feared the attacks would spit out her lungs.

He needed to call a physician, but he couldn't bear to leave her. He had never been the sort to panic easily, but he couldn't think for the terror blurring his mind and swallowing his soul. He couldn't lose Georgina. Not now. Not ever. The shouts and noises from the street below joined the anguished scream of fear inside his head.

Fighting for some form of rationality, Daniel piled pillows behind Georgina's head so she could lean against them while he unfastened her bodice. He thanked Whoever watched over them that she had worn a gown that buttoned up the front. The way his hands were shaking, he didn't think he could hold her up and unfasten back hooks.

With trembling fingers he ripped open the corset beneath, and Georgina took a gasping breath that brought another wracking attack of coughs. This time, her lashes fluttered a little, and Daniel's heart fluttered with them.

"Georgina, try to breathe easy. Don't gulp, sweetheart. It's going to be all right." The words didn't make sense even to him, but they seemed to soothe her. "I'm going to get you a cup of water. I'll be right back. Just breathe easy, and I'll be right here."

He thought she nodded slightly, and taking a deep gulp

of air for himself, Daniel hurried to fetch a cup of water, thankful whoever had condemned the building hadn't shut off the plumbing.

When he returned, she was moving restlessly on the bed. The coughs weren't so heavy now. He sat beside her and pulled her into his arms again. "I've brought you water, sweetheart. Sip it slowly. That's a girl." He was talking more to reassure himself than for Georgina's benefit. He held the cup to her lips and tilted it so the water dribbled gently down her throat. She pushed away to cough again, then reached for the cup herself.

Daniel was certain his heart had stuck in his throat as she drank thirstily. He wanted to weep and offer prayers of gratitude and wild promises to a God he had thought meant for others and not for him. He'd dutifully attended church on Sundays when forced by the women in his life, but he'd never gone on his own. That was going to change now, he promised. He would be right by Georgina's side when she marched through those church doors.

"Daniel?" Her words were uncertain, husky from her raw throat. Her gaze met his with disbelief and a thousand questions.

"You didn't really think I could stay away, did you?" He stroked her hair lightly, not daring more. "I didn't get halfway to Cincinnati before I realized I couldn't live without a heart, and you've got mine."

She made a sound that almost sounded like a giggle, and Daniel felt a foolish grin spreading across his face.

"You're a cad and a scoundrel," she whispered, burying her face in his shoulder to cough some more.

"I'm doing my damnedest to be a hero, Miss Merry, but I'm not as good at it as I ought to be. I came back to tell you I love you and to ask you to marry me. Do you think you might, if I hang around long enough?"

Georgina clung to his shirt and tried to giggle again through a spasm of coughing. She shook her head, and Daniel thought his heart just might plunge to his feet, but he set his lips and hoped. "If loving you isn't enough, what else can I do?"

"I want a husband," she coughed, "not a hero."

Daniel settled her firmly against his side and stroked her hair. Even through the smoke he could smell lilies, and he smiled dreamily. He could imagine waking up to the smell of lilies for the rest of his life. The warm pressure of Georgina's breasts against his side stirred other desires, but he resisted. Now wasn't the time. He didn't know when the time would be, but he'd find it. She was going to be his now, if he had to burn the whole damned town to the ground to prove it.

"I think I could arrange that, Georgie, if you tell me you want to be a wife. I can't promise to be a very good husband. We may have to leave this town. You'd better think long and hard before you make any decisions. I'll give you all the time you want."

"Stupid," she muttered, pounding weakly at his chest. "Stupid, stupid, stupid."

Daniel felt laughter gathering in his chest, and tears of relief followed the trails of grief marked earlier. "I've got to get you out of here, Miss Merry. I've got to get you to a doctor, but I can't let anyone know I'm back yet. I don't want my father throwing you out of your house until I'm ready to go."

He thought she muttered something that sounded like "Damn the house," but he was probably hearing things. Holding her to his side, he stood up, and she managed a wobbly footstep beside him. He peered through a crack in the boarded windows and watched the chaos below. Off to one side waited a carriage that could only be Georgina's. A very worried Blucher stalked up and down beside it.

"Your carriage is down there, Georgie. I'm going to take you to it and let Blucher take you home. Don't tell anyone you saw me, Georgie. Do you understand?"

"No," she grumbled, but the coughing prevented any further argument.

"Then you'll have to trust me." Daniel tilted her chin up until their eyes met. "I love you, Miss Merry. Can you trust me just a little bit?"

"After I kill you," she managed to get out with enough vigor to be heard.

Daniel grinned. "I'll make it easy for you. I'll loan you my gun just as soon as I get finished with what I'm going to do."

Her eyes darkened, but he didn't give her time to question. Without a word of warning, he swept her into his arms again and started for the door. There was one advantage to having a small woman for a wife—she was easy to sweep off her feet.

Blucher looked up in relief as Daniel emerged from the shadows and deposited Georgina in the carriage. She was too weak to protest and sank into the cushions with another spasm of coughing as Daniel turned to the driver. With a few words of caution and a command to find her a physician, Daniel sent the man and the carriage off. He thought he saw Georgina turn and stare through the window at him, but he didn't dare follow. Not yet.

Picking up a cap lying discarded in the street, Daniel slid it down over his forehead and worked his way into the crowd. It was time to find out what this fire was all about.

Georgina lay propped against the pillows of her bed the next morning, still coughing but not so badly after a night of rest. She sipped carefully at the medicine the doctor—Dr. Phelps and not her father's treacherous Dr. Ralph—had provided and tried to remember the horrible nightmare of the night before.

She was certain she had dreamed Daniel was there, a penitent Daniel who declared he loved her. An almost penitent Daniel, she amended, vaguely remembering some of his words. He had laughed at her, she remembered, and she had tried to hit him, but he'd said he loved her. And if her memory wasn't all askew, he had rescued her from the burning factory.

That part was almost certainly true. It would be typical of Daniel to play the hero rather than to wait for help. The declaration of love she wasn't so certain about. That could have been wishful dreaming. It didn't seem nearly as likely as Daniel playing hero. And she didn't see him here worrying over her bedside, either. She could very well have imagined that part.

Peter arrived as Georgina sipped at her breakfast. She didn't have much stomach for toast, but the juice felt good as it went down. She threw Peter a look of disdain and reached for her coffee.

"I suppose you're going to blame me for the fire, too." He flung his hat at the nearest chair and ignored it when it bounced to the floor. "My mother is in hysterics, your precious husband seems to have disappeared, and my father has been incommunicado for days. Those are probably good enough reasons for burning down one of the best garment factories in the country. I sent for your father, by the way."

"How thoughtful. I'd better eat and drink while I can. When he gets home, I won't dare touch anything."

Peter stared at her. "Maybe my father was right and you are touched in the head."

Georgina smiled sweetly at him, but a coughing fit diminished the effect. Peter continued to watch her warily, but he held out the glass of juice. After she took the glass, he picked up the bottle of medicine on the bedside table.

"This didn't come from Dr. Ralph. Maybe you better have him come over. That cough doesn't sound good."

The sound Georgina made was vaguely like a laugh. "Good. Dr. Ralph and my father, my saviors. Get out of here, Peter. I'm going to get dressed and go hide before I end up in the Shady Rest Retiring Home with my mother."

Peter set the bottle down and contemplated her carefully. "What are you talking about?"

"Don't play dumb for my benefit." Georgina set her juice aside impatiently and pulled herself straighter in the bed. "Your father and Dr. Ralph are probably playing the same game with your mother. I'd go inspect her medicines if I were you. Now leave, Peter, I want to get dressed."

"Your maid said you were supposed to rest. I practically had to beat her over the head to get in here. Now lie there and explain things a little more coherently or I'll be here all day."

Georgina scowled. "How plain do I need to be? Dr. Ralph gives my mother laudanum to keep her quiet. He gave it to me so my father could drag me out of here and hide me away in a convalescent home until your father could do something about Daniel. Any time a woman in this town tries to protest or complain, Dr. Ralph is there to solve the problem. I think maybe he's drunk too much of the stuff himself."

She pulled back the covers and started to get up, ignoring Peter's shocked expression. "Now will you get out of here?"

"After that, I don't even dare mention sending for the maid to fetch a doctor." Peter turned his back so she could reach for her robe, but he didn't leave. "I don't know how the fire happened, Georgina. You've got to believe me. I've hired some men to investigate, but I doubt that they'll find anything. The fire brigade put out the worst of it before it could destroy the machinery. I'm going to go over there and supervise moving what can be saved into an empty warehouse. We'll find a new building and go back into production as soon as possible."

"We?" Her tone was heavily laced with irony. "*We* won't do anything, Peter. You'll get your backside out of here and out of my life and never present your face to me again if you know what's good for you. I'm tired of being nice. I'm going for your father's throat. You don't want to be around when I do."

Spasms of coughing prevented her words from being as forceful as she could have wished. Peter swung around, but refrained from pushing her into the nearest chair.

Clenching his fists at his side, he waited for her to recover before speaking. "You'll have to beat me to him if anything you've said is true. I'm going to take Dr. Phelps to see my mother this morning. If there's any truth to what you're saying, I'll give the evidence to Daniel. He needs to put it in the paper and warn all the women in town. We'll drive Ralph into the ocean if need be. Where is Daniel, anyway? I've still got to persuade him to see Mother."

Georgina took the chair of her own accord and sipped at her juice while she gathered strength. "I'll give him the message, but he rather has his hands full right now. I suppose you're going to tell me you didn't know your father offered to give me the mortgage on this house if Daniel would conveniently disappear?"

Peter ran his hand through his hair in a gesture vaguely reminiscent of Daniel's. "I'm prepared to believe just about anything right now. Don't hit me with any more just yet, Georgie. Let me do one thing at a time. Tell me where to find Daniel."

"Not on your bottom dollar, Peter." This time, she managed her best vapid smile convincingly. "As far as I know, he's gone back to Texas. Be sure to tell your father that."

Swearing, Peter bent to pick up his hat. When he straightened, his handsome face was taut with anger and his eyes flashed emerald fires, but his words were carefully polite. "You promised to tell Daniel about Mother. I'm holding you to it, Georgie."

She held her smile. "I'll write him a letter. Bye-bye, Peter."

The smile faded as he scowled and walked out. It was impossible to tell whose side Peter was on. She wanted to confide in him. She had always trusted him. But then, she had always trusted her father, too. She wasn't certain she could even trust Daniel anymore. After all, he had walked out on her just as she had thought they were making progress. But he had come back. She would rely on that.

Georgina didn't bother to try to get dressed. She had no work to go to and no one she particularly wanted to see badly enough to strain her aching chest to do it. She brushed her hair and pinned it up and let the maids wait on her. As nervous and uncertain as she, they seemed to be glad of the opportunity to be doing something useful.

By the time Janice knocked on the door, Georgina was ready for sensible company. She set aside her book and gestured for her visitor to come in.

Janice slipped through the partially open door and closed it behind her. She gave Georgina a critical look. "You look better than yesterday for some reason. How do you feel?"

"Like a consumptive. I can't stop coughing. Tell me what's happening."

Janice took the chair. "Peter Mulloney is down at the factory, ordering the machines carried into the warehouse you and Daniel were using. He's had all the boards ripped off and new glass is being installed. I don't know what happened to the condemnation notice."

"He probably ordered his father to have it removed." Georgina shrugged in dismissal. "Mulloney owns all the sewing equipment anyway. My father said it was mortgaged to the hilt. I just hate going down in defeat like this." Seeing Janice's expression, she hurried to add, "Peter said he would have the factory operating again as soon as possible. I'll make certain he hires you and Audrey. I think he almost listened to me today. He thinks I've got something he wants."

Janice waited patiently for some explanation, but none was forthcoming. She frowned slightly, then embarked on the rest of her news. "Egan has disappeared. He was around yesterday trying to collect the rent, but no one has seen him since he and Emory had supper together last evening. They were both saying some rather unpleasant things about you and Daniel when they left."

Georgina felt her stomach lurch in apprehension, but she managed to maintain a look of calm. "Maybe Daniel ran him out of town on a rail," she said lightly.

It was Janice's turn to look apprehensive. "I've heard Daniel hasn't been seen in days. He's all right then?"

"Daniel is better than all right," Georgina said with certainty and a touch of bitterness. "Daniel is in his element right about now. He has more pots of trouble brewing than any one man can handle, and he's probably sitting on a roof somewhere, watching them boil and laughing. Don't ever fall in love, Janice. Men are pure hell."

Janice's normally noncommittal expression evaporated with a fleeting smile and a sound almost like a laugh. She hastily recovered, but her eyes were still smiling. "I'll remember that," she said solemnly. "At least I'll know better than to get near men with six-guns and funny-looking hats."

"Good." Georgina nodded her head vigorously. "Find yourself a nice clerk down at Mulloney's, one with a white collar and clean hands, one who's so grateful to have you that he'll satisfy your every wish."

This time, Janice did laugh out loud, her lips cracking open just enough to reveal her small white teeth. As if to keep anyone from seeing her actually laughing, she hurriedly rose and walked to the door, turning only to say, "Tomorrow's the Fourth. Make certain you get a grandstand seat for the parade."

"Oh, I'll be sure to do that," Georgina muttered as the door closed. And she had some excellent ideas on how to accomplish that and several other things on her mind.

Thirty-eight

"Your father will take care of everything, don't you worry at all." Dolly Hanover patted her daughter's hand against the bedcovers. "That charming young Peter sent us the nicest telegram. I'm certain he'll see to everything. I never did understand why you wouldn't marry him."

Georgina waited patiently for her mother to leave. It was good to know that her father hadn't left her mother behind in the convalescent home again, and she was always happy to see her; she just had other things on her mind right now. Being married to a man like Daniel had that effect.

"Peter never listened to me, Mother," Georgina answered with remarkable restraint. "And Daniel needs me." Sometimes, she amended to herself.

"Well, I'm sure that's important." Despite her words, there was a puzzled frown on Dolly's forehead as she turned to leave. "Now you get lots of sleep and don't worry about anything. We're here now."

Which was just what Georgina was worried about. Would Daniel come here if he knew her parents were back in residence? If he didn't, she was going to have to go out and hunt him down, and she didn't have the slightest idea where to begin if Peter had taken over the newspaper office.

She listened to the leaves brushing against her bedroom window and tried to imagine that it was Daniel coming for her. She had obediently sat here all day waiting for him to put in an appearance, and he hadn't even sent word. If he didn't show up soon, she was going to hang him. Shooting wasn't good enough.

She fingered the lace on the light silk robe she had donned after her bath. This was another item meant for her trousseau, and it had gone unworn until now. She had worn it for Daniel's benefit. She really must be mad. Why was she trying to please a man who had walked out on her?

All her life she had been cosseted by the men in her life, told not to worry, everything would be taken care of. Maybe that attitude worked for women like her mother, but it wasn't working for her anymore. She was beginning to realize that men needed taking care of as much as women, and the thought wasn't in the least dismaying. She wanted to take care of Daniel—if the damned man would just let her.

Georgina listened to the sounds of the house settling down for the night and swore softly to herself. A normal marriage was too much to expect, she supposed, especially after the way hers started out. And if her parents' marriage was anything to judge by, she really didn't want a normal marriage. She just wanted Daniel.

She turned off the lamp and slid down between the sheets and patted the empty pillow beside her. She didn't think she was asking for much to want to have her husband in bed beside her every night. She'd come to crave that closeness of Daniel's body next to hers. She wanted to be able to reach out and touch his shoulder, slide her foot next to his, whisper sleepy questions in his ear when she woke. And she wanted to be there when that fire lit in his eyes and he leaned over her and took her in his hands and joined their bodies until they were one. She wanted that with every fiber of her being.

Georgina closed her eyes tightly against the torture of her thoughts. The wind must be picking up. The branches outside were rubbing frantically against the glass.

The branches outside. Her eyes flew wide open again. She had lived here most of her life and the wind never blew that hard from that direction.

She was out of bed and at the window in seconds. Flinging open the sash, she glared at the shadow straddling the slender maple branch outside, his grin growing from sheepish to delighted as she raged at him.

"Daniel Ewan Mulloney, you are the most incorrigible, least intelligent, exasperating excuse for a man I have ever met in all my life! Why in heaven's name can't you come through a door like any normal human being? It would serve you right if you fell from there and broke your silly neck. Get yourself in here now before I'm picking pieces of you up off the ground."

Daniel slid his leg silently over the sill, caught the window frame, and pulled the rest of him through until he was standing so close in front of her that their toes touched. Georgina couldn't suppress a gasp as he slid his hands beneath her robe and cupped her breasts through the thin silk of her gown.

"Did I hear a hint of concern in that tirade? Or would you prefer it if I broke my silly neck and let you alone?"

"Idiot!" Georgina tried to pull away, but his touch was too compelling. Instead, her breasts seemed to surge forward to fill his hands, and the place between her thighs began to tingle. "I don't know why I married a man so prone to risking his foolish neck."

"Because your boyfriend held a gun on me?" he answered helpfully, nuzzling her neck.

"If that's all it was, I should have let him blow your head off and saved everyone a lot of grief." She kept her voice cool, but her body was growing warmer by the minute. Georgina slid her fingers into the unruly tangle of Daniel's hair and bent willingly to his embrace.

"Then tell me it was because you loved me, because you can't live without me." His lips continued their sensuous journey as he gently urged her backward toward the bed.

"You left me!" Georgina's fingers grabbed his hair tighter, jerking it from his scalp as she felt herself being maneuvered against the bed. "Why would I tell you any such thing after what you did?"

Daniel let her pull his head up until he was gazing into

the wild blue of her eyes. "Because I love you? Because I only wanted to do what was best for you?"

Georgina's grip loosened beneath the intensity of his gaze. "And I thought you were so smart," she whispered scornfully. "Only an utter idiot would think I would be better off without you."

The gray of his eyes almost became silver in the moonlight, and Daniel's mouth softened into a tender smile of delight. "Does that mean you'll take this lame hero for husband, to have and to hold, until death do us part?"

"I will." And standing on tiptoe, Georgina raised her lips to his.

With an exquisite shudder of relief, Daniel clasped her in his arms, pulling her body into his, and filling her mouth with his kisses. Georgina clung to him with all her strength, trying not to imagine what it would have been like if she'd never held him like this again. She couldn't bear even the thought of it, and she held him tighter, desperately, pleading with her mouth and body to never let her go.

Daniel lifted her gently to the bed, throwing the sheets aside and kneeling over her, worshiping her with his mouth and hands. Growing frantic under the trail of his kisses, Georgina tore at his shirt, pulling it from his trousers and running her hands beneath the cotton to the hard, warm male body beneath. Not until then was she certain she wasn't dreaming.

She wouldn't let him go long enough for him to remove his clothes. She helped him with his buttons, then deliberately stroked the hard male part of him she released from the confining cloth. With wicked delight Georgina felt Daniel's shudder of desire, and she slid her fingers deeper, testing the strength of his resistance.

"Georgina." His voice was strained as he held himself propped over her. "You'd better be certain you understand what this means."

Georgina positioned her legs on either side of him and wriggled so close she could feel the heat of him through the thin film of silk. "Probably warehouses and cockroaches and midnight rescues," she assured him as she ran her fingers provocatively up and down his arms. Her voice dropped to a whisper. "And babies, and baths together, and maybe some day a little house with roses in the front yard and horses in the back."

"How did you know?" Daniel pulled the hampering silk to her waist and touched her there, where she was warm and wet and waiting.

She arched into his hand with a moan, felt his fingers open inside her, and barely got the words between her teeth. "I read a Pecos Martin book," she murmured, and then gasped as his hand moved and something much stronger came inside her.

As Daniel surged deeper into her, his mouth covered her breasts, and a flame of desire raced through her from head to toe. With a cry of surrender Georgina flung her arms around him, letting him have complete possession of her body, letting him take control, until she no longer knew where her body ended and his began, knowing only that they were one in this. When he took her to that place they were coming to know so well, she whispered his name just as he forced her over the precipice, and she closed her eyes and clung to his shoulders as they tumbled together into weightlessness.

"I love you," she whispered as Daniel's heavy body sank onto hers, pushing her into the mattress.

Long brown fingers closed around her breast and teased at the nipple. Georgina felt him stiffen slightly at her words, but she wasn't going to take them back. She ran her hands over the powerful muscles of his back. "I love you, Daniel, and I'll kill you if you ever leave me again."

He chuckled lightly against her ear at that threat. "Make me believe that, and you'll be sorry. When I go, I'll take you with me, and you might find yourself living in a Texas desert with cactus for company."

Georgina wriggled her hips and with satisfaction, felt him growing hard again. "I'll dress them up in shirts and ties and skirts and bonnets and take turns shooting at them and serving them tea."

Daniel placed his hands on either side of her head and

propped himself over her. "You don't know anything about that kind of life, Georgina. I'd be a cad to do that to you."

Worried, Georgina wriggled against him again, hoping to distract him from the unpleasant note of this conversation. When he merely turned over and pulled her with him, she squirmed uncomfortably at his side. "Then I'm not the wife you want," she said in disappointment.

Daniel stroked her hair and wrapped his arm around her back until his fingers reached her breast on the other side. "You're all the wife I want. Why do you think I came back? I couldn't bear the thought of a future without you. We'll just have to think of some way to work this out so you can have your family and home and I can keep from killing my father."

"And he can keep from killing you." Not entirely reassured, Georgina rose up on her elbow to glare down at him. "Why don't we go to visit Natchez and your family and think of something safe to do?"

Daniel sighed. "That would probably be best. I just don't like leaving a job undone. If neither of us is here, things just might slip back to the way they've always been. But I can't risk you in another fire like the one last night."

Georgina returned to the safe curve of his arm. "I'm sure that must have been an accident. It wouldn't make sense for your father to burn down the factory he practically owns."

"It wasn't an accident." Daniel's grip on her arm tightened in anger. "Someone set fire to the crates of finished goods you had stacked in there. From what I've gathered, Egan and Emory decided to teach us a lesson that got just a little out of hand. I don't think they knew you were in the building. And they didn't plan to destroy the whole factory. Someone had given the alarm and set the fire wagon on its way before I called for help. They just meant to destroy all your hard work."

Georgina was silent. She felt the angry tension building in the man beside her, and she smoothed her hand over his chest, wishing it away. "But your father had nothing to do with that," she said carefully.

"He could have. He at least created the kind of setting that would allow it. I heard he's fired Egan and hired some other strong-arm, one who packs a gun. It's not a healthy situation, Georgina."

He left so many things unsaid. Georgina struggled with the conflicting messages she was receiving. On one hand, he was saying he wanted her to stay here where she belonged. On the other, he was saying it wasn't safe. In neither case did he say what he wanted for himself. But judging from what Evie had told her about his upbringing, Georgina very much thought what Daniel wanted was a family, and his real family was right here. She could help him start a new one, but he hadn't resolved his conflict over the old one yet. The need to know more of his family and the need to protect her were tearing him apart. If it weren't for her, he would be out there on the front lines fighting his darnedest to close that gap between himself and his family.

Georgina twisted her finger in a hair on Daniel's chest and slid her leg over his. He had such long, muscular legs. She moved closer. "We can't go anywhere or do anything until you visit your mother, Daniel," she whispered.

He stiffened. "Don't be ridiculous, Georgie. She's better off thinking I'm dead."

"Peter told her you're alive. He says she isn't eating, that she's worried sick, or sicker. They may be poisoning her with laudanum the same way they're poisoning my mother. You've got to go see her, Daniel."

"You want me to walk up to the rattlesnake's nest and ring the bell?" he asked in disbelief.

"That's just exactly what I want you to do. It's my birthday tomorrow. That's what I want for a present. I'll send a note to Peter and he can arrange it."

The Fourth of July—he'd forgotten. All hell would probably break loose tomorrow, and she wanted him to walk into the middle of it. One of them was a few nickels shy of a dollar, and Daniel didn't want it to be him. But it undoubtedly was, because he was going to do it. He wasn't going to leave this town until he'd made the acquaintance of the woman who had given him birth and then thrown him away. Artemis wouldn't let him live peacefully in this town anyway. If he meant to take Georgie with him when he left, there was no point in hiding anymore. He didn't give a damn what became of this house and the mortgage once they were gone.

"I don't suppose you have any firecrackers you can include in that note, do you?" he asked wryly as he gave in to the idea that he wasn't going to be a hero.

"One or two." She sat up and began to tug the rest of his clothes off him.

Daniel placed his hands behind his head and admired the image of his Miss Merry performing such a wifely task on him. But the juxtaposition of rounded hips to straining loins proved fatal to his complacence. With an impatient kick he removed trousers and shoes, and with a command he hadn't known he possessed, he caught Georgina's waist and pulled her over him.

She gasped with surprise at her unexpected position, but she learned quickly. With arrogant satisfaction, Daniel felt her come over him, and in a matter of minutes, he was teaching her to ride.

He was going to enjoy teaching his little firecracker the pleasure of married life, if she didn't kill him first.

A groan escaped him as Georgina carried his little trick one step further. He barely had time to hang on and hold her still before the uncontrollable explosion overtook him and he came deep inside her.

Daniel's hands clamped her waist and held her hips tightly against his.

"You're going to pay for this in the morning," he warned as the aftershocks rippled through them both.

Georgina grinned, bent over and nipped his ear, then slid off him to her side of the bed. "You ain't seen nothing yet, Pecos."

Thirty-nine

ᴇ

Dolly Hanover smiled nervously when confronted with the actuality of her son-in-law over breakfast the next morning. Daniel smiled his most boyish grin and passed her the cream for her coffee.

"Morning, ma'am, perfect day for a parade, wouldn't you say?"

She responded shyly to his charm, ducking her head, but blushing with pleasure at his attention. "We don't usually attend. George says the streets are too full of the common elements."

"Mama usually goes to the Mulloneys for their big Fourth of July picnic," Georgina said with an innocent look that wouldn't fool the pope.

Daniel regarded her warily. His impetuous wife was up to something, but he didn't even want to contemplate what it might be. He glanced at the way Georgina was holding her coffee cup, displaying the ring he had just given her this morning. The sight of his ring on her finger stirred something deep and possessive inside him. The fact that she was proud of it made him bristle with pride. He wouldn't destroy this bond forming between them by questioning her.

"The parade stays downtown," Dolly explained diffidently. "Sometimes, we can hear the music."

"Well, you just have a really good time, Mama." Georgina patted her mother's hand. "Daniel and I will meet you at the Mulloney picnic."

That was when Daniel knew she was up to something,

but he waited until they had left the breakfast table before hauling her into a quiet room where no one would hear them. "I don't know how good an idea it is for you and your family to be over there when I show my face. If my father sees me, he's likely to make a scene."

Georgina patted his cheek in much the same way as she had patted her mother's hand. "Don't worry. I sent a note to Peter telling him to keep your father otherwise occupied. He may be a villain, but he's not dumb. You'll have some privacy."

Daniel caught her hand and pulled it between them. "I'd feel a lot easier if I knew what you were up to. Where are you going to be while all this is going on?"

"Oh, I'll be just fine, don't you worry. I'll make certain I'm surrounded by people who wouldn't think of harming me. You just go see your mother and don't worry about a thing."

The more she told him not to worry, the more Daniel suspected he had something to worry about, but the sound of Georgina's father coming down the stairs kept him from questioning closer. Holding her hand captive, he pulled her into the hall to confront his nemesis.

"Good morning, sir."

The older man halted in shock when confronted with the tall stranger who had carried his daughter off. His hand went up to rake at his full side-whiskers, then to tug at his cravat. The steely gray of Daniel's eyes remained implacable. With a slight "harrumph," George Hanover managed a greeting. "I see you don't even have a home for my daughter. You ought to be ashamed of yourself."

Daniel entwined his fingers with Georgina's and smiled confidently. "On the contrary, I have several. I just wanted Georgina to have time to get used to the idea of being married before I take her away. And I thought you might feel better if you had time to get to know me better so you would be a little less concerned for Georgina's welfare."

"Likely story." George glanced at the ring on his daughter's finger and hesitated. It wasn't an inexpensive ring. He took a more calculated look at his son-in-law.

Journalists didn't make enough money to pay for that tailored frock coat he was sporting this morning. But it could have been bought on credit, on the promise of his wealthy marriage. George frowned. "I'd suggest you consider taking Georgina to one of those many homes pretty soon, then. This one isn't likely to be ours much longer."

"I can take care of that, if you'd like, but first I have a few calls to make. We'll talk later." Turning away from his frowning father-in-law, Daniel kissed the top of Georgina's head. "Stay out of trouble until I get back, will you?"

"Of course, Daniel, don't I always?"

Georgina smiled and waved him away, then turned back to her father still waiting in the hall. "I'm calling Blucher for the carriage to go to the train station. We'll be having guests to go to the Mulloneys with us today."

She didn't wait for his response. With a secretive smile she lifted the long flounces of her best organdy and hurried to summon the driver. The morning train would be arriving shortly, and Tyler and Evie had already wired they would be on it.

Blessedly oblivious to Georgina's plans for the day, Daniel walked with a nervous stride toward the house he had never thought to enter. He wondered if there was a servants' entrance he could sneak in. He still wasn't certain it was a good idea to come anywhere close to his father yet. His wild promise to take care of the Hanovers' house had been just that—a promise and nothing more. Paying off the mortgage on that place would leave him pretty close to bankrupt, and he wasn't at all certain that he could produce the income to keep it running, especially when he would have to divest himself of all his capital to buy it. It would be much better if he just left town and let Georgina carry the mortgage as he'd tried to do earlier.

But he had promised Georgie he would visit his mother, and he wasn't going to back out now. The resulting fireworks might be better than the ones downtown should he run into his father, but that remained to be seen. He would just have to take his chances.

The carriage gate was open, and Daniel walked up the drive, expecting someone with a shotgun to appear any minute to turn him away. Instead, the figure of Peter Mulloney appeared on a side porch, glanced his way, and started down the drive with long, land-eating strides.

His brother wore an imposing frown beneath the dark shock of curls, but he grabbed Daniel's hand and shook it curtly when they met. "We'll go up the side steps. My father has gone to the store, but there's no sense in alerting the household."

"What's he doing at the store on a holiday?" Daniel found himself hurrying to keep up with his younger brother. Peter might be younger, but he was several inches taller and broader of form and didn't possess the limp that had nagged Daniel all his life. He could almost resent Peter's good looks if he wasn't so worried about meeting the woman inside that house.

Peter sent him a suspicious look. "Georgina didn't tell you? The store's staying open today. Father thinks it will bring in good business with all the crowd in town for the parade."

"He's out of his mind," Daniel said flatly as they climbed the stairs and entered the cool dusk of the interior. "The people attending that parade aren't the kind of people who would dare enter the sacred portals of Mulloney's."

Peter shrugged. "That's what I told him, but he was adamant. I think he's just trying to show the employees who's in charge."

"Don't you get any say in this?" Daniel glanced with curiosity at the brother he hadn't had a chance to know.

"I might be manager, but he owns the stock. He's quite capable of firing me if he chooses." Bitterness edged Peter's voice as they took the inside stairs two at a time.

"You could try making your own way," Daniel said wryly as they reached the upper hall.

Peter sent him a controlled look of fury. "That's fine for you to say, but who's going to look after Mother and the boys? Somebody has to stand between them and the old man."

That set a whole new perspective on the subject that Daniel hadn't considered until this minute, and there was no time now to ponder it. They stopped before closed mahogany double doors.

Peter threw them open and waited for Daniel to enter first. Daniel gave his brother a sour look, then stepped inside the most elegant boudoir he had ever encountered.

Beneath the cream-colored silk half-canopy of the antique mahogany tester bed sat a fragile woman with pale brown hair streaked with silver. She wore a wine-colored bed jacket over a figured cream silk that matched the heavy satin duvet covering the bed. Wine-red roses filled the vase beside the bed. The sculptured Oriental carpet beneath his feet carried the vivid color scheme further with accents of blue and gold that matched the lounge chair in front of the floor-to-ceiling bay window. Daniel was afraid to look any farther to the huge pieces of antique furniture in the shadows along the wall.

He had no idea how to greet the woman in the bed who was regarding him so carefully. As he approached, she raised a hand to her throat, and he thought he could discern every bone and ligament and vein in it, so thin and frail was the skin. Her cheeks were covered with a light dusting of powder, but no amount of makeup could cover the fine, high cheekbones nearly protruding through their delicate covering. A good stiff wind would carry this woman off like a kite, and he was shaking a little inside as he stopped at the foot of the bed.

"I'm Daniel Mulloney, ma'am. Peter said you wished to speak with me."

She smiled faintly then, an almost mystical smile, as if she had seen other worlds beyond this one and only dwelt here temporarily. She gestured for him to come closer. "John will look like you in a few years, and you will one day look like my father. The Ewans are handsome men, but John is at that awkward age and doesn't believe me. I would like him to meet you."

Daniel took the seat indicated and glanced to Peter for

reassurance. His brother stood guarding the door, hands behind his back, his expression deliberately blank.

Daniel turned back to the woman in the bed. "I hadn't meant to disturb you, ma'am. I had no intention of imposing on the family who spent so much on seeing me raised properly."

The elegant woman made an extremely inelegant noise. "You mean you would like to royally skewer the family that threw you out, but you're too polite to say so. Nanny did raise you well, I see. Unfortunately, I find it a trifle hard to forgive her for not letting me know you were alive. She was my nanny once, not Artemis's. He must have paid her exceedingly well indeed."

Daniel looked skeptical. "Begging your pardon, ma'am, but we were told she was nanny for my adopted sister's mother. It's possible she never knew you."

Her pale brows pulled together in a frown that almost matched Daniel's before it quickly disappeared. "As I understand it from Peter's inquiries, your adopted sister's mother was Louise Howell. Louise's mother was Evangeline Ewan before she married. Louise grew up in St. Louis, as did I. My father was her uncle. Louise and I were cousins. You and Evie Monteigne are actually second cousins. It is rather unfortunate that the nanny we shared was not only the kindest nurse we had ever known, but had an affinity for money and a reprehensible ability to keep secrets she shouldn't have. I don't think I'll ever forgive her."

"She's dead, ma'am," Daniel reminded her softly. "And she was good to us. She gave us a good home and was the mother we never knew. She was a trifle old to be a mother, I suppose, but we never had reason for complaint."

Edith Mulloney's hand began to shake as she pulled unconsciously at the covers, and her voice quaked slightly. "You were my first-born child. She had to have known that. Perhaps Louise's child was born out of wedlock, and Louise had a reason to keep her hidden, but you were not. You are the legitimate heir to all my husband owns, just the same as your brothers. It's a disgrace, a shame I can never live down. I should have known. Somehow I should have known . . ."

She was crying now, and Daniel leapt to his feet, reaching for her hand even as Peter started across the room.

"Please, don't cry. I was a cripple until I was eighteen. I could easily have died without Nanny's care. It's all worked out for the best. You couldn't have known, and you couldn't have made it any better for me if you had. I'm just sorry I never had a chance to know you."

"Maybe you'd better leave now." Hands in pockets, Peter stood beside him, gesturing his head toward the door. "Dr. Phelps said she shouldn't be overexcited just yet."

"No. No, you can't leave. We have too much to talk about. Go get your brothers, Peter. They need to know about Daniel. I'm not ashamed of him, and I don't intend for him to be hidden from the rest of you anymore."

The fragile hand gripping his had a strength Daniel never expected. He turned uncertainly to Peter. "I'm not sure this is a good idea. Your father doesn't claim me. He will throw Georgie's parents out of their house if he knows I'm here. I think you'd better think about this carefully before we do anything rash."

Peter's smile was almost malicious. "Heaven forbid that we should do anything rash, big brother. You might get saddled with this whole crazy house instead of me. But one thing I can tell you for certain, if the old man says one thing to insult our mother, I'll deck him myself. You'll have to wait your turn."

The frail hand tugged at his, and Daniel turned his attention back to the beautiful woman he was being told was his mother. Chaotic emotions warred within him, and he struggled to bring them under control as she spoke.

"There isn't one iota of truth to what Artemis says!" she said indignantly. "It's true I was in love with another man before my parents agreed to his proposal, but I would never have done what he thinks I did. My father lost a great deal of money in land speculation. We would have been impoverished if I hadn't accepted Artemis's proposal. I am ashamed of myself now, but at the time, all I could think of was living without the servants and pretty frocks I was accustomed to. The man I loved was far from wealthy. I couldn't bring him any dowry. So I married Artemis, and I remained faithful to him, even though he swore otherwise. You may not have been the healthy son or image of him that he expected, but you *are* his child. He will simply have to accept that fact."

Before Daniel could find the words to reply, the bedroom door flew open and the boy he now knew as John burst through. John looked slightly disheveled and smelled of horse sweat, but he hastily brushed at his hair with his hands and straightened his shirt in his mother's presence. He glanced with curiosity at Daniel, but his attention instantly reverted to Peter.

"You'd better get down to the store. Something's going on, and it doesn't look good. All the employees seem to be in the street outside, and I don't see any sign of Father."

A younger version of Peter strolled in at a more sedate pace, his green eyes quickly veering to the room's various occupants and a frown similar to Peter's forming on his forehead. Ignoring John's warnings, he commented calmly to Daniel, "You're that newspaper editor, aren't you?" He turned to Peter. "What's he doing in here?"

Edith was the one to answer. "Boys, I want you to meet your eldest brother, Daniel."

The sudden silence that fell over the room was broken by the faint strains of a band playing "Yankee Doodle" in the distance.

Forty

ℰ

"He's dead," Paul announced flatly, glaring at Daniel through eyes so like his father's and Peter's it was eerie. "I've seen the grave in the cemetery."

"You wish," Peter answered calmly. "Undoubtedly, that was what Father wished, too. But he had the obnoxious gall to survive."

Discomfort crawled over Daniel's skin, but the woman in the bed continued to cling to his hand like a lifeline. He had always wondered what his family was like. He wasn't certain he wanted to find out all at once.

Twenty-year-old John came forward first, his eyes alight with curiosity, his message forgotten. He studied Daniel as if he were a foreign object to be catalogued. "You don't look like Father," he decided.

"He looks like my side of the family, just as you do." Edith gestured for her youngest son to come forward. "I think he's been denied enough as it is. I want you all to make him feel welcome."

"When hell freezes over." Paul crossed his arms over his chest and glared.

With a lopsided grin John held out his hand. "Paul and I don't agree on anything. You're the one who won Georgie, aren't you? I am green with envy."

As if the sound of her name caused her to materialize, a familiar voice called from the stairway. "Yoo-hoo! No one answered the door, so we let ourselves in."

Daniel felt a wave of relief sweep over him. He had a

dire need for Georgina's presence right now. Giving
John's hand a brief shake and releasing himself from his
mother's grip, he took a step toward the doorway.

Georgie was faster. And Evie. And Tyler. Daniel gaped
as the trio swept in. He must have fallen on his head
when he jumped off that train. Or maybe he ate a strange
mushroom in Mama Sukey's jambalaya last night.

Trailing lavender organdy and smelling of lilies, Georgina sailed across the room. "Mrs. Mulloney! You are
looking so much better! I trust Peter took my advice and
called in Dr. Phelps."

Laughter danced in Evie's dark eyes as she glanced
around at the men standing stiffly in various parts of the
room. Behind her, Tyler propped a shoulder against the
door frame and crossed his arms, his gaze measuring
the situation for any elements of danger. Garbed in a fawn
frock coat and low-crowned Stetson, he was nearly as elegant as Evie in her yellow traveling gown with narrow
bustle and shortened skirt.

Georgina made introductions, and the Monteignes willingly came forward to shake hands and utter pleasantries.
The stunned Mulloney brothers could scarcely take in all
the chatter at once. It was only when their mother made
an exclamation of joyous surprise that they turned in unison to the center of their world.

"So you are Louise's daughter! How much like your
mother you look, my dear. You don't know how good it
is to meet you!" Edith clasped Evie's hand in both of
hers.

With satisfaction Daniel noted it was Evie's turn to be
shocked. She stared at the woman in the bed with a mixture of hope and surprise.

"You knew my mother?"

Edith smiled gently. "She was my favorite cousin. We
grew up together. When I received word of her untimely
death, I felt sorry that she had never experienced the joy
of children. Now I know she must have had her love for
you all those years. I hated to think all that was left of my
family was gone. Now I have you. I think this has been
the best day of my life."

Tears glittered in her eyes, and Daniel looked help-lessly to the two women in the room for some clue as to what he should do. As the eldest, he felt responsible, but he'd never had a mother before. He didn't know where to begin.

Evie bent to kiss Edith's cheek, and Georgina hurried to fluff up her pillows. The music outside seemed to grow louder as the men watched each other warily.

"The store!" John remembered abruptly. "We've got to get down to the store."

A loud slam and a violent curse in the lower hall ended that thought. A roar of "Peter!" sent the crystal lamp prisms shaking.

Smiling brilliantly, Georgina slipped from the bedside to clasp Peter's arm gently with one hand, patting it with the other. "The employees went on strike this morning, Peter. You'd better calm him down and make him see rea-son or it could become very ugly shortly."

"Georgina!" Peter and Daniel exclaimed in unison at her calm statement.

Tyler abruptly moved to capture Evie's arm and pull her aside as furious footsteps resounded on the stairs. Daniel grabbed Georgina away from his brother, pushing her closer to his mother and standing guard in front of both of them. In complete accord as before, his three brothers formed a barrier between the bed and the door.

"Peter, get yourself out here now! We're going to have to straighten—"

The man in the doorway stopped abruptly at the sight of the room full of people. The barrier of his sons in front of the bed caused him no concern, but the sight of Daniel standing slightly to the side brought the mottled purple of wrath to his sagging jowls.

"You! I should have known you would be behind this. I've reached the end of my patience." He turned and stabbed a finger in Georgina's direction. "You better tell your parents to start packing their bags. They're going to be out on the streets tomorrow."

Concerted sounds of protest erupted around the room, but the silver-haired man gave no heed as he stalked toward the huge bay window at the rising sounds from the street below. "What the hell!" he demanded more than asked as he stared out to the street.

"It's a protest march," Georgina announced brightly. "Your employees are demanding better working conditions." She peered with curiosity out a smaller window. "And I rather think more than the department store employees are with them."

That was undoubtedly the understatement of the year, Daniel decided as he peered over her shoulder. Through the canopy of trees along the edge of the lawn he could discern what appeared to be the entire Independence Day parade marching up the quiet residential street. Horns blared, drums pounded, and "The Battle Hymn of the Republic" became "The Star-Spangled Banner" as they listened.

"Goddammit, stop them!" Artemis roared as the parade seemed to veer toward the open gates of the front drive.

Georgina gave her father-in-law a nervous look and tugged at Daniel's sleeve so he bent to hear her whisper. "His color isn't healthy, Daniel. Maybe you'd better calm him down."

Daniel gave her a look of incredulity. Half the town was marching across the front lawn, and she wanted him to calm his father down? "I quit being a hero," he reminded her.

"Ummm, that's true." A slight frown marred her forehead as she glanced around at the rest of the room's occupants.

Peter had gone to stand beside his father and stare at the mob of people rapidly filling the emerald lawn. Evie sat beside the woman in the bed, calmly patting her hand and casting curious looks at the rest of them, while Tyler hovered protectively near her. The two younger Mulloneys had found another window from which to watch. There really was very little any of them could do now that the scene had been set in motion.

Artemis flung open the windows and stepped out onto the small balcony beyond. Shaking his fist at the crowd forming below, he yelled, "Get yourselves out of here before I fire the lot of you! Dammit, I'm going to call the police!"

The rousing cacophony of horns and drums gradually came to a standstill while people still marched through the gates, spilling across the lawn and up the trees and onto the walls so they could watch the action. Through the open window came the sound of a male voice obviously chosen as spokesperson.

"We've come to declare our independence! We will no longer be slaves! We demand decent hours and decent pay!"

"You can have your damned independence!" Mulloney roared back. "You can all go look for jobs tomorrow."

Peter caught his father's arm and tried to pull him away. "Don't do this, Father. We can't possibly keep the store open without them. Let's hear them out first."

Artemis turned a deeper shade of purple and shook his fist at his son. "Stay out of this, you traitor. *You're* the one who brought that bastard in here." He shook his finger in Daniel's direction.

"I won't have you malign my mother like that, sir," Peter replied with calm indignation. "Daniel is as much your son as I am."

"You're no son of mine!" He shook his fist furiously. "You're . . ." With a sudden startled gasp he grabbed his chest and staggered a step forward.

Peter caught his father's arm and steered him away from the balcony. Below, someone continued the speech-making, and rousing cheers could be heard rising from the crowd.

"Let go of me, damn you!" Artemis fought off Peter's grasp and tried to straighten. He gasped as if the wind had been knocked out of him, and bent over again.

"John, go find a doctor," Daniel yelled, rushing forward to help Peter.

Both John and Paul ran out the door. Their steps clattering down the stairs mixed with the yells and noise outside the window.

Worriedly, Edith attempted to rise from her bed. Both

Georgina and Evie rushed to help her. "Bring him over here. Make him lie down," she ordered.

"Dammit, woman, I'm all right! You're not going to make an invalid out of me." Artemis tried to shake off the hold of both of his sons, but his weakness betrayed him. They led him easily in the direction of the bed.

Outside, there was a concerted chorus of yells and the explosive detonations of firecrackers. Georgina and Evie exchanged concerned glances around the frail woman now standing stiffly between them.

"Someone had better speak to them," Edith said mildly.

"I'll do that, damn you!" Artemis yelled as his sons lowered him to the bed. "Just bring me some water." He gave an inadvertent moan of pain and bent forward before passing out.

Edith clutched the hands holding her and watched as Peter and Daniel hurriedly straightened Artemis out on the bed and released his collar. The purple staining his jaws had faded to a sickly white, but he was still breathing. Edith nodded carefully, as if any movement might jar her head from her shoulders. "I'll speak to them," she announced.

Everyone turned to stare, but she was already sailing regally toward the window with Evie and Georgina as ballast. Tyler grabbed Daniel's shoulders and shoved him away from the man in the bed, taking his place there so Daniel could go to his mother.

Too stunned to comprehend all that was happening, Daniel slipped his hand beneath the elbow Evie was holding and sent her away with a nod of his head. She relinquished her place gracefully.

As Edith appeared in the window supported by Daniel and Georgina, a cheer rose from the crowd. The band began on "Yankee Doodle" again, and firecrackers exploded throughout the lawns. Children jumped and cheered for no other reason than that they enjoyed the noise. Their parents clapped and screamed because Artemis Mulloney was no longer standing there yelling threats. They could only hope that his replacements were reasonable people.

"Daniel, you must speak to them. My voice won't carry," Edith murmured beneath the roar.

"What in hell do you want me to say?" Completely shaken by events, Daniel forgot to be polite.

"You're the eldest. You say what needs to be said."

"I don't have that authority. Peter should be the one doing this."

"Peter will do what I say. My name is on all those legal papers, too. Peter has been acting in my behalf all these years. Perhaps we've failed. It's your turn now."

Daniel stared at her uncertainly, then glanced to Georgina. Her eyes were wide and bright with confidence in him, and he took strength from the look she bestowed on him. He knew what to do; he just needed that look to tell him he was right. He smiled back and waited for the roar below to grow quiet.

"Thank you for coming here today." The wry note in his voice sent ripples of laughter through the crowd. "My father has been taken ill. If there is a physician out there, I would appreciate it if he would come forward immediately." That stopped the laughter.

A figure hurried forward from the outskirts of the crowd just as John appeared on horseback with another mounted man carrying a black bag. A low murmur of concern wafted through the crowd as the two physicians raced up the front steps.

Daniel watched them disappear through the portals before turning back to his main purpose here. He scarcely knew the ill man behind him, but he was ready to shoulder the responsibility of being the partial cause of his attack. He squeezed the frail hand on his arm and sought the words that needed to be said.

"We know that you are out there today for a reason. I hold myself partially responsible for that reason, as I hold myself partially responsible for my father's illness today." A low murmur of shock and surprise rippled through the mob. The hand on Daniel's arm squeezed gently, and his mother shook her head, but Daniel continued without interruption. "And as a responsible person should, I will try to correct the errors that have been made in the past."

Daniel turned his glance to his mother, then to Georgina. All the eyes in the crowd did the same. "Knowing my wife, I'm certain a woman's judgment will be entering many of the decisions to be made." Some of the laughter that followed was derisive, but a definitely feminine cheer overrode it. Daniel gave the crowd a grin. "But I think it's time to hear the opinions of those who have made Mulloney Enterprises what it is today."

The crowd remained silent, too afraid of this change in administration to have any confidence in Daniel or his disarming grin or in what he really might mean.

Seeing that, Daniel pointed at the people in the forefront of the crowd, many of whom he recognized from late-night arguments in taverns or as friends of the Harrisons. "I want you to get together now and appoint five good people to represent you. Today's a holiday, and I want all of you to enjoy it, but tomorrow, I want those representatives to come to the store so they can sit down with Peter and myself and discuss what needs to be done. I don't know a damned thing about the business and the man who knows the most may not be able to be there, so I make no promises, but where there are problems, there have to be solutions. You're going to have to help us find them."

Shocked amazement prevented any instant response to this declaration, but as people turned to their neighbors and verified what they'd thought they heard, a murmur of approval began to grow into cheers that became an uproarious cry of triumph. The band swung into a cacophony of songs accompanied by the crazed crackle of one firecracker exploding after another, and some all at the same time.

Beneath this barrage Daniel helped his mother return to the room. Georgina clung to his other arm, and the heat of her fingers made him wish they were alone. He needed more than her reassurance right now.

But the bedroom beyond was packed with people, and there didn't seem to be any escape. Physicians bent over the inert figure on the bed. His brothers stared at him as if he'd grown two heads and horns. His mother demanded to be lowered to a chair near the bed. Tyler and Evie sent servants scurrying through the doors on a multitude of errands. Daniel could only be grateful that his in-laws had apparently been caught in the crush of the crowd and hadn't come to join them.

Through this he had Georgina's hand on his arm to comfort him and keep him calm. The damned little firecracker had set all these events in motion, and she was bravely taking them in stride. Daniel thought maybe he'd taken on more than he could handle when he had taken on his altogether too-creative bride, but he was going to learn to take big chances in the future. He put an arm around her waist and hugged her to him.

Georgina opened her mouth to say something, but the words were lost when Peter appeared in the bedroom doorway. Daniel hadn't even noticed he had left, but he was standing there now, frowning in bewilderment.

Finding Daniel, he gestured with his head. "You'd better come see this."

When Georgina started to follow her husband, Peter shook his head. "You'd better leave her here."

"Stow it, Peter Mulloney. I can go anywhere I want to." With her nose in the air, Georgina sailed into the hallway on Daniel's arm.

To Peter's dismay, a small parade of people followed them out and down the stairs. When he tried to protest, John grinned and said, "Stow it, Peter, we can go anywhere we want to."

Peter scowled at Daniel and his wife. "This lack of authority is all your fault. If you have your way, we'll have anarchy."

"Study history. Leaders eventually emerge out of chaos." Much more cheerfully than he felt, Daniel continued his pace. "Where are we going?"

"See for yourself."

They had come to the bottom of the stairs. In the front hallway, surrounded by a bevy of bemused servants including a staid butler in formal frock coat, were two men apparently trussed together. Both looked slightly battered and bruised but mostly sheepish as they tried to avoid staring eyes.

"Egan!" John whispered from behind Daniel's shoulder.

"Emory!" With a tone of awe Georgina stepped forward to examine the culprits.

Her gaze fell on a sheet of paper pinned to Egan's back. Before she could reach for it, Daniel shoved her behind him and grabbed it, ripping it from Egan's shirt.

As he scanned the note, he stared in amazement, then began to chuckle. Before Georgina could rip the paper from his hands, he handed it over, and she read it out loud.

"Anytime you need to ride round-up on your family, just drop me a line. And next time you write about Pecos Martin, make sure he's a man's man, and keep those damned women out of it."

Georgina stared at the signature on the bottom and doubled up with laughter.

It was signed "Pecos Martin."

Epilogue

❦

"Where are we going?" Georgina gathered up flounces of blue batiste and hurried after her long-striding husband.

"You'll see," he said mysteriously, offering his elbow but keeping his gaze straight ahead.

"You and Peter have been acting awfully odd lately," Georgina complained. "I'm not at all sure I like it. I'm beginning to think I was much better off when you had no family."

Daniel sent her a quick glance of concern, then seeing the laughter in her eyes, he smiled and hastened his steps. "At times, I've thought the same thing. But there are other times when there are distinct advantages to family."

Georgina sighed. "I don't know. I love my father dearly, but he just won't listen when I make suggestions about rebuilding the factory. And even though I persuaded my mother to stand up to him about all those medicines and Dr. Ralph, she still lets him walk all over her. He's a terrible tyrant."

"You can't expect a man who's had things his own way all his life to change overnight, Georgie. He did agree to let you look over the new line, and he hired a woman to act as foreman."

"It should have been Janice. I still can't understand why she all of a sudden decided to up and leave with Evie and Tyler. Just because Audrey got her job back and you gave Douglas an after-school job isn't any excuse for her to run away like that."

"Audrey and Douglas are comfortable at the boarding house. Janice and Betsy weren't. The position of school-teacher back in Mineral Springs was a good opportunity. Evie will see that Janice is paid well and provided with housing, and Betsy will benefit from the dry air. Quit being selfish, Georgina Meredith. You know they were delighted with the chance to get out of here. Janice has been raising that family for years. It's time for her to get away on her own."

Georgina considered sulking at his proprietary tone, but she was distracted by her surroundings. They had walked past the old neighborhood in which she had grown up and were traversing the recently laid streets of a new development. Gaslights had already been installed, and the streets were not only wide and straight, but sidewalks ran alongside of them. Several new houses were already occupied. Tender leaves shivered on young trees. Older trees had been left at the rear of the houses, and these provided shade for the wraparound porches and second-story turrets of the lovely homes. Georgina stared around her in surprise. She'd scarcely known this area existed.

"Daniel, are we lost?"

"Nope." He steered her up the walk to a modest, two-story, yellow house ornamented with white gingerbread scroll work. The deep front porch already sported a swing, and trailing ferns hung on the shady side porch. Georgina glanced enviously at the rose bed along the decorative iron fence. It wasn't anywhere near the size of her parents' garden, but it was a start. She wished it were hers.

Biting her lip at such a selfish thought, she followed Daniel up the steps. Daniel had given her everything she had ever wanted except a home of her own. She couldn't blame him for that. He owned part of his nanny's house in St. Louis with Evie. He owned part of a ranch in Texas with Evie's cousins and father. He even owned a share in Tyler's plantation in Natchez. And there was always the Mulloney monstrosity to call home if he wished. Then, of course, they were already living in her father's house. Why would he need still another home? There really hadn't been time to even talk about such things. What with consulting with her father about the factory and working with Peter on Mulloney Enterprises and fighting on a daily basis with his father, Daniel scarcely had time to breathe anymore. Even his press had been packed up and put away, and she knew that was his true desire.

So she didn't quite register the fact that Daniel produced the key to unlock the front door. It wasn't until Daniel swept her into his arms and crossed the threshold that Georgina gasped and clung to his neck and allowed herself to hope as he swung her around to inspect the front hall.

"Daniel! Put me down! What on earth are you doing?" But she continued clinging to his neck even when he set her feet on the polished wooden floor. Her gaze greedily took in the exquisitely carved wooden molding around the ceiling, the delicate etching of the glass-covered lamps on the walls, and the pattern of colored light from the stained-glass transom. She had never seen anything so enchanting in all her life.

"Do you like it?" Daniel watched her face worriedly, holding her waist between his hands as she looked around with an expression of wonder.

"It's magnificent. I've never seen anything so lovely. Oh, Daniel, who does it belong to? Do you think we could buy it? Please, please tell me it's for sale and we can afford it." She bit her lip suddenly and let her arms slide from his shoulders. "I'm sorry. I shouldn't have said that. There isn't any way we can afford a place like this, not with Daddy's place to keep up, too."

Daniel relaxed and caught her hand to pull her into the parlor. "The factory is starting to produce again. Your father can pay his own bills as long as you don't ask him to pay the mortgage. I can afford this on my own income, but you'll be wanting pretty gowns and servants, too. So Peter and I have come to an agreement, and whether my father likes it or not, he's going to have to accept it or find himself without anyone at all."

Georgina stared at her husband with rising hope and no small amount of trepidation. "You aren't going to play the hero again, are you, Daniel? I'd rather we stayed with my father than to risk you in some other mad scheme."

Daniel's smile was slightly lopsided as he gestured at the sun-filled parlor. "Do you like it?"

"I love it, and you know it. Just tell me what it's going to cost, and I'm not talking about money." She glared back at him, knowing this husband of only a few months too well.

He bent and nibbled at the corner of her mouth. "It's going to cost every night in your bed for the rest of our lives."

Georgina shivered as the liquid warmth of his kiss took its course. If they were married for a million years, she would never get used to this sensation. She wrapped her fingers in Daniel's vest to steady herself. "You already have that. What else, Daniel?"

His hand brushed her breast lightly before settling on her arm. He steered her back toward the hall and the lovely oak stairway leading upward. "We'll be staying here in Cutlerville rather than traveling the seven seas." He pulled her up the first step.

Georgina continued to hold back reluctantly. She couldn't keep her eyes from focusing on the beautiful details of the banister and the rooms unfolding above, but she still hadn't gotten the answer she wanted. "That's what you wanted to do anyway. You said you wanted a home and a family, and now you've got one. That isn't too high a price. There's still a catch to it." She glared at him balefully. "Who built this house?"

Daniel sighed, scooped her waist into his arm, and half carried her the rest of the way up the stairs. "Peter did. This was the house he had meant for you. I added a few details since he never had it finished. If you don't like it, just say so. There's still time to sell it to someone else."

Georgina stared into the massive bedroom filling the right wall of the upstairs. Sun streamed through a blanket of windows, pooling on a familiar piece of furniture. "Our bed," she murmured, floating out of Daniel's hands and into the room to touch the first piece of furniture they had shared together.

"We can always buy something fancier later." Daniel stuck his hands in his pockets and watched her anxiously. "I just thought it would be nice . . ."

Georgina swung around and stared at him through wide blue eyes. "We certainly will not. Our son could have been conceived in that bed. That's our bed. It stays right there."

Slapped in the face with too many possibilities at once, Daniel could only stare at the vision in pale blue standing between himself and the bed. Sunlight captured the silver-gold of her hair, but cast her beautiful blue eyes in shadow. His gaze dipped to the generous expanse of her bosom, the one he had admired blatantly every night these past few months. Then hearing her words still ringing in his ears, he couldn't help but send a look of curiosity to the loop of fabric crossing the delicate skirt pulled tightly back from her stomach and hips. He couldn't see anything different. But his eyes rose to meet Georgina's, and hope blazed in them.

"Our son?" he asked tentatively.

"Or daughter." She shrugged almost diffidently, turning away from the heat of his gaze to stroke the ornate brass footboard.

"Georgina." A warning in his voice, Daniel stepped closer, reaching out to take her chin and turn her face back to him. "Are you or are you not trying to tell me something?"

"Well . . ." She couldn't meet his gaze, but her hand absently stroked the fabric he had been eyeing earlier. "It's been three months," she said, as if that explained everything.

Heart pounding crazily, Daniel searched Georgina's averted face for some sign of certainty. A delicate flush stained her cheeks, and his thumb went to caress the slight shadow beneath her eyes. He had thought she just wasn't getting enough sleep. "Georgina," he whispered, "give it to me straight. Are we or are we not going to have a baby?"

Her lips curved bravely upward. "You're not angry? I know it's awful soon, and Evie said we ought to wait, but well ... It was probably too late even then, Dr. Phelps says. I'm almost three months along ..."

"We've only been married a little over three months!" Daniel exclaimed. Then seeing the fear rise to her eyes, he carried her up in his arms and began smothering her face with kisses. "My God, Georgina, I love you. I think I just might burst with happiness this minute."

"Really? Really, Daniel? You're not just saying that?" Georgina clung to his shoulders and arched her neck backward as his kisses found new territory. For the first time since she had learned of the child, she allowed a tingle of joy to invade her veins. He wasn't angry.

Daniel dropped her on the bed and began working at the ivory buttons of her bodice while he scattered kisses across her face and throat. "I'm the happiest man alive," he murmured in between kisses. "I just can't believe it. I'm going to be a father." Laughter instilled with pure joy burst from his throat, and he kissed her soundly on the mouth. "And you're going to be the best damned mother this world has ever seen. Have I mentioned that I love you?"

"Not in the last few minutes." Finally regaining her confidence, Georgina began to push at Daniel's shirt buttons. "We'd better put this bed to good use while we can. My mother says I will be fat and ugly before long, and you won't want anything to do with me."

"Never," Daniel whispered along the expanse of skin his fingers had uncovered. "I'll always want you. And I'll want you even more when you're filled with my child. I can never thank you enough."

"Thank me?" She caught his hair and pulled his head up where she could see his eyes. The gray glittered with unshed tears, and her heart gave an extra leap at the emotion she saw shining there. "Why would you thank me? I love you. I want to have your children."

"That's why I'm thanking you," he answered gruffly. "Now shut up, woman, and let me make love to you."

Georgina gasped as Daniel's hands unfastened her corset ribbons and his mouth found her nipple through the cotton of her chemise. Every fiber of her body tingled as

he tasted her there, and she cried out her ecstasy as he released the buttons of her chemise and touched her naked-
ness. Even after three months of marriage, this was entirely new, because her husband was a different man
every time he touched her. Today, he was proud and
greedy and demanding, and she had no intention of ever
changing him.

Their clothing fell to the polished floor in stages. The
heat of a mid-September afternoon caressed their skin as
the sun poured through the uncurtained windows. Georgina didn't think they had ever done this in sunlight before, and she opened her eyes to admire the broad
expanse of Daniel's chest hovering over her. Gray eyes
were smiling back, and his hand went between them to
touch the place where their child grew. And then his fingers slid lower, and Georgina was closing her eyes and
arching her hips and begging to receive him again.

He took her gently, with the tenderness of a husband
and the knowledge of a lover. He filled her, expanded her,
showed her horizons that she could never have experienced without him. In return, she gave him all he asked
and more, surrounding him with love, easing his needs,
and surrendering her body into his care without a qualm,
giving him the child he wanted and the future he dreamed
of. The convulsions of joy that overtook them with this
physical joining were only a small sample of the union
binding them.

Afterward, Georgina lay in Daniel's arms and watched
the sun slowly sink toward the horizon, sending a pattern
of shadows across their skin. Lazily, she traced the trail of
light hairs to his navel. "You're so beautiful," she murmured absently.

Daniel chuckled. "If that's why you married me, you
got a bad deal. I've got a couple of brothers who beat me
in the beauty department."

Georgina slapped his taut stomach. "No, they don't.
And they don't even come close when it comes to courage and intelligence and integrity. You're going to have to
show them what it takes to be real men."

Daniel grew momentarily silent, stroking her hair over

her shoulder. "It's probably too late for that. Peter's planning on leaving as soon as we get the papers signed on this house. He doesn't want anything more to do with Mulloney Enterprises. I can't talk him out of it."

Georgina bounced up and glared down at him. "That has nothing to do with you, Daniel Mulloney. He's a grown man and can make his own decisions. The only thing that matters here is whether or not you want to stay and take up where he left off."

Daniel admired the lovely globes of her breasts hovering over him. The crests were puckered and pink and begging for plucking, but he forced himself to remember her delicate condition. His gaze swerved with interest to the faint swell of her abdomen, and pride surged through him. He had found a woman who loved him enough to carry a child for him. The knowledge of that still rang hosannahs through his soul.

"Wrangling with my father will be simple enough while he's confined to that bed, and the doctors don't think he will ever be able to do more than get about in a wheelchair. Running Mulloney Enterprises won't be the problem it has been for Peter in the past, and the pay is good. If Peter wants to take off, I'll miss his help, but there's plenty more coming along. Paul and John are willing to learn."

Georgina worried at her bottom lip as she studied Daniel's expression. "What about your newspaper?" she finally demanded.

He grinned, then caught her waist and lifted her off of him. Swinging his feet to the floor, he tugged her after him. "I've got something I want to show you. It's one of the reasons it took so long to get this place finished up."

As he pulled her toward the door, Georgina pulled back. "Daniel, I'm not dressed!"

"I know."

He gave her a look that warmed her clear through her middle and made her blush from head to toe, as he could easily see. Fighting a desire to cover herself with her arms, Georgina raised her chin and followed him without further protest. They were both jaybird-naked and wandering through the house like a couple of pagan Indians. The excitement of it settled deliciously in her bones.

Daniel led her down the back stairs, through the kitchen, and to another set of stairs leading into the cellar. Georgina gave him a look of caution, then followed barefoot down the wooden steps. It was cooler down here, but she didn't feel the chill. Watching Daniel walking naked in front of her kept her warm.

He threw open a door and Georgina gave a cry of surprise. There, in all its glory, sat the printing press she remembered from the warehouse. She touched the massive steel machine with wonder, then sent Daniel a questioning look.

He shrugged and crossed his arms over his chest. "We won't need the money from it, and now I've crossed the line to Mulloney's side so I can't very well complain about myself, but there are still a lot of things in this town and state that need looking at. I don't see why I can't turn out a monthly newssheet, if I can find a few good reporters."

Georgina touched a finger to her lips and turned him an innocent look. "Like me?"

Daniel frowned. "Over my dead body. That's my child you're carrying there."

"And mine. And did you know that the railroad just laid off most of their regular employees so they could hire immigrants for half the usual wages? I've got photographs of that train wreck outside the station the other day. The conductor had next to no experience, and I talked to the regular conductor. He says there's a bridge past Jasper that's ready to collapse, but the company isn't willing to spend money to fix it. I can get more photographs over there if you can get a reporter to cover the story. I bet once the story breaks, even the Cincinnati papers will want to see those pictures."

She was just starting to get wound up. Carefully placing his hand across Georgina's mouth, Daniel lifted her from the floor and started back up the steps.

"Not on your life, Miss Merry. You're not going anywhere without me."

Georgina nipped at his fingers until he lifted them from her mouth. "Then you'll just have to go with me. Now put me down, Daniel. You're going to hurt yourself."

The kind of hurt he was developing had more to do with all that rich softness filling his hands and arms and not any muscle strain from carrying her. Her round rear end was pressed enticingly to a most interesting part of his anatomy, and at his silence, she wiggled provocatively against him.

"Give up, Daniel. I'm too quick for you."

He turned her around and laid her back against the kitchen floor as they reached the top step. Kneeling over her, Daniel trapped her between his knees. "You'll never be quick enough, Miss Merry. If you so much as try to go out there without me, I'll have my old friend Pecos come back and tie you to the fence post."

"You wouldn't dare," Georgina said, then giggled as he brushed her mouth with kisses.

"Heroes always win," he reminded her, before settling the matter in a most masculine fashion.

Georgina's cry of laughter and joy echoed through the empty kitchen, but it wasn't a cry of surrender. The sun sparkling through the leaded glass of the breakfast nook caught the smile of love and triumph on her lips as she gave her body to her husband but let her spirit soar with his.

Whatever he could do, she could do, too. Her hero had taught her that.

Be sure to look for Patricia Rice's final novel
in her *Paper* trilogy entitled

Paper Moon

coming to you next year from Topaz.

Peter Mulloney rode toward town through the shadows of the cottonwoods along a dry riverbank. It was late. The moon had already reached its zenith and was on its downward path. He was tired, filthy, and numb from the long journey. He'd only stopped to rest for the sake of his horse, and the animal was fairly dropping on its hooves now. As much as he wanted to find the Double H, he would have to wait until morning.

He found a secluded place just on the outskirts of town where a trickle still ran in the riverbed. At this hour, there were few lights in the windows of this town sprawled along the intersection of two roads. There was no doubt a hotel somewhere down that main street, but he was flat broke. It didn't matter. He was used to sleeping on the ground.

He took his horse down to water, brushed it, and unpacked his saddlebags. He lit a small fire to make coffee and ground his teeth around some beef jerky to pretend he'd eaten. The night was more than warm, and he kicked out the fire, buried it in dust, and scattered the stones to let them cool. Then he strode off into the bushes to take a leak before settling down for the night.

In the morning he'd find some way of making himself respectable before heading for the Double H. He didn't know the Hardings, but his brother, Daniel, had given him their names as people he could rely on out here. People like that were rare, and he'd traveled a mighty distance to find them. He just hoped they were the sort who were willing to risk investing in a gold mine.

Buttoning his denims, Mulloney glanced in the direction of a light flickering from a nearby window. He wondered what emergency kept anyone up at this hour. Fingering the two-weeks' growth of beard on his jaw, he almost turned and walked away until he saw a silhouette appear between the curtained window and the lamplight.

He almost swallowed his tongue as he watched the silhouette drop the bodice of her gown and bend over what must be a basin of water. She moved with the grace of a sylph, supple as a willow as she swung a cascade of long hair over her head and dipped it into the water. Mulloney had to grab a branch overhead to keep from falling on his face. He knew it had been a long time since he'd had a woman, but he'd never strained his pants at the sight of a shadow before. He really must be in bad shape.

What in hell was the damned woman doing washing her hair at this hour of the night? He had half a mind to yell at her for her foolishness, but then he told himself he was being an idiot and tried to turn back to camp. He couldn't do it.

He was fascinated by the sight of long slim arms scrubbing and lifting the thickest hair he'd ever had the pleasure of seeing. He wondered what color it was. He'd never watched a woman wash her hair before. He'd never imagined what an erotic show it could make. His pulse was throbbing as she squeezed the tendrils dry and stood up, shaking the long tresses over her shoulders. Her back was to the window and all he could see was the hourglass shape of curving hips and slender waist and supple back. He willed her to turn around.

She lifted her hair with a comb or brush, he couldn't see which—the thin muslin curtains concealed too much. He almost convinced himself he was a pervert probably watching some old lady who couldn't sleep. Then she turned slightly so her breasts were outlined against the flimsy material, and he felt his mouth go dry. She was perfect.

High full breasts sloped down to a narrow rib cage he

could almost feel in his hands right now. Thick hair flowed loose and easy past a slender waist to well-formed buttocks that would fill a man's hands. Hell, he'd hold her if she was eighty. He would bury himself inside her if she was purple with pink spots. He didn't care what the hell she looked like, as long as she had a body like that.

The lamp went out and he cursed. She must be sitting there brushing her hair in the dark. He wondered if she could use a little help. As exhausted as he was, he wouldn't be able to sleep for the rest of the night after that little show.

He ought to know better by now. Unless she was a whore, she wasn't available. He'd had his fill of whores for the moment. Catalina had been the last of a whole string of them. He didn't need the grief. Maybe when he was rich, he'd go back East and find himself a fashionable young lady and sweep her off her feet. Until then, he was better off tending to himself.

Loins aching, he curled into his bedroll. As he suspected, sleep eluded him. He wished there was enough water in the river to douse himself, but he suspected he'd need more water than it would take to douse a major fire before he cooled off. He wasn't sure he would survive long enough to make a fortune and go back East to find a willing woman. He wanted one right now. He'd denied himself a great deal over these last years. Maybe he was denying himself unnecessarily now. There was bound to be women out here somewhere who needed a man as much as he needed a woman. He just needed to find one who wasn't a whore.

Peter dozed briefly on the edge of sleep until a whicker from his horse made him push back to wakefulness. That was when he smelled the smoke.

Janice pulled her comb through a tangle of hair, wincing slightly as she worked it out. The task of washing and combing her hair had soothed her slightly, but not enough to make her face that empty bedroom. Even now, with the lights out and the whole world asleep, the little house echoed of silence. She kept listening for Betsy's breathing.

She had spent ten years listening for Betsy's breathing. In that first year, she'd been terrified every time she couldn't hear it, certain death had come to steal her away. She had slept with the baby in her bed so she could reach out and touch her chest and reassure herself every time she heard the silence. And when she knew the infant was all right, she would weep herself to sleep, ashamed because she had almost wished the child had died.

There had been times since then when the burden of living had become so grueling and painful that she had wished the angels would come carry Betsy to a better place, but those times were long past. From that terrified, guilt-ridden fifteen-year-old, she had grown into a woman who knew her own strengths and weaknesses and used them to her advantage. Betsy was her biggest weakness and her greatest strength. For her child, Janice would and could do anything. Should the world discover that Betsy was actually her bastard and not her sister, her reputation would be shredded and her means of earning a living lost. She would be forced to turn to prostitution to stay alive— the only suitable occupation for a fallen woman like herself.

It was a tightrope she walked every day of her life. Even Betsy didn't know the truth. That was the reason Janice had finally capitulated and let Betsy go with the Hardings to Natchez. A sister would be much more apt to let someone else take care of a younger sibling than a possessive mother would.

But she was suffering for it. It had been nearly a week now, and Janice couldn't sleep, couldn't eat, couldn't occupy her mind with anything but worrying about Betsy. Janice had always been the one to see that Betsy got her rest, that she ate right, that she didn't overexert herself, that she took her medicine at all the right times. Betsy had always been too weak to run and play with the other children, so she had always been right there by Janice's side whenever possible. It was like losing her right arm not to have her here now.

But someday Betsy would have to learn to live on her own. Janice knew that was the healthy outlook to take. She just had a hard time accepting it. Ellen at the dry goods store was only sixteen. In six more years, Betsy would be old enough to be married and pregnant, too. Janice couldn't bear to think about her life stretching on forever while Betsy went her own way, leaving nothing but this emptiness. But that was the way it must be if Betsy was to lead a happy life, and that was what Janice wanted more than anything.

So she consoled herself that Betsy was happy now. She was with friends who didn't mind that she couldn't keep up with them. She was with people who looked after her. She was with a teacher who could teach her to use the art set she had received for her birthday. Janice smiled at the memory of Betsy's excitement upon unwrapping the gift. She had practically been dancing up the walls. It was worth the extra hours Janice had worked at copying pages of legal text for the lawyer's office.

Her eyes ached from staying up so late tonight finishing the task, but she might as well continue earning the money since she couldn't sleep anyway. Maybe she could save enough to offer to pay James Peyton to come into town regularly to give Betsy lessons. The older man was losing his eyesight and the palsy in his hand prevented him from holding a brush, but he still knew how to teach painting and drawing. His encouragement was giving Betsy the kind of confidence she needed.

Janice pulled on her cotton nightgown and began to braid her still damp hair. Summer hadn't officially begun, but the night was hot. She'd never in her life slept without clothing because she'd always lived in a house filled with people and no privacy, but with Betsy gone, she was almost tempted. Maybe as the summer moved on, she would try it. It gave her something to think about besides Betsy.

She heard a horse whinny outside, and she frowned as she moved toward her narrow bed. There had been some problem earlier in the year with vagrants helping themselves to horses down at the livery and breaking into hen-

houses for their meals, but none had been seen lately. The
sheriff had dealt quickly and firmly with the thieves, and
word had apparently spread to avoid Mineral Springs.
Somebody must have left their animal tied up outside for
some reason.

She was just pulling the covers back on the bed when
the pounding started on the door.

"Fire! There's a house on fire! Give me some pails!"

Fear jostled briefly through Janice's insides: a brush of
panic at a strange male voice, the knowledge of what fire
could do in a town of wood like this. But she had handled
more than her fair share of emergencies in the past. Sliding on her slippers, she grabbed a wrapper, and hurried
for the water pail on the stove.

She barely noticed the shadowy figure filling her doorway as she threw open the door and thrust the pail out.
Obviously, he had to be tall and broad to fill her doorway
like that, but other than noting the bristly beard, she had
no opportunity to see anything else. He grabbed the pail
and ran for the pump, yelling for her to go find help.

He didn't have to order her. She could see the flames
leaping from the roof of the schoolhouse. The schoolhouse. Panic really did grab a lungful of air from her
then. That was her livelihood, her main source of income,
the reason she had use of this house. She set her feet to
running for the fire bell at the end of the road.

Men stumbled from houses and saloons and barns as
the bell clanged and echoed, shattering the night silence.
A rooster crowed. A donkey brayed. A shout went up
from someone who saw the flames. Pretty soon the street
was filled with running men, most half-dressed and bleary
eyed. The last time there had been a fire, they had lost almost half the town.

Women and children staggered out after them. Boys
pulling suspenders over nightshirts galloped down the
road, their hands filled with buckets. The pitiful excuse
for the town water tank was rolled out from behind the
livery by the strongest men in town, and they raced down
the street, hauling it by the traces which should have held
horses. They'd bought the fire engine after the last fire,

but the town council had never decided whether to buy horses or ask for volunteers to pull it.

Janice grabbed another pail and a washbasin and ran after them. Her house was the closest to the fire, the most likely to catch next. The generosity of a trust fund from Jason's stepmother had allowed the school board to build the little house near the school when Janice had arrived with Betsy. Teachers with children to raise had been unheard of until then. The school board had only been willing to accept Janice because she was the sole candidate available after a year's search. She'd had to sign a contract to stay on for five years when they offered to build the house. The five years were up, and if something wasn't done to stop the fire, so would be her job and the house.

She handed her containers to two children, and grabbed the pump handle away from the man filling a bucket. He didn't argue but took his bucket and ran to where the fire was spreading to the grass around the school. Janice pumped the old handle up and down, filling every bucket and pan and bowl shoved beneath the spout. She was used to the old pump. She'd had to use it every day of her life for the last five years. Her arms no longer strained at the task.

She kept glancing over her shoulder at each shout and yell from the crowd around the leaping fire. Her heart stuck in her throat as she saw the flames licking along the roof rail. There wasn't any chance of saving it now. All they could do was try to contain it.

The faces of people running up with empty containers were black with smoke, but she recognized most of them. She'd lived here long enough to know every man, woman, and child in town. The few she didn't know were most likely traveling drummers coming through town on the stage, stopping off long enough to sell their wares and moving on. The only one that didn't fit that description was the large man with the beard. He came back more times than any of the others, flying over the field with long strides and quick, incisive movements as he took charge of the most dangerous spots, lining up women in a path to the schoolhouse, sending boys to carry water to the men closest to the fire. He was too impatient to wait for the containers to be passed along the line. He grabbed them out of waiting hands to throw their contents on flames licking along the dry grass and up the trees, heading straight for the house.

"A shovel," he demanded of Janice as he shoved a bucket into someone else's hands. He looked braced to run as soon as she gave him directions.

"Toolshed, back there." Janice nodded at the precarious lean-to attached to the privy.

He was off and running before the words were scarcely out of her mouth. Minutes later, she saw him digging a trench across the schoolyard, flinging dirt on trails of fire while ordering someone else to keep an eye on the cottonwoods. The man knew what he was about. Janice breathed a sigh of relief. It was good to know there was someone who knew what they were doing.

The schoolhouse couldn't be saved. She knew that. The men futilely emptied the water tank on the blaze and succeeded only in sending billowing clouds of smoke into the air, making them cough and gag and fall back. The lines of women and children passing containers of water began to falter as smoke and exhaustion thinned the ranks. Janice could feel her own shoulders and arms and back ache and moan with every pump of the handle. She would be stiff for a week, but she couldn't stop now. There was still a chance to save her house.

The man with the beard seemed to be working toward that goal now. He yelled at the ranks of faltering water carriers to cover the side yard between the two buildings. The schoolhouse was on the outskirts of town. Dry grass and the dry riverbed were all that separated her house from the rest of town. From the river, buildings scattered to the right and left, up and down the main street. They had to stop the fire here, where there was only grass to burn.

More men ran for shovels. Children ran to the puddles in the riverbed to fill their containers. Someone shoved Janice away from the pump and began to beat it with more vigor. She staggered backward, found a pail, and wearily filled it, hauling it toward a new line of flame licking beyond the trench.

She had no concept of time. She only knew that the eastern horizon was spreading a red glow which reflected the dying fire as the schoolhouse crumbled slowly into a bed of embers. The wind died with the dawn, and the remaining small bonfires were quickly doused.

As her shoulders sagged beneath the weight of one more bucket of water, a hand reached out to take it from her.

"Go to bed. It's over. I'll bring your pail back when I find it."

His voice was raw from smoke and exhaustion, but the unfamiliar accents sent a shiver down her spine. They were crisp and precise, unlike the slow drawl of the town's inhabitants, more like the voices of her past. She took an odd comfort in that and nodded obediently.

She didn't even turn to look at him as she walked away.

SCINTILLATING ROMANCES BY PATRICIA RICE